Thor

Wine, the Vine, and the Cellar

SALZWASSER
VERLAG

Thomas George Shaw

Wine, the Vine, and the Cellar

Reprint of the original, first published in 1863.

1st Edition 2022 | ISBN: 978-3-37500-354-8

Verlag (Publisher): Salzwasser Verlag GmbH, Zeilweg 44, 60439 Frankfurt, Deutschland
Vertretungsberechtigt (Authorized to represent): E. Roepke, Zeilweg 44, 60439 Frankfurt, Deutschland
Druck (Print): Books on Demand GmbH, In de Tarpen 42, 22848 Norderstedt, Deutschland

ON WINE.

WINE,

THE VINE, AND THE CELLAR.

BY

THOMAS GEORGE SHAW.

Nullius addictus jurare in verba magistri.
HORACE.

LONDON:

1863.

TO THE

RIGHT HON. W. E. GLADSTONE,

CHANCELLOR OF THE EXCHEQUER.

SIR,

My feelings of personal respect and admiration of your talents and principles as a Statesman, have induced me to ask your permission to dedicate to you this book.

Your sanction is the more gratifying, as I have informed you that I have expressed opinions, on some points, not in accordance with your own.

I have the honour to be,

SIR,

Your obedient servant,

THOMAS GEORGE SHAW.

CONTENTS.

CHAPTER I.

GENERAL REMARKS.

CHAPTER II.

PORT—OPORTO—UPPER DOURO, ETC.

CHAPTER III.

LISBON AND LISBON WINE.

CHAPTER IV.

SHERRY, XEREZ, PORT ST. MARY, ETC.

CHAPTER V.

SOUTH-EAST OF SPAIN, BARCELONA, ETC.

CHAPTER VI.

CLARET, BORDEAUX, MÉDOC, ETC.

CHAPTER VII.

CHAMPAGNE, REIMS, EPERNAY, ETC.

CHAPTER VIII.

BURGUNDY, CÔTE D'OR, BEAUJOLAIS, ETC.

CHAPTER IX.

SOUTH OF FRANCE.—MARSEILLES, ETC.

CHAPTER X.

PARIS, BERCY.

CHAPTER XI.

RHINE AND MOSELLE.

CHAPTER XII.

MARSALA.

CHAPTER XIII.

ITALY.

CHAPTER XIV.

GREECE.

CHAPTER XV.

HUNGARY.

CHAPTER XVI.

CRIMEA.

CHAPTER XVII.

MADEIRA.

CHAPTER XVIII.

TENERIFFE, VIDONIA, CANARY, ETC.

CHAPTER XIX.

CAPE.—SOUTH AFRICAN.

CHAPTER XX.

AUSTRALIA.

CHAPTER XXI.

AMERICA—CALIFORNIA.

CHAPTER XXII.

PERU.

CHAPTER XXIII.

CELLARS—DECANTING—FININGS—BOTTLES—BOTTLING.

CHAPTER XXIV.

GOUT.

LISTS OF ALL KNOWN WINES.

APPENDIX.

LIST OF ILLUSTRATIONS.

WINE,

THE VINE, AND THE CELLAR.

CHAPTER I.

GENERAL REMARKS.

Wine Duties in 1822—Manner of Paying—East Vault Exchange—Tasting—Remarkable Cooper—Dock Company's Responsibility—Wines in Bond—Wine Trade a bad Trade—Young Gentlemen as Cellarmen—Agents in the Hunting-Field—Bribery—Treatment of Wines—Ignorance existing—South African—Elbe Sherry—Ebro Port—Adulterations—Lord Palmerston—Greek and Roman Wines—Constituents of good Wine—Mr. Ballantyne's Letter—Christopher Smith in 1750—Tavern Drinking—White Port—Teneriffe—Introduction of Sherry—Claret of first Growth, *viâ* Boulogne—Claret in Stoups—Wine-drinking in the Hebrides—Bad Cellars in modern Houses—Wine Merchants' Clerks—Tasting in the open Air—'Sinful' Prices—Wine like Horse-dealing—Drunkenness formerly not disgraceful—Tavern Bill in 1728—Recollections of 1773—Wine for Twenty in 1863—Few drunken People now—A Bishop's Claret—The Royal Sailor—The First Gentleman in Europe—Duke of York's Aide-de-camp—Jockey of Norfolk—Pepys's Memoirs—Poulett Thomson—Author's Obstinacy—Wine Committee—Duty reduced—Wine as a general Beverage—Consumption since 1855—Alcoholic Test—Song from *Punch*—Evasion of Alcoholic Rate—Statistics of 1862—The Wine Association—Uniform Rate of 1/0—Effects of Vine Disease—Prices in Montpellier—Consumption in Paris, in Mayence, and in London—Table of Rates of Duty since 1671—Statistical Table from 1791 to 1862—Wine and the Poets.

THE following details respecting excise and customs men, dock coopers, duty-paying, and similar matters, forty years ago, possess little value in themselves; but those who remember them are rapidly passing away, and it may be interesting to others to know how the wine trade was carried on in times gone by.

On the 14th of May, 1822, began my acquaintance with the wine duties, and the manner of paying them, which was very different from the present mode.

If a cask or case was to be taken out of bond, it was necessary, first, to write what was called a Require-note, which gave full particulars of the ship, entry, gauge, &c., of the cask, and stated that you *Required* to pay duty. This was taken to the Excise office at the dock-gate, and, if found correct, was initialled. Furnished with this authority, another paper was necessary, called the warrant, besides two more, with the number of gallons in figures.

All these were for the Excise, whose office was on Tower Hill; and as there was only one collector through whom all had to pass, it may be imagined how tired we poor clerks often were of waiting our turn.

For the Customs, one paper written in full, with another in figures, was demanded; but on these were placed the letters C. A., which, being interpreted, were found to denote 'cum aliis,' *with others*; proving the classical knowledge of Her Majesty's Commissioners of Customs, and that they were always wanting something more. Few, if any, merchants attempted to pass their entries with the Customs themselves, preferring to employ agents; some of whom, though receiving salaries of only 300*l.* or 400*l.*, left fortunes of 100,000*l.* at their decease. Many firms paid 4/6 for each entry; and when it was of importance to get the cask off on the same day, what was called a *Reading-out* entry was necessary, for which an additional 1/6 was charged. The next day, on showing the excise warrant, a permit was granted for the party to whom the wine was to be sent; and this being shown to the excise officer at the vault, he compared it with the delivery order of the dock company. If the customs officer happened to be near, the delay might not be very great; but as it was necessary that the two should be present together to 'pass' the cask, a most tedious waste of time was often the result.

Increase, or reductions of the duty, at that time, and until 1824, were made by adding or deducting so much per tun; and this, being divided by the number of gallons in the tun, gave the rates per old gallon. Part was paid to the Excise, and the remainder to the Customs. The whole, upon Port, Sherry, Cape, &c., was 7/7, of which the Excise received 4/2, and the Customs 3/5. On Madeira it was 7/8, on Rhenish 9/5, and on French 11/5; each branch of the revenue receiving its proportion of these sums.

After wine was 'permitted' out of the docks into the dealers' cellars, French and Cape had to be kept separate from port, &c.; and all stocks were under excise supervision, so that even twelve bottles were not allowed to be sent out without a permit; which caused much trouble and loss of time.

It was generally known on which day the officer's visit might be expected; and as he could often find means to give annoyance, a dinner and a good bottle of wine were usually ready for him.

I recollect an instance, in my own experience, of the way these officers sometimes acted. On a shelf in my counting-house there stood sixteen or seventeen bottles of French wines which had been sent as samples, and for which I could show no permit. To my astonishment, I received a letter, nearly a foot long, freighted with, at least, a quarter of a pound of wax; and on opening it, I found that it was from the 'Honourable Sirs' in the old Excise Office, in Old Broad Street, ordering me to appear before them for breaking the law, for which I was liable to a penalty of 50*l.* I went as commanded, and was ushered into a large room with a green table, round which were three very solemn-looking gentlemen, and the officer standing at the end. He told his story, and I told mine, and the Honourable Sirs were so kind as to let me off, with the forfeiture of the wine, and two guineas, one of which the officer got. I do not know how the unfortunate sixteen bottles were appropriated.

All goes on so easily now, that some may doubt whether such things could have existed only a comparatively short time ago, but I can assure the incredulous that her Majesty's revenue officers were almost ubiquitous. There are few who have not had experience of their presence on arriving *from* a foreign country, but I can state from personal knowledge that on one occasion I was not allowed to go *to* a foreign country without having my portmanteau searched: it was in 1823, when, embarking at Newhaven for Dieppe, a strict examination was made to discover if I was carrying abroad any models or plans of machinery! A few years previously, just after the war, great distress existed, and many weavers from Paisley wished to emigrate. It was feared that they would carry with them our skill in weaving, and the customs officers in Greenock, and, I suppose, in other parts, had instructions to examine the hands of emigrants, and to stop those who had soft, weaver-like hands!

The excise officers were generally men who had been trained to, and understood, their work; but many of the customs officers were old butlers, gardeners, &c., who got their appointments by parliamentary influence, and were of course entirely ignorant of their duties. Even their superiors, both at the Excise and Customs Boards, at that time consisted, with few exceptions, of men whose lives had been passed in occupations unfitted to qualify them for such important posts.

The whole system, in short, was a mass of confusion, annoyance, delay, and expense; but I remember that, bad as it was, it was keenly defended by all the old clerks and others who had surmounted its difficulties and mysteries, and were therefore opposed to every change which tended to deprive them of their monopoly by facilitating the despatch of business.

There is still much room for simplification and improvement, but those who have now to do with revenue officers can have but a slight conception of the very superior class of men they are, in contrast with those of former years.

Since that period a great change has taken place in the way of conducting the wholesale part of the trade. Then, it was very unusual to purchase even a single cask without going to the docks to taste it; but now, sales are almost invariably made by samples. Formerly, every house of importance had a partner or a representative to show their bonded stock; and there were generally from fifteen to twenty to be found, every afternoon, at their usual exchange, at the East Vault, London Docks. The only shelter being an open shed, it was often cold shivering work in the winter, waiting without anything to do but to gossip about people and things, and scandal, true or false.

It was also necessary to attend to the landing of wines, to see that they were properly laid up for gauging, to have them sampled, to taste them, to report opinion, and to have those housed on which duty had not been paid. I have often thought of an amusing piece of red-tapism connected with these proceedings. The Act of Parliament stated that all casks brought into the docks must be bonded; and thus a cask that was to be sent from the quay would be actually placed in the slings, lowered into the vaults till it touched the ground, and then hoisted up into the wagon waiting for it. Without this ceremony it was feared that there would be an infringement of the Act.

No casks smaller than a hogshead, nor cases of less than three dozen, were then admitted for home use. The 'broad arrow' was put upon them, but the Honourable Board generally condescended to let them pass after a week's deliberation, with 'a fine.'

When a west-end, or country, or other dealer came down, he was probably the known customer of one of the houses; and, addressing himself to its representative, he would enter one of the vaults. Supposing it to be the East Vault, the man who attended to the lamps, handed one to each person, and called the cooper whose turn it was. He enquired the names of the import ships, by whom bonded, the date, and the marks and numbers of the casks; and if he did not know where they were, referred to a book.

On being told which wine the dealer wished to taste first, he would probably have to squeeze himself in between casks in one of the narrow gangways off the main one, would drive his fret into the cask named, and bring forward a large glassful.

When this had been duly criticised, more of the same or of other importations might be tasted; or the 'customer' would perhaps return to the quay, and go into other vaults with some one else.

The coopers were a shrewd intelligent set of men, and never did I see one of them tipsy. But other temptations were held out, too powerful to resist. From the conversations they overheard, and from being frequently asked to give their opinion about wines, they picked up a good deal of knowledge, and especially became acquainted with many of the dealers who came to the docks to buy. By speaking to them in a confidential way, of certain casks they could privately show, that were worth notice for goodness and cheapness, they were considered men whose services were worth securing.

Accordingly, it was known that several were in the pay of houses, and that they took every opportunity they safely could to show the wines of those firms. They also managed to *fine* a cask or two of each parcel, which was thus bright, and with a 'beautiful face;' while others were out of condition. It is also alleged, probably not without grounds, that when a glass of another cask was desired to be brought forward, still the same '*fined*' cask was the one drawn from, and its contents exhibited to the dealer.

One of these coopers was a remarkable man, with

a memory so retentive, that there was scarcely a cask in the vault that he could not take you to at once, without reference to the book; and such a favourite was he that I have often waited a quarter of an hour, when it was near closing time, being sure that if I secured him I should get through my work sooner than by taking another who might be ready to accompany me. The cooper of whom I speak was well known to be paid by a city firm, in whose employment he afterwards served as dock clerk for many years; and seldom, indeed, has a house had a more zealous, able, profitable clerk. He has been for some years at the head of one of the first wine houses in the city; and it is due to him to state that he has invariably upheld his character for shrewdness, fair dealing, and *inflexibility* of opinion.

The success with him was so great and evident that it became quite a fashion for houses to take coopers out of the docks as clerks; but I am not aware of another instance in which the experiment has been successful.

About the year 1853 it was discovered that great frauds were carried on, and almost every cooper in the East Vault was dismissed.

As soon as a cask is in the slings of the dock company to be hoisted from the hold of the ship, the company become responsible, and continue so while it remains in the docks. If it is taken away at once, there are certain charges for landing, cooperage, wharfage, &c.; but if it is placed in the vault, there is a charge of about 20*s.* per pipe per annum, called the consolidated rate, which includes everything, and three months' rent; but is exclusive of tasting, which is 2*d.* per cask each time.

For this consolidated rate, the cask is under the care of the company, and if any accident occurs before it has been placed on the merchant's cart, they must pay all damage. They are, however, not responsible for a loss of less than one gallon per cask per annum, it being considered that this may arise from natural evaporation and leakage; and thus, if a cask of 100 gallons were housed on the 31st of December, 1861, and taken away on the 30th of December, 1862, the quantity being found on regauging to be 99 gallons, the merchant could make no claim; but if it were 98 gallons, he would be entitled to send an invoice to the company for 1 gallon.

The dock charges are somewhat higher than at wharves, and in bonded vaults in provincial towns; but the security, and the satisfaction of knowing that the casks are properly attended to, are worth an extra charge. It is, of course, impossible to prevent frauds occasionally in these and other establishments, but great care is used to check their occurrence.

It is, however, to be hoped that the habit of keeping wines in bond will not be continued, for it is ruinous to every cask of pure natural wine from any and every country. Such kinds as port, sherry, marsala, &c., with 35 to 45 per cent. of proof spirit, will stand any amount of maltreatment and knocking about; and, generally, the longer they have been in bond the better they are; but it is very different with wines that have not been dosed with spirit, and which, therefore, require constant care and attention.

In the docks this is quite impracticable; and when it is stated that, in every country where the slightest anxiety is felt for the quality of its wines, every cask is racked from the lees two or three times a year during the first two years, and is filled to the bung every week, this alone will convince all that it must be destructive to them to remain where the sole care from year's end to year's end is that the dock company shall lose none of the liquid. In many cellars in France there are 6,000, 8,000, and 10,000 hogsheads which require daily supervision; but, even in the bonded cellars at Bercy, near Paris, every merchant has entire control of his stock, and employs his own men. This is also the case in Holland and Belgium; and it must also become the case here, if we are to have a larger consumption of unbrandied wines.

The following remarks, which I extract from a weekly French paper devoted to wine affairs, show what is thought in France on this point:—

There are in London vast docks, in which are deposited wines on which the duty is not paid when they are landed.

The company to whom the docks belong employ only their own servants. When a cask is placed in their cellars, it must remain till the duty is paid or it is exported, without being either filled up or racked from its lees; and in this state it is delivered. The buyer has tasted bright wine, but when he receives his cask it seems a mass of lees; and it is little wonder that the exclamation is often made, 'What stuff this French wine is!'

There is another evil. Merchants and retailers are equally ignorant of the treatment of all wines not loaded with brandy. This is not surprising, as they are not permitted to have any charge of their wines in the docks. We ought not, therefore, to send any wine to the docks in London, till there shall be arrangements, as in Paris, by which every merchant may be enabled to take charge of his own wines, and to employ his own men to do what is required. This is allowed in Holland and Belgium, and we advise all to avoid sending to the docks in England any wine that is not as strong as port and sherry, while such regulations exist.

It seems to be a general habit to speak of one's own trade as a bad one. This is, of course, not correct generally, but it is easy to prove, by facts and by reasoning, that it is quite true as regards the wine trade. No trade can be healthy, if, while others are increasing in a wonderful degree, it remains stationary. Taking the average of each ten years from 1791 to 1858, the consumption of wine has been 6,513,019; 6,304,085; 4,929,129; 5,987,745; 6,503,188; 6,163,377; 6,748,975 gallons; with a population which has increased from fourteen and a half to nearly thirty millions, and with exports of manufactures which have increased from about thirty to nearly one hundred and thirty millions sterling; while the revenue from wine has kept below two millions sterling for the last fifty years. Surely this is a sufficient proof of a wretched, languid trade; and it is melancholy to hear old wine merchants talking over their personal recollections of numerous firms, once of excellent standing, now broken down and vanished. A few have been successful, through industry and knowledge of the trade; but even these qualities could seldom have enabled them to make money, had they not also possessed considerable capital, or the means of borrowing it when wanted. Without such advantages, it is generally a desperate affair to go into the wine trade; and I fear I am expressing nearly the truth, when declaring my belief that, if all who deal in wine were to be called upon to pay whatever they owe in business and otherwise, more than a half would be found insolvent.

This is a bold assertion; but it is not made without having asked the opinion of men who well know the realities on which it is grounded. It would be entering too much into details to show how certainly anyone becoming a wine merchant in the private trade, with small capital, or whose business improves and increases, and consequently absorbs more and more money, must place himself under obligations to one or more of the shipping, or bottling houses.

This is a dangerous and unfortunate position for him, although there may be a few firms which will conscientiously discourage his increasing his liabilities; but, so long as he is supposed to have property, he will find plenty eager to offer him facilities for wine and duties; and, as they can discount his acceptances, this can be done with no outlay on their part. Acceptances will fall due, and private customers are often long in paying; favours have to be asked; more wine is bought, price must not be narrowly scanned; and thus the wheel revolves till the oil is dried up. Such is 'ow'r true a talé' about many a one.

The prices of all wines have lately risen so high that there is not now the same scope for profit as formerly; and, therefore, the temptation to offer the advance of duty, with one or two years' credit, is not so strong as it was. It will be in the recollection of many, that the head of a very old and first-rate house made up his mind about thirty-five years ago to realise his property, and to retire from the trade; and they cannot have forgotten what a tumbling down there was when he decided on demanding payment from those indebted to his firm. I have been informed by one of his customers, very honest and very industrious, but poor, that he had a running account with this rich man, who rarely hesitated to lend him 500*l.* or 1,000*l.*, but invariably made him increase his stock by ten pipes, on which it was not difficult to see that the profit must have been 150*l.* or 200*l.*

In other trades, I believe there is a great deal of pawning and pledging to raise money, but I do not suppose that it is carried to the same extent as in the wine trade. It being impossible for anyone to fix a precise value on wine, it is a convenient article for all sorts of representations; and wine warrants are often mentioned in police reports.

The placing of a son in a trade or profession is an anxious question with most parents; but I would urge upon all *not* to make a wine merchant of him, unless there are substantial grounds for believing that he will be admitted into an established business; and even when this is certain, he should be taught the trade as if his only hope of success depended upon his own exertions. It is impossible for anyone to be a good practical wine merchant in the shipping, the city-bottling, or the private trade, unless he knows every detail, not only at the docks and wharves, but in the cellar; and this latter part can only be learned by being able to do a cellarman's work. Some of the first wine merchants in the country induce London houses with whom they deal to take their sons for two or three years to teach them the trade; and these young gentlemen may often be seen in the cellar with their leathern apron and cap. Father and son thus show their good sense, and both will reap their reward. But, besides the practical knowledge to be got here, it is essential that he should go abroad, not only to acquire the languages, but to gain as much knowledge of vineyards and of wine-making as will be communicated to him. Without this, he can know very little about wine, and has to take for granted what is told him by the old firms whose trade is with England, or by their 'travellers.' He cannot correspond or speak with the growers themselves.

People seldom care to learn what they see no use in knowing; and formerly there was little in most cellars but port, sherry, madeira, marsala, and bucellas, which, owing to their strength, required little attention. These were supposed to be the only kinds the English would drink, and it was therefore thought needless to disturb themselves about others. The shipping and large bottling houses, also, being naturally opposed to any change which would derange their course of trade, used their powerful influence to prevent a reduction of duty, fearing it would cause the general introduction of other kinds, and overturn the monopoly which they had so long enjoyed.

However, there is now scope, which did not previously exist, for a young energetic man to make an income, by availing himself of the advantages of a practical training here and abroad, and by his knowledge of foreign languages, and of growers from whom he may purchase direct, instead of from the great merchants with palaces abroad and agencies at home. Such a youth, if possessed of the other essential qualifications, is sure to be valued and respected by good wholesale houses; and, with a 1,000*l.* of capital, he will carry on a large business more easily than another, who is ignorant and indolent, can do with 5,000*l.*; while his prospects of success will be infinitely better.

Such a young man as I describe will not have much difficulty in getting a partner with money; and if he meets with one who has been brought up to the trade, and will apply himself to promote the interest of both, he will be fortunate; but I would strongly advise him and his father to allow no amount of money to tempt him to connect himself with anyone, young or old, who has not been bred to the trade. This may do well enough, perhaps, when a 'young gentleman' with money is admitted into a firm whose business is already formed, and in which there is an able partner or manager; but if the youth has not the good sense to refrain from interfering with what he knows nothing about, he will certainly do much harm, even in such an establishment.

But where a trade has to be made, and it is scarcely known where to rely on selling 100*l.* worth the first year, such a person is often worse than useless; because, if he were willing to go through the disagreeable necessity of begging and seeking for orders, he does not know how to set about it; and few sales are made by those who show that they are speaking of what they do not understand. Interest is payable upon his capital; expenses are in all probability increased; and the loss of a portion of the profits is the consequence of the partnership. As to connections who, it may have been honestly represented, would be ready to buy their wines, and would recommend others—let little dependence be placed upon this. If the connection is among rich tradesmen and shopkeepers, who think and talk much of good living and good wine, and give good prices, and pay quickly—these are valuable, as are also some others; but people do not now generally have 'their wine merchant,' as formerly. Many years ago the wine trade used to be considered peculiarly gentlemanly, but now it is somewhat differently regarded.

Wine merchants are generally considered very troublesome; but it is a necessary part of this disagreeable trade to be constantly seeking for orders, even amongst intimate friends. More means and instruments are used to accomplish this than is generally supposed; for it is not seldom that a finely-booted and spurred independent-looking gentleman in the hunting-field is, in reality, *sub rosâ*, a wine merchant's 'help;' and, by 'incidental' hints, there and at table, about Château this and Château that, he earns profits for his employer and commissions for himself.

However good a stock may be, there is so much competition that the merchant's sales will be very slow indeed, if he imagines that the excellence of his cellar will absolve him from practising such solicitations; with much, besides, very repugnant to the feelings of a gentleman. Not the least of these is the payment to servants of money which, properly, should be given to their masters, and favours of various kinds to persons of influence in clubs, &c. These are understood matters, of course, and I doubt if there are any in the private wine trade who can declare they have not conformed to this bad custom.

In dealing in almost any other article, the value is approximately known on both sides; the purchase is made for the sake of a profit, and there is no favour felt or bestowed. But in wine, excepting among some of the wholesale houses who buy and sell in the market, all sell to the consumers, who purchase for their own use, and not as a money-making investment.

The wine trade is generally supposed to be easily understood; but no one who knows it will say so, though there has been little else imported than the usual strong wines, which bear almost any temperature and treatment; for even claret and other kinds from France, &c., have been nursed and matured before being brought over. This cannot possibly continue; since Frenchmen and others will establish themselves, buying growths by the tun, as the Belgians, Dutch, and Germans do, when it is yet scarcely wine, and attending to it themselves in their capacious cellars.

There are several branches of the trade. There is, for instance, the firm in England which is partner with, or agent for, a house in Oporto, Xerez, Bordeaux, &c., and whose business it is to procure orders for their house abroad, or to sell their stock in bond.

ever been a favourite subject; and the last good joke on this head is from no less an authority than Lord Palmerston himself. It is related that, when a deputation waited upon him, he told them the following story:—

> I remember my grandfather, Lord Pembroke, when he placed wine before his guests, said, 'There, gentlemen, is my champagne, my claret, &c. I am no great judge, and I give you these on the authority of my wine merchant; but I can answer for my port, for *I made it myself.*'

In reference to adulterations, I see in a book on Wine, often quoted, the following description:—

> A very inferior French wine, sold to the adulterators at a few sous the bottle, is now frequently mingled with rough cyder, and coloured to resemble claret, with cochineal, turnsole, and similar matters. This is pronounced fine quality, and sold as such in this country. Certain drugs are added as they appear to be wanted; and the medley, to which a large profit is attached, from the imposition, is frequently drunk without hesitation, and without any discovery of the cheat.

In another work we are told—

> Port wine, or what is often sold as such, affords an example of the skill and cunning employed in adulteration. First, the wine itself is compounded of logwood, sugar, and spirit; next, the crust on the bottle is precipitated by artificial means, with a view to give it the appearance of age; the corks are stained for the same object; and even the very cobwebs which envelope the bottles are often borrowed.

I believe that if a hundred wine merchants were called upon to state their opinion whether there was any truth in these and similar descriptions, all would declare that, from Lord Palmerston's grandfather to the borrowed cobwebs, they did not believe a word of it.

It need not be doubted that there are the full proportion of men, among those who sell wine, who will use any means whatever to make money; but, often as I have asked if it were possible to make a drinkable, saleable wine according to the descriptions and receipts quoted, I have got the same answer—that it was simply *impossible*. Pepper, mustard, milk, everything is adulterated, and so is wine; but not in the way that those who have little practical knowledge represent. While cape paid only half duty, almost the whole of it was used for lowering the cost of sherry, &c., and thus underselling those who would not resort to such a deceitful practice. Now, by the equalisation of duty, this is stopped; but many are still seeking the same object of underselling, by mixing 'Hamburg (Elbe) sherry,' or any other handy liquid, and making a profit by offering the result as sherry, at a lower price than others can sell theirs, which has not been thus cheapened. I have before me the following report of such an 'operation' in mixing, which was lately performed in a bonded vault in the city:—

6,550 gallons of French red wine, with 2,100 gallons of proof spirit and 65 gallons of capillaire.

There is nothing in this compound of upwards of

4,000 dozens very injurious to health, but those who drink it are not to be envied. Capillaire is a preparation of sugar and water, and is much used to sweeten wines which are thin and poor.

There are so many corroborative proofs in favour of the opinion, that it cannot be doubted that the wine which the Greeks and Romans made and praised was so compounded, as to render it inconceivable how any person could have swallowed it. For instance, a pint, and sometimes two or three pints, of salt water were added to about six gallons of wine. To impart pungency, powdered pitch or resin was sprinkled on the must, during fermentation; and when this was completed, the flowers of the vine, the leaves of the pine or cypress, bruised myrtle-berries, the shavings of cedar-wood, southern-wood, bitter almonds, &c. &c., were infused in the wine. Another way to gain the desired taste and flavour was, after putting these ingredients in must, to boil the whole together till it became of a thick consistency, and to add, more or less, to the wines that were fermenting. Here is another recommendation :—

To 90 amphoræ (about 500 gallons) of must, which has been evaporated to one-third, put 10 sextarii ($1\frac{1}{10}$th gallon) of tar, washed in boiled sea-water, a pound and a half of turpentine, and the same of resin. These being further reduced by boiling, add six pounds of crude pitch in powder, with a judicious but liberal allowance of various herbs, such as spikenard, fleur-de-lis, myrrh, calamus, saffron, melitot, cassia, &c., well bruised and sifted.

The wines of the ancients have been described as

'thick and fat,' owing to their having been usually boiled in the 'fumarium' to a consolidated state, so that they could not be poured out of the vessel until dissolved by hot water. Aristotle tells us that some of the stronger kinds became a concrete mass, from exposure, in skins, to heat and smoke.

The component parts of the produce of the grape are as follows, varying in degree, and thus insuring a variety of qualities:—Saccharine matter, extractive or mucilaginous and colouring matter, acids, essential oils, alcohol, water.

1. *Saccharine Matter.* — This, when fermented, produces a new principle, from which alcohol, by another process, is derived.

2. *Extractive or Mucilaginous or Colouring Matters.*—These are chiefly produced in the course of fermentation from the skin and pellicule (the thick part) of the grape, and from the stalks, when fermented with the juice.

3. *Acids.*—Tartaric acid is found in great abundance in the unfermented juice. Much of it is decomposed during fermentation, and, a considerable quantity afterwards combining with the colouring and other matters, falls to the bottom of the cask or bottle, sometimes in a loose state, and in some wines remains more or less fixed as 'a crust.' In most kinds there are malic, citric, and acetic acid; while sparkling wines contain carbonic acid gas, evolved during fermentation, and confined in the bottle.

4. *Essential Oil* is a volatile but indispensable

principle, by which the vinous and peculiar flavours and qualities are generated and distinguished.

5. *Alcohol or Spirit* is produced from the saccharine matter which has undergone fermentation.

6. *Water* is necessary to allow the process of fermentation to operate.

Each of these principles is required in order to form good wine, and upon their due combination it mainly depends. If the season be too hot the grapes will wither and ripen before their proper qualities have been developed, and the saccharine and extractive matters will so greatly predominate, that it will be necessary to use water or juice, to allow the fermentative principle to operate.

On the other hand, if the season be cold and wet the saccharine will be deficient, and the juice must then either be boiled until a part of the water has been got rid of, or it must be enriched or strengthened by the infusion of sugar or sweet must.

No one can feel otherwise than astonished that the Greeks and Romans could have drunk such abominable decoctions as those described; but the more I investigate this subject, the more do I become convinced that it is not much more than a hundred years since the favourite kind of wine drunk by ourselves was somewhat similar; and that it is an erroneous idea to suppose that pure, natural, or fine wines were the general or favourite kinds in use by our ancestors. Even independent of many facts which lead to this conclusion, every experienced wine merchant would infer that it is very improbable that good old wine was easily procurable at that period; because he learns in his travels among wine growers that it is impossible to have it good and mature, unless there be considerable capital invested in vineyards and in cellars, joined to such an amount of industry, skill, and patience as we have reason to believe was not usual in olden times. Every country was also overrun by wars; and there was but little security, without which there is little provision made for the morrow.

The conviction has forced itself upon me that vineyards were as slovenly attended to as agriculture generally; that the wine was very badly and crudely made; and that it was drunk or sent off quite new, mixed with various compounds, either in the country where it was grown or was going to.

I am much confirmed in this opinion by the letter of Mr. Ballantyne, which may be seen in the Appendix. With the exception of this letter, I have nowhere met with any document, in reference to the wines in use about a century ago, which a wine merchant cannot immediately discover to have been written by persons ignorant of the trade.

On the contrary, Mr. Ballantyne can be seen at once to have been a man thoroughly acquainted with it, from the fermentation to the mixing and compounding; and his professed object was, not to attempt to prove that no adulterations took place, but that these were confined to a few, and that good wine was procurable if persons would go to dealers of character and position. Although the whole appears in the Appendix, the letter contains so much that is interesting and new that I offer no apology for giving here the following extracts:—

I made acquaintance also with Mr. Christopher Smith, a very old wine merchant, who told me that when he had come to a state of manhood (about the year 1750), and drinking wine at taverns, it was eightpence per quart, served up in a curious pewter measure, which turned round upon a little swivel, with a spout, and, if ten were in company, one glass served them all. The call was only for red wine or white wine, but frequently the red was called claret, and the white sherry. *Sherry was then generally, like other white wines, kept in a state of fermentation, by sweet malaga, meade, cider, or honey.* Pale wine was but just coming home (about 1768) on the lees, with which was mixed Spanish or small French wine; and a similar mixture was made of the various sorts of white wines. The dexterity of the wine cooper then was shown in making the most palatable at the lowest prices; but now (referring to 1807, the date of his letter) all wine comes in so clean and so perfect that the skill of the wine cooper of former days is not required. With white port, being subject to ferment in summer and grow foul in winter, we mixed a little Teneriffe, which improved its flavour, and prevented any further fermentation.

I think three years had elapsed before I had seen a butt of sherry; but when I did, I recommended it in preference to white port. A man of quality recommended to me Mr. Duff, our late consul at Cadiz, to whom I sent orders from several friends, and white port soon became despised, although it had been in such esteem that, even as late as 1782, I got orders in one week for eighty pipes. Now it is forgotten, and sherry has prevailed.

What is now considered true sherry, from Xerez, was not known in England previous to the shipments of Mr. Duff, and it is very clear that he did not ship any before 1760; therefore the speculations about 'sherris sack' having been our sherry must be incorrect. I believe the Spanish wines alluded to in olden times were from Malaga and the Mediterranean coast; with which there was a great trade, when Cadiz or Xerez were scarcely known to shippers. Mr. Ballantyne adds:—

I believe it was not before the year 1750 that the first growth claret, properly prepared and of proper age, came to England from *Boulogne* (!) to Mr. Stewart of York Buildings, and Mr. Allan of Mark Lane; but of late years the Forsters, the Johnstons, and two or more houses at Bordeaux, can ship it in the same excellent condition as formally from Boulogne.

For further information on this point, I refer to my remarks about claret.

Although not easy to comprehend, it is a fact that the shipments of wines from Bordeaux and Rochelle were enormous, even so early as the fourteenth century, when it appears that upwards of two hundred vessels were loaded at Bordeaux for England. It is recorded that in the reign of Edward VI. in 1546, 'for wines, we have continually from France and Spain, as also out of Almaine and out of Candia, great quantity of the best that grow in those parts.' In Scotland it was often so abundant that, upon the arrival of ships at Leith from Bordeaux, casks were placed on wheelbarrows, and the 'claret' sold in the streets in stoups. Scott and others, describing the Scotch in old times, often allude to the 'stoup of claret,' which was probably the usual way of buying and also of drinking it: but it could not have been a 'vin de Bordeaux' from the Médoc; for this, as it is now sent, will not bear such rough usage without becoming soon undrinkable. Being so common and plentiful, we may be sure that it was new, strong, and cheap, and rarely bottled.

We can understand the gentry, the inhabitants of the towns and the Lowlands drinking wine, but can scarcely imagine that it would be necessary for the Scotch Privy Council in the beginning of the seventeenth century to pass Acts to prevent 'the excess of drinking of wines in the Isles' (the Hebrides, or continent adjacent).

These were, then, in a state of greater poverty than any other parts of Scotland, and what they drank as claret must have been grown up the river above Bordeaux, probably in the Clairette district. In 1609 the introduction of wine into the Isles from the mainland was forbidden. In 1616 its *use* was forbidden. In 1622, finding that 'a great quantity of wines is yearly carried to the Isles, with the insatiable desire whereof the inhabitants are so far possessed that, when there arrives any ship or other vessel there, they spend both days and nights in their excess of drinking, and seldom do they leave their drinking so long as there is any of the wine remaining,' its sale by any person whatever was finally prohibited.

This, however, applied only to the 'commons and tenants,' for the chiefs were allowed a quantity yearly according to their rank. MacLean of Coll, and MacLean of Lochbuy, were each restricted to four hogsheads; Clanranald had twelve; MacLeod of Dunvegan, sixteen. This last is fifteen bottles daily, which seems a liberal allowance. The acts of the Privy Council, in their quaint old language, will be found in the Appendix.

> Vina probantur odore, sapore, nitore, calore;
> Si bona vina cupis, quinque F laudantur in illis:
> Fortia, Formosa et Fragrantia, Frigida, Frisca.

The habit of drinking is less common than formerly, and the proportion of wine merchants who become drunkards is not greater than among other classes: but it is unfortunately the fact that many youths, in the counting-houses of wine and spirit merchants, cannot resist the temptation of sipping the wine and brandy samples always within their reach; the consequences of which may be inferred.

Partners and agents, especially those who seek for business among small hotel-keepers, publicans, and that class, are subject to a dreadful life; for, with many, no bargain can be concluded without 'something to drink.' This practice cannot be continued without destroying the delicacy of the palate, and rendering it unfit to discriminate the shades of difference in any but the coarsest kinds. The same may be said of many wine merchants in London and elsewhere who are constantly tasting the strong 'market' wines of every colour and quality, besides rum, brandy, gin, &c.

Tasting should be in the open air, or in a well-ventilated room; for it is impossible to distinguish a delicate bouquet in confined close places impregnated with the flavour of strong wines and spirits. A similar remark applies to wine after dinner; and this reminds me of an excellent arrangement in the club of Oporto. When dinner is over, all move to another room with a similar table, on which the dessert is laid. True judges attach as much importance to the bouquet as to the taste of wine; but this part of its excellence is generally lost at a dinner-table; for then, even the most indifferent about what may be thought of him will scarcely venture to hold the glass to his nose, sniffing the flavour, and still less to roll the wine in his mouth, looking very solemn, as he may have observed is the custom in the 'wine market.' Yet, without smelling and tasting thus, much of the excellency of the finest wines is lost.

If wine merchants could feel sure that those to whom they send wine were capable of appreciating it, and would do it justice, the trade would be comparatively easy; but the reverse is generally the case. With sherry it does not much matter whether it is sent to-day and drunk to-morrow; neither does it greatly affect champagne, unless of fine old kinds; but every dealer must feel regret, when making his invoice for choice old port, claret, burgundy, &c. at a high price, to be told that it is for 'immediate use.'

Another serious injury arises from the (so-called) wine-cellars in almost every modern house. Were it not a known fact, it would scarcely be believed possible that such little poking holes should be found, even in large mansions; displaying, too, such thoughtlessness and ignorance, that they are often placed next the kitchen fire, or out of doors, exposed to constant change of temperature. In another chapter I treat of this point, so essential to the good keeping of wine.

I was much struck lately by the remark of a gentleman worth, probably, 10,000*l.* a year, and very generous and liberal. I had been recommending some remarkably fine hock, which I had met with in Germany, at six guineas a dozen, and he wrote in reply that he considered it 'sinful' to expend 10/6 on a bottle of any wine. I entirely agree with him; yet there are still many who are ready to pay any sum to possess certain kinds in great repute, and produced in such limited quantities that the possessors may demand almost any price. Wine, in this respect, is somewhat similar to the traffic in horses. A horse, handsome and good enough for any one, may be bought for 70*l.*; while another, with some particular beauty, will fetch 100*l.* or 200*l.*

Few have any idea how difficult it is to get perfectly fine wine. It often combines all that could be desired, with one imperfection, which may be an objectionable amount of sweetness or of dryness;

but the latter, instead of being a soft, or general dryness, may be of a harsh and hard character. In the same way there are two kinds of sweetness; that which is merely *sweet*, and the other, arising from the richness of fine, well-ripened grapes. The former kind will always remain sweet, unless in a wine of body, with fermentative matter sufficient to reduce it; but the latter, though it shows that more age is required, will develope into dryness.

Until the great questions of Catholic and Negro Emancipation, Reform, the Corn Laws, &c. were settled, gentlemen could seldom meet without keen, and often violent, discussions on these questions; and late hours and much drinking were the usual consequence. But, even thirty or forty years ago, no disgrace attached to any one who was tipsy, or came to the drawing room in a state which showed that he had been drinking. On the contrary, it was rather expected, as a matter of course; and the jollity exhibited was thought to add to the pleasure of the evening.

Recurring to periods of older date, we shall find that the tipsiness and 'hilarity,' within our own memory, were 'temperance' in comparison with the habits of our forefathers.

Take, for instance, the following description given by Professor Cosmo Innes, in his *Sketches of Early Scottish History*. The gentleman to whom it relates was Mr. Rose, of Kilravock, in the county of Moray, stated to be usually a sober man, who *indulged* occasionally. The scene is in the public-house in Findhorn, and the authority is the clergyman of the parish, who gives the *bill*, the date of which is 1728.

Bill for Kilraick (Kilravock) and Colonel Rose, from Tuesday 12 o'clock, till Thursday 7 o'clock, afternoon :—

Tuesday, for 23 botles wine, at 1*s.* 6*d.* each botle.	£1	14	6
Wednesday, for 26 botles	1	19	0
Thursday, for 8 botles	0	12	0
To 5 ds. sugar	0	5	0
To 8 pints 'eall'	0	1	4
To eating	0	5	0
To 2 gills brandie	0	0	6
To 2 servants eating	0	3	0
To their drink—12 pints 'eall'	0	2	0
	5	2	4

N.B.—£5 2*s.* Scots is 8*s.* 6*d.* sterling.

In contrast with the above, I may mention that I was talking over these matters with a gentleman noted for his good dinners, capital wine, and no stint of it; and, wishing for information, I begged him to tell me how much was usually drunk at his table. He answered :—

'I have a dinner party this very day of ten ladies and ten gentlemen, and here is a list of the wine I have given out, to which I add what I believe will be used.'

For twenty persons :—

8 pint decanters of Sherry. Much of this will be left.
5 bottles of Champagne. All will be used.
1 ,, Sauterne. Ditto.
2 ,, Madeira. 1½ will be used.
2 ,, Sherry. All used.
1 ,, Port. Not all will be used.
2 ,, Claret. 1 used.

Dr. Somerville informs us that about 1760, in Scotland, when visitors called in the forenoon, ale or brandy were usually offered; and, to persons of importance, claret, and brandy-punch.

The following account of the state of society in the south-west of Scotland about a hundred years ago, was communicated to me by one who had a vivid recollection of the events described. It was in the country of Dirk Hatteraick's exploits:—

In the county in which I lived from the year 1773, drunkenness was not only frequent, but general. Social meetings were held almost daily, and intoxication was expected, as a matter of course, to conclude the evening's entertainment. During day the streets were sprinkled with staggerers of both sexes, cursing, swearing and fighting. Meanwhile, smuggling flourished, and the rugged coasts of that part of Scotland afforded secret nooks, where the French luggers could be concealed while landing their goods. Money was made, and houses built; and so little disgrace was attached to it, that the smugglers and their wives were often admitted by the chief landed proprietors as visitors, while their contraband goods were received into their houses and cellars. It was common for the ladies to commission from the *ladies* of the smugglers, tea, lace, silks, shoes, gloves, &c., from France. From these coast recesses frequently issued hundreds of horses loaded with tea, brandy, wine, tobacco, &c., traversing the wild moors, in co-operation with many of the gentlemen of this and neighbouring districts, and by arrangement with the shopkeepers of the towns and villages. Sometimes there were dreadful conflicts between these desperate, well-armed drivers and the revenue officers, supported by dragoons. The Isle of Man, being a smuggling depôt, and quite close, afforded great facilities for carrying on this trade—so destructive to every good habit and principle.

I believe that, although few parts of Scotland were so bad as Galloway, owing to its convenient position, yet smuggling was carried on in every part.

Drunkenness still prevails, but is rarely seen except in the lowest ranks; and even among those not to the same extent as formerly. I know it is said that it is as bad as ever; but let any one carry his recollection back to the streets of London forty years ago, especially on a Saturday night and Sunday morning, and he must admit that there is a great improvement. It is unusual to see a drunken person now; but I remember when the streets on a Sunday were swarming with both men and women in a state of intoxication; and going still further back, especially to Scotland, it may be said to have been there almost universal.

As an instance of the habits and manners prevailing in that country, I recollect that there were always numerous drunken people on a certain racecourse; so that boys went in the evening, on the road to the course, to see the fights which were sure to be going on, accompanied by a due amount of cursing and swearing, then habitual with high as well as low. Were it not impressed upon the memory, one could scarcely believe in the improvement which has taken place in the very appearance of people; especially when one remembers the ragged state of the clothes of many, even of the better sort, which was matched by their dirty faces and hands.*

* The following gives a fair idea of the natural love(!) of cleanliness in the North at this period:—An English lady, visiting

The passions and opinions of all classes were then violent; and that these were early instilled into children may be inferred from a *toast* they were called upon to repeat, when placed upon the dining-room table—'Bless the King and damn Buonaparte.' The whiskey-bottle was always at hand, and a servant girl could hardly bring a note without being asked to 'pree' (*i.e.* to take, or taste). Few things were done without being cemented by 'half a mutchkin.' Almost all the whiskey in private houses was 'smuggled,' for it was made in small stills, slowly; while the 'legal' was distilled in large quantities within certain hours, and was, therefore, hot and coarse.

At gentlemen's tables there was usually wine (madeira or lisbon) during dinner; and after dinner, either tumblers were brought for each person, or the general toddy bowl; after which few continued to drink wine, though the port was such as is now rarely seen. A glass of whiskey was thought beneficial for the stomach after the fish; and, if useful then, was quite as much so after the cheese. During dinner each gentleman was usually called upon for 'a sentiment' or 'a statesman,' or a lady, as a toast to drink to; and it may be supposed there was no lack of them. Five o'clock

her husband's birthplace, was introduced to his old nurse, from whom she felt sure she would hear some delightful anecdotes of his childhood. The nurse on being informed who she was, and of her object, said, 'Oh, mem, he was an unco laddie; aw could ne'er catch a grupp o' um te hae his heed kaim'd or his face wussen.' The astonishment of the English lady, on hearing the translation of this specimen of broad Scotch, may be supposed.

dinners required substantial suppers, when ladies 'of a certain age' were privileged—and did not neglect their privilege—to have a 'tumbler;' with the choice of wine, whiskey, brandy, rum, or hollands, which were on the sideboard. Before retiring for the night, the practice was invariable to have a tray brought up with the various kinds of spirits.

I believe that similar habits then prevailed throughout the kingdom, and that it was greatly worse at an earlier period than I can personally refer to. To prove this would not be difficult, but I shall give only the following instance, from Thackeray's *Four Georges*, to show the manners, about the year 1780, of royal people and of those called the 'higher classes.'

'Pray, my lord bishop,' says Hay, 'how much of the claret have you, that you wish to remove?'

The bishop said, six dozen.

'If that is all,' Hay answered, 'you have but to ask me six times to dinner, and I will carry it all away myself.'

We come to yet higher personages, and find their doings recorded in the blushing pages of little Miss Burney's 'Memoirs.' She represents a prince of the blood in quite a royal condition. The loudness, the bigness, boisterousness, creaking boots, and rattling oaths of the young princes, appear to have frightened the prim household of Windsor, and set all the teacups twittering on the tray. On the night of a ball and birthday, when one of the pretty kind princesses was to come out, it was agreed that her brother, Prince William Henry, should dance the opening minuet with her, and he came to visit the household at their dinner.

'At dinner, Mrs. Schwellenberg presided, attired magnificently; Miss Goldsworthy, Mrs. Stanforth, Messrs. Du

Luc and Stanhope, dined with us; and while we were still eating fruit, the Duke of Clarence entered.

'He was just risen from the king's table, and waiting for his equipage to go home and prepare for the ball. To give you an idea of the energy of his royal highness's language, I ought to set apart an objection to writing, or rather intimating, certain forcible words, and beg leave to show you in genuine colours a royal sailor.

'We all rose, of course, upon his entrance, and the two gentlemen placed themselves behind their chairs, while the footmen left the room. But he ordered us all to sit down, and called the men back to hand about some wine. He was in exceeding high spirits, and in the utmost good humour. He placed himself at the head of the table, next Mrs. Schwellenberg, and looked remarkably well, gay, and full of sport and mischief; yet clever withal, as well as comical.

'"Well, this is the first day I have ever dined with the king at St. James's on his birthday. Pray, have you all drunk his Majesty's health?"

'"No, your royal highness; your royal highness might make dem do dat," said Mrs. Schwellenberg.

'"Oh, by G——, I will! Here, you (to the footman), bring champagne; I'll drink the king's health again, if I die for it. Yes, I have done it pretty well already; so has the king, I promise you! I believe his majesty was never taken such good care of before; we have kept his spirits up, I promise you; we have enabled him to go through his fatigues; and I should have done more still, but for the ball and Mary;—I have promised to dance with Mary. I must keep sober for Mary."'

Indefatigable Miss Burney continues for a dozen pages reporting the conversation of the young sailor prince, who drank more and more champagne, stopped old Mrs. Schwellenberg's remonstrances by giving the old lady a kiss, and telling her to hold her potato-trap; and who did not 'keep sober for Mary.' Mary had to find another partner that night, for the royal William Henry could not keep his legs.

Will you have a picture of the amusements of another royal prince? It is the Duke of York, the brother with whom George IV. had had many a midnight carouse, and who continued his habits of pleasure almost until death seized his stout body.

In Pückler Muskau's 'Letters,' that German prince describes a bout with his royal highness, who in his best time was such a powerful toper, that 'six bottles of claret after dinner scarce made a perceptible change in his countenance.'

'I remember,' says Pückler, 'that one evening — indeed, it was past midnight — he took some of his guests, among whom were the Austrian ambassador, Count Meervelt, Count Beroldingen, and myself, into his beautiful armoury. We tried to swing several Turkish sabres, but none of us had a very firm grasp; whence it happened that the duke and Meervelt both scratched themselves with a sort of straight Indian sword, so as to draw blood. Meervelt then wished to try if the sword cut as well as a Damascus, and attempted to cut through one of the wax candles that stood on the table. The experiment answered so ill, that both the candles, candlesticks and all, fell to the ground and were extinguished. While we were groping in the dark and trying to find the door, the duke's aide-de-camp stammered out in great agitation, "By G——, sir, I remember the sword is poisoned!"

'You may conceive the agreeable feelings of the wounded at this intelligence! Happily, on further examination, it appeared that claret, and not poison, was at the bottom of the colonel's exclamation.'

And now I have one more story of the bacchanalian sort, in which Clarence and York, and the very highest personage of the realm, the great Prince Regent, all play parts. The feast took place at the Pavilion at Brighton, and was described to me by a gentleman who was present at the scene. In Gilray's caricatures, and amongst Fox's jolly associates, there figures a great nobleman, the Duke of Norfolk, called Jockey of Norfolk in his time, and celebrated for his table exploits. He had quarrelled with the prince, like the rest of the Whigs; but a sort of reconciliation had taken place; and now, being a very old man, the prince invited him to dine and sleep at the Pavilion; and the old duke drove over from his Castle of Arundel with his famous equipage of grey horses, still remembered in Sussex.

The Prince of Wales had concocted with his royal brothers a notable scheme for making the old man drunk. Every person at table was enjoined to drink wine with the duke—a challenge which the old toper did not refuse. He soon began to see that there was a conspiracy against him; he drank glass for glass; he overthrew many of the brave. At last the First Gentleman of Europe proposed bumpers of brandy. One of the royal brothers filled a great glass for the duke. He stood up and tossed off the drink. 'Now,' says he, 'I will have my carriage, and go home.' The prince urged upon him his previous promise to sleep under the roof where he had been so generously entertained. 'No,' he said, he had had enough of such hospitality. A trap had been set for him; he would leave the place at once and never enter its doors more.

I have tried to find in Pepys's and other memoirs, details of the drinking habits of the English, as of the Scotch, at the same period, but unsuccessfully. Pepys seems to have felt more interest in eating than in drinking. For instance, he writes, in 1659, 26th January,

Dined at my lord's lodgings, where my wife had got ready a very fine dinner—viz., a dish of marrow-bones, a leg of mutton, a loin of veal, a dish of fowls, three pullets, and a dozen larks all in a dish; a great tart, a neat's tongue, a dish of anchovies, a dish of prawns, and cheese.

But not a word about wine. On the 18th of February:

> The city is very openhanded to the soldiers, that they are drunk all day. Two of them were hanged in the Strand for their mutiny at Somerset House.

But two years later we have a little more about drinking, though, whether wine or brandy, he does not state. For the sake of Mrs. Pepys and Mrs. Franklyn's memories, we shall hope that it was not the latter: —

> April 3rd, 1661.—Took my wife and Mrs. Franklyn to Axe Yard, where there were three great bonfires, and many gallants, men and women, who laid hold of us, and would have us drink the king's health upon our knees, kneeling upon a faggot, which we all did. Wonderful to see how the ladies did tipple.

It is now above thirty-six years since I had an interview about the wine duties, with Mr. Poulett Thomson, then Vice-President of the Board of Trade; and twelve years since the first of a series of letters appeared in *The Times*, advocating the reduction on every kind to *one shilling* per gallon. From that period, few months have elapsed without letters written for the same object, besides numerous communications with men in and out of office. I could mention the names of a few, very few, wine merchants who were equally zealous for a reduction; but, without exception, all were opposed to my proposal of such a low rate as 1/, and insisted that it would not be granted, wishing me to try for

2/ or 2/6. My resistance was called obstinacy; but although it probably embraced a share of that useful quality, yet it was grounded on what is now an admitted principle—viz., that no duty ought to exceed 10 per cent. of the cost of the article; so that even 1/ would be 100 per cent. on a large proportion of the common class of wines, and was therefore as high a rate as should be charged.

In consequence of the numerous letters in favour of and against a reduction, which appeared in 1850 and 1851, Mr. Disraeli, then Chancellor of the Exchequer, could not resist granting a committee; hoping thereby to stop the agitation and disturbance caused by myself and a few others. The keenest exertions were used on both sides, and not a little personal animosity was aroused; for the feelings and opinions of the two parties were very divided. The committee dissolved without being able to agree to a report, but the ball had been moved; the question was not allowed to rest; and the conviction was gradually driven into the minds of even the greatest opponents of any alteration, that it was inevitably coming upon them, after all. Much anxiety was also felt as to whether the government would allow the return of the difference of duty on duty-paid stocks, according to the Treasury Minute of July 1843.

On the 29th of February, 1860, the duty on every description of wine was made 3/ per gallon (having been since 1831, 5/6 and 5/9 on all, except Cape, which were 2/9 and 2/11); and government acted in a very liberal, trustful way in regard to the Treasury Minute.

On the 1st of January, 1861, this uniform rate of 3/ per gallon ceased, and the duties, taking the degrees of strength, according to Sykes's hydrometer, were as follows: —

Under 18°	1/	per gallon.
„ 26°	1/9	„
„ 40°	2/5	„
„ 45°	2/11	„
On *all* in bottle	2/5	„

Although rejoiced to see 1/ per gallon realised, my disappointment was great to find it accompanied by not only one, but three other rates; besides the unjust charge laid on even the weakest, if imported in glass instead of wood.

During the first six months the 'tests' of strength by the Customs were 72,031; while it is impossible to say how many were tried by dealers and those they employed. The Chancellor of the Exchequer got little rest from complaints and representations, public and private, addressed to him on this head; yet often have I been astonished by the way in which, in the midst of apparently overwhelming questions, he has immediately replied to long letters full of details, as if he had nothing to think of but the wine duties and the alcoholic test.

It would be very ungracious to express aught but gratitude to him for having effected even a partial reduction, for he had much opposition to encounter;

and, of course, the only persons he could consult were a few Customs and Excise officials, who rarely know much of the practical workings of trade, and have no objection to formalities and delays. As he could not communicate with any wine merchants, he was obliged to receive other opinions; and the result was the grievous mistake of the variety of rates of duty.

As the feeling against these was very strong and general, Mr. Gladstone again yielded; and announced, on the 3rd of April, 1862, that the duties should be as under:—

Rates of duty on wines imported into Great Britain and Ireland on and after April 4, 1862:—

	Containing less than the following rates of proof spirit, verified by Sykes's hydrometer, viz.:—		If imported in bottles, and containing less than 42 degrees
	26 degrees	42 degrees	
	s d	*s d*	*s d*
Wine, Red . the Gallon	1 0	2 6	2 6
Ditto, White . "	1 0	2 6	2 6
Lees of such Wines "	1 0	2 6	2 6

And for every degree of strength beyond the highest above specified, an additional duty of 3*d.* per gallon.

This is a great improvement upon the former tariff, but the evil of a differential rate is still retained.

The most important question now connected with wine is, whether it is to become a general beverage; or, at least, whether it will be drunk so commonly as to make it, to some extent, supersede spirits, and yield a large revenue.

Reference to the accompanying calculations, shows that the total annual consumption (quantity on which duty has been paid) was:

	Gallons.		Gallons.
In 1855 .	6,669,784	in 1856 .	7,368,071
1857 .	7,042,301	1858 .	6,697,178
1859 .	7,263,007	1860 .	7,357,652
1861 .	10,787,209	1862 .	9,803,046

The average revenue during the five years of the old duty, from 1855 to 1859, was 1,878,666*l.* In 1860, it was 1,144,794*l.*; in 1861, 1,223,240*l.*; and in 1862, 1,123,640*l.*

Those in the trade (and they were almost all) who opposed the reduction, may point to these figures triumphantly; and I believe that they will be able to point to similar, though not to equally bad results, as long as the intolerable differential rate remains on the statute book.

The proposal for a uniform rate of *one shilling per gallon* happens, as I have said, to have been my proposal. I fought for it during many years, and shall never cease to fight till there is a shilling, and nothing but a shilling, laid on all wines; whether it be the weakest claret, or the strongest port, imported in wood or in glass.

The arguments offered, were supported by the able writer of the Money article in *The Times;* and even *Punch* took up the cause of cheap wine, as may be seen in the following *jeu d'esprit.* I believe there is much truth in the remark made when this appeared: 'When *The Times* and *Punch* take up a question, there is a certainty that it will be carried.'

LIGHT FRENCH WINE!

A BACCHANALIAN AND PACIFIC SONG.

SUGGESTED BY MR. SHAW'S LETTER IN 'THE TIMES,' MONEY ARTICLE.

(From *Punch*, January 30, 1851.)

AIR—'*Gaily still the moments roll.*'

All away the sessions roll,
Whilst we quaff the brandied bowl,
Which can never be so whole-
-Some, sure, as light French wine.
(*Chorus.*) Not, sure, as light French wi-i-ine &c.

Rum, the liver gnaws like grief;
'Something short,' makes being brief;
Much disease would find relief,
Did we drink light French wine.
(*Chorus.*) Did we, &c. &c.

Drink, from malt which Britain brews,
Doth the noddle oft bemuse;
So much beer we should not use
Could we get light French wine.
(*Chorus.*) Could we get, &c. &c.

HEAD need ne'er his brain engage
How with France a war to wage,
Did we but our thirst assuage
By drinking light French wine.
(*Chorus.*) By drinking, &c. &c.

No; our neighbours o'er the sea
Never would the boobies be
To fall out with us, if we
Consumed their light French wine.
(*Chorus.*) Consumed their, &c. &c.

Burgundy, Champagne, Bordeaux,
Would in many a goblet flow;
But the Custom House says, 'No;
You shan't drink light French wine.'
(*Chorus.*) 'You shan't,' &c. &c.

Why not, then, the duty lower?
If you plead that you're too poor,
Mind, that we should drink the more,
Could we get cheap French wine.
(*Chorus.*) Could we get, &c. &c.

You'd lose nothing in finance,
Whilst retrenchment would advance,
Since there'd be no fear of France,
If we drank light French wine.
(*Chorus.*) If we drank, &c. &c.

It is an old saying and a useful truth, that the smuggler keeps Chancellors of the Exchequer in order; and I am glad to see the following description of a mode by which the differential rate can be legally evaded. It is extracted from a wine circular:

A rather ingenious method of evading payment of a considerable portion of the difference between the 1/ and 2/6 rates of duty is now being adopted by dealers who supply the public with low-priced beverages, popularly known as Elbe sherry &c. The Hamburg wines (?) hitherto imported were generally found to contain from 36 to 38 per cent. of spirit, and, as such, 100 gallons were liable to 12*l.* 10*s.* duty. Now, we are informed by shippers that they are taking orders at from 8*l.* to 9*l.* per butt, *guaranteed to contain less than* 26 *per cent.*; the parties who retail them having made a calculation that they can, after payment of duty, augment the strength to 36, and effect a saving of 25*l.* per cent. For example, the duty on ninety gallons of wine amounts to 4*l.* 10*s.*, and ten gallons of spirit at 10s. is 5*l*., making together 9*l*. 10s. for 200 gallons of 36 degrees, instead of 12*l*. 10s., if imported of that strength.

A very serious evil of the 2/6 rate, is that it greatly injures the export part of a wine merchant's business; for, as the return of the duty when wine is sent abroad is no longer allowed, there is a loss of 5/ on every dozen imported in bottle, and above 26° of strength, sent out of the duty-paid cellar. A great many orders are for small quantities of various kinds, which would be bottled, or taken from bins, but the amount of the duty must in that case be lost; and, consequently, although there may be plenty in the merchant's cellar, he finds himself compelled to purchase more in bond.

If it is for port or sherry, he buys what he requires from some one who has it ready in the bottling vault, or he sends a cask there, from his bonded stock. These latter wines require, of course, to be fined, which for sherry, occupies at least three weeks; when there is the trouble of sending corks, &c., and then paying dock companies to do what would be more satisfactorily done in the merchant's own cellar. If there were only the rate of 1/ per gallon, merchants would willingly lose the 2/ per dozen on wine from their own cellars, and would still have the option of shipping from bond.

The Tables of Trade and Revenue for 1862 having now been published, the effect of the reduction is seen in the following statement:—

Number of Gallons, and Amounts received, on each degree of strength, in 1862.

	Rate of Duty	Red and White	Per Cent. of Total	Amount of Duty on Red & White	Per Cent. of Total Duty	Red	Per Cent. of Red	White	Per Cent. of White
	per gallon	*galls.*		*£*		*galls.*		*galls.*	
Under 26° .	1/	1,287,511	13·13	64,375	6·4	1,102,927	25·21	184,584	3·41
Under 45° to 3d April, and under 42° from that date .	2/6	7,616,796	77·70	952,099	84·2	3,022,779	69·8	4,594,017	84·62
42° and upwards from 3d April . .	2/11	73,427	·75	10,709	·10	21,366	·48	52,061	·97
In bottles: under 40° to 3d April, and under 42° from that date .	2/6	825,312	8·42	103,164	9·84	228,394	5·28	596,918	11·0
		9,803,046	100	*1,123,605	100	4,375,466	100	5,427,580	100

I have already written so often against the differential rates, that I shall refrain from entering into much detail here; for I could only reiterate the facts and opinions already published. In order to enable those who desire it to understand the question, some of the letters will be found in the Appendix.

The calculations, derived from the official statements of wine last year (1862), as above, show that—

1,287,511	gallons were charged	1/	, producing	£ 64,375
7,616,796	,, ,,	2/6	,,	952,099
73,427	,, ,,	2/11	,,	10,709
825,312	,, (in bottle)	2/6	,,	103,164
9,803,046 gallons				*£1,123,605

Thus it appears that, after all the much talked of

* I cannot get the amount of the duty on each class to agree with the total sum received upon Wine, within about £6,000; which arises, probably, from certain old arrears having been carried from former years. This does not affect the argument, and but very slightly the per centage of duty.

reduction to a low rate, the quantity charged 1/ per gallon is only 1,287,511 gallons, while that charged 2/6 and 2/11 is 8,515,535 gallons. In other words, the 1/ is little more than an eighth part, being exactly 13·13 per cent. of the whole; and yet the Wine Association in their last Report express themselves as *satisfied* with this result!

Including Champagne, we here see that the total of all wine, of every kind and country, imported in bottles, is only 825,312 gallons, or 412,656 dozens. It must be remembered that, as regards sparkling kinds, it is not optional but compulsory, to bring them over in bottle; and consequently even the very weakest and cheapest must pay 5/ per dozen. But, although it cannot be said that others must be thus imported, yet it is a practical fact that the high rate on such importations greatly militates against the introduction of many kinds, which therefore remain unknown. Every wine merchant who endeavours to extend his trade in natural wines, must have found that he can procure orders for a case or two of some variety of the low-priced kinds, with a view to a trial; but very few gentlemen will order this quality in cask; and the merchant is not disposed to purchase a hogshead for the sake of selling only six or eight dozen, which he is aware may not be liked, and may be returned to him.

The loss of 3/ per dozen from his profit may be easily submitted to on high-priced qualities; and he knows that when he imports good full-bodied kinds he is naturally timid about the lower priced. But there is another serious objection to this intolerable regulation.

In visiting a wine-cellar abroad, the very kind that is wanted may be found in the most brilliant condition for bottling, having lain, perhaps, for months undisturbed; and now, what is to be done? Supposing it to be a hogshead of claret, of forty-six gallons—if imported in the hogshead, the duty at 1/ will be 2*l.* 6*s.*; but if the contents be transferred, there, from wood to glass, the rate will be 2/6 per gallon, or 5*l.* 15/ for the hogshead. Rather than let the wine be disturbed, and thereby more or less injured, and having, also, to wait at least a month after its arrival in cask, before it will be again fit for bottling, he will probably resolve to pay the additional 150 per cent. duty, by importing it in bottle.

Another evil of the 2/6 rate is that its amount still causes wines to be kept in bond, which would not be done if there were only the shilling rate; and it is not using too strong a word to apply *destructive* to the manner in which natural and young wines are (mal-) treated in all bonded vaults.

I have already offered some remarks on this point, but having met with similar opinions in the French *Parfait Vigneron*, I copy them here, hoping that they may prove useful.

Great ignorance prevails in England about the proper management of French wines, whether in cask or in bottle. Port and sherry are carefully decanted, and drunk in the most brilliant condition; but our wines are almost always kept in the original bottles, and, consequently, are seldom bright. This, of course, deteriorates not only the quality, but the appearance, and raises against them an unjust prejudice.

It is needless to expect our wines to make much way in London, while importers allow casks to remain in the docks, constantly disturbed by the removal of others near them, and never filled up. What would be thought of any wine merchant in France who would treat his stock in such a manner?

Although London is very deficient in cellars — and those existing are seldom suited for natural delicate wines —it would be infinitely better to have every cask brought at once from the public dock vaults than to leave them where there is no care paid to them, except to see that there is no leakage.

It should also be added that, as few, if any, English cellarmen have knowledge or experience of the management of any but strong brandied kinds, which scarcely anything can hurt, and only of our ripe well-fermented qualities, merchants who desire to purchase new wines, and to rear them themselves, will find it absolutely necessary to engage experienced French cellarmen.

There is no man for whom I feel a greater respect than for Mr. Gladstone; and I believe that no one else in the present or in any other Government would have had the courage to propose the shilling rate. But my respect for him must not deter me from expressing the conviction that he has been led by revenue officials to clog the measure with regulations of a very injurious tendency.

First, the duty was made, for about a year, 3/ per gallon on every kind; then, for about the same period, 1/, 1/9, 2/6, and 2/11; and, now, it is 1/ and 2/6.

The 3/ still left a rate of 6/ per dozen. The next change, the admission at 1/, of wines up to 18° of strength, produced constant annoyance, and allowed only the weakest to be introduced. The extension of the boon to 26° of strength is a great improvement, but it still excludes some natural wines, with others having a very small portion of spirit added.

Passing 26° by even the tenth of a degree, the duty payable is increased 150 per cent.; so that if 1,000 gallons are within the 26°, the charge, at 1/, will be 50*l.*; but, if exceeding 26°, it will be, at 2/6, 125*l.*

If the strength instead of being $26\frac{1}{10}$° is $41\frac{9}{10}$°, or 16° stronger (but this side of 42°), it will still be charged only 2/6 per gallon. Surely this cannot be allowed to continue; and yet is not the law by which every gallon imported in bottle, be it weak or be it strong, is charged the highest rate, even more inconsistent?

These are strong expressions, but they are justified by the circumstances of the case; though I believe that if twenty of the first wine merchants in London were consulted, eighteen would be opposed to any change; because the high duty continues to capitalists that practical monopoly which they possessed in a still greater degree under the old duty.

The champagne houses with well-known brands, prefer the duty at 2/6 rather than at 1/, because the latter would cause more competition. Port and sherry houses prefer it, because with a low rate, many strong kinds of a cheaper class would be introduced as substitutes.

But it would be giving a very incorrect and unfair impression, were I to omit the mention of a powerful cause which has contributed to prevent the success of Mr. Gladstone's measure.

This is the enormous rise in the prices of all wines since the oïdium, or wine disease, of 1851. The reduction of duty on a butt of sherry and a pipe of port is about 18*l.*; but the increased price of the wine itself is more than 20*l.* higher than for similar quality formerly; so that the lower duty has scarcely compensated for the higher price. It may be fairly argued that the increased price of sherry is to some extent attributable to the extended demand, especially if the shipments now made to other parts of the world be taken into account; but, even with all this, the present exportations from a country of such wine-producing powers, as Spain, are very small.

The wine disease seems now to have run its course; and if there were only three or four vintages in the wine countries, as abundant as have occasionally occurred, empty cellars would be replenished, and wine would fall to the old normal prices.

With two or three exceptions, the grapes suffered everywhere. In my remarks on the wines of the

South of France, I give an extract furnished by the Chamber of Commerce of Montpellier, showing the prices before and after the oïdium; and it was not worse there than in other places it attacked. The prices were, per twenty-two gallons, in 1851, 15/; 1852, 1*l.* 5/; 1853, 2*l.* 10/; 1856, 3*l.* 7/; 1857, 2*l.* 7/.

Prices are lower now, owing to several good vintages in the South; but stocks throughout France have become low, and the production in some districts having been small, the consequent fall in price has not been so great as it would otherwise have been.

The '*satisfactory*' result of the reduction is sometimes alluded to, as I have already observed; but with little reason, in my opinion. In the year 1851, before the reduction, the consumption was 7,263,026 gallons, yielding 1,982,329*l.* Last year the gallons were 9,803,046, and the revenue 1,123,640*l.*

Can this be justly called satisfactory? I call it very unsatisfactory, and have no doubt that it will continue to be so, until there is a uniform rate of 1/; when, although we may not expect to reach the average annual consumption of 360 bottles for each man, as in Mayence, or of 185 bottles for each man, woman, and child, as in Paris, we may yet hope that our last year's two bottles per head will be replaced by at least twelve bottles; which, at 1/ per gallon, would yield 3,000,000*l.* of revenue.

The Consumption of Wine, the Revenue from it, the Population, the Rates of Duty, the year 1791

Years	Port		Sherry		French		Marsala		Madeira		Rhenish		Unenu-
	Gallons	Consumption, per cent.	Gallons	Consumption, per cent.	Gallons	Consumption, per cent.	Gallons	Consumption, per cent.	Gallons	Consumption, per cent.	Gallons	Consumption, per cent.	Gallons
1791 to 1800 (average)		70 to 75		16 to 24		1 to 3							
1801 to 1810 (do.)		60 to 65		18 to 24		1 to 2							
1811 to 1820 (do.)		68 to 62		20 to 25		2 to 4							
1821 to 1830 (do.)		44 to 54		24 to 32		4 to 6							
1831	2,707,734	43.58	2,089,582	33.63	254,366	4.09	259,916	4.18	109,127	3.56	57,888	0.93	Not specified
1841	2,387,017	38.59	2,500,760	38.36	358,740	5.72	401,439	6.49	107,701	1.58	55,242	0.87	
1851	2,524,775	40.20	2,533,389	40.33	447,566	7.12	394,225	6.28	71,025	1.14	58,957	0.94	
1859	2,020,561	27.82	2,876,554	39.60	695,913	9.60	227,657	3.13	29,566	0.41	125,408	1.72	501,465
1860	1,776,138	24.14	2,975,769	40.44	1,125,599	15.30	209,154	2.84	28,942	0.39	222,725	3.3	592,167
1861	2,709,649	25.06	4,082,274	37.38	2,227,662	20.65	231,270	2.13	28,749	0.27	345,647	3.20	878,838
1862	2,349,954	23.97	3,956,213	40.35	1,900,344	19.38	214,125	2.18	31,906	0.32	316,440	3.22	851,782

This Table, showing the Consumption, Revenue, &c. since 1791, will be found to give a clear and succinct history of the wine trade from that period to the end of 1862; and a miserable picture it offers of a stationary, or rather of a retrograding, trade. In making comparisons, it should not be forgotten, that if a thousand gallons, three years ago, are still a thousand, this proves retrogression; because the population increases nearly a million every three years, with a corresponding annual increase of wealth.

and the Number of Bottles for each Person, calculated in average periods, from to the year 1862.

…nerated	Cape		Total Gallons duty paid	Revenue from Wine	Population	Bottles per head, per annum	Rates of Duty per Gallon		Red Wine		White Wine	
Consumption, per cent.	Gallons	Consumption, per cent.					On Port, &c.	On French, &c.	Gallons	Per cent. of Total	Gallons	Per cent. of Total
			6,513,019	£ 1,412,120	14,500,000	2.9-10ths	4/10 to 6/1	7/1 to 9/1				
			6,314,065	2,469,239	16,580,994	2.2-10ths	6/9 to 9/1	10/2 to 13/8				
			4,912,139	1,974,095	19,754,618	1.5-10ths	9/1	19/8 to 13/2				
			5,987,785	1,688,806	22,941,950	1.6-10ths	9/1 to 4/10	13/9 to 7/3				
	539,584	8.48	6,212,264	1,585,484	24,419,421	1.5-10ths	Cape 2/9	all other kinds 5/6				
	441,288	7.10	6,184,960	1,720,479	27,019,558	1.3-10ths	2/11	5/9				
	234,672	3.74	6,280,653	1,776,249	27,831,781	1.3-10ths	2/11	5/9				
6.90	785,926	10.82	7,263,046	1,982,327	estimate 29,750,000	1.5-10ths	2/11	5/9	2,972,192	40.92	4,290,778	59.8
8.5	427,698	5.81	7,358,192	1,144,794	estimate 29,000,000	1.5-10ths	From 29th Feb. 1860, 3/ on all		3,001,413	40.79	4,356,779	59.21
8.15	340,082	3.16	10,787,171	1,223,240	29,307,199	2.2-10ths	1/ 1/9 2/5 and 2/11		5,110,210	47.37	5,676,961	52.63
8.68	182,282	1.86	9,803,046	1,123,640	estimate 29,500,000	2.0	1/under 26 degrees, and 2/6 under 42 degrees		4,375,466	44.63	5,427,580	55.37

With the old duty, the rate charged was 5/9, whether it was vin ordinaire, roussillon, or still stronger sherry or port; and the only instance, of which I am personally cognisant of wine having been seized on account of its strength, was about forty years ago. This was two hogsheads of white port, which tasted more like brandy than wine.

The temptation, *then*, to deceive was much greater than now; because the benefit, if successful, was the difference between 5/9 on wine and 22/10 on brandy, which was 17/1; while, now, all that could be gained is between 1/ and 10/4, or 9/4 per gallon. The gain, therefore, by smuggling, was 7/9 per gallon greater than it is now.

It is alleged, by some, that if strongly-brandied wines are allowed to be introduced, they will be converted into spirit, and the Government defrauded of the duty, under the guise of wine. The answer to this is, that a wine merchant imports only that which he believes to be merchantable; and if his wine is brandied to such an extent as to taste more like brandy than wine, it will be unsaleable. As to getting it distilled and the spirit sold profitably as brandy, not even the most suspicious Customs or Inland Officer believes that this could be done.

By referring to the letters in the Appendix these complications will be found more fully explained. Already they are admitted by many who previously argued in their favour, to be injudicious.

Exclusive of the importations in bottle, the quantity on which the rate of 2/6 was paid in 1862 is above 77 per cent. of the whole; a convincing proof that the people of this country still prefer strong wines. This, no doubt, is a bad and corrupted taste, the result of a vicious course of legislation.

What else could be expected, when reference is made to the following Table; which shows that from 1693 to 1831, or 138 years, the rates of duty against the wines of France were never less than 50 per cent., and for 85 years of the time were about 120 per cent. Even in the northern parts of Europe people drink bordeaux and similar wines; but, here, all natural unbrandied kinds were so long interdicted that few ever tasted them; and, although they are becoming more known and appreciated, a nation's habits and tastes cannot be altered even in a generation.

Rates of Duty per Gallon, on the Wines of France, Portugal, and Spain, from 1671 *to* 1850; *showing the relative increase and reductions, and the differential charge against those of France, down to* 1831, *when they were equalised.*

Years	Period	Duty on French s.	Duty on French d.	Raised, per cent.	Lowered, per cent.	Duty on Portugal and Spanish s.	Duty on Portugal and Spanish d.	Raised, per cent.	Lowered, per cent.	Difference against French, per cent.
1671 to 1678. .	8	0	4	...	...	0	4	...	...	equal
1678—1688. .	10	0	8	100	...	0	8	100	...	equal
1688—1693. .	5	1	4	100	...	1	4	100	...	equal
1693—1697. .	4	2	1	56	...	1	8	25	...	25
1697—1707. .	10	4	10	132	...	2	0	20	...	142
1707—1745. .	38	5	3	9	...	2	5	21	...	117
1745—1782. .	37	6	0	14	...	2	9	14	...	118
1782—1786. .	4	9	5	57	...	4	10	76	...	95
1786—1794. .	8	4	10	...	49	3	1	...	36	57
1795	1	7	4	52	...	4	10	57	...	51
1795—1797. .	2	10	2	39	...	6	9	40	...	51
1797—1800. .	3	10	6	3	...	6	11	2	...	52
1801	1	10	2	...	3	6	9	...	2	51
1802	1	10	7	4	...	7	0	4	...	51
1803	1	12	5	17	...	8	3	18	...	51
1804	1	10	6	...	15	9	0	9	...	17
1804—1812. .	8	13	8	30	...	9	1	1	...	50
1813	1	19	8	44	...	9	1	...	...	117
1814—1825. .	11	13	9	...	30	9	1	...	...	51
1825—1831. .	6	7	3	...	47	4	10	...	47	50
1831, and since	...	5	6	...	...	5	6	...	...	equal

The very earliest allusion to wine is :—

'Noah began to be an husbandman, and he planted a vineyard. And he drank of the wine, and was drunken.'

A Latin poet has ingeniously and beautifully represented the wine as a gift from the gods, to console mankind for the miseries entailed upon them by the Deluge :—

Omnia vastatis ergo quum cerneret arvis
Desolata Deus, nobis felicia vini
Dona dedit, tristes hominum quo munere fovit
Reliquias, mundi solatus vite ruinam.

Ovid gives the following prudent advice :—

I own, I think of wine the moderate use
More suits the sex and sooner finds excuse.
It warms the blood, adds lustre to the eyes,
And Wine and Love have ever been allies;
But carefully from all intemperance keep,
Nor drink till you see double, lisp, or sleep.

In another, we find :—

More fruitful than the accumulated board,
Of pain and misery; for, the subtile draught
Faster and surer swells the vital tide,
And with more active poison fills our frame.
Ah, sly deceiver! branded o'er and o'er,
Yet still believed! exulting o'er the wreck
Of sober vows.

Another sings in a similar strain :—

Three cups of wine a prudent man may take:
The first of them for constitution sake;
The second, to the girl he loves the best;
The third and last, to lull him to his rest—
Then home to bed. But, if a fourth he pours,
That is the cup of folly, and not ours.
Loud noisy talking on the fifth attends;
The sixth breeds feuds, and falling out of friends;
Seven beget blows, and faces stained with gore;

Eight, and the watch patrole breaks ope' the door;
Mad with the ninth, another cup goes round,
And the swilled sot drops senseless on the ground.

As the size of these 'cups' is not stated we must suppose that they were very capacious; otherwise three of them would be a small allowance for the author of the following ingenious piece of logic:—

Good wine makes good blood,
Good blood causeth good humours,
Good humours cause good thoughts,
Good thoughts bring forth good works,
Good works carry a man to heaven.

Ergo,
Good wine carrieth a man to heaven.

He is borne out by what the Frenchman says:—

Qui ne sait d'une heureuse ivresse,
Qui ne sait les heureux effets?
Elle prodigue la sagesse,
Elle revèle les secrets;
Des chimères de l'espérance
Elle sait nous faire jouir.
C'est dans la coupe du plaisir
Que l'ignorant boit la science;
Au lâche, elle rend la vaillance;
Au fourbe, la sincérité;
Et dans le sein de l'indigence
Fait trouver la félicité.
Gaieté, franchise, confiance,
Talents, vous êtes ses bienfaits;
Eh! quel buveur manqua jamais,
Ou de courage, ou d'éloquence!

Cowley, in his imitation of Anacreon, rises to this pitch of extravagance:—

The thirsty earth soaks up the rain,
And drinks and gapes for drink again;

The plants suck in the earth, and are,
With constant drinking, fresh and fair;
The sea itself (which, one would think,
Should have but little need of drink)
Drinks twice ten thousand rivers up,
So filled that they o'erflow the cup.
The busy sun (and one would guess
By 's drunken, fiery face, no less)
Drinks up the sea; and, when he 's done,
The moon and stars drink up the sun.
They drink and dance by their own light;
They drink and revel all the night.
Nothing in Nature's sober found,
But an eternal health goes round.
Fill up the bowl, then, fill it high,
Fill all the glasses there; for why
Should every creature drink but I?
Why, man of morals, tell me why?

Even the learned Bacon does not consider it beneath him to declare:—

The use of wine in dry and consumed bodies is hurtful; in moist and full bodies it is good. The cause is, for that the spirits of the wine do prey upon the dew, or radical moisture of the body, and so deceive the animal spirits; but where there is moisture enough, or superfluous, there wine helpeth to digest and to dessicate the moisture.

These being the sentiments of the author of the *Novum Organum*, I shall not presume to say more of them than that they do not appear to me to be very wise; neither does Plato's interdict against the use of wine by all under twenty years of age. Aristotle approved of it 'for all except children and nurses.'

CHAPTER II.

PORT—OPORTO—UPPER DOURO, ETC.

The Foz—The Douro—Vigo—Minho—Oporto—Alto Douro Company—Baron Forrester—To make Port—Wine Tasters—Elderberries—Jeropiga—Rise in Prices—The Future of Port—Rates of Duty since 1671—Methuen Treaty—White Port—Lisbons—Tom's Coffee House—Lyne Stephens—Letter from Lisbon, 1798—The Port Trade Artificial—Difficulty of giving just Views—Head of the Wine Trade—Bottle-stink—Dining Hours—Horse Shoe—Gronow's Reminiscences—The Cheeryble Brothers—Old Port in Lancashire—Monopoly—Alto Douro Company's Tasters—Old and Present Prices—Few Shippers formerly—Crusts—Racking and Fining—Mr. Ballantyne's Letter—Mr. Gassiot's Description—Estimates of Cost—Rua Ingleza—Prison of Oporto—Siege—To Fight and be Fighted—Steamer Signalled—Man and Wife—Escape—Consumption and Percentage since 1831—Statistics.

OPORTO may be reached by landing from the steamer, which stops, when the weather permits, opposite the fort, or Foz. The powerful mail-boat, with a crew of twenty men, crossing the dangerous bar at the mouth of the Douro, is a fine sight; and the walk to the town along the high banks of the river is very beautiful. On my second visit, in 1844, I disembarked there; but I would advise every lover of scenery to leave the steamer at Vigo and ride to Oporto.

From the hill on the brow of which Vigo is built the view is very extensive and splendid, and so it continues the whole way, with the sea beating against the rocks on the right; while the varying prospects of valley and mountain, luxuriant foliage and fields, never fail to delight the eye.

I have seen many lands, but I recollect none which equal in beauty the great valley of the Entre-Minho-e-Douro; especially when coming upon the River Minho, that separates Spain from Portugal.

On arriving at Oporto, the porter at the inn conducted me to the house of a friend, where I first met with the fine, high-flavoured, light, old port that the English merchants have for their own use; and most excellent it is.

I ventured to return to my hotel without a guide, but, losing my way, I wandered up and down the precipitous streets for two or three hours, having forgotten the name of the inn; could I have recollected it, I was unable to make inquiries, from my ignorance of the language. At length I stumbled against two men, who stopped and spoke to me; and even in the darkness of those southern climes, I could perceive they were policemen with guns. The fear of sleeping in the streets, and of the large rats running about and fighting and screaming, brought into play the old proverb of 'necessity being the mother of invention.' I remembered that my inn was in the high part of the town, and that close to it was a large open space where many men were spinning ropes. This seemed my only way of explaining my wish, so turning my face to the policemen, I began to walk backwards, moving my hands in front as if rope-spinning, and then pointing up the street; they seemed amused, and talking together beckoned me to follow; when shortly I found myself on the great square, and in a few minutes more in my *posada.*

The next morning, I first beheld by daylight the beautifully situated towns of Oporto and Villa Nova on opposite sides of the river; and the surrounding country, with its quintas and mansions, many of them in the midst of orange groves, which diffused their fragrance around.

Unless the vintage be very bad, it is usual for the partner or manager of each foreign house in Oporto to go up to the wine district, where many of them have country quarters, and live very comfortably during their sojourn. As the reputation of their firm depends upon their selection, there is, of course, much anxiety and rivalry among the numerous buyers congregated in this little privileged tract, called the Upper Corgo; which begins about sixty miles up the Douro, and is about twenty-four miles in length, and twelve in breadth, on both sides of the river.

What can more strikingly demonstrate the evils of the system connected with the supply of port wine than the fact, that not one gallon can be legally exported to any part of Europe unless it has been passed by the Alto Douro Company as suitable? This company has also the power of fixing each year the quantity that it considers sufficient; and often a farmer, with twenty pipes of the very same wine, gets a bilhete (*i. e.* a certificate of goodness) for only ten pipes, while the other ten, having no bilhete, lose half their value; as they must be placed among those for country use, or for importation to any place not in Europe.

Some years ago, this and an export duty of about 6*d.* per pipe to America, while it was about 6*l.* to Europe (*i.e.* England), occasioned large shipments to that country and Canada, and reshipments of the same wine to Britain; till the practice was put a stop to by oaths and bonds, and informers abroad. There is now a reduction from the former high export rate, to about 1*l.* per pipe. These bilhetes are bought and sold as openly as railway stock here, at a price varying from 3*l.* to 6*l.* per pipe, according as the company permits more or less exportation of the yearly produce. Protected by them, wines entirely different from those for which they were granted, with others actually made out of the bounds of the company's limits, are brought to the river-boats, and to the *lodges* in Villa Nova, where the wines are stored. There is no feeling that there is anything wrong in this; indeed, bad as port wine generally is, it would be much worse if the merchants were compelled to adhere to the qualities often approved by the men who are sent up by the Alto Douro Company to pronounce their verdicts, and for which it receives a yearly subsidy of about 35,000*l.*,—being about the half of the duty on all wine exported to Europe.

In the year 1833 the old company, which had

existed since 1756, was abolished, and for about ten years all was free; but in 1843, the government in Lisbon was induced to reestablish it; lopping off, however, many of its powers and privileges, though still retaining sufficient to do a great deal of injury. It is probably not any exaggeration to add that, were it not for this incubus, we should have wines, not only from the present district (the Upper Corgo), but likewise from the former favourite ground, the Lower Corgo, at much more moderate prices than ports have long averaged.

It is also notorious that there are some of the finest vine-growing land and aspects in the world out of the bounds of demarcation; and nothing but railroads and perfect freedom of operations are required to open up great districts teeming with vegetable and mineral wealth, and with a fine laborious population.

The truth of the old proverb, that 'two of a trade can never agree,' has been well proved by 'port,' and port making; and many a fight and dispute there have been on the subject; especially since the day that the talented Baron Forrester (who was drowned in the Douro two years ago) struck out, right and left, against all his factory neighbours and fellow-countrymen who had hitherto lived an easy-going life, undisturbed by intestine discord and untroubled by the pestilent 'agitators,' who for some years past have left nothing alone, from princes and palaces down to port wines. Even Cobden himself has not been more abused, nor have more attempts been made to put him down, than were made against Baron Forrester; but he was one of those men, who, conscious that he understood his subject, and could give good reasons for his statements, would not be driven from his point. I have been again reading the documents on his side, and on that of his opponents, and have no hesitation in declaring my conviction that he was right, and that they were wrong. Without in the least expressing approval of many of his ways, it cannot be denied that no man knew better, and few if any so well as he, the port wine country, the people, and everything connected with the Douro, from the Foz to Spain.

In all his letters I can see nothing but recommendations to make wine of grapes alone, excluding elderberries, jeropiga, and brandy—at least the use of the last to the extent to which it is applied for stopping the fermentation of the must.

So far as I could learn from himself or his writings, this was the grand principle he always advocated; and if such be the case, surely no one can reasonably object to his recommendations.

The following extract is from his description of the usual way that ports are made, and I believe it is correct.

To produce black strong and rich wine, the following are the expedients resorted to:—The grapes being flung into the open vat indiscriminately with the stalks, sound and unsound, are trodden by men till they are completely smashed, and then left to ferment. When the wine is about half fermented it is transferred from the vat to tonels; and brandy (several degrees above proof) is thrown in, in the proportion of twelve to twenty-five gallons to the pipe of must, by which the fermentation is generally checked. About two months afterwards, this mixture is coloured thus:—a quantity of dried elderberries is put into coarse bags; these are placed in vats, and a part of the wine to be coloured being thrown over them, they are trodden by men till the whole of the colouring matter is expressed, when the husks are thrown away. The dye thus formed, is applied according to the fancy of the owner, from twenty-eight to fifty-six pounds of the dried elderberries being used to the pipe of wine! Another addition of brandy, of from four to six gallons per pipe, is now made to the mixture, which is then allowed to rest for about two months. At the end of this time it is, if sold, sent to Villa Nova, where it is racked two or three times; and receives probably two gallons more of brandy per pipe, and it is then considered fit to be shipped to England, it being about nine months' old. At the time of shipment one gallon more of brandy is usually added to each pipe. The wine thus having received at least twenty gallons of brandy per pipe, is considered by the merchant sufficiently strong.

The criterion by which the official tasters deputed by the Alto Douro Company form their judgments of new wines, is whether they possess the qualities of dark colour, strong body, and richness; indeed, their instructions are to pass as good only those wines which have enough of such qualities, not only 'for themselves, but to spare for others.' The inevitable result is that the farmers and growers, in order to receive bilhetes, grow grapes, such as the tintas and mourisco, producing colour and body, but also coarseness; and to these they add the juice of elder-berries, sugar, jeropiga (syrup made from must prevented from fermenting by means of spirit), and also large quantities of strong brandy.

It may be easily understood how little inducement there is for exertion while such a despotic and injurious system exists; and every evil that it ought to entail would follow, were it not for the beneficial effects of bribery, corruption, and smuggling, which in this, as in many other instances, help to counteract the follies of governments. The happy possessors of bilhetes sell them within the district to others, who, by this protection, pass wines for which they were not granted, or smuggle in wines from the proscribed neighbourhood, in which some of the choicest growths are made.

We now come to the much vexed question, whether port wine can be safely sent away without a large admixture of spirit. I do not know one Oporto man who does not declare decidedly that it cannot; and I am of the same opinion, if the question refers to the wine long known here as port.

But I do not believe that there is anything so peculiar in the soil or climate of Portugal as to render the juice of its grapes different from that of every other wine-growing country; though I can understand that black grapes, of the deepest tint and heaviest substance, fermented with the husks and stalks, besides extraneous matters, to give all the colour and body possible, must contain an amount of fermentative principle destructive to its preservation.

The percentage of proof spirit, in the best port, evolved in fermentation, may be averaged at 20 per cent.; but in addition to this there is usually added, in quantities of three, four or five gallons, from fifteen to eighteen gallons to every pipe before it is shipped to England. That sent to the Brazils has usually about half the quantity.

It is not because the shippers desire to add brandy; for this is always dearer, and is now greatly dearer than the same quantity of wine; but they act on the same general principle as other dealers, in supplying the article demanded by their customers. No one can object more than I do to additions of spirit, but port drinkers *will* have port such as it is usually seen; and those very persons and writers who abuse port wine, would not place it on their tables, were it to come to them in a pure and natural state.

Any shipper will send it without additional spirit, if it be previously agreed that there shall be no complaint should it become bad; but few, if any, dealers will give such an order even when assured of its good keeping; because, a merchant buying to sell, knows that if he sends it to any of his old port customers they will return it to him, and if he tries to sell it he will have much difficulty and trouble, entailing explanations, &c. I can speak from experience; for I once selected a hogshead which was stated to be without the addition of brandy;

but although much liked by several wine merchants to whom I showed it, they all declared it to be more like claret than port, and that they could not sell it. At length, a gentleman tasted and bought it, and, about three years afterwards, told me that he never had such port; and that on leaving his house in the country his successor offered him three guineas a dozen for all that remained.

He and others remarked that it had a strange flavour, very different from port, and resembling burgundy; which was quite intelligible, as it had not been deadened and made heavy by quantities of spirit. Although I was assured there was no admixture of brandy, I could perceive by the taste and flavour that a little had been added; and that the claret flavour and taste would have been more predominant had it not been for that addition. It is amusing to hear some of the old city wine merchants calling the unbrandied red wines of every country 'like claret;' solely because claret has been almost the only red wine in its natural state they have been in the habit of tasting. They seem to forget that grapes, whether from the Médoc, the Côte d'Or, the Rhône, Hungary or Italy, Portugal or Spain, have, after all, a very similar taste when eaten, and that the fermented juice, allowing for various peculiarities from soil and sun, &c., retains its natural flavour.

Those who have not been in Oporto can hardly conceive the difficulty which shippers sometimes have in executing the orders sent out; and many wine merchants of high standing here would feel their dignity rather offended if they heard the remarks and gossip in the Rua Ingleza on the arrival of the English mail. One shipper gets an order for twenty pipes of real 'true, old, mature wine with no refreshing, but with plenty of deep colour.' Another tells of an order for ten pipes of a 'vintage five years old, but full of colour.' If those who send such orders saw wine that is truly old and unrefreshed (no newer wine added to it), they would see wine that has been depositing its colouring and other heavy parts during four or five years, and that in the course of nature has lost much of its colour and body.

At the period of my visit the cry was for colour! colour! colour! And I remember that, in a first-rate lodge in Villa Nova, some thousands of pipes of beautiful old wine, which would now fetch 60*l.* or 70*l.*, were then absolutely unsaleable; and had it not been that the fine vintages of 1840, 1842, and 1844, gave the means of darkening them, the loss would have been very serious to the holders. Many may still remember G. W., than whom no man was a better judge of port; he kept resolutely to fine old wine, and would have nothing to do with the dark, strong kinds then in vogue; so he could get no orders, and his stock, when sold by auction, fetched only about 20*l.* per pipe. Somewhat later, the well-known house of K. L. and Co., noted for fine old ports lighter than the usual shipments, sold their stock by auction, and what was the result?—an average price of 17*l.* or 18*l.* per pipe.

Rarely have finer wines been imported than Baron Forrester shipped when he left his old firm; but dealers wanted colour, strength, and dryness, *alias* harshness, and even his best were sold at very low prices.

Similar cases may be remembered. One occurs to me, of J. B., near Pountney Lane, an old respectable house; known by its adherence to the old-fashioned, light-coloured, and tawny ports, and from never bottling the dark, new kinds. But the fashion had changed, and although the stock was well known, it was unsaleable, and the house suffered the fate of innumerable others.

Yet if similar quality to these had been adhered to, I believe port would not have fallen into its present disrepute; for it cannot be denied that it is now generally regarded as an intoxicating, vulgar wine. Whether it will regain its prestige is very doubtful; at all events, this can only be attained by using means similar to those used by growers in the Médoc, Côte d'Or, and other places; where the finest varieties of grapes are sought, and science, skill, and care are applied in all the processes of development.

Upon analysis, the great proportion of port wine is found to be a black, coarse compound; the colour alone proving that, besides new spirit, there must be something else, for no grape could give such depth of darkness. That the elderberry is used is often perceptible when the glass is half a foot from one's nose; and the luscious sweetness is evidently not entirely from the grape. The quantity of this low quality that comes over proves how badly the official Wine Company carries out its professed object; and this is ever the case with such fiscal interference.

All dealers are naturally anxious to have it supposed that their stock is excellent; but every wine merchant knows that the shipping houses send, at certain prices, exactly the same wine to one as to another; and therefore any peculiarity must arise from management in the cellar here.

The question now the most interesting to wine merchants is, what is to be the future history and fate of the port?

The fact is as well authenticated as any historical fact can be, that the wines of France formed the great proportion of the consumption of Great Britain previous to our Revolution of 1688; when the duty on them was raised, in fifteen years, from 1/4 to 4/10 per gallon, being 360 per cent.: and in 1703 the Methuen Treaty was entered into with Portugal, binding ourselves to receive her produce at a rate of one-third less than on that of France. Since that date down to 1831, the differential rates against the French wines were never less than 50 per cent., as I have already shown. (See Table, p. 61.)

Looking at those calculations, we see that French wines have not had fair play; and they who read the domestic history of Scotland or Ireland, or who have conversed with old people from those countries, do not require to be told that French was their usual wine. Holland is a cold damp country, but there, as also in Hamburg, Sweden, &c., the wines of France are generally drunk.

In England the hatred against the French at the end of the seventeenth century, and long afterwards, was violent; and as there was not here, the same facilities for smuggling as in other parts of the kingdom, the English government succeeded better in excluding everything French. It is comparatively easy to extract figures, as I have done, from all the books, documents, and old Acts of Parliament I could find upon this subject, and to give the results as reliable information; but although for many years I have had much to do with that kind of work (and without such searching and calculations there can be no just basis of reasoning), yet I have always been conscious that the 'facts and figures' often give a very unsatisfactory view of the case.

In the instance of port, the word suggests only the kind of wine which is made up in the Douro and shipped from Oporto. The usual way in Portugal of spelling the name of this town is Porto, or with an O prefixed for *the*, to denote 'the port,' or harbour; but I have little doubt that port (wine) derived its name, not from Oporto, the place, but from Portugal, the country.

There are no means of tracing the quantities of each kind imported, but no doubt exists that there were considerable importations of white ports, not only from Lisbon, but likewise from Oporto.

In the plate of old families there are decanter labels—'Red Port,' 'White Port,' and 'Lisbon.' Within my own recollection, a large business was done in lisbon, distinguished as rich, mellow, and dry; and I remember an old merchant telling me that, when he was young (about 1780), it was the daily custom with the merchants to go to a coffee room—*Tom's*, in Cornhill, he mentioned—to have for their luncheon a gill of lisbon, with bread and cheese.

The following letter from Lisbon, dated in 1798, referring to transactions ten years previously, confirms, in some measure, my remarks as to the extent of the wine trade between Lisbon and England. I doubt whether all the houses in London now order in a year much more lisbon and calcavellos than is shown in that one letter. In treating of lisbons I shall refer more particularly to this. The Mr. Stephens alluded to became enormously rich, by contracts and the monopoly in the manufacture of glass, granted to him by the Portuguese government, as well as by severe economy. He left about 600,000*l.* to his relative Mr. Lyne, then a partner in the firm of Lyne, Hathorn, and Roberts, agents for Kopke's port and Gordon's sherry; who upon his accession of fortune, assumed the name of Lyne Stephens, which became well known, through his own great wealth, and, afterwards, by the extravagance of his heir and his carrying off the beautiful Duvernay.

Lisbon, 17th February, 1798.

Mr. Samuel Brown, Love Lane, London.

SIR,—Before us is your esteemed favour of 30th ult., with advice that our mutual friend, Mr. John Parker, had communicated to you an abstract of our letter to him dated 10th ult., in which we quoted the then shipping prices of wines. You mention a probability of Mr. William Tonkin handing us the few orders you had sent to him for wines since he left England, and which as yet we have not seen. In consequence of the prices quoted to Mr. Parker of our wines the 10th ult., you had favoured us with an order for twenty-six pipes of lisbon and six pipes of calcavella for Messrs. John and Walter Grey, of Water Lane, Tower Street; for John Allnutt, Esq., Mark Lane, ten pipes of lisbon; and for Mr. George Bridges, Water Lane, Tower Street, twelve pipes of lisbon and three pipes of bucellas; in all fifty-seven pipes of lisbon, calcavella and bucellas, of the vintages 1795 and 1796, and one pipe of bucellas, vintage 1794, as per the list in your letter, whose further contents we duly note. Particular attention will be shown to the quality of the wines and full gauge of the pipes; also to the credit of twelve months to Mr. George Bridges, seeing his orders will be considerable; but our general credit is nine months from the date of bill of lading, by bills drawn, payable at the Exchange, on Lloyd's list, on the date thereof.

Since we wrote Mr. Parker, the merchants in London (who have their houses here in the wine trade) have fixed a second time the prices of wine as at foot, and which is to govern during all the present year, to serve for your information, if you should happen not to be apprised thereof; and, as we are given to understand that there will be no convoy for England these four months, you will have time to confirm your order or annul it, as you please, observing to you that our stock of wine, vintage 1795, is so far exhausted that we cannot, with credit to our brand, engage to ship more than your present order.

Respecting the vintage of 1796, we have as good a stock as any of our neighbours, though the vintage, in quality and in quantity, was indifferent; but we have very little of 1795, and it is generally so throughout the trade here, owing to the alarm this country has, and is yet in, that few of the houses have ventured to purchase, dreading the consequences of an invasion, so that all of us are unprovided with vintages 1794 and 1795; which we are particular in mentioning that you may not call on us for them; and vintage 1796 are not very good. The last vintage, 1797, are excellent in quality, but remarkably short in quantity, which caused the prices to be double of the 1796, and gave rise to the second arrangement of prices in London. God grant that the times may soon become serene again, that we may engage as largely in purchases for supplying you and other friends to fullest satisfaction as to quality, price, and full gauge of pipes.

Mr. Stephens was married to our Premier's daughter. He took to the wine business, from passing the summer with our family in the country up the river, where our wine magazines are. Observing the great exports, he commenced in 1788 upon a large scale, induced also from its being a large and plentiful vintage; and it gave him an opportunity of shipping the best wines, and gaining in the first outset a name for choice wines. To gain good customers he let them go a little under the current shipping prices; and, as you remark, had he pursued the business, he would have been the first shipper in Lisbon.

We are sorry for these critical times: when they become more tranquil you will find all your orders will be punctually executed, and have no doubt (from your experience of the solidity of your friends) to mutual satisfaction, being persuaded you will touch no orders but what are of the most solid responsibility.

Sir, your obedient humble Servants,

(Signed) John Bulkeley & Son.

I fear to recur to the wine of the Douro, feeling how impossible it is to write about it so as to satisfy myself; and therefore how much more difficult it must be to make it intelligible to others. That trade has been so artificial, and there have been so many laws, rules, and regulations respecting it, that one might argue in favour of or against the whole system, and there would be keen supporters on either side.

It is generally necessary to hold and to express opinions, but every year's experience tends to modify the boldness with which some of these were formerly uttered. The truth of this was lately brought vividly to my mind by the remark of a gentleman who is admitted to be at the head of the wine trade, and who justly merits this distinction, not only on account of the extent of his business, but still more so by his character as an excellent man.

On consulting him on some question connected with port, (about which, if any one may be supposed to understand every circumstance and detail, *he* ought, for he has passed many of his fifty years of experience in Oporto and on the Douro), after giving me the information I desired, he added:— 'But I become more conscious every year I live, of reasons for doubt upon many points on which I was at one time quite confident.' Most truly can I reiterate his words.

I recollect the landing of the famous 1820, which caused quite a sensation throughout the kingdom; more especially, as the vintages 1816, 1817, 1818, and 1819, were all decidedly bad, and there was a rush upon the wine of 1820. But that year in Portugal was hot, and the grapes were so ripe and luscious that the wine was much too sweet and clammy.

Its very excellence also, after four years of failures, caused it to be badly treated; for there was so great a demand that it was brought over almost in a state of must, insufficiently fermented; instead of having been kept for at least a couple of years, with one or two rackings. But it was put into bottle at once, on the argument, as I remember, of some of the so-called wise men of the docks — 'Get it into glass, get the cork on the top of it, and then you will keep in all the good.'

Many had substantial grounds for regretting having followed such ignorant counsel; because on drawing corks four or five years afterwards, they found plenty of 'crust' and plenty of colour in the wine, and a 'well-stained cork,' but their 1820 very much the same as on the day when it was bottled. As it was a desperate affair to wait for such wine becoming fit to be sent out, numerous bins were *started* into pipes, older wine added, fined, racked, and bottled; and in two or three years there was another fine 1820 fit for use.

I believe that any old wine merchants will agree that the 1821 and 1822 were more perfect than the celebrated 1820, though it may seem heresy to say a word against that famous year. I am convinced that the sweet 1820, succeeding so many bad years, and followed by two similar, though not such very saccharine years, was the origin of the bad repute into which port has gradually fallen since that period.

There arose a taste for a sweet wine; and when this could not be supplied from the juice of the grape, other means were used to meet the prevailing demand; the consequence of which was, that for some time there was scarcely any but sweet port to be had. It was excellent in quality when solely from grapes; but almost all that was compounded, though seemingly substantial at first, gave way in colour, and became a sweetish, flavourless wine. Not a few houses will remember this serious fact.

The most perfect vintage that I recollect was the 1827, about which there was nothing in the least peculiar, or what is called 'striking.' The wine was evidently from well, not over-ripened grapes; and there was in it a fine firm fulness, with sufficient richness, but no hard stalkiness or dryness; so that it was certain to go forward improving. This kind has also the great advantage that it does not require absurdly long keeping in bottle.

Such a vintage as is here described, if it had had less brandy than is generally given, and had remained two years longer in Portugal, properly attended to by racking, &c., might have been shipped to London, bottled in three months, and in two years would have been fitter for use, than if bottled green and kept for ten years in bin. It would also be finer, because it is scarcely possible for wine to continue for many years in contact with the crust and cork without being deteriorated in bouquet.

I know this is a most heterodox opinion about old port, but I have often seen proofs of its correctness; and it is a well-known fact that almost every third cork, containing very old wine, is decayed and has a bad smell, which it of course imparts to the wine. I do not say that port ever has a delicate bouquet; for only a drop of brandy let fall into the finest glass of any wine will immediately deaden its flavour, and ports have often twenty-five gallons of proof spirit added to a pipe; but even port, with all its strength, when it has been twelve, fifteen, or twenty, or more years in bottle, has generally what is known among wine-merchants as the 'bottle-stink;' and if, with this same 'bottle-stink,' it is declared to be, and buyers believe it to be, a 'real vintage 1820,' ten guineas per dozen will be a small price for it.

A few years ago anything black enough, and with a touch of the elegant 'bottle-stink,' was immediately saleable at high prices; and much ransacking at public sales, as well as in public-houses, there was, to find such profitable merchandise.

I have never heard a satisfactory reason, nor can I comprehend, why port, if it be really fine and mature, should not be quite as good when drunk from the wood as from bottle; indeed, I believe that if it were carefully matured to a perfectly ripe state in the cask, it would be generally much better than it is usually found in bottle. I know to what comments I expose myself in expressing such opinions, but am ready to give my reasons for them. The famous wine of 1834 resembled 1820, with as much sweetness but less body. It was also brought over and put in bottle too soon, which many had afterwards cause to repent. The '34's lost colour rapidly; and after that vintage there were large stocks in Villa Nova and in bottle here, with more sweetness, but without the full rich vinosity which ensures goodness if kept long enough.

From 1834 there was no fine vintage till 1840, which was firm, dry, and stout, with colour; which proved invaluable, by enabling the holders of the unsaleable pale sweet stocks to give them colour and dryness. Vintages '42 and '44 were first-rate years; and '47 was excellent, though generally much overrated, being devoid of that delicate softness which is so agreeable. Some of that vintage, early bottled, is scarcely fit for use even now, and will never be equal to those which were allowed to get rid of their coarse parts in wood.

Since 1847, there have been several very good vintages; but it is unquestionable that port is losing caste, and is seldom seen on the table of the 'higher classes;' and we all know that when anything in this country has become 'vulgar' its fate is sealed.

Not forgetful of the difference in strength, of the

body and the stomach, at thirty and at sixty, yet in bringing back to memory the fine, soft, silky bins of olden times, and the pleasant ease with which half-a-dozen friends would empty a dozen bottles, it is difficult to suppose that this could have been a very usual occurrence had the wine been as strong as it now generally is. It should be recollected, also, that in those days, especially among bachelors, a party seldom broke up without a tumbler or two of brandy and water after all the wine. These were bad habits, undoubtedly; I am not defending them, but only stating facts.

It is true, that the dinner hour was early, and, among many, the hour of rising from table was late; the guardians of the night were 'Charleys,' indulgent to the sounds of loud merriment, and in all respects a contrast to 'Peel's police.' Those who recur to that period, cannot have forgotten that when gentlemen dined alone, they seldom left the table before eleven o'clock, and were generally tipsy. So it was, also, at public dinners, where at least two bottles were drunk by each. Port was the invariable wine after dinner, and any one drinking white wine was then considered peculiar.

Now, *tempora mutantur, et nos mutamur in illis;* and a good change it is. There are, of course, many jolly drinking parties still; but the late hour of dinner in general renders it now impossible, even if it were desired, to remain long at table afterwards; and almost all that is used during dinner is sherry, champagne, with other white wines. The days of the 'horse-shoe round the fire,' and the exciting but agreeable discussions of port and politics, are things of the past, except among a few 'veterans.'

At the period to which I refer, drinking was mere child's play in comparison with the extent to which it had formerly been carried; and the descriptions which elderly men gave of their 'social' recollections were rather astounding, as I have mentioned in my 'General Remarks.'

Since that chapter was written, I have met with the following description of the habits and manners of 'the best society' about the year 1815, in Captain Gronow's curious and interesting *Reminiscences.* My own recollection does not extend to 'six bottles,' but there is no doubt of the facts, although they may appear almost incredible to this sober generation:—

Drinking and play were more universally indulged in then than at the present time, and many men still living must remember the couple of bottles of port, at least, which accompanied his dinner in those days. Indeed, female society, amongst the upper classes, was most notoriously neglected; except, perhaps, by romantic foreigners, who were the heroes of many a fashionable adventure that fed the clubs with ever acceptable scandal. How could it be otherwise, when husbands spent their days in the hunting-field, or were entirely occupied with politics, and always away from home during the day; whilst the dinner party, commencing at seven or eight, frequently did not break up before one in the morning. There were then four and even five bottle men; and the only thing that saved them was drinking very slowly, and out of very small glasses. The learned head of the law, Lord Eldon, and his brother, Lord Stowell, used to say that they had drunk more bad port than any two men in England; indeed, the former was rather apt to be overtaken, and to speak occasionally somewhat thicker than natural after long and heavy potations. The late Lords Panmure, Dufferin, and Blayney, wonderful to relate, were six bottle men at this time; and I really think that if 'the good society of 1815' could appear before their more moderate descendants, in the state they were generally reduced to after dinner, the moderns would pronounce their ancestors fit for nothing but bed.

I venture to make the following further extracts from Captain Gronow, not only in reference to drinking, but to eating. It is often stated, probably with a good deal of truth, that heavy joints require heavy wine, and that nothing will have a more powerful influence in inducing a taste for light, or natural wine, than lighter and more scientific cookery.

Even in the best houses, when I was a young man, the dinners were wonderfully solid, hot, and stimulating. The *menu* of a grand dinner was thus composed:—

Mulligatawny and turtle soups were the first dishes placed before you; a little lower, the eye met with the familiar salmon at one end of the table, and the turbot, surrounded by smelts, at the other. The first course was sure to be followed by a saddle of mutton or a piece of roast beef; and then you could take your oath that fowls, tongue, and ham, would as assuredly succeed, as darkness after day. A prime difficulty to overcome was the placing on your fork, and finally in your mouth, some half dozen different eatables which occupied your plate at the same time. For example, your plate would contain, say, a slice of turkey, a piece of stuffing, a sausage, pickles, a slice of tongue, cauliflower, and potatoes. According to habit and custom, a judicious and careful selection from this little bazaar of good things was to be made, with an endeavour to place a portion of each in your mouth at the same moment; in fact, it appeared to me that we used to do all our compound cookery between our jaws.

The wines were chiefly port, sherry, and hock; claret, and even burgundy, being then designated 'poor, thin, washy stuff.'

A perpetual thirst seemed to come over people, both men and women, as soon as they had tasted their soup; as from that moment everybody was taking wine with everybody else till the close of the dinner; and such wine as produced that class of cordiality which frequently wanders into stupefaction.

How all this sort of eating and drinking ended was obvious, from the prevalence of gout, and the necessity of everyone making the pill-box his constant bedroom companion.

It may serve to explain, also, why early deaths were more common then than at the present time.

It was a usual custom in Manchester for merchants and manufacturers to have a dinner on the chief market-day for all who chose to partake of it; and it is related of the 'Cheeryble Brothers,' who thought nothing of buying eight or ten pipes at a time, that they and their friends would sit down after 'Change on Tuesday and not rise again till 'Change hour on Thursday. I remember well the first time I heard a gentleman in Manchester ask those at his table, not long after dinner, whether they would have more wine or adjourn to the drawing-room. This is now usual, but at that time it was thought a strange innovation, and was highly disapproved of by many.

In no part of the kingdom was better port to be had than among the manufacturers in the north of England; because many bought pipes of the best vintages, and kept a succession in their cellars, priding themselves on having their wine old and of the highest quality. Port was a constant subject of discussion and rivalry. Now they expend more of their money on paintings and fine arts, and, unless it be among a few intimate friends, the word wine is rarely mentioned; and when its use becomes general it will be as little alluded to as beef or mutton.

Oporto merchants and growers must exert themselves to meet the changes which have occurred already, and still more those which are sure to follow. For more than a century and a half Portugal has had a practical monopoly in its trade with England, to their mutual disadvantage; but those days are gone, and she must henceforth fight her own battle unaided. I have no doubt she is quite able to do so; but to succeed she must throw off all shackles and enter into the field of free trade; otherwise nothing can prevent Oporto dwindling down to the condition into which Lisbon has fallen from her once prominent position for enterprise and extent of her commerce.

Excepting a considerable amount of British manufactures imported into Oporto, chiefly for smuggling into Spain, her wealth is nearly dependent upon wine; and that portion formerly sent to the Brazils (at a much lower price than shipments to England), has been latterly seriously diminished by the cheap, strong, and excellent kinds from the south of France. The proportion of wines of Portugal to all kinds consumed in England, from 1787 to 1795, averaged above 70 per cent., and the quantity about 4,000,000 gallons for a population of 12,500,000. In 1831, the proportion was 44 per cent., the quantity 2,707,734 gallons, the population about 23,000,000. In 1862, the proportion was 23·97 per cent., the quantity 2,349,954 gallons, the population about 29,000,000.

The duty per gallon, during that period, has been 3/1, 4/10, 6/9, 7/, 8/3, 9/ 4/10 (in 1825), 5/6, and 5/9. By the late reduction, at the mininum strength of port, 3/, 2/6, 2/11, and 2/6 up to 42° of strength. Until 1815, wars alone, independent of other circumstances, caused such interruptions to the natural course of trade, that anyone looking at the rate of duty, and inferring thence an increase or diminution of consumption, would ground his argument upon a fallacious basis; especially if he does not at the same time take into calculation the price of the wine itself.

Without going back one hundred years, when the price of a pipe of port is said to have been from 6*l.* to 8*l.*, there is no doubt that the price at the latter end of the last century was from 14*l.* to 18*l.*; and it is also unquestionable that the prices since the beginning of the century have been from 30*l.* to 70*l.*; though, before the vine disease, fine parcels could often be picked up in the docks at 8*l.* or 10*l.* below the lowest of the quotations of the houses with known brands.

As I have already stated, those fine old kinds which by time had thrown off their coarseness were long almost valueless; and I remember others which, from their richness and fruitiness and newness, could scarcely be called wine, bringing 70*l.* and more.

Besides the houses with a foreign connection, there are Portuguese, usually called speculators, some of them very rich, whose business it is to invest large amounts in wine for shipment to the Brazils, and for supplying shippers whose capital is small, but to whom, if trustworthy, credit for two or three years is often given.

However high the opinion of some, in respect to the fine quality of port, may be, it is not shared by the official tasters appointed by the Alto Douro Company; for so late as 1858, after representing to the government that 'it can never be brought into proper estimation without the aid of protective laws,' they go on to state that, by the sale of bilhetes, or permits, wines 'are introduced for exportation which have not been qualified by the jury created by law;' and thus, 'the purchasers of such permits, infringing the law, convey wines under a false denomination to foreign markets, and carry on a fraudulent trade.' This is rather strong language in reference to 'British merchants,' but, were it not extracted from an official document, the concluding sentence would scarcely be believed authentic: —

> The Douro farmers are of opinion that the promptest and most efficacious measures for establishing the commercial credit of Oporto would be to examine every pipe of port wine actually existing in the merchants' stocks, approved and legalised for exportation; to purify these deposits, and to reduce the rejected wines to brandy, or to sell them in this country (Portugal) for what they will fetch, for account of their owners.

These tasters, even had they originally good palates, must get them destroyed by their constant tasting of new wines, the jeropiga, and the brandies; and their instructions are to reject all that are not only strong, but which could spare some of their strength and colour.

It is declared by all Oporto merchants that we must never again expect ports at 14*l.* to 18*l.* as they were about 1798, when the very choicest did not exceed 20*l.*; but notwithstanding these opinions, I am convinced that were all restrictions abolished, it would soon follow that ports would not be much higher priced than at those quotations. There would be wines from many other localities outside the present lines of demarcation; they would be not only of a lighter kind, naturally, but they would have less spirit added; and would cost the grower much less than those grown on the favoured twenty-four miles on the Upper Douro, or smuggled in from the neighbourhood by means of surreptitious bilhetes.

Before the introduction of the bonding system in England, in 1802, wines were landed at wharves; and I have been told that Tower Hill was often completely covered with casks; by which the loss, the pillaging, and the tricks to cheat the revenue were constant and enormous.

Ports came, then, almost entirely from the Lower Corgo, nearer Oporto than the Upper Corgo; they were lighter than those now made, and had less spirit added. They were usually kept for two or three years before shipment, being carefully fined and racked during that period. On arrival, the shipping houses placed those which were not already sold in their bonded cellars; and those who bought them placed them in their own cellars, where they again racked or treated them according to their judgment. Two houses in the private trade still existing, were very noted for their ports—one of them for having a light pleasant kind, and the other for a clarety flavour and dryness. The first is supposed to have been owing to frequent fining and racking; and the other to the house being large importers of claret, and using the claret lees and a little of the wine to *dry* and flavour the port.

At that period, also, there seems to have been a

certain demand for whatever quantity could be offered of any fine vintage; and it was only necessary for the few English firms then existing in Oporto to write to their customers, informing them that a vintage was very fine, to receive replies begging that 50, 100, or 200 pipes might be kept for them. There were then comparatively few wine merchants in the kingdom, and these bought largely, supplying the smaller dealers.

The quantities formerly shipped to England are astonishing. In 1799 it exceeded 57,000 pipes, and from that time to 1810, it averaged about 44,000. In 1820, it was 21,196; in 1830, 19,038; in 1840, 23,204; in 1850, 25,400; and in 1862, 24,832 pipes.

During the period from 1799 to 1860, the population of the United Kingdom increased from about 15,000,000 to above 29,000,000.

A statement made by me on another occasion as to the price at which port was formerly sold to private customers in bottle has often been questioned; nevertheless it is perfectly true, and I now give my authorities, both of whom will be remembered by many. I was informed by Mr. Thomas Henshaw and Mr. Bennett that they were fellow-apprentices, and recollected well that the usual and understood price of port was 21/ per dozen, and that thirteen bottles were then always sent as a dozen. They both described the port of that time as greatly lighter than that which came afterwards into vogue, and that it consequently became earlier fit for use.

A firm-holding crust is, of course, of great importance, but the desire for a heavy crust and a dark stained cork seems a mistake; and for my own part I should be disposed to form a more favourable impression by seeing it light, and the cork little stained—not owing to its having been a short time in bottle, but to the wine having been ripe for bottling.

No one seems able to give a satisfactory reason why some crusts slip and others adhere. My own idea is that a new wine will rarely give a firm crust, because the gross parts fall too rapidly and in too great quantities to be able to fix themselves to the rough parts of the glass; and therefore when the bottle is moved it slips off and injures the limpidity.

When the wine is older, and has been racked from its lees and fined, the deposits will fall more slowly in smaller particles, and will be more likely to take hold of projections or hollows in the lower side of the bottle.

In bottling port it is customary, even when new bottles are known to be perfectly clean, to rinse them with shot, as it is believed that this makes the crust hold better; which is probably caused by the shot roughening the inner sides and knocking off the smooth 'bloom' on new bottles.

Port, from the quantity of colour, &c., it contains, is very easily 'chilled,' as its constituent parts on that account require more heat to hold them in solution than any other wine. If it be a strong heavy kind its fermentative principle will rectify this; but if old and light, it often takes a long time to become bright again.

A warm cellar, and still more quickly the heat of a fire, or placing the bottle in warm water, will dissolve the floating opaque parts.

It is not surprising that there are grievous complaints against 'sweet' port, for it is often like syrup; but this fault will continue while dealers and drinkers require more colour and body than the juice of any grape can supply. The natural consequence has been a call for 'dry;' but this frequently leads to disappointment, because dryness is generally the result of bad seasons, when there is a deficiency of the qualities necessary to constitute a perfect wine.

I have no doubt the demand for port may be resuscitated by any house of capital, experience, and energy which will resume the course practised previous to 1820, when port was the favourite wine of this country. There is not, and was not any mystery about it; for it was simply to retain the wine in Oporto about three years, racking and fining it two or three times, and then shipping it. If originally good and well fermented, and with less spirit than is now added, it will be a fine, fresh, good wine with sufficient colour, and will be in perfection in four or five years.

On arrival it may, perhaps, be desirable to give it another fining and racking, to put it still earlier forward. The albumen in whites of eggs and isinglass, both from their weight and their combination with portions constituting the wine, carry to the bottom of the cask some of the colour as well as of the body, and should therefore be used cautiously. Racking has less effect, being little more than drawing off the bright part from the lees.

As a rule almost invariable, ports with the hard stalky dryness, which are often liked from their contrast to those with sweetness, are the produce of a cold and unfavourable season.

I remember once getting thirty or forty dozens of this kind from a gentleman's cellar — very old, and as black and dry as a piece of burned stick, with a dead heavy flavour. It was very different from what I considered fine old port; but a few professed connoisseurs having tasted it, immediately divided it among them at a high price, and I often heard it praised afterwards.

Very excellent white port is still produced, though in small quantities. In good years, the common red kind used in wine-shops is very pleasant; but ever since the vine disease, it has been beyond the reach of many who could formerly afford to drink wine.

When the produce of very hot seasons has been

put into bottle before being allowed, by fermentation in bulk, to reduce the saccharine and deposit a portion of the vegetable matter, little change can be expected to take place for many years; simply because, owing to the small quantity in a bottle, there is not fermentative matter sufficient to enable the process to operate except at a very slow rate.

But the same wine, if it has been kept in cask until it has ripened by the deposit of its lees, and has been occasionally freed from them by racking, will turn out in bottle the best that can be expected of any wine with twenty or thirty gallons of spirit added to its own natural strength.

While offering these remarks, the letter which appeared in *The Times*, of December 24, 1807, and from which I have already quoted, was sent to me. It will be found in the Appendix, but I here make the following extracts. The Mr. Ballantyne whose name is attached was evidently an experienced wine merchant, and he gives an insight into the practical working of the trade and the social habits of the people, in a more vivid and truthful manner than I have ever before seen. It is strange to read the description by Christopher Smith (in all probability Alderman Smith, the head of the still existing firm of Sebastian Smith and Co.) of the manner of drinking at that period:—

> When he attained manhood, he drank wine at taverns at 8*d.* per quart, served up in a curious pewter measure. . . . When a good pipe of port on draught was grown flat, a hogshead was filled, and in time put on

draught, and lastly was put in a half-hogshead; and those casks were seldom clean, and therefore it was often very bad in inns and taverns. . . .

Wines long kept at Oporto grow tawny, vapid, and get what we call in Oporto the country taste. Those who took my advice ordered two-year-old wine, and obtained more praise from their customers than ever before. . . .

About the year 1790 and 1791, I had about 170 wine merchants chiefly taking their port wine from me (among all of whom there were not ten who sought cheap wine), and these mostly great importers, who sold to publicans and the lesser dealers, making no pretensions to supply gentlemen's tables. . . .

White port was very subject to ferment in summer and to grow foul in winter, when we mixed a little Teneriffe, which improved its flavour, and prevented any further fermentation; and when a pipe of red port became too old for our customers, we enriched it to their taste with newer wine; for at that time superannuated port was not esteemed.

The writer states that when he wrote (in 1807) the shipment to England of port, red and white, was 38,973 pipes, and of sherry 11,000 butts. In 1862 the quantities were 24,832 pipes of port, and 52,876 butts of sherry.

We learn from this valuable letter that sherry was scarcely known till about 1780, and that previous to its introduction white port was much used; as also wines from Lisbon, as may be seen more at length in treating of lisbon. In a former chapter, I have stated my belief, after a good deal of investigation, that it is altogether a mistake to suppose that our forefathers drank 'light wines;' and that, on the contrary, they drank coarse, ill-made, compounded wines, such as would now be abominated.

I am glad to be able to give here a drawing of a lodge in Villa Nova, and a description of the whole process of the trade there, so clear and excellent

WINE LODGE AT VILLA NOVA.

that it cannot be otherwise than generally interesting. It is from the evidence of Mr. Gassiot, the able head of the firm of Messrs. Martinez, Gassiot, & Co., on the occasion of a trial lately against the London Dock Company.

The *lodges*, as they are called in Villa Nova, in which the wines are kept, are large isolated warehouses, from the bottom to the top of the rocky hill; and present a very pleasing effect, looking across the river from Oporto.

In his evidence, M. Gassiot says.:—

The wines that arrive from the wine country after the vintage, about March, April, and May, are entered immediately in this manner: Bought, No. so-and-so, ten pipes, eleven pipes, twelve pipes; generally about seventy pipes at a time. The fact is entered in the lodge diary; that is the first operation. When the vintage wines have all come down, they are tasted, one by one, by the proper authorised cooper, who examines each. He exercises his judgment, and separates the wines into one, two, or more lots; and, when the entire purchase that was made in the wine country has been received, then comes the operation of general lotting for that vintage.

Afterwards follows the operation of blending, and bringing the lots into perfect uniformity together; and the mode in which that has been done, I can better exemplify by this drawing of a lodge of wine stores in Oporto. Twenty-one casks, or forty-two, or sixty-three, in twenty-ones, are made up according to the number of pipes it is intended to make of this particular lot; a can, containing an almude, which is about five gallons and a half (the twenty-first part of a pipe) is filled out of one of these pipes.

This is a drawing of a lodge at Villa Nova. The can that you see on the head of one of the coopers is a can that contains an almude of wine out of one of the pipes; another can resting on one of the pipes also contains an almude, the twenty-first part of a pipe.

From the pipe that is intended to be operated upon first, one almude at a time is taken and put into each of the other pipes, that is, one almude into each pipe. We have now got rid of one pipe; we have put it into twenty-one empty casks; I will confine myself to the twenty-one. We then take another pipe, as near the same quality as it is possible for us to judge, and divide that in the same way, putting one almude of that pipe into each of the other twenty-one pipes, and so we go on until we have taken twenty-one pipes of wine that come from the Douro and blended them together. Then, having done that, it is sometimes necessary to add a little brandy. There is a measure called a canada; it is the twelfth part of an almude; and sometimes half a canada, or a canada, or a canada and a half, is put into each cask: a pipe consists of twenty-one almudes and six canadas. I have now gone through the process that is adopted, and made you acquainted with the secrets of my trade, as regards making up the vintage wines.

The next operation I will describe to you is the purchases of wine made in Villa Nova from speculators. The way in which all shipping houses, before the oïdium, used to manage, was this: all the wines that are purchased in the wine country are of course obliged to be paid for in ready money; at least, I am obliged to pay what is called a *signal* on shipment, the moment I make my bargain with the farmers. At midsummer and Michaelmas I give what are called *escritos*, or what would be called bills here, payable in Oporto; and at Michaelmas I have paid for every pipe of wine I have bought in the Douro.

I pay a deposit the moment I make my purchase; I receive my wines in February, but I do not make my second payment till midsummer; at Michaelmas I have paid for all my vintage wines. I am not able to ship my wines at once; they are not fit for shipping till the year after, and I need not point out to your lordships and the jury that it would require a very large capital to ship 2,000 pipes of wine per annum. The mode in which the business is done by wealthy and respectable houses with capital is to purchase as many wines as they can afford to pay for. 'If it is a fine vintage,' my late partner used to say, 'sell your shirt to buy wine.'

There are speculators at Oporto, many of them men of great wealth and very great respectability: many are Fidalgos. Persons of that class are always buyers, and the farmers know it; therefore we cannot buy the moderate-priced wines so cheaply as they can. We are jealous at Oporto as well as in London; all are desirous to get the best wines they can, and give sometimes ridiculous prices for them. The farmers know that, and keep up their prices; they know that they can always sell their wines to the Portuguese speculators, and we cannot buy wine of that class so cheaply as they can.

These Portuguese speculators have large stocks of wine; I know that when I was in Oporto one of them had 10,000 or 15,000 pipes of wine; I purchased very largely of him, and I think he must have had as many as that. In former times (and I am now speaking of a time when there was more wine than would have flooded the docks), these parties used to have large quantities of wine; and we might at any time, or within a week, buy 1,000 pipes or 10,000 pipes, and they would give us two, three, four, or five years' credit. My house was offered 3,000 pipes of wine at five years' credit, by Visconde Ferreira, if I would buy them.

You see, then, our operations were very simple, and we could carry on a large business with a comparatively moderate amount of capital, because the large trade in this country is not a trade in fine wine, but for good, useful, honest, sound wine—wine that will not turn out bad, but which has no pretensions to be called superlative wine.

I purchase in Villa Nova a quantity of wine of a speculator, say a couple of hundred pipes; those wines are received into the lodge, as I have already described to you, and they are treated in precisely the same way as I have described with regard to the vintage wines.

We exercise the best judgment we can; we do not buy these wines for the purpose of keeping them, but the moment we get them, perhaps within a week of the time of our receiving them into the lodge, comes the operation of blending them, refreshing them with some of our fine new wines, and making them fit for the English market.

If you will allow me I will go through my statement; I will get rid of the lodge diary altogether, and you will never have occasion to refer to it again. I have described to your lordships and the jury the operations that are gone through with regard to the vintage wines and the wines I buy at Villa Nova; I will now describe, if you please, the mode in which I export my wines.

In the first place, every house has its distinctive mark; they have, first of all, their brand, about which you have heard a great deal, which is a burnt mark at the end of the cask; you will see it on one of those (referring to the drawing before produced). There is a burnt mark at the end of the cask; that is our distinctive brand, which is our property, and which cannot be imitated by other houses, or they would be brought before a court of law for it; but, besides that, there is also a mark cut in, not branded, which every house also uses.

For instance, the plaintiffs in this case have, ever since I can recollect them, had a distinctive mark; it has been a house of the highest respectability, in former years particularly. They had a distinctive mark — a double diamond; and Dixon's double diamond wines are known by every house all over the country, and would be bought without being tasted, their character being so high and so well known.

We have also distinctive marks. Instead of having one mark, we have three marks: we have three diamonds with grape, O, and a single grape; and those marks are well known throughout the trade; there are other houses who ship double diamonds like Mr. Dixon, and there are others, I am sorry to say, who put on three diamonds, the grape, and O's; but they must not put on our brand; when I speak, therefore, of a distinctive mark, I mean a distinctive mark coupled with a brand.

Now, having thus described the brand, I will now proceed to tell you what we do. I will assume that one of my friends (and I see many here who are listening to what I say with great attention) gives me an order for ten pipes of my three-diamond wine; I will describe to you the mode in which I should execute his order.

I have a large lot prepared of three-diamond wine, as well as of all these marks. The cooper would have instructions on a slip of paper similar to what has been shown to you in the evidence of D'Almeida, who is the cooper of Messrs. Gubian; that slip would be handed over by my manager at Oporto, who holds my procuration, and he would say, 'Prepare ten pipes of wine for Mr. Jones' (or rather 'to be marked J,' for the cooper knows nothing of the buyer). He takes out the ten pipes; they are tasted very carefully, and in all probability, having been made up three or four months, they may be a little light; and a little new wine, or a little peculiarly choice wine, which we keep for that purpose, to preserve identity of colour, would be put in, and then those wines would be shipped.

But I may get an order from London, not for my fine wine, but for my lower-priced wine, and then the operation would be this: I will take my own prices at the finest times, when the price was 40*l.*, and when I used to ship good useful wines at 18*l.* Suppose some gentleman gives me an order for fifty or one hundred pipes at 25*l.*, I send that order out to my house at Oporto.

My eldest son, who is present, as well as his brother (both are my partners), if in Oporto, exercises his judgment; he might say, 'These wines are wanted at 25*l.* Presuming we have never shipped any of that sort before, we think ten almudes out of the lot we bought of such a person at Oporto, and five almudes out of the lot we bought of such another person (that would be fifteen), and six almudes out of our fine wine, will make up a very good wine.' They then make up a sample cask.

We make up the sample to the best of our ability, and having tasted that sample, we find perhaps that it is not quite so good as we intended it to be; or it may be too good, and we then make up another pipe; and, having made up our mind upon the subject, and perfectly satisfied ourselves as to its quality, the shipment is made up. Now the whole of that operation, including everything, appears in figures in our lodge diary; and it does so in every diary of every house.

To this information I will add extracts from my note-book, when last in Oporto.

The first is the calculation of the cost of a pipe of fine wine at that date.

				£	s.	d.
Cost at the farmer's, say for a fine 1840 .				12	0	0
Cask				1	8	0
Cartage to river				1	0	0
Boatage to Oporto and oxen hire to lodge .				1	0	0
Brandy, 3 almudes (16 gallons), 20° over proof,						
at 4/6 per gallon	£4	10	0			
Less 16 gallons wine	1	12	0			
				2	18	0
Leakage and evaporation, at 4 per cent. on 17*l*.				0	15	0
Export duty and fees				3	0	0
Shipping charges				0	5	0
Interest from (say) January 1, for two years on 17*l*.				1	14	0
Rent, say 3*d*. per week				0	15	0
Interest, nine months from date of shipping, on 25*l*.				0	18	0
Proportion of traveller's expenses in England, sampling, &c., say				1	0	0
Commission and guarantee in England, 8 per cent. on (say) 40*l*.				3	2	0
				£29	15	0

In looking at this calculation it should be remembered that wines of every class and brandy have risen immensely since the oïdium; which, however, has now almost disappeared, and would probably disappear entirely if sulphur were as judiciously applied as in some parts of France.

Note of tasting in Villa Nova, May 1844, in Lodge of —— :

Lot	W	at 30*l*., clean, old, mature: good at price.
„	FVS	at 45*l*., full, firm, colour, flavour: refreshed.
„	FSS	at 50*l*., very fine, colour, mature, flavour.
„	$\frac{\text{R}}{1834}$.	at 55*l*., high character, soft, flavour, not much colour.

To make up a quantity to be shipped at 34*l*., I took

16 almudes,		88 gallons of		W
5	„	27	„	FVS
		115 gallons		

For a quantity to be shipped at 47*l*., I took

14 almudes,		77 gallons of		FVS
6	„	33	„	FSS
1	„	5½	„	$\frac{\text{R}}{1834}$
		115½ gallons		

This shows how wines are made up from the 'lots' of certain qualities.

Orders are received for so many varieties of colour—'dark' 'not deep colour,' 'tawny,' etc.—that it would be a never-ending confusion were it attempted to keep all ready to meet every demand.

When I was there, the fashion was in favour of a deep dark colour, and, as already mentioned in another place, there used to be not a little joking among the gossips on the Rua Ingleza about the injunctions received to send 'fine mature wine, but with deep colour.' The deep colour could only be given by adding new wine to the old.

I began Oporto with the police, and *à propos* not of ports but of police, I will finish it with a visit to its prison; a subject which may be interesting just now, when prisons and their inmates are attracting so much attention among ourselves.

The Prison of Oporto.—The Portuguese seem to be at present in about the same state of advancement, in regard to prison discipline, that we were a century ago. A coarse principle of vengeance rules in the management of criminals; and whether the unhappy sufferer survive or die under the pains of incarceration seems to be a matter of indifference.

While on a visit to Oporto, in 1844, I had an opportunity of seeing the manner in which prisoners are treated in the common jail of that city. Not being in the habit of visiting such places, I should not have entered this one, but for a circumstance which attracted my attention.

In daily passing the prison, a large building of handsome architecture, I saw what was very painful to contemplate. From the unglazed windows long poles were projected, and to each was attached a string and bag, the whole being kept in motion, accompanied with screams and wailing lamentations from the inmates.

On looking up, wretched faces, sallow, and matted long beards, were seen crowding against the gratings; and the appeals made by them to the passers-by for food or money were among the most dismal sounds which had ever fallen on my ear.

Interested, as well as shocked, I resolved to visit this abode of misery:

Homo sum; humani nihil a me alienum puto.

On consulting with some friends as to the best manner of gaining admission, all endeavoured to dissuade me from the attempt, assuring me that no one ever entered willingly; as the scenes I should there witness were dreadful, and the danger from infectious diseases great.

A feeling, however, greater than curiosity induced me to persevere, and I succeeded in procuring an order from one of the magistrates. This was attended with some difficulty, as, at the period of my visit, one of those insurrections or revolutions which are so common in the Peninsula had just broken out; in consequence of which the town was under martial law and many arrests were made.

At each corner of the prison a sentry was placed, who challenged all who passed after sunset. I was admitted into a large hall, where there was a strong guard of soldiers; and from thence I ascended a long flight of steps, at the top of which was an iron gate.

I showed the order and the gate was opened. I was requested to inscribe my name in a book, after which the jailer desired me to follow him, informing me that it was the prisoners' dinner hour. I accompanied him and his four assistants, and, passing through a long vaulted passage, we came to a hall about forty feet square; in its centre there was an immense tub containing soup, and close to it a pile of loaves. I tasted the soup, which was made of beans and other vegetables, with a large portion of oil, and it was not unpalatable.

In a little time I followed my guide through another passage, and my attention was directed to a trap-door, on which the jailer gave three loud knocks with a heavy stick; and being almost instantly responded to from below, the bolts were withdrawn, the door lifted up, and immediately there issued, first one, and then another, of most miserable-looking creatures, each holding his ration-can. Both were tall men, very thin, of sallow, unhealthy complexion, long hair over their faces, and most repulsive melancholy expression.

Casting their eyes upward on mounting from below, they walked quickly to the soup-can, held out their ration-tin, and received from an under-jailer a piece of bread, and without a syllable having been uttered, returned to the trap-door and descended. The door was closed over them, the iron bars padlocked, and there they were to remain until rations were again distributed.

I thought I had never seen such wretched-looking fellow-creatures; but I confess my sympathy in their fate was not increased on being told that these two men were the executioners of the prison. Having been condemned to death for murder they had availed themselves of the option offered, either to suffer themselves, or to put others to death. One of them had been confined for thirteen and the other for seven years, during which time they had lived in the same apartment.

We then proceeded to a trap-door in another

passage; and, being desirous of seeing the room in which the prisoners were kept, I accompanied one of the jailers. After descending a long, narrow, winding staircase, nearly blocked up by the prisoners, anxious to ascend for their rations, I found myself in a large high-vaulted apartment, with unglazed windows, but barred. The jailer climbed up and sounded each bar with a short piece of iron, to discover if any of them had been filed. There were eighty-one prisoners in the room, among whom were several deserters, young fellows in military costume; others were murderers and robbers. Some were still untried; others had long been sentenced to the galleys, or death; all were huddled together, whether their crimes were great or small.

I felt that I had got into strange company; but, although a very melancholy, it was a rather interesting scene, to be in the midst of so many human beings, whose features betrayed the violent passions which had caused the perpetration of the bloody deeds which had brought them there. Among them were some handsome men, and the variety of dress had a singular and picturesque effect. Many were well clothed, others were in straw cloaks or sheepskins, and others had nothing but a shawl for covering. Some had provided themselves with mattresses, but most of them had the bare floor for their couch. A very few were working as carpenters and weavers. All were very polite; and, on the whole, I found their quarters greatly superior to what I had been led to imagine. From there being no glass in the windows, it must be extremely cold during the winter; but there is, however, a current of fresh air, to counteract the close atmosphere and pestilential diseases which would otherwise arise.

I was much struck by the proof which even these lawless men exhibit of the necessity for a distinction of rank and power, for they invariably elect from among themselves a judge or chief, whom all must implicitly obey; and the one whom they had selected while I was there was a very tall, gentleman-like man, who had committed some half-dozen murders. On receiving permission, the whole, provided with ration-cans, mounted the steps, ranged themselves in the hall, and one by one marched past the man dealing out the soup and the bread, and again immediately descended.

Some had complaints to make; and one man became violently excited, and gesticulated with an elegance and energy which would have called down rounds of applause, had he been on the stage. I afterwards descended into another room where there were about fifty men, and into another with the same number of women. Many of them had children, and the rations for all were served out in the same way as to the men. We then proceeded up another staircase, and entered various rooms occupied by those who could afford to pay for superior accommodation, many of them being gentlemen and tradesmen who had been arrested in consequence of the existing insurrection. I had reason to believe that some of the prisoners were kept concealed from visitors; and, on a small door being opened by the jailer, I entered (though at first held back by one of the assistants) a cell so dark that at first I could see nothing; but shortly I observed an object, covered with a white cloth, moving in the corner. This man was no doubt a political prisoner; and, without a syllable being uttered, his rations were left with him, and the door closed.

While waiting in the hall, a man, apparently a farmer, was brought in upon suspicion of being connected with the rebels, and underwent a most minute examination, in order to discover if he was the bearer of any treasonable papers; and so searching was this scrutiny that his shoes were actually taken off, and the soles ripped open. Nothing suspicious was found; yet the jailer ordered one of the trap-doors to be raised, and closed over this unfortunate creature, who, unless he had some friend with influence, or with money to bribe the officers or judges, would probably remain in prison for years; but, even if condemned to death, he might have the execution deferred as long as money was 'judiciously' applied.

Within the last two or three years, the town and country police has been rendered so efficient that murders or robberies are comparatively rare in the neighbourhood; and the prison is not nearly so full as formerly, when frequently, owing to its crowded state, the wretched creatures became so excited and violent that it was thought necessary to order the sentries to fire through the windows indiscriminately among them.

During the time of Don Miguel's usurpation,—a time still spoken of with horror by the inhabitants of Oporto,—the prison was crammed so full that it was represented to the governor of the town (the notorious Telles Jourdão) that there was no space for more. 'Is it full to the ceiling?' he demanded. 'No.' 'Then,' added he, 'do n't tell me that it is full.' At that dreadful period, there was scarcely a respectable family in the town who had not relatives in this prison, and many of them were beheaded in the adjoining square. When Don Pedro entered Oporto, the doors of the jail were broken open, and all were liberated; with the exception of the jailer, whose skull was fractured by the mob as he tried to escape.

Since the period of my visit to this horrible place of confinement, the Portuguese legislature has had under consideration the state of the national prisons, and the establishment of penitentiaries; but I have not heard that any improvement has yet resulted from these deliberations.

The beautiful Douro becomes very turbid and high after much rain in the upper country, and in Spain; and as it had risen so much that no boat would venture to cross the bar to meet the mail steamer, I had the prospect of a long detention before me.

There was much kind hospitality in the evenings; and it was easy to pass the forenoons, when not engaged in the lodges, in rambling over the beautiful and interesting neighbourhood. There were few parts with which historical associations of the old war were not connected; while the town itself, and every spot around, showed the marks of the memorable siege ten years before my visit. The effects of round shot and musketry, and of fire, were visible everywhere; and I looked with deep interest on many a field and building of which I had had vivid descriptions from a dear relative who had received many wounds in their defence against the usurper, Don Miguel. In the enthusiasm of the moment, I said to my guide, 'Manuel, would not you like to be a soldier?' and he replied, 'Yes, sar, ver much I like fight, but no like be fighted.'

One morning, however, I received a warning that made me very cautious afterwards. Having climbed over several walls, I was sauntering through a field, when I was startled by a loud voice, and, on turning round, was horrified to see a soldier holding his rifle straight at me, and looking very angry. Not knowing what he said, I held up my hands in the most supplicatory manner, and, taking off my hat, made him a low bow; which had the desired effect, for he put down his rifle and beckoned to me to move off. I obeyed his order with the utmost alacrity, and did not look back till I had sprung over several walls. I learned afterwards that the building which I had observed in the field was a powder magazine, over which the soldier was sentry.

Becoming tired of waiting in Oporto, I had decided on riding with a guide to Vigo, to meet the steamer on her calling there; but just as I was setting off, the flag announcing that she was in sight made me give up the land journey, and hurry down to the Foz; where I was informed the mail boat would embark the passengers for Lisbon at a place on the shore, about two miles from the mouth of the river. This point, called the Rocks, forms a projecting pier from which it is safe to communicate with passing ships, unless the sea be very rough.

While waiting, I wandered about the little town, and had an opportunity of learning practically the truth of the old adage, that you should never interfere in the quarrels of man and wife.

Passing along a narrow street I heard loud voices, and the screams of a woman issuing from a house, the door of which being open, I entered, and there saw a man in a fearful passion, holding his wife by the hair and beating her, while she resisted vigorously. I hesitated for a moment whether it were not best to let them fight it out, but gallantry overcoming prudence, I watched till the man's back was towards me, when I rushed in, seized him by the throat *à la garotte*, and, placing my knee to his back, held him so that he could not move. Flattering myself that the lady would feel the deepest gratitude, I looked to her for approbation, when, to my dismay, she cast upon me a look of fury; and seeing her clench her hands, I thought it was time to escape, so, giving her beloved a push into her arms, I rushed out of the door, scarcely halting till I found myself in the boat, protected from the sweet pair by twelve stout rowers. They soon put me on board the steamer Iberia, which landed me the next morning in Lisbon.

It is seen by the Table of Consumption, &c. (p. 58), that the consumption and the per centage which port bore to all other kinds, was—

In 1831,	consumption	2,707,734	gallons,	43·58	per cent.
„ 1841,	„	2,387,017	„	38·59	„
„ 1851,	„	2,524,775	„	40·20	„
„ 1859,	„	2,020,561	„	27·82	„
„ 1860,	„	1,776,138	„	24·14	„
„ 1861,	„	2,702,649	„	25·06	„
„ 1862,	„	2,349,954	„	23·97	„

The following tabular statement of the prices, the amount of duty per pipe, and the shipments to this country annually, since 1787, is interesting; and I believe it is nearly as correct as it can be made. But I must beg a reference to the remarks on a similar statement of sherry shipments, as these apply equally to port (see p. 151).

Shipping Prices, and Duty, per Pipe of Port, and Shipments of Pipes to Great Britain, from 1787 *to* 1862.

Years	Price per Pipe	Duty on a Pipe	Quantity Shipped to Great Britain Pipes	Years	Price per Pipe	Duty on a Pipe	Quantity Shipped to Great Britain Pipes
	£ £	£	£		£ £	£	£
1787	16 to 20	18	32,174	1825	36 to 45	28	40,322
1788	16 „ 20	„	36,087	1826	36 „ 42	„	18,548
1789	16 „ 20	„	39,678	1827	36 „ 46	„	24,549
1790	16 „ 20	„	42,862	1828	30 „ 40	„	26,164
1791	20 „ 24	„	47,212	1829	30 „ 50	„	17,981
1792	20 „ 24	„	54,981	1830	30 „ 50	„	19,038
1793	20 „ 24	„	31,194	1831	32 „ 50	32	20,243
1794	20 „ 24	„	50,002	1832	26 „ 48	„	24,025
1795	19 „ 22	28	52,763	1833	26 „ 54	„	22,760
1796	22 „ 30	39	37,626	1834	28 „ 58	„	24,177
1797	22 „ 30	40	22,340	1835	32 „ 48	„	24,174
1798	22 „ 30	„	54,801	1836	38 „ 48	„	25,029
1799	22 „ 30	„	52,783	1837	30 „ 46	„	22,376
1800	22 „ 30	„	54,203	1838	22 „ 44	„	25,221
1801	22 „ 30	„	64,859	1839	26 „ 48	„	25,464
1802	22 „ 30	„	37,051	1840	24 „ 50	33	23,205
1803	34 „ 38	47	52,947	1841	24 „ 42	„	20,757
1804	32 „ 34	52	19,698	1842	24 „ 42	„	11,208
1805	32 „ 34	„	40,006	1843	26 „ 42	„	21,893
1806	32 „ 34	„	39,696	1844	26 „ 42	„	25,109
1807	32 „ 34	„	47,828	1845	28 „ 50	„	23,383
1808	32 „ 34	„	44,186	1846	24 „ 46	„	23,477
1809	32 „ 34	„	41,156	1847	24 „ 50	„	20,529
1810	32 „ 34	„	54,720	1848	22 „ 42	„	21,277
1811	40 „ 70	„	18,520	1849	22 „ 42	„	23,028
1812	40 „ 70	„	30,014	1850	25 „ 48	„	25,400
1813	40 „ 70	„	Custom House burned	1851	28 „ 48	„	20,780
1814	40 „ 70	„	30,996	1852	30 „ 48	„	19,219
1815	40 „ 70	„	31,641	1853	24 „ 42	„	46,834
1816	40 „ 70	„	16,430	1854	36 „ 65	„	33,831
1817	40 „ 55	„	28,250	1855	40 „ 70	„	26,755
1818	40 „ 55	„	35,888	1856	42 „ 70	„	29,216
1819	40 „ 55	„	20,622	1857	45 „ 70	„	23,615
1820	40 „ 55	„	21,196	1858	42 „ 63	„	11,592
1821	30 „ 40	„	23,394	1859	44 „ 66	„	14,530
1822	30 „ 40	„	27,758	1860	42 „ 70	17	22,424
1823	30 „ 40	„	23,208	1861	42 „ 80	„	22,945
1824	34 „ 42	„	19,992	1862	40 „ 80	14	24,832

CHAPTER III.

LISBON AND LISBON WINE.

Lisbon—Belem—'Charley' Napier—Don Miguel—Don Pedro—Espoz y Mina—O'Connell—Sacavem—Calcavellos—Arinto—Termo—Colares—Lavradio—Bucellas—Cintra—A Bottle of Colares—Conde de Piedade—St. Ubes—Estramadura—Memorandum of Tasting—Letter from Lisbon in 1806.

LISBON!—what a change has taken place in the importation of wines from that place!

It may be seen in my remarks upon port, that I believe a very large portion of the shipments from Portugal were formerly from this district; and some idea may be formed of the extent of that trade by the perusal of the letter of 1798 (page 80).

I have also mentioned that about the same period it was the daily habit, among City men, to go to Tom's, or some other coffee-room, to have bread and cheese and a gill of lisbon, as it is now to go to Garraway's for a sandwich and a glass of sherry. Old wine-merchants will remember when constant orders used to be received for lisbon; while now they do not probably receive one in six months.

It shows how fashions unaccountably change; for there is scarcely a better or more agreeable wine than real, old, rich, mellow, or dry lisbon; but its name is nearly forgotten, since nothing passes now that has not the name of sherry, however coarse much of this is, and not to be compared to good lisbon. With the exception of an order for a quarter-cask, some months ago, I have not been asked for it for years past.

Among our forefathers it was the favourite white wine; and in many an old residence may be seen the silver label, 'Lisbon.' The city of Lisbon was at one time second only to London, for commerce; but it is melancholy to look on its splendid houses, so beautifully situated, and the still-existing remains of churches and palaces, rent by the earthquake of 1756.

On passing the fort of Belem, we come upon a view of the town and its streets, ascending the steep hills, varied by the numerous churches and spires, all glittering in a brilliant morning sun. The sight, as we passed Belem, reminded me of the late 'Charley' Napier, who dined with me the day before he set off on his daring resolution to take Don Miguel's fleet. With several active supporters of Don Pedro, there was the Spanish guerilla chief, Espoz y Mina, so renowned in the old Spanish War, and so denounced at a later period by O'Connell, for shooting the mother of Cabrera.

Napier was a slovenly-looking man; his trowsers, for instance, had evidently been once white, but were now the worse for wear, and had become of a brown yellow. He was fond of saying eccentric things, and of pretending to be in a great passion, while it was evident he was merely affecting it in words and manner, and had all his wits about him. Although he wished to be thought impelled by romantic feelings to help a young queen to her throne, still it was not difficult to see that no man ever entered on an enterprise with more cool calculation than he did, before agreeing to lead this expedition ; or more resolved to be well paid, alive or dead, by prize money or insurance. Well do I remember, on that evening, his declaring to my friend George Bell, that unless the steamers were provided with certain things, they must look out for some one else. When asked what he would do if he did not meet with Don Miguel's fleet, he replied :—'I'll look for a black night; I'll try to slip past Belem; I'll run on to Lisbon, land there, and —then we shall see what we shall see.'

Now, again, for wines. On arriving, I called on Mr. L., of the old house H. L. & Co., who kindly accompanied me in a boat about eight miles up the Tagus—a delightful sail, past hill and dale, and vineyards and quintas, till we arrived at Sacavem, where the wine stores, similar to the lodges in Villa Nova, are chiefly collected. Here, lisbon, with bucellas, arinto, and termo, is found. These are white; while the colares, lavradio, &c., are red; but, to enumerate the various kinds and qualities would occupy many pages, without affording much information; for there is scarcely any quality which may not be grown in this province of Estramadura.

Of lisbon, there are the dry, the mellow, and the rich kinds; with calcavellos, which is still richer and sweeter, and is made near Belem. Arinto is usually half and half of mellow lisbon and bucellas; and termo is somewhat similar. About the year 1824, there was an extraordinary run upon bucellas, so much so that it rose 20*l.* per pipe in a very short period; but the fine old, but small, stock was soon exhausted, and the shippers had recourse to a new and inferior quality; so that it fell out of repute almost as rapidly as it had jumped into it. As an instance of its general estimation before it lost caste, I recollect that at public dinners, for the one bottle of sherry placed on the table, there were at least two of bucellas.

The following day I went with Mr. C. to his delightful quinta, three miles up the river, where we dined; and I had an excellent opportunity of tasting all kinds, in perfection. He was an enthusiast about the wines of Lisbon; but it is impossible to fight against the overwhelming power of fashion; and his money was, consequently, badly invested. The next day I accompanied another kind friend to that wonderfully lovely spot, Cintra; and, ascending to the old Moorish palace, then the Peña Convent, now the King's summer palace, had a view such as there are few like it in the world.

We walked down to Colares, paying sixpence in a wine-shop for a bottle of the well-known wine of this name; which is never, I think, agreeable, being hard and stalky. It is stated that, if sent to this country, it spoils in a year, even if a little spirit be added. My authority for this is the agent of one of the first Lisbon houses, who assures me that such has been his experience with casks for his own private cellar; but, still, I have doubts of any wine whatever, of such body as colares, going wrong, if it has been properly fermented and made.

I went also across the river and tasted very nice white wine, grown on the estate of Barrocas-Piedade, presented by the Portuguese government to Admiral Sartorius, Conde de Piedade. Near St. Ubes a pleasant sweet wine is grown; in short, the variety is immense; there is scarcely a limit to the quantity that *might* be produced in this district, if there were the demand for it.

A pipe of lisbon is 117 gallons; a hogshead 58; a quarter-cask, 29.

I see in my memorandum made at the time:—

> About 4 gallons of brandy, 24° over proof, are put in, just after fermentation, 2 gallons on the first racking, and the same on shipping. I tasted some 1840, with only 1 gallon, and thought it much better than the others. Mr. L. fears it will not stand, but it tastes firm and solid, and I shall try a hogshead.

I got the hogshead over; it was much liked during more than a year that it remained unsold; and I never afterwards heard a complaint of it.

The following letter, dated 1806, shows the prices at that time.

Lisbon, February 22, 1806.

Samuel Brown, Esq., London.

SIR,—We have the pleasure to acknowledge receipt of your much-esteemed favour of the 8th ultimo, and note contents. Having occasion to make a remittance by the packet, we have taken the liberty to value on your wine account, as follows:—

£	*s.*	*d.*		£	*s.*	*d.*
63	0	0	per your letter of August 13, 1805, at nine months, date from July 27, less 5 per cent. commission	59	17	0
432	0	0	per ditto, 8th ult., at nine months, date from December 16, less 5 per cent. commission . .	410	8	0
495	0	0				
24	15	0	Commission, at 5 per cent. .	£470	5	0
470	5	0	to our own order, and which, we doubt not,			

you will honour with your usual punctuality, debiting our account for the same.

We beg leave to hand you a list of the present shipping prices of wines, the qualities of which we can particularly recommend to you and your friends.

We remain, &c.,

(Signed) FITZGIBBON, FRENCH, & DUFF.

Lisbon wine,	1805, 23*l.*	
Do.	1804, 25*l.*	
Do.	1803, 24*l.*	
Bucellas,	1805, 25*l.*	per pipe.
Do.	1804, 27*l.*	
Calcavellos,	1805, 26*l.*	
Do.	1804, 28*l.*	

CHAPTER IV.

SHERRY, XEREZ, PORT ST. MARY, ETC.

Xerez-de-la-Frontera — Port St. Mary — Cadiz — Map of Cadiz and neighbourhood—Bodega tasting—Capitaz—San Lucar—Cordova—Rock-water Sherry—Colouring—Napoleon butts—How Sherry is made—Manzanilla—The Doctor—Soleras—Spanish earth — Macharnudo—Extent of production of Sherry—Increasing demand—Rise in price—Deterioration of quality—Railways—The Guadalquivir—Seville—Dancing Gipsy Girls—Valdepeñas—Dinner at one A.M.—Kicking a Muleteer—Amontillado—Chamomile—Montilla—Vino de Pasto—Paxarété—Rota Tent—Gordon & Co.'s Circular, 1802—'Sherris Sack'—Mr. Ballantyne's description—Mr. Duff—Table of Consumption since 1831—Prices, &c., from 1787 to 1862.

THE word Sherry is derived from the name of the town of Xerez-de-la Frontera, in Andalusia, one of the wealthiest in Spain. It is about twenty miles from Cadiz, and about ten inland from Port St. Mary across the bay, reached when I was last there (in 1844) by a steamer; but a railway now runs from Cadiz through Xerez and Seville, on to Cordova, to be continued to Madrid. On entering the bay of Cadiz there is a view worth travelling many miles to see.

Cadiz itself is like a city of white marble palaces; and although the old walls and fortifications are in a dilapidated state, recalling many an interesting historical recollection, they possess a beauty of their own; which is much enhanced by the breaking and rushing of the waves into the breaches made by war and time. Some of the streets have a charming appearance, owing to the balconies being filled with flowers, and painted in the gayest and most brilliant colours. On looking up, each side seems as if it were a hanging flower-garden. This is especially striking in the principal street, the Calle Ancha, narrow as all are in the south, but laid out at such an angle as to afford shelter from the rays of the sun, except when in the meridian.

CADIZ, XEREZ, AND NEIGHBOURHOOD.

Crossing in the steamer to Port St. Mary, I took a calesa to Xerez, five or six miles distant, and arriving in the evening, went to the principal inn, which reminded me forcibly of *Don Quixote*, and *Roderick Random*, and some of the scenes so amusingly described in those works. It must be rather trying to English travellers to observe the indifference with which they are received and treated in Peninsular hotels. No bowing or ready waiter, or Boots, will be found to welcome you, or to carry your portmanteau; and on entering the doorway you will probably see a large room, full of muleteers, labourers, and proprietors, drinking, smoking, and chatting.

When the landlord or a servant takes the trouble of escorting you to a sleeping-place, it will probably be found to contain a dozen wooden bedsteads, with several of them occupied, even at mid-day, by tired muleteers.

If you express a desire to have a room for yourself, instead of with a dozen or two companions, you are considered very fastidious, and are shown to another, where you can be in solitary grandeur, with a wooden bed, two chairs to match, and a looking-glass six inches square that reflects a countenance of a shape not easily recognised, and far from flattering. It is often said that the beds and linen in Spain and Portugal are dirty and full of vermin, but, as far as my own experience enables me to judge, I should express a very different opinion.

On returning to the room below I got some of the capital acorn-fed ham, fowl and rice, and eggs, with a few tumblers of the pleasant refreshing wine of the country. What I paid in a wine-shop was, I think, a penny for a glass containing about half a pint.

At both my visits to Xerez, I resided with a friend who thoroughly understood the sherry trade, having been, so to say, born in it, and having worked at it all his life. After breakfast, with the capitaz (manager of the bodega or stores) we begun tasting, first the various Soleras lots, from which orders are executed according to the kind described, and the price to be charged; and, after knowing the groundwork, I stated what I thought would please those for whom I had orders to select sherries. We then took certain proportions from lots, putting them together to decide which blend we most approved; or we found that what we had made up was not perfect of its kind, and might have the fault remedied by a 'topping' of a couple of gallons to the butt, of a rich luscious wine called the doctor, or else of the light amontillado; which produced the very effect desired.

After a couple of hours of this work, finding the palate a little wearied, we would ride till three or four o'clock, when we returned to the bodega; and again tried the various samples, making notes of our opinions. At other times, we prepared samples on one day, giving them a night's rest to mix well together—which is too often forgotten—and then compared them carefully, the next day.

It is an easy matter when one has only to prepare a certain number of butts of the best quality, at certain prices, of gold, pale, or brown sherry; but it is different when orders arrive to ship, 5, 10, or 50 butts, of exactly the same as were sent by such a ship, two years ago. Samples of shipments are always retained, and heads and mouths are kept hard at work to meet the requisition.

After much tasting, perhaps the identical quality seems to have been reached, yet there may be evidently a shade more or less colour, which would cause the rejection of the shipment; and there is no way of assimilating the colour, except by an addition of dark or of pale wine, which would distinctly alter the flavour and character; and so the operation must be recommenced.

This proves how impossible it is for any sherry shipping house to continue to give satisfaction, without possessing or having the use of a large capital; for nothing but age will give sherries the flavour and peculiarity which this alone imparts. There are a few very rich firms in Xerez, one especially; others, possessed of insufficient capital, connect themselves with a capitalist, who purchases from the growers or others, and nurses the wine in his own bodega for two or three years, until it is merchantable. He then arranges with the houses to take it into their stock, or otherwise, for its sale; or he may have a mortgage upon all or part of the houses' stock. Such firms must of course, there as here, carry on their business at a disadvantage.

There is not much difficulty in describing the trade of the few old firms; for it consists simply in buying the best new wine, and nursing it until ready for shipment to any part of the world.

There are a few houses at Port St. Mary, also, whose trade is probably equally simple; but, until some years ago, there was a prejudice against the wines from that place.

I remember my old master, who was in Xerez till driven away by the French in 1806 or '7, telling me that when he left, every acre which could produce real sherry had been appropriated. I dare say this was almost correct, for it is well known that an immense quantity of the white wine put on board ship in the Bay of Cadiz is not Xerez wine, but that much of it is brought from Malaga, and other places on the coast; where it is shipped in vessels loading for England and other countries, and arrives with a bill of lading identical in every respect with that of true sherry. There are also quantities grown between Xerez and San Lucar, and on every piece of ground that will produce anything approaching to sherry. Some very nice wine is also made on the hills about Cordova, which has been found to diminish the dead heaviness of much of the present sherry.

On the road to San Lucar is a large extent of vines on a red, sandy soil, on which I was told some wine was grown, which I remembered to be in such demand in 1825, that the partner and myself were kept very busy while the run upon it lasted. It was so pale that it was called Rock-water sherry, and was therefore supposed to be very light. On the contrary, it was poor and thin, with little sherry flavour; and a large quantity of spirit was added, to enable it to be shipped very young, to meet orders.

Three or four times I have seen the fashion for

dark brown, for brown, for gold, and for pale, change. The browns are coloured usually by juice of the grape, boiled before fermentation to a thick consistency; this, when kept to a great age, gives not only colour, but softness and richness. Sherry acquires a slight colour by age, but is usually coloured by the addition of a little of the boiled mosto, or must.

Sherries were shown to me, in one great bodega, for a butt of which it was declared (how truly, I know not) that 1,000*l.* would not be taken. It is not for a moment pretended that the wine is worth any such money, but it is valued as a curiosity and ornament to the bodegas, as a painting may be to a dining-room. It has, however, a very substantial value, because the addition of even four or five gallons of such sherry to ten butts of very fine, worth 100*l.*, may so greatly improve them that each will bear the charge of 120*l.*

These wonderful wines are known as the Napoleons; because it is stated that when the first Emperor Napoleon was in Spain, in 1808 or 1809, he honoured the wine and the proprietor by condescending to approve of a butt of this description, as his soldiers did of the less *recherché* kinds by drinking them all up! This, by the by, is an awkward historical fact against the reputed ages of some of these wines. But even in 1844 there was a long interval since Napoleon's visit; and there could not be a moment's doubt of the great age and original fine quality of some of them.

In these wines one catches the true old Xerez flavour, which is very powerful; and can discover the peculiar bitterness, which is a characteristic of the finest growths of this locality. In fact, there is far too much of it to be pleasant; and a fine old kind with a few gallons of Napoleon added is much more agreeable than the strong original.

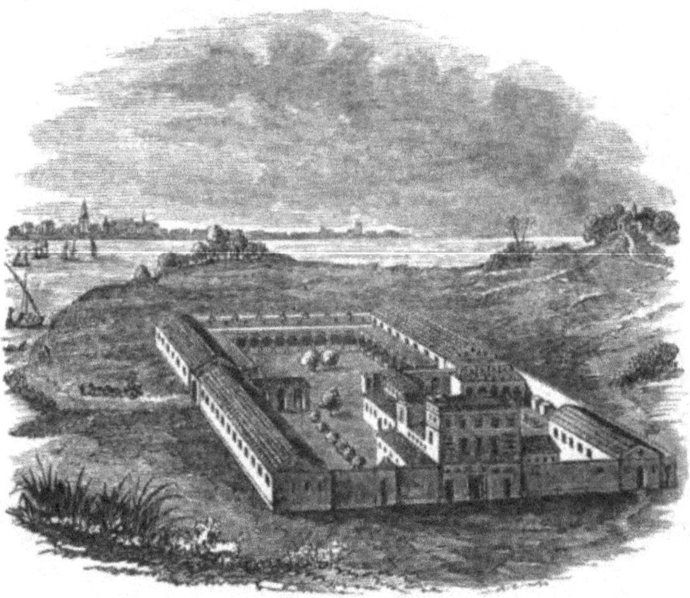

RESIDENCE AND BODEGA AT PORT ST. MARY.

Notwithstanding what I have already written, it may perhaps make the whole process of sherry-making still more intelligible if I transcribe my notes made on the spot. Blank and Co. have beautiful stores called, here, bodegas; the whole, with cooperage, stables, dwelling-houses, and small garden, enclosed within a high wall. The bodegas themselves consist of various buildings containing about 4,000 butts, each store having wines usually about the same age.

They have only one vineyard of their own, about two miles from Xerez, on a low sandy soil, producing very inferior quality. They bought it for the purpose of making their own brandy, but they generally ship the wine off as a cheap kind. When the grapes are gathered, they are put into a vat sixteen feet square and four deep, where they are trodden by men, and the juice is allowed to run into a large tub, from which the butts are filled, and then rolled into an adjoining bodega. Here the wines remain to ferment, and, except being racked from the lees, are kept in the same casks for two or three years, when they are considered fit for being brought into the merchantable stock; but it must not be supposed that any, except the best kinds, remain so long on hand.

Many, by racking, by fining, and by adding spirit, bring their wine into an exportable state within eighteen months after the vintage; and this is especially the case with the light, poor kinds grown near San Lucar. Even of the identically same kind carried to a bodega in San Lucar and to Xerez, one portion will have crossed the sea from the former place, while the other portion is ripening in Xerez, to be improved by age, and then used for cheapening some of the dearer, stouter classes.

It is on the light sandy grounds between Xerez and San Lucar, on the Guadalquivir, that the wines generally known as Manzanilla are produced; it is this kind which is sold in the wine-shops, being the usual drink of high and low; and it is most excellent.

One can no more drink, in Spain, the sherry usually consumed in England, than they can, in Oporto, the usual English port.

About six gallons of spirits are put into a butt of sherry after fermentation, and generally about four gallons more previous to its being shipped. It is almost quite pale at first. The very dark brown is made at San Lucar in the following manner:—Twenty or thirty gallons of must (unfermented juice) are put into an earthen vessel and heated until not more than a fifth part remains, when it looks and tastes like treacle. This is turned into a cask containing more must, which causes it to ferment; and the result is a very full luscious wine, which, if originally good, becomes after many years invaluable for giving softness, richness, and colour to others.

Large quantities of this product, when new, are used to colour and to cover the harsh thinness of poor qualities. It is for this reason that it is called the Doctor; and many a butt that comes to England, to be sold as 'curious old brown,' at an immense price, has to thank the old boiled mosto stocks for its character.

Stocks are kept in casks of all sizes, generally double butts, called soleras; which are never sent away, being the standards or basis on which a shipper's reputation depends; for from these he executes his orders. For common kinds he probably buys from the *capitaz*, or other speculators; and on such, a house of high standing will not place its known brand.

As with the old proverb of the 'sow's ear,' so is it with bad soleras. But, even with the finest, there are required, for their proper treatment, correct taste, experience, and knowledge of the market for which the wine is intended. I mention this, because in more than one Xerez bodega, with excellent old soleras, there seemed to me great want of skill in the making up of what I was shown; the makers apparently supposing that all that was necessary to produce the best quality at certain prices, was to put two kinds together whose respective value averaged the price wanted.

Daily experience shows that this is a mistake; for two kinds often do not go well together; each, although blended, is tasted in the blend. But as a rule, I am sure that when, for instance, a good 50*l.* per butt is required, and the half and half blend of a 60*l.* and a 40*l.* do not amalgamate pleasantly, it is better to put these aside, and to try with others, rather than endeavour to reconcile those that will evidently not be friends.

Very often the best way to gain flavour, body, and life, is by the judicious proportioning from three or four soleras; a little doctor, or amontillado, is frequently beneficial; but these require to be handled very cautiously, for the effect is seldom seen correctly at first.

They have a very effectual way of cleaning the inside of the casks and knocking off all tartar or other matters. Two heavy chains, joined by a piece of leather, are put into the cask, the bung being driven over the leather so as to enable the chains to be drawn out. A little water having been poured into the cask, it is rolled violently up and down, and every way, so that the chains may strike upon every part of the interior. Water is then put in, until it comes out perfectly clear, when the cask is well rinsed with wine, and a sulphur match burned inside.

For finings, whites of eggs are invariably used first; then, about twenty-four hours afterwards, Spanish earth, a hard clay procured a few miles from Xerez, is employed. For a butt, a piece the size of a turkey's egg is broken off, and allowed to soak in about a bottle of wine, in a large earthen basin, during the night. It will be found so soft in the morning, that it may be worked by the hands into a liquid, frothy state. This is poured in at the bung, and the contents stirred about for a considerable time by means of the iron *rousser*, and in a couple of days the wine will be brilliant. Mr. Blank says this is the custom, but that he cannot see the use of the eggs previously.

The iron *rousser* is a long and very strong piece of iron with a handle, and, at the end, a hole through which a small hard wisp made of cane is put, and fastened. This is passed through the bung, and a man seating himself on the cask, stirs the wine well for a considerable time.

Sherries are always tasted from the bung, by means of a long thick piece of whalebone, to which is attached a hollow cane, which is dipped into the cask, and the wine transferred to a glass; or (as in Oporto, and in various parts of France) to a silver tasting-cup.

The bungs of the soleras are never driven home, and it is not to be wondered at that the annual loss by evaporation in that climate is considerable, being estimated at five per cent.; so that 2,000 butts on the 1st of January must be expected to be only 1,900 on the 31st of December.

P. D.'s stock is said to be 15,000 butts, and he requires no capitaz to help him. It is a wonderful sight to see his immense bodega with its gangway, and to pass through rows and tiers of soleras, new, old, and very old. His vineyard at Macharnudo, on a hill a little way from his stores, is considered the finest in the district.

It is calculated that the Xerez and Port St. Mary district is about 25,000 acres, and the produce about 150,000 butts; but if the parts occupied by grain were planted with vines, the quantity would be much increased. It is probable that the best (the Albarizza) soil and aspects are already appropriated for that purpose, so that the production of truly fine Xerez cannot be much extended. This, however, cannot be said of the growths from the red earth (barros), nor of those from the sandy grounds (arenas), which are light and pleasant when in their natural state.

But it is a truth that for some years the demand for sherry has quite surpassed the supply. This cannot be in the least (as in the instance of port) attributed to any interference on the part of the Spanish government; since an entire and perfect freedom prevails in the conduct of this trade. The cause does not appear very difficult to explain. It is said that the 'first gentleman of Europe,' in his usual polite language, d—d Madeira as gouty, and swore he would in future drink only sherry; which, of course, gave a lift to the one, and a fall to the other, 'in high society.'

Since that time the export of sherry has been gradually increasing, and the shipments last year were 52,876 butts.

The vine disease that began in 1851 was bad about Xerez, and the seasons likewise have been unfavourable, so that stocks have become very low, and the prices consequently exceedingly high; but high as they had risen already, an additional increase has just been made on the price lately—on 40*l.* of 4*l.* per butt; on 60*l.* of 5*l.* per butt; on 80*l.* of 10*l.* per butt; and on 100*l.* of 20*l.* per butt.

Those shippers, who are resolved to uphold the reputation of their brand, are right to insist on a higher price, rather than consent to deteriorate their reputation; but some do not now possess sufficient old soleras to enable them to ship wine commensurate with the rise in price; and one finds, among brands and marks of old firms, young and coarse-flavoured wine.

There has been no rise lately, but the reverse, in the common kinds; for these can be got not only in the Xerez district, but all along the Spanish coast. They are brought to the Bay of Cadiz, where they are landed at a place called Aguada, and prepared for shipment as sherry.

Such things are done in all trades, and will be continued as long as trade exists; and, although two blacks do not make a white, there is no more deceit in it than is daily practised by grand and small houses, which ship and sell Château Lafitte, Margaux, &c., of vintage this and that; Schloss Johannisberg 1758, 1788, or 1808; Port 1815, 1820, or 1840; besides other kinds, with names and titles which, ninety-nine times out of a hundred, neither they themselves, nor anyone else who knows anything about it, believe a word of.

But often downright frauds are committed, one of which has just been reported. It appears that some dealers considered that it would be a profitable speculation to purchase, in the docks, the cheapest things they could find, which when put together would taste like sherry; to ship it to Cadiz, and to bring it back, with a bill of lading dated in Cadiz, as genuine sherry.

The Customs authorities profess to use means, by branding the word *mixed* on the cask, and by cutting in the names of the vatters, to make what has been done, evident to all; but there seem to be ways of getting certain words erased, and marks inscribed or retained, which remind one of O'Connell driving his coach and six through acts of parliament.

I copy from a well-known wine circular an account of one or two of these fraudulent transactions:—

Our present business is to unfold a novel system of sending inferior 'mixed' wines a short round, from London to Gibraltar and Cadiz, and home again, at a cost of about 35*s.* per butt, whereby their nominal value is enhanced some 100 per cent. This ingenious traffic is carried on with great despatch, and certain operators are apparently deeply engaged in such 'roundabout' commerce. The following are the particulars:—

Twenty butts, mixed by Gordon, March 11, 1863, composed of ten butts Hambro' white, 6¾ butts Sherry, one quarter-cask E. I. Madeira, spirit, &c., entered out for Cadiz in the name of J. Barber, per 'Cadiz,' March 13; returned per same ship, and entered in the name of Barclay, April 13; marked <OS> No. 1/20; housed at Cooper's Row Warehouses.

Twenty-three butts, vatted by Camp, March 26, 1863, composed entirely of Hambro' white, spirit, &c.; entered out for Cadiz in the name of J. Barber, per 'London,' April 2; returned per same ship, and entered by W. Slade, 4th inst.; marked WZ, No. 1/23; housed at Metropolitan Bonded Warehouses.

It will be observed that these liquids are vatted in the names of 'Gordon' and 'Camp,' and the nominal shipper, by bills of lading, is 'A. Cross;' all clerks and office boys in the employ of a well-known firm of sworn brokers, who enjoy a celebrity for extraordinary shrewdness.

Sherry has long been the favourite wine, but the quantity of bad quality now shipped and sold under its name has already injured its reputation; while the high prices of any that is good and old offer an opening for the introduction of another white kind.

The Xerez and Port St. Mary district is a mere speck in the map of Spain, and it is not to be doubted that railways will soon bring into play severe competition with those hitherto favoured spots on the border of the sea and of a fine harbour. The whole of Spain, from Gibraltar in the south to Ferrol in the north, and to Gerona in the east, is capable of producing unlimited quantities of wines, both white and red, of which many are excellent.

Already a railway is open from Cadiz, through Xerez to Seville, and to Cordova; and will soon be finished to Madrid, whence lines are to diverge northwards to Corunna, Santander, and Irun, with branches to other towns.

On the south-east, one has been open for some time from Alicante to Madrid; and Madrid and Barcelona will, ere long, be joined. Another very important line, now open as far as Badajoz, is in progress from Lisbon to Madrid; besides that from Lisbon to Oporto, which will open this year.

When I was in Xerez, the only easy and pleasant way of going to Seville was by driving over to San Lucar, and thence by the Cadiz steamer which touched there, up the Guadalquivir, to that interesting and beautiful town, full of fine old Moorish and Spanish buildings, and gipsies, not forgetting the gipsy dancing-girls, and their more than questionable dances. From Seville it took two days and two nights to reach Madrid; but I had the satisfaction of seeing the conductor of the diligence fill his large leather bottle at Valdepeñas, and the gratification of helping him and our mule-driver to empty it. Railways are supplanting diligence travelling, which is preferable for viewing the country when not pressed for time, eating as the natives eat, and drinking as the natives drink.

I found that almost all the wine along the road, and in Madrid, was called Valdepeñas; but nowhere did I meet with any to be compared to the contents of my friend the conductor's leather bottle—no, not even in a room about 100 feet long, where we stopped to *dine* about one o'clock in the morning.

In various parts were flickering lights, and at the farther end a blazing fire, to which I was making my way, when I nearly tripped over something from which issued a loud guttural sound. As my eyes became accustomed to the obscurity, I discovered several mules tied up all round, and the ground covered with muleteers, one of whom I had kicked. Remembering the stories about Spanish knives, I was excessively careful in picking my way up to the fire, which I was very anxious to reach; not because I was cold, but because I saw a very large thing like a boiler in the act of being swung from the open fireplace to a cool distance; and as we had been promised dinner six hours earlier, I was now in a most ravenous state. A number of us sat round the pot, from which issued odoriferous fumes that reminded me of Meg Merrilies and Dominie Sampson; each was provided with a spoon and a large brown plate, and each helped himself; and never have I more enjoyed a meal than this midnight dinner, not even at the old Rocher de Cancale. It consisted of kid, rice, quantities of olives, and plenty of garlic.

I know this is a digression; but I seem to have been doing nothing for forty years past but thinking and writing and talking about wine, and I am glad of a little change. Now, to resume. Almost all wine-merchants agree that sherry is better, drawn from the cask than from bottle; and this is my own opinion; and were it not that it is often inconvenient to have it in wood, owing to the danger of pillage, I would recommend none to be bottled which is not intended to be kept for years.

Very often in tasting sherry which has been a year or two in bottle, we find a hardness that the wine had not before bottling, and this generally continues; though occasionally, after having been four or five years in bottle, it becomes soft and much improved.

In every wine, without exception, but especially in those with colour, a portion of the vegetable and other matters which constitute its 'distinctiveness' must inevitably be precipitated to the bottom of the vessel in which it is kept; this is called lees in the cask, and crust, or deposit, in bottle. Brown sherry often forms a considerable crust; and even very old pale, which has been racked and shipped perfectly bright, and again fined here, will be found, if well examined, to have numerous what are called 'fliers,' which have shown themselves since the bottling; but it is probable that if such wine were kept twenty years it would be found that the last drop was as bright as the first, these particles having become crystallized by age.

It is, however, very different with the general run of sherries, especially gold or brown; for let these be bottled in the most brilliant condition, in twelve or eighteen months there will be a sediment, rendering it necessary to decant them very carefully. If the wines had been thoroughly fermented, with little or no spirit added; and if they were not coloured by the boiled must, nor worked up with others just before shipment, this evil would be slight; and we should not have sherries all reduced to one heavy, flavourless standard.

I will add what I have remarked in reference to port, that there are plenty of first-rate houses in Xerez and Port St. Mary ready to give the purest wines, if people here would buy them. Brandy has been for some years, and is still, enormously dear; and it is a very heavy item in the cost that would gladly be avoided; but were none, or only a very small quantity, put to sherry, it would to a certainty meet with the same reception, in England, as pure, unbrandied port.

There seems no doubt of the truth that no explanation can be given how it is that some casks, apparently exactly the same as twenty or fifty others, become afterwards an entirely different wine. This is stated to be the case with the well-known amontillado; the origin of which name is *à la montilla* —the mountain wine, grown on the hills about Montilla, near Cordova.

True, very old amontillado is a remarkably delicate, fine-flavoured wine, quite pale, much too light and delicate to please generally, but invaluable for giving character to sherries that require some of their heaviness knocked off. Indeed, a great deal is sold as amontillado that is evidently only clean light sherry, but, like the real kind, is charged at a high price.

Manzanilla derives its name from the similarity of its flavour to the camomile, which in Spanish is manzanilla: and I have no doubt, from the strong camomile flavour in some I have tasted, that this flower is not unfrequently used to increase the peculiarity; as the flower of elderberries is used on the Rhine to give the peculiar bouquet to what is (supposed to be) sparkling moselle. It is grown on the Barros and Arenas grounds between Xerez and San Lucar; from which, until the dearness of all kinds available for exportation had driven them more to the plains on the Guadalquivir, the inhabitants of the district were supplied with their daily beverage.

That which is intended for manzanilla is well fermented and carefully prepared, and, when of a good year, is a very nice wholesome wine, although scarcely meriting the encomiums which have been bestowed upon it.

'Vino de pasto' means the wine of breakfast, or of repast. When fine of its kind, it is very pleasant, and is generally on the best tables in Xerez. There is no particular spot where it is grown; it being selected from any that may appear of high quality when young.

Montilla, as before stated, is produced on the hills about Montilla, near Cordova, and is very pleasant, with much flavour. A large property has been lately bought there by an English firm, which has risen within a few years into high repute for their sherries,—attributable probably to the judicious blending of a portion of this with their heavier Xerez wines.

Paxarété comes from a place about fifteen miles to the south. The grapes are allowed to become very ripe, almost like raisins; the fermentation is early checked, and consequently the wine is very luscious. When old, it is an excellent liqueur, and a little of it has often a very beneficial effect in giving a mellow softness to sherries that are deficient in that quality.

Rota, on the bay opposite Cadiz, is known for its rota tent (from *tinto*, dark), prepared from black grapes, similarly to the paxarété; but, of course, being dark, the husks of the grapes have been allowed to ferment with the juice.

I think these are all the peculiar kinds which are shipped from Cadiz. Formerly almost every butt of sherry came first to England, and was thence transhipped to any other country; but now many ships load direct (as also in Oporto) for America, Australia, Russia, &c. A butt of sherry is 108 gallons, a hogshead 54, and a quarter-cask 27.

The following letter, dated in 1802, from the well-known house, Gordon & Co., is interesting. By it we see that their quotations began at 24*l.*, and their highest was 40*l.* This is rather a contrast to present prices of the same and other houses—40*l.* to 100*l.*, 150*l.*, and 200*l.*! There are now plenty of (so-called) sherries as low as 24*l.* I do not know whether, at the date of the circular, Gordon or other houses shipped at lower prices, but I suppose they did not.

Xerez de la Frontera, May 1, 1802.

Messrs. Yeats, Brown, & Co., London.

SIRS,—The death of our partner, Mr. Robert Gordon, in January 1802, and cessation of his concern in our house on the 31st December last, have induced us to give a share of the business to Mr. Gideon Granstoun, who is entitled in every respect to this mark of our friendship and confidence.

Our firm will continue to be Gordon & Co., of which our signatures are here annexed. We shall henceforward devote our whole attention to the wine trade; and we shall study to support the long-established reputation of our brand-mark D G by the shipment of sherries and rota tents of the best quality on the most moderate terms.

The unprecedented scarcity of wines, from the failure of three successive vintages, is the real cause of their enhanced value. Those now in our cellars are very select, and their prices are quoted below.

Messrs. Hathorn & Roberts, of London, will have the entire management of our concerns in Great Britain and Ireland. In soliciting, therefore, a continuance of your favours, we request you will address to us here, or to our friends, Messrs. Hathorn & Roberts, of London, as none but they or their agents will have permission to take orders for us.

We hope to be favoured with your commands, and remain, with respect,

Sirs, your obliged and very obedient servant,

Per James Gordon & Co.,

JOHN DAVID GORDON.

SHIPPING PRICES—1802.

Brand-Mark D G.

	£	s.	
Sherry at	24		per butt, free on board, in Cadiz Bay.
„	25	10	
„	27		
„	28	10	
„	30		
„	32		
„	34		
„	37		
„	40		
Paxarété	45		
Tent	.	.	per hogshead ditto.

The signature of Y. O. S. James Gordon (Gordon & Co.)
„ Y. O. S. John David Gordon. „
„ Y. O. S. Gideon Granstoun. „

Sherries, and the kinds which come to this country from Spain under that name, are never in pig-skins;

but almost all those grown in the interior are carried in them, swung across the backs of mules. After the skins have been well seasoned, there is no reason why they should injure the quality; but there is generally very little attention paid to keeping either the exterior or the interior clean, and consequently a bad flavour and taste are frequently imparted.

The more we investigate, the more do we find preconceived ideas and theories overturned by unwelcome facts, which nullify opinions that appeared well-founded and have been received as axioms. It has long appeared to me very doubtful whether the wine we now call sherry, from Xerez, was known in this country even 150 years ago. I can trace no authority for it, except the words in Shakespeare, 'sherris sack,' which is usually supposed to be 'dry sherry;' but we find also in old books, 'sack with sugar,' and sack in so many ways, that it is evidently not derived from the French word 'sec,' dry. Indeed, I have come to the conclusion that, at that period and to a much later date, little if any dry wines were drunk, and that all had honey, sugar, mead, or other things added to them.

I am not aware that either Cadiz or Xerez is mentioned, till a comparatively late period, as places whence wine was brought. Malaga furnished the Spanish wines so long known under the names of malaga and mountain, both of which are quoted in all old wine circulars.

Mr. Ballantyne, in his letter, to which I have already alluded, states:—

In taverns, the call was only for red or white, but frequently the red was called claret, and the white, sherry. Sherry was then generally, like other white wines, kept in a state of fermentation by sweet malaga, meade, cyder, or honey. Pale wine was but just coming home on the lees, with which was mixed Spanish, or small French wine; and a similar mixture was made of the various sorts of white wine. The dexterity of the wine cooper then was making the most palatable, at the lowest prices. But now all wine comes in so clean, and in so perfect a state, that the wine cooper's skill of former days is not required. From 1767 to 1774 no pale wine was bottled but for immediate use; only draft wine of all kinds was used in the principal taverns, and it was often very bad, not from tricks of the vintners, but from bad management. . . . With white port (being subject to ferment in summer, and to grow foul in winter) we mixed a little fine Teneriffe, which improved its flavour and prevented any farther fermentation. . . . I think three years of the above time had passed before I had seen a butt of sherry, but, when I did, I recommended it in preference to white port. A man of quality recommended to me Mr. Duff, our late Consul at Cadiz, to whom I sent orders from several friends; and white port soon became despised, although it had been in such esteem that, even as late as 1782, I got orders in one week for shipping 80 pipes. Now (1807) it is forgotten, and sherry has prevailed. But I beg, as many of you as have given up your affection for your palates to gratify your eyes with what is extremely pale, when you discover a hot, pungent, bitter taste, such as no grapes could ever give, will not impute it to the wine-merchant, many of whom, with reluctance, import it to gratify your perverted tastes.

The accompanying statement of the shipping prices,

amount of duty, and shipments from the years 1787 to 1862, is as correct as I can make it; but I offer it only as an approximation to the truth. (See p. 155.)

I may here state that, for my own part, I attach very little confidence to any wine statistics of an earlier date than 1821; and this is not said without a good deal of practical experience. Since the Parliamentary Committee on Wine sat in 1852, there has been no difficulty in referring to any amount of statistics; but when I began, twenty years before that time, I had to search in old Acts of Parliament and innumerable documents, and was sometimes disposed to give it up in despair, as errors and confusion were so palpable.

Duties, until 1825, were also increased or diminished by the *tun*, which explains such rates as 7/7 and 11/5 per old gallon; and as it was necessary to reduce all, from the earliest date, to the imperial *gallon*, with the rate upon *it*, by which alone a just comparison could be made, it may well be supposed that the labour was not light. Previous to 1821, the 'United Kingdom' sometimes included Scotland and sometimes not. As to Ireland, it was impossible to comprehend the customs arrangements; but I recollect that the documents required in sending wines there were similar to those for shipment to Holland, &c.

Wine-merchants will immediately perceive that the prices quoted here, show neither the lowest nor the highest that they have often known to have been given; but, while referring to circulars, I have recurred also to memory, not only for quotations, but for qualities.

I can recur personally to 1822, when the lowest shipping prices of the then eight or ten old sherry houses was 28*l.* to 57*l.* 10*s.*, and occasionally 65*l.*, though higher for 'very old and very choice;' and I am much mistaken if the sherries of that period, had not a flavour and 'character' in them that are now rarely found.

By reference to Gordon & Co.'s list of 1802, it is seen that the lowest price was then 24*l.*, rising to 40*l.* for the best. This has been described to me as very fine, but not so bright and well-made as at a later date; though not improbably its brightness and freedom from fermentation now may be, in some degree, owing to larger additions of brandy. For a considerable length of time, before the vine disease broke out in 1852, sherries—at least, white wines shipped in Cadiz Bay—could be had, at very low prices, of good drinkable quality. Many will concur with me in thinking that a more agreeable wine could then be bought for 20*l.* per butt than can now easily be met with at 40*l.*

The consumption and per centage which sherry bore to all other kinds (p. 58) were:

In 1831,	consumption	2,089,532	gallons, and	43·58	per centage
1841	„	2,500,760	„	38·59	„
1851	„	2,533,389	„	40·20	„
1859	„	2,876,554	„	27·82	„
1860	„	2,975,769	„	24·14	„
1861	„	4,032,274	„	25·06	„
1862	„	3,956,213	„	23·97	„

Shipping Prices of Sherry, and Duty per Butt, and Quantity shipped to Great Britain, from 1787 *to* 1862.

Years	Price at Cadiz per Butt	Duty per Butt	Quantities Shipped to Great Britain—Butts	Years	Price at Cadiz per Butt	Duty per Butt	Quantities Shipped to Great Britain—Butts
	£ £	£	£		£ £	£	£
1787	24 to 40	17	8,432	1825	30 to 65	26	26,489
1788	24 „ 40	„	9,402	1826	33 „ 63	„	22,736
1789	24 „ 40	„	7,998	1827	31 „ 60	„	23,395
1790	24 „ 40	„	9,736	1828	30 „ 60	„	30,657
1791	24 „ 40	„	13,038	1829	31 „ 65	„	27,327
1792	24 „ 44	„	10,790	1830	30 „ 65	„	24,127
1793	24 „ 46	„	8,726	1831	31 „ 65	30	25,021
1794	24 „ 46	„	12,320	1832	30 „ 65	„	23,519
1795	24 „ 46	26	16,176	1833	30 „ 65	„	32,390
1796	23 „ 52	36	12,184	1834	31 „ 70	„	33,138
1797	23 „ 52	38	4,518	1835	31 „ 75	„	35,885
1798	23 „ 52	„	7,142	1836	31 „ 65	„	30,429
1799	21 „ 48	„	13,352	1837	30 „ 65	„	27,332
1800	21 „ 48	„	16,708	1838	31 „ 70	„	32,460
1801	25 „ 48	„	12,670	1839	31 „ 65	„	39,719
1802	24 „ 48	„	10,740	1840	31 „ 65	31	38,676
1803	26 „ 48	45	13,742	1841	31 „ 65	„	30,810
1804	28 „ 48	49	13,292	1842	25 „ 90	„	25,887
1805	26 „ 48	„	18,786	1843	22 „ 90	„	25,469
1806	27 „ 44	„	16,528	1844	25 „ 80	„	33,141
1807	27 „ 44	„	15,280	1845	22 „ 60	„	33,697
1808	27 „ 44	„	23,972	1846	31 „ 65	„	30,907
1809	30 „ 50	„	21,878	1847	28 „ 75	„	32,799
1810	38 „ 60	„	20,336	1848	31 „ 70	„	25,952
1811	40 „ 70	„	9,082	1849	28 „ 70	„	31,829
1812	45 „ 70	„	16,136	1850	28 „ 70	„	35,433
1813	45 „ 70	„	Custom House burned	1851	31 „ 80	„	36,157
1814	45 „ 85	„	11,270	1852	28 „ 80	„	29,461
1815	43 „ 85	„	10,296	1853	24 „ 90	„	36,233
1816	38 „ 60	„	6,784	1854	24 „ 70	„	41,251
1817	36 „ 60	„	9,592	1855	36 „ 85	„	35,759
1818	34 „ 65	„	13,870	1856	36 „ 85	„	37,415
1819	45 „ 65	„	8,726	1857	36 „ 85	„	42,860
1820	47 „ 65	„	8,604	1858	36 „ 120	„	22,781
1821	28 „ 65	„	8,572	1859	36 „ 150	„	33,605
1822	30 „ 65	„	10,950	1860	40 „ 150	31 & 16 4/	49,314
1823	30 „ 60	„	15,564	1861	40 „ 200	13 1/	50,052
1824	34 „ 65	„	18,800	1862	40 „ 200	13 1/ & 13 10/	52,876

CHAPTER V.

SOUTH-EAST OF SPAIN, BARCELONA, ETC.

Gibraltar—Sir David Wilkie—Smuggling—Malaga—Old Mountain—Almeria—Carthagena—The Old Guide—Pobre España—Alicante—Valencia—Barcelona—Custom House—Burning and Dancing—Tarragona—Old Rancio—Catalonia—Marseilles—Saguntum.

ON visiting the wine districts of Spain and Portugal, in 1844, I returned home from Xerez by Seville, Madrid, Vittoria, Irun, Bayonne, and Bordeaux—the mail being escorted out of the capital, by three dragoons, to Buitrago, not far from Vittoria, where Wellington gained one of his many victories.

At my former visit, in 1841, I steamed from Cadiz to Gibraltar, where I had to remain during two days on that wonderful rock; and it is scarcely less wonderful to think that we hold a portion of the land of the Spaniards. While at the signal station, the very highest point, looking through the old sergeant's glass at the houses and hills in Africa, we were surprised to see the English steamer, which had left on her way home two hours previously, turning round and coming back to the rock. We soon learned that this was caused by the death of Sir David Wilkie, on his return from Egypt.

The governor was applied to to allow his body to

be landed and buried; but Gibraltar being a fortification, and ships from Alexandria being then placed under quarantine, permission could not be granted; and the body therefore was consigned to the deep, as represented in Turner's well-known painting.

Almost the sole trade of Gibraltar is smuggling, which is very efficiently protected by our vessels and the guns of the fort, which are brought to bear upon any Spanish *guarda costa* that ventures within three miles of them. At that time, there was great excitement and correspondence relative to a Spanish cruiser, which, after having chased a smuggler for a great distance, overtook her within the prescribed three miles' distance, and carried her off to Carthagena; but no sooner was this seen and known than an English brig-of-war was despatched, with orders to enter Carthagena, and to bring the smuggler back to her protectors. The chagrin of the people of Carthagena may be imagined on seeing this done; nor can we wonder that Spanish pride was roused against those daring Ingleses.

Leaving Gibraltar at night, accompanied by half a dozen handsome smuggling boats, designed for various parts of the coast, we reached Malaga the next morning at six; and I had the pleasure of being useful to the well-known blind traveller, Lieutenant Holman, who was then travelling through Spain that he might describe its beauties. It was evident that all his descriptions were founded upon answers to his numerous questions.

It is impossible to overrate the beauty of the position of Malaga, surrounded by luxuriant hills, and the snow-covered Sierra Nevada rising to the skies, with ranges of mountains extending as far as the eye can reach.

But, *revenons à nos moutons*, Malaga wines. As usual, I introduced myself to the principal wine-merchants, and invariably met with a courteous reception. I was shown the cellars of two or three, but would have been sorry to have drunk a pint of any wine I tasted there; they were all heavy, coarse, and ill-made. The only tolerable quality was that which was destined for transmission to Cadiz, to be there mixed with the thin so-called sherries.

I saw some of the dark old 'mountain,' which used to be well known as a forenoon or liqueur wine; but better kinds have superseded it.

The very circumstance of the grapes grown here being so excellent is a proof that, if the making of wine were found as profitable as the sale of grapes, very fine wine would be produced. I do not mean because the grapes are so large and fine — for it is a fact that large, fine-eating grapes invariably produce inferior wine—but because the soil, the heat, and the aspect of the various hills, are so admirably adapted for wine that the result might be looked upon as certain. At the *table d'hôte*, both the white and red kinds were little better than vinegar.

The next day I passed in Almeria, famous for its grapes, but I could not hear of a wine-merchant. It is a small miserable place; but it is said that when the Moors were being driven out of Spain by the Spaniards, many fled hither on their way to Africa, and, not being able to get away, were allowed to remain. I can well believe this, for the inhabitants are wild-looking beings, with black sparkling eyes, very little clothing, and the habit of sitting cross-legged on the ground. Few of the windows are glazed, and the roofs are flat, as in Eastern countries.

From Almeria we steamed—as usual, during the night—to Carthagena. There is this great comfort in the Mediterranean, one is not troubled about the tide 'serving,' the ebb and flow being almost imperceptible.

All that can be seen of Carthagena, until you are alongside the houses, are forts in the rocks on each side of a narrow entrance, through which you pass into an immense basin surrounded by rocks, and so deep, to the very water's edge, that you may almost step ashore from any-sized ship.

This basin is a natural opening from the sea, in which a Spanish fleet has many a time reposed. Farther inward is another very fine basin; and around both are the dilapidated ruins of buildings, such as one would expect to see were Portsmouth or Plymouth allowed to fall into a similar state of neglect.

My old and worn-out guide, whose dress seemed to be of the days of the Armada, and whose figure suited the scene, looked depressed and ashamed. When he saw me drawing the attention of a travelling companion to a copper bolt attached to a pillar, which had withstood the ravages of time, and making a remark which he justly attributed to the fallen state of Spain, he could not help exclaiming—'Si, señor, pobre España, pobre España!' We left the old man in his solitude, giving him a couple of pesetos, for which he expressed his thanks by a low bow, holding in his hand his large cocked hat, still adorned with tattered remnants of faded gold lace.

We sailed that evening for the interesting town of Alicante, where, and indeed as far as Barcelona, I could meet with nothing but the same dark, coarse, red wine, universally drunk with water at meals along this eastern coast. Alicante has lately regained some of its former importance, as it is a favourite route to Madrid, for passengers coming by steam from Marseilles; but the railway is now opened to Valencia further north.

We passed the next day at Valencia, walking from the landing-place to the town, along a beautiful road shaded by fine trees, and on each side such luxuriant fertility as I never saw before. Indeed, it is said, there are few things grown in the tropics which do not thrive there.

I was much struck with the beauty, elegance, and good taste of the dresses of the women, while the costume of the men is remarkable and graceful. It consists of a white shirt, open on the neck and chest, a small green vest, the arms bare to the elbows, a wide red sash, white linen *kilt* descending to the knee, hose of several brilliant colours, rolled so as to hold them up just below the knee, the usual Spanish canvass shoes, and the overhanging red cap with blue and white border.

On entering Valencia one is struck with astonishment at the rows of magnificent houses with marble staircases and pillars profusely carved, and the beautiful courts with fountains and statuary, seen through the massive iron gates—all denoting the wealth which once belonged to Spain. Material decay proceeds slowly in this fine climate; there was little appearance of dilapidation or of age; but it was easy to perceive that these palaces had not been built for their present occupiers, and that Valencia, like many other cities in Spain, was a place of the past, whose glory had departed.

Here, as everywhere else, I made a point of seeking for wine, but, although it was very abundant, I could only find such as had evidently been made without the slightest care.

After a passage of about fifteen hours, we reached Barcelona, landing at Barcelonette. On putting my foot on shore, I was accosted by a man in broken English: 'Sar, there be one great fire this night; custom house to be burned.'

Not knowing how to pass the evening pleasantly, I confess I was glad to hear of this variety; and, getting my portmanteau out of the steamer, and depositing it in an inn, I accompanied him to the scene of action. Following his advice, I covered the lower part of my face with a large wrapper, and put on an old, loose, great coat.

I learned that the customs authorities having hitherto exported all the contraband goods they seized, had now advertised some to be sold in Barcelona, which the manufacturing people had declared they would not permit; and that, if it were attempted, they would burn the custom house down. My guide stated that the goods were French, but that, as little discrimination might be made between French and English, I had better not utter a word, and be as unlike a foreigner as I could.

Proceeding to that beautiful boulevard, the Rambla, we saw an immense concourse of people, many with torches; and in the midst of them a wagon with two horses for carrying off the goods. We joined the procession and marched down to the custom house in the plaza, when there was a halt, and the noise of the ponderous knockers on the custom house gate was heard. Being desirous to have a full view of this extraordinary scene, I was working my way towards the principal actors, when my guide friend declared 'he not go no farder;' so I went 'farder' alone, wondering, I confess, what I should do if a troop of the fine-looking yellow dragoons were let loose among us; but they had the kindness not to interfere..

The knocking at the door and the noise became louder, but the gates stood motionless, till the cries of my friends the goods-destroyers became so decided and their perseverance (till success should crown their efforts) so evident, that the gate was seen to swing on its hinges; being unlocked from within.

In a moment the square resounded with cheers, torches were waved aloft, and a general excitement prevailed. The wagon was backed in, the goods loaded, the custom-house people assisting, and in a little time the order was given to march up to the Plaza do Commercio. Resolved to see it out, I joined the procession, arm in arm with a couple of fellows with clothing exceedingly suitable to a very hot climate, and with bare, brown, brawny arms, and the red cap. I could cheer and make a noise as loud as the lustiest, but, as to speaking, I remembered the old Scotch saying, that it is sometimes prudent to 'keep a calm sough.'

After half a mile's march, we reached the square, where there was prepared a blazing fire, upon which the goods were thrown; and no sooner did they begin to burn than a grand cheer arose and we all danced round, rejoicing in their destruction; after which I retired to my inn.

I learned the next day that the true history of this outbreak was, that some of the principal manufacturers, or dealers in cottons, were afraid that, if the custom house once began to sell seizures, they would continue to do so, which would greatly injure them; and they therefore paid their workmen and others, to put a stop to it in the summary way above described.

Barcelona carries on a large trade; the inhabitants are an industrious people, possessing some mills; but I was assured they did not produce one half the quantity of goods sold as their manufacture; that the greater proportion was smuggled over the Pyrenees from France, and by Gibraltar from England.

EL CONTRABANDISTA.

Yo que soy Contrabandista, y campo por mi respeto.
Yo que soy Contrabandista, y campo por mi respeto.
A todos los desafio,
Pues á nadie tengo miedo.
A todos los desafio,
Pues á nadie tengo miedo.
Ay! ay! ay! jaleo muchachas!
Quien me merca el hilo negro
Mi caballo es tan cansado,
Y yo me marcho corriendo.
Ay! ay! ay! ay!
Ay! que viene la ronda,
Y se oye el tiroteo.
Ay! ay! caballito mio,
Caballito mio, carito! ay! jaleo!

There is an immense quantity of wine produced at Tarragona and in that neighbourhood; but no endeavour seems to be made to grow any but the coarse red kind, which is exported to all parts of the world; and even to France, to give body and colour to others that are deficient in these qualities.

No country possesses greater advantages than the eastern coast of Spain for growing every class of wine, and in quantities so enormous that figures can give but a very slight idea of the amount. Within these few years more attention has been directed to this favoured spot; and although a long time elapses before new vines give wine at all, and still longer before the grapes are in perfection, yet with more attention to the vines in existence, and more skill and care in converting the grapes into wine, it has already been shown that an excellent quality can be produced.

I had a proof that, even then, carelessly and unskilfully as it was made, it becomes good when mellowed by age; for observing some old dusty bottles on a shelf in a wine shop, two Frenchmen and myself bought a few, and found them to be capital rancio (old); nearly the colour of brown sherry, and very different from the dark new kind. Tarragona is the great port of shipment for Catalonian wines, which at that time and before the vine disease, were sold at very low prices, viz. 4*l.* or 5*l.* per pipe. The rancio, when of good quality, and its tawny colour is not produced by the mixture of white wine with the red, is worth from 12*l.* to 14*l.* per pipe. The usual way of selling all along this coast is per tun of 252 gallons, which is equal to two pipes of 126 gallons each. I was told they put in no brandy, but this I do not believe. Very large shipments were made to Cette, Marseilles, and other ports in France, a few years ago, on account of their comparative cheapness, and also to give strength and colour to many of the French wines; and the same is still done to a great extent.

Leaving Barcelona in the comfortable Spanish steamer in which I embarked at Gibraltar, I landed on the following day in Marseilles; and thus ended the steaming portion of a very interesting journey; for although we sailed usually during the night, yet we had daily a few hours of light, early in the morning, or in the evening, when we embarked after having passed the day at one of the principal towns.

The whole coast from Gibraltar to Marseilles is a continued variety of beautiful hills running to the sea, pierced by fertile valleys, with almost always a village; and the elegant feluccas with their white sails skimming along the clear blue Mediterranean. Frequently the captain pointed out the ruins of towns whose names are familiar to schoolboys; and in all my travels I think I have never been more astonished, than when a place on a hill was pointed out to me, and I was told it was Saguntum. The name instantly brought back many recollections, not the most agreeable; for I remembered long lessons about a long siege, and long pieces of Latin to be learnt about that tiresome siege.

It also reminded me of the venerable Professor Pillans, then (1813) head master of the Edinburgh High School; and equally vividly did Saguntum make me think of a class-fellow, Archie Campbell, much given to fall asleep, but who was quite awake to the story that the Saguntines when sorely pressed by hunger sowed turnips on their ramparts; for when Mr. Pillans called out, 'Campbell, what did the Saguntines do?' he immediately replied, 'Sawed neeps, Sir.'

CHAPTER VI.

CLARET, BORDEAUX, MÉDOC, ETC.

The Médoc and Neighbourhood — The fine Growths — Vins de Graves — Haut Brion — Rothschild — Vins de Côtes — Blaye — English Wine-Merchants — Fermentation — Fining — Dinner at Château Lagrange — Château Margaux, 1834 — Hôtel de Margaux — Price of Lafitte, 1858 and 1860 — Profits of the old English Houses — Dutch, German, and Belgians — White Growths — Differently made — Produce of Bordeaux and Neighbourhood — Broker's Quotations, 1858 to 1862 — Was the Médoc a barren Waste 150 years ago? — Letter from Professor Michel — Wines used in Scotland — Mr. Ballantyne, curious Information — Result of Testing of different Years — Consumption and per Centages from 1831 to 1862.

THE red wines from Bordeaux, which pass under the name of claret in England, come from several districts in the neighbourhood of that city. Those from the Médoc are of the highest quality. After them come the growths of St. Emilion, in the arondissement of Libourne; those about Bordeaux itself, called the Graves; and, lastly, the wines of the Côtes of Blaye, of Quinsac, of Camblannes, and of the Palus, ranked as first, second, third, fourth, and fifth; the last two being called 'bourgcois supérieur' and 'petit bourgeois.'

In the Médoc are the celebrated vineyards—Château Lafitte, Château Margaux, Château Latour, Mouton, Larose, Léoville, Pichon-Longueville, &c.

These are distinguished by much delicacy of taste, and a bouquet varying according to the locality.

The parishes in which are the most celebrated vineyards are Margaux, Pauillac, St. Jullien, St. Estèphe, Listrac, St. Laurent, St. Seurin de Cadourne, and several others.

VINTAGE IN THE MÉDOC.

Châteaux Lafitte, Margaux, and Latour are decidedly superior to those that rank as second growths. This is attributable, not only to their excellent positions, but almost equally to the great care bestowed to uphold their reputation, which has long enabled the proprietors to get prices much higher than their neighbours.

Demanding incessant care and attention in every way, one of the most anxious and difficult parts is to have a good combination of vines; for no more in the vegetable than in the animal world can a successful result be derived from only one stock, however pure and perfect this stock at first may be. One vine gives delicacy, another body, another flavour; and the grapes from those and two or three more, with other characteristics, produce wine superior to any that could be got from any one kind.

But it is not always that these first growths are superior to the second, for occasionally the latter, and even third growths, prove better. The St. Emilions are fuller and stouter, and have a deeper colour, than the Médocs; and, although less delicate and fine, have a very agreeable taste, and are generally much liked. The Vins de Graves are also favourites, though not equal to the Médocs. The parishes which produce the best wines of this class are Talence, Pessac, Mérignac, Léognan. The Vins de Côtes, Blaye, &c., though deficient in flavour, and not to be compared to many of the Médocs, when of a good year, are very pleasant, and are much used in Bordeaux.

I remember, when dining a few years ago with a friend at an inn in the village of Margaux, within a stone's throw of the Château, we were much amused on finding the wine so very bad that we could drink it only with water.

When in Bordeaux, a few months back, I tasted

Château Lafitte 1858, which could not be bought for less than 100*l.*, and the same growth of 1860, which could be had for 5*l.* per hogshead.

This proves what I have stated, and if wine-merchants will go over themselves to select according

CHÂTEAU LAFITTE.

Si, parjure à son nom, à sa vertu première,
Laffitte n'ouvre pas les yeux à la lumière;
S'il ne s'arrête pas dans son essor fatal,
C'en est fait pour toujours de son éclat natal.

to their judgement and the opinion of respectable brokers or merchants, they should mention no name at all, but describe clearly what is wanted, with the limit of price. It is certainly more satisfactory to go to the place, to taste and compare the contents of various cellars; but, unless there be a knowledge of the language of the country, the tasting and comparison must be confined to the cellars of the few houses who are in the habit of dealing with England (and not even in London are there more highly respectable merchants). Yet they have long been accustomed to prices and profits very different from many equally respectable French houses, who possess as good wine, and have not been allowed by their native fellow-dealers to get habituated to such gains.

Formerly, every Bordeaux house of note that shipped to England added large quantities of hermitage, which gave the appearance of body, but, at the same time, deadened the flavour; and, after a few years in bottle, the wine became of a brownish hue, hard, and flavourless.

Shipments are now much purer, but claret will never be appreciated while the fear of a deposit exists. Except rhenish, no pure natural wine will preserve its qualities longer than médoc, if properly attended to; but I doubt if it be judicious to keep even the fullest-bodied vintage above three years in cask, and of course light kinds require less time to ripen. Three years, with the usual racking, will be long enough for even the stoutest growth to have deposited its coarse parts, while retaining its generous vinosity. No time can be specified when it will be in the best state for bottling and use, this being mainly dependent on its birthplace, constitution, and management.

If it is intended to sell it in bottle, it is fined with whites of eggs, and in about four weeks it may be bottled.

But I repeat, no specific rules as to time can be laid down; for one wine may be light and unfit for keeping

CHÂTEAU LATOUR.

Voyez à Saint-Lambert cette petite tour:
C'est là qu'est le fameux domaine de Latour.
C'est le vin le plus riche et le plus coloré
Et pourtant il est fin, vif, délicat, ambré.
Quand il est dépouillé de son tannin par l'âge,
D'œnantine et d'alcool c'est un noble assemblage.

long, especially in wood, and ought to be bottled within a year, while another may be a stout kind, with much unfermented saccharine, requiring several years to develope its inherent qualities, and to get rid of the coarse constituents by the natural process of fermentation; which never ceases in any vegetable matter, but proceeds more rapidly when in large bulk than when in a small quantity and space.

CHÂTEAU DE LAGRANGE.

Vous voyez près d'ici le château de Lagrange.
Quatrième d'abord, une opulente main,
Pour un titre plus haut, changea son parchemin.

Although it is usual to *fine*, I believe it would be better to give such wines as claret, or others not very strong-bodied, time to become bright without fining, as this carries down mechanically, and attracts chemically, much that forms the bouquet, the softness, and delicacy which are so agreeable.

I remember, some years ago, being struck with

the truth of the opinions I have just expressed. Being on a visit to a friend in the Médoc, I accompanied him to dine with the proprietor of Château Lagrange, who was formerly one of the Ministers of Louis Philippe. There was a handsome dinner, and the choicest wines. The servant, in filling the glasses, always added Château Larose, Château Lagrange, Château Lafitte, &c., naming the vintages. Some of them, from their great age, had lost much of their flavour. All were decanted, which ought never to be neglected; and upon this important point some remarks are offered under the head of Decanting.

In olden times the cultivation of the vine was carried on in the most slovenly way. There were no trellises, no training, no engrafting, no seeking for the best vines, and no studying of the finest results from a judicious planting of the best varieties, and the blending of several growths to produce an improved whole. These are the results of experience, science, and capital. Good roads are also a very modern invention; and it is within the recollection of men still living that the horse and pack-saddle was the usual conveyance even in this country; and when such is the case, heavy, bulky articles can be carried only by rivers. Were it not for the Douro, we could receive very little port; and were not Xerez and Port St. Mary so near the Bay of Cadiz, we could not import much sherry.

Owing to railways, Bordeaux merchants can now easily procure wine from every part of France; and an immense proportion of so-called claret is brought from the banks of the Rhône, from the Herault, Roussillon, &c., which are blended in more or less quantities with bordelais, and sold as such with almost any name that is desired.

CHÂTEAU PICHON DE LONGUEVILLE.

Pichon de Longueville, en face de Latour,
Est élégant, musqué comme un homme de cour.
Dans son parfum, son ton, enfin dans tout son être,
Il a l'étincelant éclat d'un petit-maître :
Et, quoiqu'il soit léger, coquet et sémillant,
Son esprit est solide autant qu'il est brillant.

If buyers demand Lafitte, Pichon de Longueville, St. Estèphe, &c., there are very few indeed who will decline the order on the plea that they have none, but will feel themselves justified in executing it by sending the best they can at the specified price, and invoicing it according to the growth ordered.

It would be much better if no names were mentioned, as they are rarely to be relied upon, and often mislead; for, not unfrequently, what are con-

CHÂTEAU MARGAUX.

Inclinez votre front, fléchissez les genoux,
Amis, Château-Margaux s'élève devant nous!
Voilà l'un des trois rois, l'un des trois dieux du monde!
Quand de ses feux d'été le soleil nous inonde.

sidered second growths prove superior in some years to those of high repute. Such was the case in 1834, when the Château Margaux proved a failure; but, although averaging yearly about 400 hogsheads, it was extolled as much as the other great growths of that remarkable season, and probably 4,000 hogsheads were sold throughout the world.

Belgian, Hamburg, and Dutch houses carry on a large trade in bordeaux wines through a broker, purchasing vineyards while in grapes, or just fermented, and having them carefully attended to till the spring, when they may be safely exported. They are then shipped to Holland, &c., while quite young.

As they purchase probably one or two hundred tuns, equal to four or eight hundred hogsheads, it is worth their while to charter a vessel to carry them; and thus every means are used to make their wine cost as little as to the Bordeaux merchants themselves. When arrived in Amsterdam or Rotterdam, they are placed in the cellars belonging to the merchant, where he may rack, blend, or do anything with them he likes, until he sells and sends them out in wood or in bottle. It is known that the Dutch generally buy very cheap growths, and that they are large importers from Marseilles, Cette, &c., in the south; and certainly I have nowhere tasted such bad so-called Bordeaux wine as one gets in hotels in their heavily taxed country.

Many Belgian, Russian, and Hamburg dealers lay in their stocks in a similar way, but Burgundy is gaining favour rapidly, especially in Belgium, as in many other places; which may be accounted for by the whole Burgundy district having wonderfully escaped the oïdium, while the Bordelais suffered terribly; but it may be also attributed to the late facility of communication by railways. This has been the means of introducing the many delightful wines of that great central country of vineyards, which produces not only the most exquisite, expensive kinds, but also others of excellent quality, and others again, that are pleasant, though very cheap.

CHÂTEAU D'IQUEM.

Là, les vins les plus fins de Sauterne et de Bomme
Vont aux nobles chasseurs prodiguer leur arome.
Le vénérable Iquem paraît au premier rang ;
L'Iquem, si savoureux, si limpide et si blanc,
Qui porte le cachet de sa noble origine,
Et brille, transparent, comme une aigue-marine.

An advantage which the wines of Burgundy, Macon, Beaune, Beaujolais, &c., possess over those of Bordelais (clarets) is, that the latter are hard, and marked by a bitterness when of a poor growth, with little flavour, while almost even the commonest and lowest of the burgundy class possesses flavour; and the general characteristics are smoothness, a certain richness of taste, without thinness and harshness, and always a decided bouquet, varying according to the quality, soil, &c. Most connoisseurs give the preference to fine Claret, which, when good of its kind, whether it be a first, second, or third growth, is as perfect a wine as can be imagined, and is said to be more wholesome than Burgundy.

The white wines are classed much in the same way as the red. The parish producing the best is Sauternes, where the famous Château d'Iquem is situated, and where there are many vineyards of Sauterne of various qualities.

After this come the parishes of Bommes, Barsac, Preignac, Cérons, and the general kinds known as the white wines of Graves. The last are dry and somewhat hard; while the others, especially in years such as 1847, 1851, 1852, 1858, and 1859, are rich and fruity when young.

These white wines are made quite differently from the red, and occupy much more time and attention. Growers anxious to have the best quality leave the grapes till they are over ripe, and first gather those which are nearest the ground. The care required can scarcely be comprehended by those who have not seen it.

The red also require constant and skillful attention,

for no sooner are they put in cask than there is a loss by evaporation and fermentation which necessitates their being filled up every week, otherwise they would certainly soon spoil.

This continues for about six months, when the bright portion is drawn into another cask, which is kept constantly filled up, and the same operation of racking off the lees is again performed in about six months afterwards.

There are splendid cellars in Bordeaux, and probably nowhere else in the world is there such a range as along the *Chartrons*, facing the river. It is stated that, in more than one, there is wine to the value of 100,000*l.*

The annual average produce of the Médoc alone is about 20,000 hogsheads; but, independent of vine disease or any similar infliction, sometimes a single night's frost almost entirely destroys the best prospects.

Last year (1862) was an instance, for rarely have the vines shown such abundance of fine grapes; but a night of frost in May, and a few weeks of such heat as has been rarely experienced in Europe in July and August, caused such havoc, that, with some exceptions, instead of a remarkably abundant and fine vintage, it has been a very small one, though, in several important districts, of very excellent quality.

Although mere names of properties, their extent, and the names of the proprietors, and the quantity that each annually produces on an average, are seldom interesting, yet as clarets are so much talked of, and many of the names known, I insert here the designations of the vineyards (with their parishes) of the first, second, third, fourth, and fifth growths of the red, and the most noted of the white.

RED WINES.

AVERAGE ANNUAL PRODUCE.

	Acres	Hhds.
FIRST GROWTHS (PREMIERS CRÛS)		
Château-Lafitte (Pauillac), Sir Samuel Scott	167	560
Château-Margaux (Margaux), Aguado	200	400
Château-Latour (Pauillac), de Courtivron et de Flers . .	105	320
Château Haut-Brion (Pessac), Eugène Larrieu . . .	260	480
SECOND GROWTHS (DEUXIÈMES CRÛS).		
Mouton (Pauillac), baron N. de Rothschild	130	360
Rauzan (*Segla Gassie*) (Margaux), comtesse de Castelpers Viguerie	127	280
Léoville (Saint-Julien) marquis de Lascases . . .	162	520
Léoville (Saint-Julien) baron de Poyféré	75	240
Léoville (Saint-Julien) Barton	62	200
Vivens-Durfort (Margaux), de Puységur	80	180
Gruaud-Laroze (Saint-Julien), de Bethmann, baron Sarget de Boisgérard	127	480
Lascombe (Margaux), Mlle Hue	512	80
Branne (Cantenac), baron de Branne	112	280
Pichon-Longueville (Pauillac), comtesse Sophie de Pichon, baron de Pichon-Longueville, comtesse de Lalande . .	125	400
Ducru-Maucaillou (Saint-Julien), Ducru-Ravez . . .	87	320
Cos-d'Estournel (Saint-Estèphe), Martyns	70	240
Montrose (Saint-Estèphe), Dumoulin	112	400
THIRD GROWTHS (TROISIÈMES CRÛS).		
Kirwan (Cantenac), Deschryver	60	144
Château d'Issan (Cantenac), veuve Blanchy	107	240
Lagrange (Saint-Julien), comte Duchâtel	305	1000
Langoa (Saint-Julien), Barton	—	—
Giscours (Labarde), J. P. Pescatore	112	320
Saint-Exupéry (Margaux), Fourcade	125	280
Boyd (Cantenac), plusieurs propriétaires	225	160
Palmer (Cantenac), Emile Pereire	212	440
La Lagune (Ludon), veuve Jouffroy-Piston	75	160
Desmirail (Margaux), Sipière	35	80
Dubignon (Margaux), Philippe Dubignon, Marcelin Dubignon	32	40
Calon (Saint-Estèphe), Firmin Lestapis	137	480
Ferrière (Margaux), veuve J. Ferrière	10	24
Becker (Margaux), Szjarderski et Rolland	10	24

RED WINES—*continued.*

AVERAGE ANNUAL PRODUCE.

	Acres	Hhds.
FOURTH GROWTHS (QUATRIÈMES CRÛS).		
Saint-Pierre (Saint-Julien), Bontemps-Dubary, veuve Roullet, veuve Galloupeau	94	80
Talbot (Saint-Julien), marquis d'Aux	150	480
Duluc aîné (Saint-Julien), Duluc aîné	150	480
Milon-Duhart (Pauillac), Castéja	75	280
Pouget-Lassale (Cantenac), Izan	40	88
Pouget (Cantenac), de Chavaille	28	80
Carnet (Saint-Laurent), de Luetkens	130	400
Rochet (Saint-Estèphe), veuve Lafon de Camarsac (héritiers) .	55	200
Château de Beychevelle (Saint-Julien), P.-F. Guestier junior .	100	320
Le Prieuré (Cantenac), veuve Pagès	28	80
Thermes (Margaux), Oscar Sollberg	75	120
FIFTH GROWTHS (CINQUIÈMES CRÛS).		
Canet (Pauillac), de Pontet	167	560
Batailley (Pauillac), P.-F. Guestier junior	85	180
Grand-Puy (Pauillac), Lacoste aîné	130	400
Artigarnaud (Pauillac), Duroy	83	400
Lynch (Pauillac), Jurine	100	320
Lynch-Moussas (Pauillac), Vasquez	50	160
Dauzac (Labarde), Wiebrock	83	260
Mouton-d'Armailhacq (Pauillac), d'Armailhacq . . .	158	520
Le Tertre (Arsac), Henry	80	200
Haut-Bages (Pauillac), Libéral	25	80
Pédesclaux (Pauillac), Pédesclaux	25	100
Coutenceau (Saint-Laurent), Bruno Devez	115	320
Camensac (Saint-Laurent), Popp	60	288
Cos-Labory (Saint-Estèphe), Martyns	75	280
Clerc-Milon (Pauillac), Clerc (héritiers)	88	80
Croizet-Bages (Pauillac), Julien Calve	85	180
Château de Cantemerle (Macau), B^{ne} de Villeneuve-Durfort .	227	640

The following estimate of the quantities of each class may be considered nearly correct :—

First growths	1600 hhds.
Second growths	3200 „
Third and fourth growths	6200 „
Fifth growths	7200 „
Total	18,200 hhds.

WHITE WINES.

	Hhds.
SUPERIOR FIRST GROWTH (PREMIER CRÛ SUPÉRIEUR).	
D'Iquem (Sauternes), de Lur-Saluces (Bertrand)	720
FIRST GROWTHS (PREMIERS CRÛS).	
La Tour Blanche (Bommes), veuve Focke	220
Peyraguey (Bommes), Lafaurie aîné	220
Vigneau (Bommes), veuve de Reyne	240
Suduiraut (Preignac), Guillot frères	480
Coutet (Barsac), de Lur-Saluces (Bertrand)	480
Climens (Barsac), Élie Lacoste	240
Bayle (Sauternes), Dupous et autres	320
Rieusec (Sauternes), Mayé	120
Rabeaud (Bommes), Deyme	80
SECOND GROWTHS (DEUXIÈMES CRÛS).	
Mirat (Barsac), Moller	140
Doisy (Barsac), Deane	48
Peixoto (Bommes), veuve Lacoste	100
D'Arche (Sauternes), Lafaurie jeune	100
Filhot (Sauternes), de Lur-Saluces (Bertrand)	480
Broustet-Nérac (Barsac), Capdeville	160
Caillou (Barsac), Saraute	100
Suau (Barsac), Pédesclaux	72
Malle (Preignac), de Lur-Saluces (Henri)	400
Romer (Preignac), de la Myre-Mory	160
Lamothe (Sauternes), veuve Baptiste	120

The following extracts from the official quotations by the committee of wine-brokers in Bordeaux show the prices by the tun (four hogsheads) in the years 1858, 1859, 1860, 1861, and 1862. The difference of value placed upon the produce of the same vineyards, according to good or bad seasons, ought to convince wine-merchants and others how fallacious *names* are. The few hogsheads annually produced of each kind prove how few purchasers can get even a hogshead of the growths celebrated throughout the world. The whole of the finest vineyards together are seen to average less, annually, than 1800 hogsheads. The prices are in francs.

DERNIER COURS OFFICIEL DES VINS ÉTABLI À BORDEAUX.

PAR LE TONNEAU (ABOUT FOUR HOGSHEADS).

VINS ROUGES	1858		1859		1860		1861		1862	
	francs		francs		francs		francs		francs	
1ers crûs.—Château-Lafitte, Château-Latour, Château-Margaux	11000	--	6500	—	550	—	5500	6600	4000	—
1 crû. —Graves, Château-Haut-Brion	—	—	—	—	—	—	—	—	—	—
2es crûs.—Mouton	6800	7000	5500	5800	550	—	—	—	3600	—
Larose, Léoville, Rauzan, etc.	6000	6500	4500	4800	—	—	4000	—	3000	3200
3es crûs.—	4500	5000	3000	3500	—	—	3060	—	2500	—
4es crûs.—	3500	4000	2800	3000	450	—	2500	—	1800	2000
5es crûs.—	3300	3500	2000	2600	—	—	2000	2500	1400	1500
Bourgeois supérieurs	2800	3200	1600	2200	300	350	1600	1850	1200	1400
Bourgeois ordinairies	2400	2600	1400	1600	275	280	1300	1400	1050	1100
Paysans des paroisses supérieurs . .	1800	2000	1300	1200	200	250	1100	1300	850	1050
Paysans des paroisses ordinaires . .	—	—	800	900	200	250	880	1000	550	650
Bourgeois et Paysans bas Médoc . .	950	1100	750	950	200	250	650	950	400	600
2es crûs.—De Graves	2000	2400	—	—	—	—	—	—	—	—
3e crû et Paysans	1000	1200	—	—	—	—	—	—	—	—
Saint-Emilion et Canon, 1er crû . .	2800	2400	1800	2000	300	—	1500	1600	1050	1200
— — 2e et 3e qualité	1400	1600	1200	1500	225	—	800	1100	600	900
Queyries et 1res côtes	1100	1200	800	950	225	300	800	—	500	600
Montferrand, Bassens et bonnes côtes .	1000	1100	775	875	190	210	650	700	450	500
Floirac, La Souys, Bouillac, Latresne, etc.	1000	1100	750	800	—	—	650	700	450	500
Ison, Vayres, Ambarès, etc.	850	900	600	700	180	200	600	650	400	500
Blaye et Bourg (1), 1ers crus . . .	1000	1050	750	850	190	210	700	—	500	550
— — Paysans	700	750	600	650	180	200	550	—	—	—
Saint-Macaire, Palus de Libourne, Cubzagais	—	—	—	—	160	190	575	625	350	400
Cahors, 1re qualité	—	—	—	—	—	—	425	450	350	400
— 2e et 3e qualité	—	—	—	—	—	—	400	425	—	—

DERNIER COURS OFFICIEL DES VINS ÉTABLI À BORDEAUX.

PAR LE TONNEAU (ABOUT FOUR HOGSHEADS).

VINS BLANCS	1858		1859		1860		1861	
Château d'Iquem	10000	—	7000	8000	1000	1100	—	
Bourgeois de Haut-Barsac, Haut-Preignac, Haut-Bommes, Haut-Sauterne . . .	3500	5000	3500	5000	560	600	—	—
Paysans ditto	2200	2500	1800	2000	500	525	—	—
Bas-Barsac, B.-Preignac, B. Bommes, B. Sauterne	1800	2000	900	1200	375	400	1000	1200
Podensac et Cérons	1100	1250	600	850	300	350	—	—
Arbanats et Landiras	900	1050	525	550	300	—	—	—
Saint-Pey, Langon, Fargues, Pujols, Toulenne	1000	1250	650	950	300	350	900	1200
Loupiac et Sainte-Croix-du-Mont . . .	800	1000	650	850	380	375	—	—
Illats, Landiras et Budos	750	800	450	550	—	—	—	—
Cadillac et Langoiran	650	800	450	700	275	300	475	700
Côtes et Rions	600	650	425	500	—	—	450	500
Entre-deux-Mers	400	450	325	400	180	210	270	310
Graves 1re qualité	Invendus		—	—	—	—	—	—
— 2e et 3e qualités	950	1500	600	700	—	—	600	750
Petites Graves	550	650	450	500	250	300	400	450

In a letter of mine which appeared in the *The Times* in January 1851, I state as follows: —

With the exception of some of the rich luscious kinds from Greece and the shores of the Mediterranean, introduced at the time of the Crusades, the whole of our supplies were received from France; and so extensive was the trade, even in the fourteenth century, that 200 vessels appear to have loaded for this country. At that period, the Médoc, which now furnishes the few casks we receive known as claret, was a barren waste; those imported then being the stout, full-bodied kinds from the higher banks of the Garonne and the south; and it is only necessary to travel in those parts of France to be aware of the amazing powers she possesses to supply, apparently, the whole world with every variety of white and red wine that could be desired.

I did not make that statement in 1851, about the Médoc, without much previous research, and I add my conviction, that the wines drunk in England, Scotland, and Ireland in olden times had little similarity to those now made about Bordeaux and in the Médoc.

I believe that they were not even red, but that they were generally white, grown south-eastwards in the interior, and brought by land and the Garonne to be embarked at Bordeaux; and probably also at some of the ports in the Gulf of Lyons. I am not blind to the fact, that I may be called very presumptuous to attempt to overturn all the preconceived ideas about claret having been the wine brought from France in olden times. After having searched for information in many quarters, and applied to antiquarians at home and abroad, I cannot discover at what period the bordeaux or the médoc wines became known, but there is little trace of them so long ago as 200 years. Looking even at the map, one sees the Médoc to be like a strip of land rescued from the sea. Among the innumerable writers about claret, it has always struck me as strange that no one seems to have speculated on the singular circumstance, or to have attempted to explain how it is, that, although this wine is known among all other nations, it is only among Englishmen that it gets the name of claret, being everywhere else called Wine of Bordeaux.

A few years ago the French government, alarmed by the consequences of the vine disease, appointed M. Victor Rendu to investigate the subject. M. Rendu is the highest authority in France, and has published a very interesting book upon the wines of that country, from which I make the following extracts.

The wines of Picardan are white, sweet, and dry (doux et sec), according to the way they are made. They take their name from the *Clairette grape*, which has entirely supplanted the old Picardan, growing to a great size and producing strong wine, which may be made very similar to that of sherry, malaga, &c. There is also the malvoisie from which is made a very delicious sweet kind.

Until the Dutch drove the Spaniards from their country, England was the only northern nation which had a navy and merchantmen; and this explains to some extent how others, when they went to

Bordeaux for wine, gave it the name of the town from whence they brought it, while the English probably were in the habit, at an earlier period, of going up to purchase their supplies near the place called Clairette, and thus the wine among the English got the name of claret. It is argued by many that it derives its name from *clair* (light), and *clairet* (rather lighter), but this seems an ill-grounded theory. It is evident that the English carried on a large trade in wine at an early period. We see by records published by Mr. Froude in his History of Henry VIII.'s reign, that much was imported even in the time of Edward VI. in 1546 —

> And for wines we have continually from France and Spain, and also out of Almaine, and out of Candia, great quantity of the best that is grown in these parts. The Flemyngs do buy much of our *beer*, because it is better than theirs, and they pay almost as much for it as we do to the Frenchmen for their wine.

It is stated likewise by unquestionable authorities, that French wines were used in Scotland by all classes, even by the poorest in the Hebrides.

There are good reasons for thinking that, in neither country, was this wine, although called and supposed to have been *claret*, in the least like médoc of the present day, because it is not of the kind to have pleased those people, and it must have become acid by the tedious journeys in wood.

Assuming it to have been generally strong white wine, either sweet or sec (dry), the malvoisy (or malmsey) is made intelligible, for it enables us to understand the frequent allusions to the sec or sack of old times.

Much more might be added to prove that Bordeaux was formerly merely the shipping port for wine of a quality entirely different from what is now understood to come from that town.

After having bestowed much time in investigating this question, I entered into correspondence with the very learned scholar and antiquarian, Professor Francisque Michel, of Bordeaux, who has devoted almost a lifetime to the study of its history. I do not obliterate my own lucubrations, but the Professor has given me so many curious and interesting historical facts, that I feel it would be vain and presumptuous on my part were I not to state that I now believe that his views must be correct, and mine erroneous.

The following letter extracted from a newspaper sent to me by the Professor, contains a few of his arguments against my theory. As regards the derivation of the word *claret*, which the English (alone) employ for 'vin de Bordeaux,' I still feel satisfied that my explanation is the correct one. I am somewhat strengthened in this conviction by seeing that now, since our correspondence, instead of tracing its origin to the word *clair* (clear, light), the name is stated to be derived from *claré*—a drink prepared in Bordeaux for the English when they possessed that district, similar to a beverage in use in England.

However, in a short time M. Michel will publish a work containing much interesting matter on these points.

Extrait du Horticulteur. *Sur l'ancienneté des vignes en Médoc, et l'étymologie du mot* Claret.

À quelle époque peut-on faire remonter la plantation et la culture de la vigne dans le Médoc? Telle est la question qui m'est journellement adressée par des propriétaires de cette terre bénie, dont les annales domestiques sont encore à écrire. En possession de la plus grande partie des documents qui peuvent aider à combler cette lacune, je vais commencer par répondre à mes honorables correspondants par la voie de votre feuille.

La partie la plus ancienne des Rôles gascons est muette sur ce que nous voudrions savoir; mais des registres des douanes de Bordeaux et de Libourne, dressés au commencement du XIVe siècle et conservés au *Public Record Office*, à Londres, nous montrent les navires anglais complétant leur chargement à Castillon, à Macau, à Margaux, et autres points du Médoc, ce qui annonce bien que ce *sauvage et inculte pays* ne l'était pas autant que l'on a voulu le dire, et que ses vignobles ne datent point d'hier. Comme nouvelle preuve à l'appui, on peut encore citer un acte publié par Rymer, dans lequel il est fait mention des vignes de Margaux en 1399, bien près de l'époque où le Médoc était présenté à Henry IV., roi d'Angleterre, comme abondant en vivres.

Les navires qui descendaient la Gironde et faisaient escale aux ports alors existants sur la rive gauche, ne venaient pas tous de Bordeaux; nombre commençaient par monter à Libourne, et, après avoir chargé des vins de Périgord, ils ramassaient ceux de Bourg et de Blaye, qui paraissent avoir été très-anciennement estimés. Si l'on ajoute foi à une tradition qui s'est perpétuée dans le département de la Gironde, ils étaient encore tellement prisés au siècle dernier, que les particuliers qui possédaient des biens dans le Bourgès et dans le Médoc ne vendaient leurs vins de Bourg qu'à la condition qu'on leur achèterait en même temps ceux du Médoc. Un pareil usage, si l'on peut le faire remonter jusqu'au XIVe siècle, expliquerait les haltes des navires étrangers pour compléter leur chargement dans ce pays, alors moins florissant que ses voisins.

D'autres curieux me demandent aussi la raison du nom particulier que nos vins ont reçu des Anglais, qui les appellent *claret.* Voici, en deux mots, ma réponse, en attendant que je sois en position de l'appuyer de preuves positives. Au moyen âge, on donnait le nom de *claré* à une boisson préparée comme il s'en consomme encore chez nos voisins, et les vins de Bordeaux reçurent le nom comme ils avaient reçu la préparation. M. Thomas George Shaw, dont il était dernièrement question dans le *Courrier de la Gironde*, comme de l'un des plus chauds propagateurs de l'usage de nos produits vinicoles, possède une précieuse lettre écrite en 1807, dans laquelle un habile négociant fait connaître son opinion sur la question qui nous occupe : 'Je crois, dit-il, que ce ne fut pas avant 1750 que le *claret* de première tête (*the first growth claret*), convenablement préparé et suffisamment agé, vint en Angleterre, de Boulogne, aux Stewarts, d'York Buildings, et aux Allans, de Mark Lane. Il avait été arrangé à Boulogne par la maison dont mes parents John et James Ballantyne avaient eu la direction principale pendant plus de cinquante ans ; mais, dans ces dernières années, les Forsters, les Johnstons, et deux ou trois autres maisons de Bordeaux, sont en état de charger des *clarets* en aussi bonne condition que celui qui avait été autrefois expédié de Boulogne.'

Veuillez agréer, &c.

FRANCISQUE MICHEL.

BORDEAUX : *Février* 28*me*, 1863.

The following extract from the letter of another learned antiquarian is very curious:—

I am unable to give you any further information either as to the kind of wine used in the Hebrides, or as to the way in which it reached the islands.

The wine generally consumed in Scotland before 1688 was French wine, and was imported directly from France, but we have little information as to the kinds. I find Beaune in use about 1450, and Gascony about 1500. Rhenish is not named at that period; and Spanish occurs in the seventeenth century, under the general name of Spanish wine. The wines imported in 1612, are thus described and classed in the Scotch custom-house tariff:

'Gascoigne and Frenche wynes, and all other wynes of the Frenche kings dominions.

'Muscadels, malmaseis, and all other wynes of the growths of the Levant seas.

'Sacks, canaries, malagas, romneyis, hullokis, bastardes, teynts, and allacants.'

All these were subject to one rate of 32*l.* 8*s.* Scots, per Scots tun. The tun is equal to 219 imperial gallons, and 32*l.* 8*s.* is 3*l.* 4*s.* 2*d.* sterling, so that the duty was then (1612) equal to 3¼*d.* per present gallon.

The French antiquaries, such as M. Francisque Michel, are better able to answer your inquiries about the claret of old times than anyone in this country. M. Viollet le Duc describes it as the wine of the south of France, mixed with honey. The name does not seem very old in Scotland. I have observed it in 1589.

In Scotland it was so abundant, that when ships from Bordeaux or Rochelle arrived in Leith, casks were placed on wheelbarrows and the claret sold off in the streets in stoups. Very little seems to have been bottled, being mostly sold in stoups, which are constantly referred to in descriptions of the manners of the Scotch. I recollect an old wine firm in Edinburgh in 1825 issuing a circular that 'they intended selling French wines by the stoup, as was formerly the custom.' The attempt was unsuccessful, as might have been expected by wine-merchants who know how unfit our present claret is for such rough usage.

But the letter of Mr. Ballantyne, to which I have already alluded as possessing the peculiar merit of being written by an experienced wine-merchant, gives information about the trade in claret which will probably astonish others as much as myself. He writes:—

> I believe it was not before the year 1750 that the first-growth claret, properly prepared, and of proper age, came to England from Boulogne, to Mr. Stewart of York Buildings, and Mr. Allan of Mark Lane. It was managed by the house of which my relatives, John and James Ballantyne, had the chief charge for more than fifty years; but of late the Forsters, the Johnstons, and two or more houses at Bordeaux, can ship it in the same excellent condition as formerly from Boulogne.

Although I have made remarks in another place on the management of claret in wood and in bottle, I copy here instructions which have been transmitted by a friend in Bordeaux. These apply equally to burgundy, &c.

The quality of the wine must not be judged on its arrival, because it is affected by the voyage.

If the hogshead is cased, uncase it.

Place the cask in the cellar, so that the bung is on its side and covered by the wine, to prevent the air from penetrating.

Avoid frequent tasting.

After a rest of about a month, draw off the wine into bottles—the latter must be quite clean.

Take great care that the cask is not moved, or the wine will become cloudy, and there will be a deposit in the bottles.

The corks must be new, and of good quality, and firmly driven in.

By attending to the above precautions the wine will never become acid.

Use only the best sealing-wax; the common kind has always an unpleasant smell, which is often communicated to the cork and to the wine.

When the drawing-off is nearly completed, raise the cask very gently, so that what still remains may be rendered as little thick as possible.

Lay aside the last drawn bottles, which are inferior, and from which the quality must not be judged.

The bottles should be laid on their sides in a dry cellar.

Great attention should be paid not to put the wine into bottle until it is in good condition, and the weather is fine and clear.

Although the wine can be drunk immediately after it is bottled, it is only after several months that its quality can be appreciated; more especially the high growths, in which the flavour and bouquet are only gradually developed during several years.

It often happens that a house which has received our wines in cask one year, write for exactly the same the next.

If the wine first sent remains in the cask, there will be

no difference between the first and the second. If, on the contrary, the first has been put into bottle, it will be better; Bordeaux wines improving much more in bottle than in cask.

These precautions are necessary in order to drink the wines of Bordeaux with pleasure. Old bottled wines will inevitably form a little deposit, and, if this is mixed with the wine, it detracts considerably from the taste and delicacy of the bouquet. It is therefore indispensable, before tasting the wine, to let it rest for about a month; then, when it is required, uncork without shaking or moving it, and, almost without changing its position, decant it slowly into another bottle, leaving the deposit at the bottom of the first.

This operation, which only occupies a few minutes, is generally practised in Bordeaux, and wherever fine wines are appreciated.

While the rates of duty were 1/, 1/9, 2/5, and 2/11, only those kinds under 18 degrees of strength being 1/ per gallon, there were constant difficulties, with clarets especially; which may be well supposed, on referring to the following note of the testing of strengths made at our Custom-House.

There are good grounds for believing that all the samples were pure, and without any addition of spirit to that evolved by the fermentation.

It is seen from the Custom-House testing how wines vary according to the season—affording another proof of the fallacy of the 'scientific' statements in books upon wine, that such a one contains so many degrees, and another kind so many more or less. When this is the case with that which is pure, how utterly impossible it must be to ascertain the actual amount of spirit from the saccharine matter in the grape, when testing those that have had spirit added.

Very often, wine may be found exactly as it was fermented in the cellars of growers, but rarely in those of merchants, who almost invariably blend different kinds together, adding often a little spirit.

As 1858 was a remarkably fine vintage, few would have expected 1859 to be fuller in spirit. Comparing 1859 with the very bad 1860, there are seen to be 29 degrees more proof spirit in these eleven samples in the former than in the latter year.

To prove still more strikingly the fallacy of the idea, that full-bodied strong wines are therefore more expensive than the lighter kinds, I may state that some growths of the Roussillon, which furnishes as cheap wine as any district in the south of France, contain even 27 per cent. of proof spirit, when tested by Sykes's hydrometer, used by our revenue officers.

TESTED IN THE CUSTOM-HOUSE LABORATORY, 1861.

Description of Wine	1858	1859	1860
	Per cent. of Proof Spirit	Per cent. of Proof Spirit	Per cent. of Proof Spirit
Château Lafitte	16·5	17·7	14·8
Langoa	17·7	17·7	16·0
Palmer	17·1	17·7	16·0
St. Estèphe, supérieur	17·7	18·3	13·7
Médoc-paysan	17·7	18·3	14·8
Grâves	17·7	18·3	14·2
St Emilion, supérieur	18·9	18·9	16·0
St. Emilion, bourgeois	16·5	15·4	16·0
Blaye, bourgeois	18·3	17·1	14·8
Blaye-paysan	17·1	17·1	14·8
Latour, blanche	23·9	26·5	20·8

It is seen by the following table that the consumption and the per-centage which French wine bore to all other kinds, was:—

In 1831	Consumption	254,366 gallons,	and	4·09	per centage
1841	"	353,470	"	5·72	"
1851	"	447,566	"	7·12	"
1859	"	695,913	"	9·60	"
1860	"	1,125,599	"	15·30	"
1861	"	2,227,662	"	20·65	"
1862	"	1,900,344	"	19·38	"

It must, however, not be assumed from this statement, that French wines, such as claret, champagne, burgundy, &c. have been increasing, as would be inferred from these figures. There are no means of ascertaining the respective proportions, but if this were practicable, I have no doubt it would be found that a large part consisted of wines from the south, some of them as strong as natural port and sherry, and many made as strong by similar additions of spirit. These are imported, not to be used as 'French wine,' but as a substitute for port, &c. or for mixing with and cheapening it and other kinds, mostly red.

I have already mentioned that Professor Francisque-Michel, of Bordeaux, had convinced me that I was incorrect in affirming that the Médoc was little else than a barren waste two hundred years ago.

My opinion was not expressed on hasty grounds, and I cannot take much blame to myself for this and other statements, as not one of them has been made without reference to every book I could hear of on the subject, as well as to all authorities likely to give information.

But having now become personally acquainted with the Professor, who has shown me the MS. of a work upon the Trade and Navigation of Bordeaux, since the time of the Romans, I see that there is nothing existing that is for a moment to be compared to his work, in respect to the valuable information it contains on these heads. It has occupied him many years, during which period he has searched the archives of Bordeaux, Bayonne, Paris, the British Museum, the Record Office, as well as the municipal documents in various towns in England and Scotland. When the result of his labours is arranged and applied as he so well knows how to do, one of the most curious and interesting historical works ever published may be expected. The motto on the titlepage of my book is—

Nullius addictus jurare in verba magistri:

but, on this subject, I bow most willingly to M. Francisque-Michel, as my *magister.*

He has kindly acceded to my request that he would enable me to insert a short history of the trade in wine between France and this country, from the earliest period that can be relied upon; which I here subjoin:—

London, June 30, 1863.

MY DEAR SIR,

The extremely flattering reception which the English press has accorded to my works has induced you to ask me to throw some light upon the commerce and consumption of French wines in Great Britain and Ireland, prior to the middle of last century; a task from which a much better qualified writer than myself might well recoil. In France, as with you, the history of commerce, although so interesting, is not yet popular; scarcely delivered from the Greeks and Romans, we have fallen again still more completely under their yoke. But, now, imitating a prince whom the laurels of Cæsar hinder from sleeping, all the academicians, even provincials, are at the feet of the conqueror of Gaul. Fashion everywhere is on the search for monuments of antiquity, though at the risk of presenting pickle-jars in the place of Roman urns.

Amongst the numerous investigations to which the district of Bordeaux has been subjected at different times, it does not appear that they have ever dug up 'amphoræ;' nevertheless, the existence of the vine in Aquitania is undeniable, Ausonius having positively mentioned it. With regard to the exportation of the wines of Gascony and Guienne into Britain, this must have commenced after the marriage of Henry II. with Eleanor. Not but that the Saxons drank wine; but it was an expensive article, and was in a great measure restricted to persons above the common rank. According to Alfric's colloquy, quoted by Mr. Thomas Wright in his 'History of Domestic Manners and Sentiments in England during the Middle Ages,' the merchants brought from foreign countries wine and oil; and when the scholar is asked why he does not drink wine, he says he is not rich enough to buy it, 'and wine is not the drink of children or fools, but of elders and wise men.' There were, however, vineyards in England in the times of the Saxons, and wine was made from them; but they were probably rare, and chiefly attached to the monastic establishments. William of Malmesbury speaks of a vineyard attached to his monastery, which was first planted at the beginning of the eleventh century by a Greek monk who settled there, and who spent all his time in cultivating it.

At all events, the wine of the south (ȝebꞃohꞇ ƿin ꞅuðan), on which the Saxons, according to the Saxon Chronicle, caroused in 1012, could not have come from Spain. The

Peninsula was then under the rule of the Moors, who were opposed by their religion to the cultivation of the vine; and as wine was necessary, if only for the celebration of the mass, this article was exported to Valencia, to Cordova, and Seville, by the merchants of Bordeaux and Bayonne; and this was still done in the time of Matthew Paris, who mentions the fact in the year 1252.

At this period the wines of Guienne, besides the markets which Spain and Flanders offered, found a still larger one in England. The same policy which for a long time closed the ports of that country against our French wines, then opened them to those of a province which was under English rule; and Normandy, which was under the same sceptre, slaked her thirst at the same source, whilst her grain crops went to feed Guienne. The continuer of the Chronicle of Sigebert makes mention of a great storm which, in the year 1177, scattered the regular fleet laden with the wines of Poictou for Normandy; the great roll of the exchequer of Normandy under the English kings contains an entry relating to a purchase of oats destined to be sent to Bordeaux for the king's use; another roll relating to the same province informs us that King John gave six tuns of Gascon wine to Henri de Ferrières, undoubtedly a descendant of the nobleman of the same name on the land of whom, at Bistesham in Berkshire, 'xii. arpendi vineæ' are entered in the 'Domesday Book.'

From what precedes, it must not be inferred that the vine was unknown in Normandy at that time. It appears from the charters so ably made use of by my learned friend, Mons. Léopold Delisle, that most abbeys had vineyards. Without doubt, as Dr. Lappenberg remarks, this branch of husbandry was in use there before the settlement of the Northmen, and might have afforded the Vikings an additional motive for choosing that province. But as almost everything was given to the Church, it is probable that wine fell to the share of the monks, and that the people retained only beer and cider. Wace, in his Chronicle of the Dukes of Normandy, relates that the

French gave the Normans the nicknames of *bigots* and *beer-drinkers*.

Philip Augustus struck a fatal blow against the commerce of Bordeaux, by prohibiting the transport of the wines of Poictou, Gascony, and Anjou, by sea to Rouen; but, for the advantage of Paris and the central provinces, he allowed the transport by the same route of the wines of Berri, Burgundy, and of France, properly so called; which at Rouen came into the hands of the burgesses, and from thence often passed into England, where it is not uncommon to meet with them under the generic name of French wines.

Chrestien de Troyes, a trouvère, who is generally supposed to have written during the reign of Henry II., makes his heroes in England to be served with the 'good wines of Auxerre, Soissons, Poictou, and Rochelle.' A contemporary writer, William Fitzstephen, informs us that the Thames at London was fringed with vessels laden with wine, and with cellars. If Henri d'Andeli, another trouvère, later it is true, may be believed, Rochelle wine was the only wine consumed in Great Britain and Ireland; that is to say, under the name of Vins de Rochelle were then comprised those of Poictou and Saintonge; which were still drunk at the end of the fourteenth century in Flanders, Brabant, Hainault, in the country about Liége, and even in Picardy. We have elsewhere a statute of King John which fixes the prices of wine in his kingdom, by which we learn the kinds drunk towards the end of the twelfth century; but if there exist ancient traces of the wine trade which the capital of Aunis formerly carried on with England through the inhabitants of Bordeaux, one meets quite as often with documents dating from the commencement of the thirteenth century, in which express mention is made of the wines of Gascony in that country, of Gascon merchants who went thither to sell them; and of those of Bordeaux, who doubtless sold the produce of their own soil.

At the same period King John ordered his chamberlains to pay Bernard of Bordeaux twenty-six livres sterling for thirty-six tuns of wine, and afterwards to Gerold of the same town 325 marks for 50 tuns of wine purchased for His Majesty. The same monarch charges the customs and dues payable on all wine quitting Bordeaux, La Réole, or any other place in Gascony, with the payment of the wines bought in England from the merchants named in the deed, though we still find him debtor to the commune of Bordeaux in a considerable sum for the purchase of the same commodity; and that when a certain Raymond d'Ujac, a burgess of that town, was appointed to demand this debt from that king's successor, he would not consent to pay it, except on the condition that it should be reduced from 1,080 marks to 600.

The connection of Henry III. with the commerce of Bordeaux was not confined to these transactions; in 1214 he directed the Archbishop, his seneschal in Guienne, to see justice done to a petition from his subjects in Bordeaux and La Rochelle, backed by a recommendation from the prelate, and presented by Arnauld de Reisac, a burgess of that town, who sued for payment for 20 tuns of wine taken by King John for the provisioning of Dover Castle. His son Henry III. ordered payment to be made out of the revenues of the seneschalty at the rate of 2½ marks per tun.

One may judge of the flourishing state of the trade of Bordeaux with England by the large quantity of wine which one finds in that country at that time, and by the purchases made by this prince from the merchants of that town. In 1224, he directed the Bishop of London to choose, by means of honest and loyal men of that city, 100 tuns of the cargo of Gerard Colum and Co., which had been stayed there, paying for it 40 sous the tun, if it could not be got for less. The same year he ordered his bailiffs at Bristol to pay Arnaud Guilhem, for 30 tuns of wine which they had taken for his consumption; and other officers to deliver 26 livres 5 sous to Guillaume Arthur and Arnaud of Bordeaux for 15 tuns of wine, at the rate of 35 sous per tun, the price paid to Etienne of Bordeaux, and Guilhem Colum, who had sold to the same prince, the one 38 tuns of wine for 56 livres 15 sous, and the other 25 tuns for 43 livres 15 sous; whilst Semirette and Galhart of Bordeaux obtained for their wines only 33 sous, and Raymond de Grave and Le Loué, of the same town, 2½ marks; half a mark more than King John paid for the wines of Auxerre.

Besides the wines which Henry III. bought of the merchants of Bordeaux, he also furnished himself from the great proprietors of vineyards, and even traded for the same purpose with the Archbishop. In 1242, he acknowledged himself debtor in the sum of 1,110 marks 11 sous 4 deniers sterling, the price of 100 tuns of wine sold to him by the agents of the prelate; and caused all his purchases to be shipped.

The king himself dealt largely in wine. In 1243, being at Bordeaux, he commanded all his bailiffs and sheriffs not to suffer that within the boundaries of their jurisdictions any wine should be sold before his, which Master Wyberd of Kent had carried into England. In the same year he ordered payment to be made to two notable burgesses of Bordeaux, Pierre and Arnaud Caillau, of 270 livres sterling for 300 tuns of wine bought on his account.

A roll of ten years later informs us that the first of these traders purchased through Matthieu Mercer, his merchant, that is to say, his agent, 30 tuns of Bergerac wine; but one must investigate further in order to throw light on the manner in which commerce was transacted in this troubled age.

The merchants accompanied their wines into England, but they also took with them other wines, of which they undertook to manage the sale for the benefit of the owners; which often led them into difficulties when these last happened to be at war with their sovereign. Suspected of covering with his name the wines belonging to some rebel, a Bordeaux merchant had 66 tuns seized, which were detained at Portsmouth until he swore that they were actually his own property, and that no person at war with the king of England had the least interest in them.

War was then, so to say, chronic; the ships that carried the wines to the British Isles did not sail singly, as they do now. If the land routes were insecure, the sea was still more so; and in the same manner as people never thought of crossing the desert except in company with a caravan, so it was only a fleet that dared face the perils of the passage. Froissart leaves no doubt of the manner in which the trade of Bordeaux with Great Britain was carried on in his time, when he tells us that 'Two hundred sail of merchant ships from England, Wales, and Scotland, arrived in this port, which came for wine.'

Usually, the ships which formed the convoy had to manage their own defence. John de Tutbury, who was bailiff of Hull in 1395, embarked at Bordeaux 260 tuns of wine and other merchandise on board his ship, called the Christopher of Hull; and having joined the English fleet, which was then on the point of setting sail, this vessel was chosen to be one of the admirals during the voyage, 'for the salvation and safeguard of all the said fleet.' The principal merchants, shipmasters and seamen, took oath before the Constable of Bordeaux, 'according to the ancient custom always used there,' that none would separate themselves from their admirals until their arrival in England. During the passage, some carricks, most probably Spanish, met the fleet in question, and, amongst other vessels, attacked the Christopher, which made a gallant resistance; but, being abandoned by the rest, who took to flight in spite of their oath, was captured by the enemy, who plundered the cargo.

On their arrival in England, John de Tutbury, Robert Sharp, and several other merchants and seamen of Hull, who, doubtless, had some share in the Christopher or her cargo, petitioned Parliament to declare the fugitives responsible for their loss, each according to the quantity and value of his freight. Their petition was fully granted, and it was directed that those who had formed part of the said fleet should be summoned before the Chancellor, to have their shares determined; and that this great officer of the Crown should be authorised to compel the defendants to indemnify John of Tutbury and his partners, with power to put them in prison, 'by the advice of three or four of the king's justices.' This custom of going to fetch the wines of Bordeaux *en caravane* was kept up until quite modern times.

As yet I have not told you what sort of wine Bordeaux sent to the foreign markets, particularly to that of Great Britain; yet it is not without interest to mark the changes and transformations of taste, and to learn the fortune of the productions destined to satisfy them. At present, at least in France, we prefer delicate, perfumed, and mellow wines; our ancestors, whose stomachs were more robust than ours, preferred those which they found 'strong, sharp, and full flavoured'—that is to say, coarse wines, like those grown chiefly in the centre of France, in the country of 'fabliaux,' the strong and heady wines of the south of Spain, and those of Galicia; which country was formerly so much frequented by the pilgrims of all Christendom.

The strong and foaming wine of Champagne was found so injurious that Henry V. was obliged, after the battle of Agincourt, to forbid its use in his army, except when tempered with water. They liked, above all, the liqueur wines; and it was on this account that they found the Greek wines so agreeable. The English then kept to the wines of Bergerac, which now are drunk almost exclusively in Holland, and to the wines of Gaillac, Rabastens, and other parts of the south-west of France. Froissart speaks of the good wines and muscadines which the Prince of Wales's army drank in 1356 on the banks of the Aude. Later, they began to like the Spanish and Portuguese wines, more especially after Bordeaux came under the rule of the king of France. In the Spanish correspondence for 1561, the English ambassador, alluding to the hot wines of Andalusia, says that his countrymen were the chief consumers, to the extent of 500,000 ducats per annum in them and fruits. Perhaps it is not superfluous to add that, in the same correspondence, mention is made of some English ships taken near the Azores, which were greatly suspected of piracy, on account of some casks of wine found on board them, and which were 'hooped with iron,' as was customary with wine-casks on board ships bound to the Indies.

As for Rhenish wines, we know, by the records of the City of London, that the merchants of Lorraine brought their wines for sale in England at a very early period. Mr. Riley has drawn from these venerable relics of the past the following information, the value of which cannot be questioned:—No wine-taverner was to mix unsound wine with good, or old with new, under certain penalties; and (greatly the converse of the present day) new wines appear to have been much preferred to old: it being enacted that, after the arrival of new wine at a tavern, none of it should be sold before the old was disposed of. Let us add that, in 1226, Henry III. caused a distribution to be made to the poor of old and spoiled wines, which fact conveys a curious idea of the English butlers of the time; and he ordered the keepers of his wines at Bristol to sell the old, and to buy new with the price of the former.

Taverners who sold 'sweet' wines were forbidden to deal in the other kinds, and the number of their taverns was limited. It was illegal also for the dealer in the non-sweet classes of wine to keep white wine of Gascony, Rochelle wine, or Spanish, in the same cellar as Rhenish; the object of this enactment being probably to prevent the former kinds being fraudulently substituted for Rhenish. The few sweet wines named in the 'Liber

Albus' so ably edited by Mr. Riley, are malvesie, the modern malmsey, a Greek wine, sold in the reign of Richard II., at 16*d.* per gallon; vernage, which may be either vernaccia, a red Tuscan wine, or what we call now grenache, sold at 2/; Crete, sold at 1/; and wine of Provence, sold at the same price; under which last name probably Roussillon, or a kindred wine, is meant. In addition to which, in another book of the City records are named these following wines:—Candie (a variety perhaps of Crete); Trubidiane (probably wine of Trebbio); Mountross (perhaps Rosas, a Catalonian wine); Greek and clairé (probably a French wine, sweetened and boiled, as suggested by Mr. Riley, whose opinion will be discussed at length elsewhere). All these wines were sold, 47 Edward III., at 12*d.* per gallon, with a Portuguese wine 'de la Rebasele;' what sort of wine this is I do not know.

Another, called 'ryvere'(probably a Navarrese wine from a district called *la Ribera,* unless it be the wine of the 'rivière d'Aude,' as mentioned by Froissart), was sold at 16*d.*; at which price, in this reign, Romaney was also sold, which came not from Romanée-Conti in Burgundy, but from Romagne in Italy; being consequently a variety of malvesie, and held, as it appears, in such estimation that it was fraudulently imitated in the time of Henry V. Other kinds named under Richard II., and not belonging to the class of sweet wines, as Rhenish, sold at 8*d.* per gallon, and red at 6*d.*, by which, perhaps, an inferior claret is meant. Besides there was another inferior wine sold at an earlier period at 3*d.* per gallon (a little more than twice the price of ale). As Mr. Riley remarks, these wines were consumed wholly in draught: at all events, no allusion to wine in bottles or flasks is to be met with in the records of the City of London; and I believe that glass bottles were manufactured in England at a late period, wicker bottles being still imported from France in 1630, as we learn from a petition of a certain William Deane, a French merchant, to King Charles I.

No wine was permitted to be sold till it had been subjected to a scrutiny, and had been duly gauged; in the reign, too, of Edward III., four vintners were chosen to assess the prices of wines. The forestalling of wines in the Pool of the Thames, or elsewhere, was strictly prohibited. King's prisage, or customs, was taken according to a fixed scale, on all imported wines.

The business of the wine-drawers seems to have been limited to the loading, carriage, and unloading of tuns and pipes of wine from the quay cellars to other parts of the City. Their charges were restricted by enactment to certain prices, according to the distance; tenpence being the largest sum allowed for the carriage of a tun of wine to any part within the walls, and eightpence for a pipe.

We will now return to the French wines; the only ones whose history I intend to trace in the British Isles.

At present we know them under their true names, but it was not so in the middle ages; they had not then thought of distinguishing the growths, nor of establishing those lists which have since multiplied to infinity. Henry III. having borrowed a tun of Gascon wine from a merchant, Michel d'Ambly, and wishing to discharge his debt, directed the keepers of his wines at Southampton to deliver to his creditor a tun of Gascon wine, without specifying the locality of its production.

At present, if we want to know with what kinds of Bordeaux wines the vessels that came to Great Britain and Ireland were freighted, we shall find all the desired information in a Register of the Customs preserved in the Record Office in London, which goes back to the year 1305, at which period the writer, Master Jordan Moraunt, was Constable of the Castle of Bordeaux, and in this office collected the customs on the wines there embarked. It commences on the 11th of September, with the entry of the Plantea of Sandwich, of thirty-eight tons burden, freighted by the burgesses; and therefore there is nothing entered for the 'grande coutume'—'*summa magne custume nihil*;' an entry which appears after a great number of other vessels specified in the same way, and belonging to the ports of Teignmouth, Southampton, Wareham, Chester, Bristol, Sidmouth, Exmouth, Winchelsea, Plymouth, &c. On the 4th of October, the wines of the burgesses of Bordeaux being exhausted, they began to lade with those that had been made outside the district. As mentioned above, the vessels that were freighted with them belonged to different ports, mostly English.

As for the wines, they came from Bazas, Ste.-Bazeille, Marmande, Port Ste.-Marie, Clérac, Mas d'Agenais, Castelmoron, Agen, Villeneuve, Ste.-Pierre, Pène, Montauban, Moissac, Castel-Sarrazin, St.-Livrade, Castel-Sacrat, Rabastens, Haut-Villars, Gaillac, Condom, Layrac, Mirabel, Villedieu, Cordes, Bayonne, Cahors, Gontaut, and a number of other places, whose names would only uselessly swell this list. After having taken in a certain number of tuns and pipes at Bordeaux, the vessels filled up their cargo at Bec-d'Ambès, Macau, Castillon, Margaux, and other places in Médoc; which pretty well shows that this 'sauvage et inculte pays' was not quite such a wretched place as some people try to make out, and that its cultivation of the vine does not date from yesterday. A ship of Dartmouth is entered as not having paid the duty for forty-four tuns, laden beyond the little river Jalle; and another of Lynn as only having discharged the dues called *de Royan* for a part of its cargo. There are also many similar entries, many of them relating to Blaye.

The ships which descended the Gironde and put into these different ports, did not all come from Bordeaux: a number of them ascended at once to Libourne, a town founded by the English, as its name (Leyburn) implies; and after having taken in the wine of Périgord, they filled up with those of Bourg and Blaye, which appear anciently to have been much esteemed. If one can believe a tradition which has been handed down in the département of the Gironde, they were still of so much account a century later, that individuals who possessed land in the Bourgez and Médoc would nòt sell their wines of Bourg, except under the condition that at the same time the purchaser should take those of Médoc. If one could show a similar custom in the fourteenth century, it would explain the stoppages of the foreign ships in filling up their cargoes in this district, which was then less flourishing than its neighbours.

In 1290, Edward I. seeing the great increase of Libourne and its trade, wrote to the Constable of Bordeaux, Itier d'Angoulême, and ordered him to consult with Master Osbert de Daggeston, for the purpose of appointing, without delay, a provost to reside in the new town. The secret but precise instructions of this officer directed him to make an entry of the names of all the ships which were laden in the Dordogne, with those of their masters or captains. He was directed, besides, to make a note of their destination, of the port to which they belonged, and of the nature of their cargoes, and to forward this information twice a year to the Constable of Bordeaux, who had orders to transmit them under seal to England at Easter and Michaelmas, the appointed times of sitting for the Court of Exchequer. We do not possess the first registers which were made in accordance with this order; but that which remains of the first year of Edward II. is sufficient to enable us to judge of the commercial progress of the ports of Bourg and Libourne at the commencement of the fourteenth century. In this register we find quite as many ships as in that which we have just considered, and, moreover, a greater variety. Of the whole number the greatest proportion belonged to England, and the next to Brittany and Normandy.

The majority took in their cargo equally at Bourg, Libourne, Blaye, and Macau in Médoc; but there are other places mentioned in this register as being visited for this purpose by the foreign seamen; amongst others,

Talmont-sur-Gironde, Royan, Margaux, and Castillon. How, then, after this (I repeat) can we believe in all that has been cast upon this 'sauvage et inculte pays de Médoc?'

I will not detain you by speaking about the dues which were levied at Bordeaux on the wine exported to the British Islands, but will content myself with a few words on the exactions to which they were subjected in England, simply referring you to the curious chapter which Madox has devoted to this subject in his 'History and Antiquities of the Exchequer of the Kings of England,' vol. i. p. 764–786. Besides the dues called 'prisa' and 'recta prisa,' the wine which entered the port of Sandwich was obliged to pay to the Priory of the Trinity at Canterbury, better known under the name of Christ Church, a duty of 2*d.* per ship, which was certainly not very oppressive on the commerce of our country; but it had also to submit to a number of other fiscal exactions, except when exempted by a special mandate from the king.

Henry III. abolished all the exactions and arbitrary tolls to which the trade of Bordeaux had been subjected in England and Ireland; in which latter country an ancient grant to the ancestors of the Earls of Ormond had put that family in possession of all the tolls on wine levied in that island, especially at Waterford. The wine merchants of the corporation were only to be subjected to the ancient toll, consisting of two tuns per ship, one from before the mast and the other from behind the mast. It was, moreover, specified that they should pay it according to the custom of the different ports. For this purpose the king appointed at each two sworn appraisers, who were charged with the valuation and levying of the duty on the wines both in the interest of the merchant and that of the crown. It was also forbidden that any bailiff or other officer should seize wine for the king, except by virtue of letters patent, containing the specific number of tuns. As regards payment, the wines taken at vintage-time had a claim on the Exchequer on the following Easter, and those taken afterwards were paid for by the Exchequer at the Michaelmas following. Except under these two conditions, no wine was allowed to be taken, unless paid for at the time. The king added, that wishing particularly to favour the inhabitants of Bordeaux, he willed and granted that, immediately on the arrival of a ship laden with wine, the property of one or more of the burgesses of Bordeaux, the bailiff who had charge of the tolls should be bound to receive the two tuns in question within five days.

More than a quarter of a century after he had been on the throne, Edward III. made a decree, which took its place amongst the statutes of the realm. A proclamation was issued that no English merchant, under the most severe penalties, should ingross or forestall wine in Gascony, nor take them by way of bargain, from any Gascon or other man, by paying dearer in England than they were sold in their own country, on the plea of preparation, peril of the seas, or any other reason whatsoever. All Gascon, or foreign merchants, might bring their wines without hindrance into England to any port they chose, and there make their profit of them, on the condition that the royal butler should be able to make provision for his master whenever he had need, by paying at forty days from date, according to custom. No English merchant, his servants, or agents, was allowed to reside in Gascony for the purpose of trafficking in or buying wine, under any pretence whatever, before the time of the vintage or that of 'reik:' that is to say, before the regular time for going to Guienne for the purpose of bringing the wines over; and it was not permitted that any should traffic in wine except at Bordeaux or Bayonne. Those that offended were to be arrested by the Seneschal of Gascony, or the Constable of Bordeaux, and sent to the Tower of London.

These regulations caused so many complaints, that it was not possible to enforce them. Ten years later,

Edward III. made a decree by which he allowed any merchant who possessed the freedom of the city, not being a mechanic, to pass into Gascony for the purpose of bringing over wine, in order that there might be a sufficiency in the realm; and Gascons and other foreigners might come and trade there freely without let or hindrance, the king's dues only excepted.

This measure caused complaints which were heard in Parliament. The English merchants who crossed into Gascony to buy wines, exported gold in large quantities, and the Gascons, seeing their haste to return home from a foreign land, where they could not continue for any length of time without great expense, raised the price of their wine during their abode, so that if they took it themselves into England it would be very much cheaper. It, therefore, seemed good to the Commons to rescind for a time the licence given to the English for going to bring over wine, in order to see if that would influence the prices. They demanded, besides, that no special warrant, that is to say, no exemption, should be granted to Englishmen, and that on their arrival in England the wines should be landed and gauged, without reservation, for the benefit of the kingdom.

By this regulation it was enacted that no Englishman should pass into Gascony to bring thence wines, but that they should be brought into England by Gascons or other foreigners. Moreover, it was to be prohibited for any Englishman to remit or send over any gold, silver, or merchandise, to any Gascon or other foreigner, for the purchase of wine, as they had been accustomed, under pain of forfeiting the gold, silver, or merchandise thus sent. They also required that all English or Gascon vessels going into the latter country should be first freighted with wine for England before all others, and that no Englishman should trade in or buy such wines before they had been landed, in accordance with the regulations prescribed by the statute, &c.

These regulations were included in those of 1368, and it was not long before complaints were again raised. Although the law by which foreigners only were allowed to import wine into England seemed beneficial to the whole kingdom, still, since the Prince of Wales, who was at that time Duke of Aquitaine, complained that his revenues were decreased by the absence of the English purchasers, and that large quantities of wine remained unsold, to the great loss of the Gascons, who, for the most part, subsisted on that commerce; it was decreed that any native of England, Ireland, or Wales, not being a mechanic, might go into Gascony to purchase wine, giving security to the magistrates of the port from whence he sailed that he would buy at least 100 tuns, and would not take them into any foreign country, under pain of the confiscation of his ship and cargo, and imprisonment.

At the same time, the statute of 1353 was not repealed, but was in full force, at least, in 1371. In that year, the wine merchants of Gascony, acknowledging the good reception that they met with in England, and the privileges they found there for their trade, granted to the king a duty of two sous sterling per tun, under the name of 'custume.'

In 1381, the dearness of wine having attracted the attention of the authorities, the king issued a decree on the sale of that article, by which it was prohibited to retail in any part of the kingdom any sort of sweet wine or claret, under pain of confiscation. As for other wines, such as Gascon, Rochelle, Rhenish, d'Oseye, and Spanish, if any Englishman should cross the sea to procure and bring them into any part of the kingdom, he was not to sell them dearer than at the following prices, under pain of forfeiture:—The best Gascon, Oseye, and Spanish wines, 100 sous per tun; and the inferior qualities 7, 6½, and 6 marks per tun; the best Rochelle wine, 6 marks and under, according to value; as, for example, 5½, 5, 4½, and 4 marks. Pipes and other measures of less capacity were to be sold according to the size of the cask and the quality of the wine. As for the retail sale of Gascon, Oseye, and Spanish wines, the best class was not to be sold within the kingdom for more than 6*d.*, and on the spot (e dedeins), according to quality, under pain of confiscation of the whole stock; the price of Rochelle wine was not to exceed four deniers. With respect to Rhenish, as the vessels in which it was kept had no fixed measurement, it was decreed that a gallon of the best sort should not be sold, either wholesale or retail, at more than 6*d.* in any part of the kingdom, under the same penalty. These were the same prices as those fixed by the regulations of the 26th of November, 1342.

However, the prohibition on the sale of sweet wine, except by retail, until the feast of St. John, in the year 1382, and after that period, except wholesale, gave rise to complaints, which were carried to Parliament, where the king, in order to give satisfaction, ordered that these sorts of wine should be placed in the same category as the rest.

In the following year, the legislation on wines was still more modified; the recent decrees respecting this commodity were repealed, and the statute of the 31 Edward III. put in force.

In 1420, the Commons petitioned that no Malvoisie, Romagne, or any other sort of sweet wine, should be sold by retail, under the penalty of 100 sous fine to the king for each offence, besides the forfeiture of the price of the wine. They also asked that no Gascon wine should be sold for less than 6*d.* per gallon, under pain of a fine of 6*l.*, and a like forfeiture for each offence; whilst, for Rhenish and Rochelle wine, the tariff should be at least 4*d.* per gallon, under the same penalties, &c. The Parliament replied, 'Soit-il comme est désiré par la pétition, s'il plest au roy.'

Henry IV. also busied himself with regulating the retail trade. The jubilee which took place in 1420 at Canterbury, and which attracted to the shrine of St. Thomas à

Becket about 100,000 pilgrims from every part of Great Britain and Ireland, and even from the Continent, appears to have had a beneficial effect upon the commerce of Bordeaux. At least, a document of the period states that Gascon wine was so plentiful in the metropolis that a bottle of red wine was sold for 3*d.*, and a bottle of white wine for 6*d.*

That war, which lasted 100 years, and which was then raging, doubtless made communication with La Rochelle and Bordeaux difficult and dangerous; but it did not, however, prevent the consumption of wine by our neighbours from being greater than one would imagine. In 1410, a truce having been concluded between the two belligerents, it was stipulated that the English merchants might go to the first of these two towns, either by land or sea, to lade with wines, and return into their own country, with reciprocity to the inhabitants of La Rochelle who chose to go and sell their wines in England; and a proclamation notified this arrangement in all the ports situated to the west of that district.

A complaint, not very creditable to the wine trade of Bordeaux, was made some years later to Parliament. The petitioners declared that formerly the wines of Gascony and Guienne were well and conscientiously made, as they ought to be; they were of a good colour and quality, pleasant to the taste, kept well for four or five seasons, and had only four or five inches of dregs in the tun, and two or three in the pipe; but that now, in consequence of their dishonest manufacture, that is to say, in consequence of a deficiency of eight or nine inches in the casks in which they were placed on coming out of the press, the said wines were unable to have their natural fermentation, and throw off their scum, as they ought. From whence, not only did great inconvenience and annoyance result to owners of great houses, who thought that they were sufficiently provided with this article of consumption, but also serious damage and loss to other buyers and sellers in the present and past times; and, to all appearance, it would be so for the future, unless a prompt remedy should be found for this state of things.

In order to effect this, the petitioners besought the king to direct the Seneschal of Guienne, by letters under the privy seal, addressed to all the towns and boroughs of that province, and especially to the mayor and council of the town of Bordeaux, to order that in every place in the wine-growing districts experienced men should be appointed to investigate, or cause to be investigated, the abuses recently introduced, and to introduce again the honest system anciently used; and that it should not be lawful to bring any cask of wine from the place where it was grown to any market for the purpose of selling it for exportation, unless it had been first tested, and marked as good and genuine, with a known seal and trade mark, accompanied with the stamp of the persons commissioned to inspect and test the said casks, under pain of the confiscation of the wine exposed for sale against the said regulations. If, in any of the said towns or boroughs, the wine was found to be adulterated or spoilt, the head of the cask was to be started, and the wine publicly poured out, according to the custom of the City of London. The petitioners also desired that it should be forbidden to sell, or load with, in Gascony or Guienne, for England, any wine except that which came up to the standard, and at such times when the said wine should have been sufficiently and properly tested in the manner and form above mentioned, so that there should not be more than four or five inches of lees in the tun, and three in the pipe; and, for the satisfaction of the buyer, the gauge of each vessel was to be certified.

During the next year, or rather longer, the wine trade between Gascony and England was interrupted; at least, the English merchants were no longer allowed to cross over to buy wine at vintage time.

In 1444, the Commons again petitioned the king in

Parliament to consider the points which they submitted to him. From time immemorial, a great part of the wine grown in the Duchy of Guienne had been usually brought to the ports of Bordeaux and Bayonne, both by land and by the rivers Gironde and Dordogne, at the feast of St. Martin. This was, as it still is, said the petitioners, the best and most wholesome of all the wine grown in those districts. At this period, a great quantity of this wine, and of that grown in the neighbourhood of these parts, came to England, and was there sold cheaper and in greater plenty than at present. There used to be also a great number of wealthy English merchants in that country, on account of their being able to buy and sell wine and other merchandise in every part of the duchy; as, also, great numbers of the Gascon merchants of Bordeaux, and other places in the said duchy, used to resort yearly to England at the vintage-time with their wine, because they were not able to sell it at Bordeaux or other places of the said duchy to the English merchants. So that, at that time, England owned more than half as many ships again than at present, which was a great source of pride and wealth for all classes; and, moreover, the power of such a marine was a great defence for the realm, and cause of fear for all its enemies. 'And at present,' the petitioners added, 'the said English merchants are obliged to buy their wine and sell their merchandise at Bordeaux or Bayonne, and at no other place, to the great loss of the whole country, and to the diminution of its trade and mercantile marine.' Further, they desired Parliament to decree that all classes of wine grown in the said duchy, under the sway of the king of England, should be admitted into the said ports; and that the English merchants should be allowed to buy and sell wine and every sort of merchandise freely throughout the whole of Guienne, as they had been wont to do of old, without let or hindrance, with a penalty of 1,000*l.* sterling for those who transgressed; promising for their part to pay to the king and his heirs all customs, subsidies, tolls, dues, and other rights which were customary, &c. This declaration, as well as that which terminated the petition, although it had for its object the common advantage of the realm, and a beneficial end, did not produce any effect on Henry VI. and his council; and it was answered by the formal 'Le roy s'advisera,' which was equivalent to a refusal.

Another document of the same date throws a new and curious light on the commerce between Bordeaux and England in the fifteenth century. I refer to the register of the custom-house at Hull, containing a detailed account of all the wines which arrived at that port during the month of September. It begins with the customary ejaculation, *Jesu Maria*, and after a sort of summary containing the name of the vessel, together with that of her captain, as well as the number of tuns of which her cargo was composed, mentions the names of all those owning them, with the share belonging to each. For instance, we find in the very first part of the register, that on the 15th of September, A.D. 1444, 23 Henry VI., a ship called the Saubade of Bayonne, commanded by Etienne de Jeuberry, entered inward; and that she was freighted with 136 tuns and a pipe, of which 70 tuns and a pipe belonged to Fortin de Cantelop; 42 barrels to the same; 18 tuns 12 barrels to Lorens La Boria; 3 tuns 1 pipe to Monyn Jeuven de la Layve; 3 tuns 1 pipe 8 barrels to Pey Estort; 3 tuns to Naudin de Lastage; 2 tuns to Johan Jeustay; 8 tuns to Bernard Julian; 1 pipe to Johan Buscat; and 2 tuns to Pey Bachey.

To these details I could easily add a great many others, perhaps more interesting; but I must not forget that I am writing a letter and not a book (I will write that hereafter). In the meantime, however, I must beg leave to call your attention to a circumstance well worthy of notice, which is, that this register is written in Latin and Gascon. I do not, of course, mean to deduce from this that the patois of Guienne was ever spoken at Hull; but that they registered in this dialect, at their ports of departure, the vessels that were laden with wine in Guienne, which brought to their ports of destination bills of lading made out for this purpose, and which the officers of the English customs were bound to reproduce.

We have now, my dear sir, arrived at the middle of the fifteenth century, an epoch memorable and distinguished, amongst other events, by the loss of Guienne by the English. This affords me a good opportunity of concluding my letter, which I am afraid has been already too long, and which must startle you like Macbeth, if only by the long series of effigies of the Sovereign which the envelope must bear for postage before it can reach you.

I have certainly not said all that I might have done on this subject, and I have scarcely mentioned the names of Scotland and Ireland; but, as I have already handled the history of the commerce between the northern parts of Great Britain and France in my work, 'Les Ecossais en France,' &c., I must be excused from reverting to that subject, at least here. I am ready, however, to take up again the sketch of the history of this commerce, which I have commenced, and to carry it down to the period preceding ours, if you should so desire.

I remain, yours truly,

FRANCISQUE-MICHEL, F.S.A. Lond. and Edinb.,
Correspondent of the Institute of France, &c.

CHAPTER VII.

CHAMPAGNE, REIMS, EPERNAY, ETC.

Vin de Champagne—Reims—Chalons—Epernay—Cramant—Bouzy—Partridge-Eye —Fermentation—Blending—Fining—Racking—The Montagne—Bottling—Saccharometer—Old Still Wine in Cask—Great Breakage—Binning—Disgorging—Liqueuring—Corking—Wiring—Papering—Injured by Icing—Château Sillery—Sillery-sec-non-Mousseux — Secrets and Mysteries — Liqueur to different Countries—Immense Fortunes—Palaces in Epernay—The celebrated Madame Mater Filiæ — Fraudulent Trade Marks — Statistical Tables.

LE VIN DE CHAMPAGNE.

Que le Vieillard cherche un reste de vie
Dans le Bordeaux qui réchauffe les sens,
Pour charmer ses banquets la Jeunesse n'envie
Que le Champagne aux flots resplendissants.

Auprès de lui qu'est cette liqueur blonde
Du vieux Falerne au reflet si vermeil?
Notre Champagne a fait le tour du monde
À nos drapeaux victorieux pareil;
Il rit, joyeux, sous la mousse qui tremble,
Et semble,
Dans le cristal, un rayon de soleil!

Invoque-le, Poète, dont la lyre
Devient rebelle, et ne rend plus de sons!
Cevin inspirateur te versant le délire
Fera gaîment pétiller tes chansons!

Auprès de lui la Muse est inféconde,
Phœbus n'est bon qu'à donner du sommeil:

Notre Champagne a fait le tour du monde
À nos drapeaux victorieux pareil ;
Il rit, joyeux, sous la mousse qui tremble,
Et semble,
Dans le cristal, un rayon de soleil !

Vous, froids Anglais, qui vantez notre France,
Et ses enfants au rire toujours prets,
Avez-vous soif d'amour, de gaîté, d'espérance,
Buvez ! Buvez ! et vous rirez après !

Et vous verrez les brouillards de votre onde
Fuir dans les cieux en nuage vermeil !
Notre Champagne a fait le tour du monde
À nos drapeaux victorieux pareil !
Il rit, joyeux, sous la mousse qui tremble,
Et semble,
Dans le cristal, un rayon de soleil !

AMAURY DE CAZANOVE.

THE fine old town of Reims, with its magnificent cathedral, is the capital of Champagne, so celebrated for its sparkling wine. In the same Department are also the important cities Chalons and Epernay, and, unless it be Cognac, I doubt if there exists any other small place where such an amount of wealth exists — all derived from Champagne!

The district is a very extensive plain with numerous undulations, and hills high enough to offer the most perfect exposures to the rays of the sun; and, as far as the eye can carry, these are seen clothed in the deep green of the vine-leaf.

The subsoil is generally white chalk. Above this, in geological order, is the argile-lignites. It is on these that are grown the qualities possessing great delicacy, and delicious bouquet.

In the best vineyards there are parts planted with vines called Crayons, and Gouttes d'Or, upon the chalk and argile, and from these the choicest wine is got. That the value of this soil is appreciated, may be seen by the numerous excavations about Cramant, Mont-Saran, Bouzy, &c.

The chemical analysis of this argile-lignites (called in the country, *cendrières*) proves that it contains the constituent parts of the vine, the grape, and the wine of the district.

It is much to be regretted that, with the possession of such an abundance of this excellent natural assistant, manures should be used in some of the best vineyards, which alter the character of the grapes, and consequently of the wine.

To have good wine, it is of course essential to have good grapes; and, as a general rate of price is established among the principal houses at the vintage, all are on the same footing. Everyone has the same opportunity as another of purchasing whatever quality he chooses, the only difference being that some houses having a larger trade, purchase a much greater quantity than their neighbours. Some makers have fine vineyards of their own, but not one of them producing a tenth part of their stock. In favourable years, however, these form an excellent basis for their cuvées (bins); but in middling and bad seasons they cannot sell them, and are compelled to work them up the best way they can. The operation of pressing the grapes is done as rapidly as possible. The three first pressures produce the choicest, or the 'flower of the wine,' which is put aside by itself. A few houses will only admit into their cuvées those three pressures, which do not yield above three-fifths of the juice of the grape. The fourth, the fifth, and the sixth are each put into separate vessels; and it is not unusual to see the fourth and fifth used for stock, but they are sure to give a reddish colour, arising from the severe pressure on the pulp of the grape. Even the sixth is sometimes introduced, but even without it the fourth and fifth frequently cause a coarse taste and flavour, and harsh bitterness—usually called in the country, 'goût de taille.'

Strange to say, these very wines, when fortified by brandy, to add to their apparent body, are often preferred in England to the purest and best; a perversion of taste which Frenchmen can account for only by supposing that our palates have been so long habituated to strong, dark, brandied wines, that we prefer this inferior champagne. However, within these few years, tastes here are improving, and instead of the former brown, and amber, and partridge-eye, and other kinds that looked like, and tasted nearly as strong as, 'golden sherry,' the natural colour and grape flavour are preferred by all who know what true good wine is. But it is right to add, that in some years of great heat, the skin and the pellicule (the part by which the grape hangs) become so ripe that they give natural colour to the juice; especially when rain falls at the period of the gathering, which makes the skins tender.

But to return to the new wine. It should remain from fifteen to twenty hours in the fermenting tub, into which it had run from the press, and in which it deposits its gross lees. It is then drawn off into hogsheads. These are laid up in large airy storerooms, generally looking towards the north, the bungs being put loosely in to allow the carbonic acid gas of the first fermentation to escape slowly. The wine at first is not clear, appearing almost like milk; but when the frost begins, it becomes bright; it is then racked, and soon after the blending and fining commence.

The *coupage*, literally the *cutting*, or, as it is usually called, the blending, is an operation requiring the most anxious thought of the maker, with much experience and a discriminating palate; for upon the skill and judgment with which this is done depends the character of the cuvées.

Until not many years ago, champagnes were made from the grapes of certain vineyards; from whence has, no doubt, arisen the names of Vin d'Ay, Vin de Silleri, Fleur de Silleri, &c., so widely and beautifully exhibited in splendid labels. But now, all the wine of the best houses is composed of various growths mixed together; for experience has proved that when this is done the quality may be made not only superior to any one kind, but the wine thus blended is also hardier, and not subject to the diseases that formerly prevailed. The following are actual instances of cuvées of 50 hogsheads, about 1,200 dozens each, made in the fine years 1857 and 1858 :—

1. Black grapes Verzenay 16 hogsheads
Do. do. Ay 16 „
White do. Cramant and Avize 18 „

50 hogsheads

2. Another.
Black grapes Bouzy 16 hogsheads
Do. do. Pierry 16 „
White do. Cramant and Avize 18 „

50 hogsheads

3. Another (which has proved exceedingly fine).

Black grapes	Verzenay	5	hogsheads
Do. do.	Bouzy	5	„
Do. do.	Chigny	2½	„
Do. do.	Ay	5	„
Do. do.	Champillon	2½	„
Do. do.	Pierry	5	„
Do. do.	Vertus	5	„
White do.	Cramant and Avize	10	„
Do. do.	Mesnil	5	„
Do. do.	Chouilly	2½	„
Do. do.	Crayons de St. Martin	2½	„
		50	hogsheads

The black grapes form generally about two-thirds, giving strength and body; while the white impart richness, delicacy, and bouquet; and the cuvée, with these proportions, will turn out to be champagne of the finest quality.

Shortly after being 'put together,' each cask is slightly fined; and in about a fortnight, when the wine is bright, it should be drawn off very carefully into a fresh cask, using the utmost precaution to allow none of the lees to enter.

The vintage, in favourable seasons, begins about the middle of September, but it is more often about the 10th of October. This is the time that calls forth all the activity and powers of the maker. He is sometimes compared to the bee, passing from flower to flower, as he passes from vine to vine, examining the grapes, comparing them, and searching in all directions for those that will enable him to surpass others in the excellence of his cuvées.

It may easily be imagined what an advantage one residing in the country—in the midst of the vines and the growers, personally acquainted with these, and having watched them in the cultivation of their vineyards—has over those in the towns.

To produce a hogshead of wine, it is calculated that from 760 to 960 pounds of grapes are required, according to the quantity of juice from the three first *pressings.* In Verzenay, Bouzy, Ambonnay, and other parts of the Montagne, the sales are by *caques* (tubs), of which there are from 5½ to 6½ to a hogshead of wine. The temptation to increase the quantity at the expense of the quality has been as powerful here as elsewhere; and not a few vineyards, once celebrated for their excellence, have fallen into such disrepute that many houses will not allow a grape from them to enter their cellar. There is a large extent of ground covered with vines, yielding the very choicest, and also a fine second class. The champagne sold at very low prices is from the low-lying grounds in the neighbouring districts, and from the bad vintages which are rejected by houses who desire to uphold the character of their brands.

The wine is next drawn off the lees into fresh casks, placed in stores above ground, where it remains till the month of March, when the important operation of bottling begins. This is a peculiarly anxious affair, for two results are desired: first, that the wine shall sparkle; and next, that its effervescence shall not be so forcible as to break too many bottles. As a guide and protection, a Gleucoœnomêtre is used, to show the quantity of natural sugar, an overabundance of which causes great breakage. If it is found, for instance, that there are 9 degrees, there will be added 4 or 5 degrees of dissolved sugar-candy, so as to bring it up to 13 or 14 degrees, which is the quantity of saccharine usually required to produce a beautiful sparkling (*mousse*). Some firms have a constant stock of stout old wines in wood, nearly still, which is used to diminish the effervescence of the young kinds, by the addition of more or less at the time of bottling.

By this means, the appearance of age is given; and wine which, without this process, would be unfit for travelling, is often sent off when not a year old. The violence of the fermentation being thus subdued, the carbonic acid gas becomes less powerful, and the amount of breakage is diminished. Some bottles are much better and stronger than others, and no consideration of price should deter the purchase of the very best glass, as the one or the other may make a difference of 20 per cent. in the breakage. The use of the Saccharometer, the skilful blendings of different growths, and greater experience, have all tended to diminish this serious item in the cost of champagne. In former years, it was frequently enormous, especially in very hot seasons. I have known it as much as 60 and 70 per cent. In such years, when the grape is rich in saccharine, peculiar care is directed to place the young wines in the deepest and coldest vaults, and ice is frequently placed in them. In some cellars there are large ice-houses. The average breakage is now from 6 to 10 per cent.

If it is wished that the effervescence should come quickly, the bottles are kept in the store above ground, and binned there; but if this is not desired, they are lowered into the cold deep cellars, binned in masses of thousands of bottles, in a most ingenious way, in the centre of the vault, the whole supported by a few laths; and, although perfectly safe, the bin may be moved by pushing with the hand. An English cellarman laughs when told of it, and will not believe in its safety.

But even in the cold cellar, with the thermometer at 36° of Fahrenheit, the wine is not long in beginning to 'work,' which shows itself by a slight bubbling in the bottles, reports as of pistols in all directions, and glass flying about, so that at this period wire-gauze protectors over the face are worn, when passing the bins. I know one cellar in which there are three men, who have each lost an eye owing to this cause. Along each bin a narrow gutter is cut, through which the lost liquid flows.

Notwithstanding the depth and the cold of the cellar, the changes in the external atmosphere produce a very decided effect; and the breakage is always greater in the spring, when the grape is budding, and in the autumn, when it is ripening, than at any other period of the year. The same is observed with other kinds in our docks, and it is attributed to the sympathy of the produce of the grape with the plant of its origin; but it would probably be more correct to trace it to the moisture and the atmospheric changes which usually then prevail. Some bottles break so entirely that all the contents pass to the floor and gutter; others retain a portion of the wine, which would soon become acid, if not removed; and, if this is not practicable, buckets of very cold water are thrown over them, to wash away any wine remaining in the broken bottles. Were this not carefully attended to, and the conduits and the floor kept clear of wine, fermentation would arise, and the cellar would become impregnated with carbonic acid gas and putridity. The wine of the previous vintage being bottled in March, if it has been well made, will have attained its full effervescence by the end of October; when each bottle of the cuvée is examined, to see whether there are any on ullage—that is, that have leaked; these are filled up from other bottles.

The whole are then removed to another cellar, where they are re-binned; but, before doing this, each bottle is turned upside down, and shaken, so as to remove the deposit which has fallen, to the lowest interior side. They now remain untouched, except by their own occasional breakages, till a merchant of Reims, Epernay, &c., purchases them for preparation in his own way. They are then sent in their 'brût' (raw) state; and it would somewhat astonish those accustomed to the limpid fluid, to see it and to taste it before it has undergone the process of disgorging and sugar-candying. If its destination is out of the district or abroad, it must undergo much manipulation.

Whatever quantity is wanted, is taken from the large bin, every bottle is well shaken, in order to distribute the sediment through the bottle, which is then placed on a table full of holes, cut in such a way that it lies, mouth downwards, at an angle of about 45°. This is called placing on point. In a few days, the deposit will be found on the lower shoulder. A peculiar sharp movement with the hand is given, to cause the deposit to get nearer the bottom of the cork; and this is done daily to every bottle for about three weeks, gradually bringing them all nearer the perpendicular. On examination, it will be found that the wine in the bottle is perfectly brilliant, and that the whole of the deposit has been brought to the bottom of the cork. To get rid of this with as little loss as possible and the prevention of any falling back into the wine, requires skill, experience, and a steady hand. The operation is called disgorging—that is, taking from the neck.

The *dégorgeur* (disgorger), standing at the place represented in the accompanying sketch (p. 232), lifts the bottle very carefully, head slanting down, and cuts the string which holds the cork; this immediately flies, the wine rushes out, but at the same moment he jerks the bottle up and turns the mouth once or twice round, so as to let a little flow and carry off any bits of cork, &c., that might otherwise fall back into the bottle. He pushes a cork in, and his part is finished, probably with the loss of less than a glass.

The bottle is now taken by the *vidangeur* (familiarly called *chopineur*), who pours out a certain quantity, according to the per-centage of saccharine which he has been told is to be added. The third sharer in the labour, called the *opéreur*, now comes into play. He has before him, usually in a tin vessel, liquid sugar-candy, of which he puts into each bottle the quantity ordered, by means of a small measure, of which there are several sizes. In all respectable champagne houses this is the only 'adulteration' which the wine undergoes, and, were it not for the liqueur, few—those not excepted

OPERATIONS IN CHAMPAGNE.

who talk about liking it very *dry*—would care to drink champagne.

It may be overdone as well as underdone; and, as in most things the difficulty is to attain the *juste-milieu*, no rule can be laid down; for some qualities require more than others; and this is the case when one year has well ripened the grapes, and another has left them green and harsh. Generally about 12 or 13 per cent. is enough, but some houses add even 15, 16, or more. Supposing the *vin brut* to be the same, the distinguishing character belonging to certain houses arises almost entirely from their liqueur, and how they apply it. Some have it perfectly pure and white, with a very slight addition of brandy or colour; others add a good deal of brandy, and also of colour, giving the appearance of body and the various shades of 'amber,' 'partridge-eye,' &c.; others consider that their liqueur is improved by being boiled.

Liqueurs, however prepared, but especially with colour and spirit, are very much improved by being kept for many years, as is frequently done, to render them soft and mellow, and less likely to deposit in bottle. Let anyone, however, who can appreciate and distinguish pure from brandied and coloured champagne, compare one with liqueur neither brandied nor coloured, against the other; and he will immediately perceive in the former a fine delicate bouquet with purity of taste, while there is in the other coarseness both of taste and flavour, and a frequent want of brilliancy, if long in bottle.

Till lately, champagne was considered thin and poor, unless altered from its natural state; and the only kind in vogue was such as no man in Champagne, and few anywhere else, except in England, would drink. For liqueuring, there has lately been a beautiful little machine invented, by which each bottle receives a certain quantity only. It possesses the further advantage of a very slight escape of gas in comparison with the process by hand.

The bottle now passes to the *récouleur*, whose duty it is to fill up to the proper height. It then comes to the fifth, the *boucheur*, or corker. The sixth, the *ficeleur*, or stringer, fastens down the cork by string. The seventh, the *ficeleur au fil de fer*, performs a similar operation with wire. The eighth, usually a woman, places the silver or gold foil over the cork and neck; and the ninth wraps the bottle in paper, when it is ready for packing.

The illustration, at page 232, of the various operations in a champagne establishment, taken from life, will assist in making my descriptions intelligible.

Every house has its own *brand* or mark. The corks used for keeping the wine in the cellar for ripening and sale, are much cheaper than those by which they are replaced when it is sold and sent off, branded sometimes with the name of the grower or merchant, but often of the purchaser, who may prefer having his own name. Before despatching, it is desirable to keep the wine for a couple of weeks after re-corking, when every bottle ought to be examined, to see if there is the slightest appearance of weeping (leakage). The force of the carbonic acid gas is so powerful, that great care and the best corks are required. The brand on the end of the cork is effected by a slight pressure against the heated branding-iron.

With one or two exceptions, every house or grower is willing to cork with any brand desired, if it be not the counterfeit of that of some other firm. (It will be seen, under the head of *the Rhine*, that no such fear or compunction there prevails, at least as regards champagne brands.) When packed in cases, a similar brand is usually burned on the case.

The loss of wine from the cork is now much less than it was formerly, the cause of which is attributable not only to the use of superior and larger corks, but chiefly to their being driven in by the corking machines now employed, much farther and tighter than was possible in the old way. Indeed, they are now often so tightly driven that a corkscrew is required; but although this may interfere with the agreeable and exciting pop, and flight of the cork, it is hardly an objection, as the preservation of the wine ought to be first considered. Gold or silver foil is now almost invariably used to cover the cork; it is ornamental, but is scarcely of the slightest use. Cement protects the cork a little, but is very disagreeable, especially in hot weather. The only true safeguard is a good cork, well driven home.

Here is a sketch of the corking machines generally used.

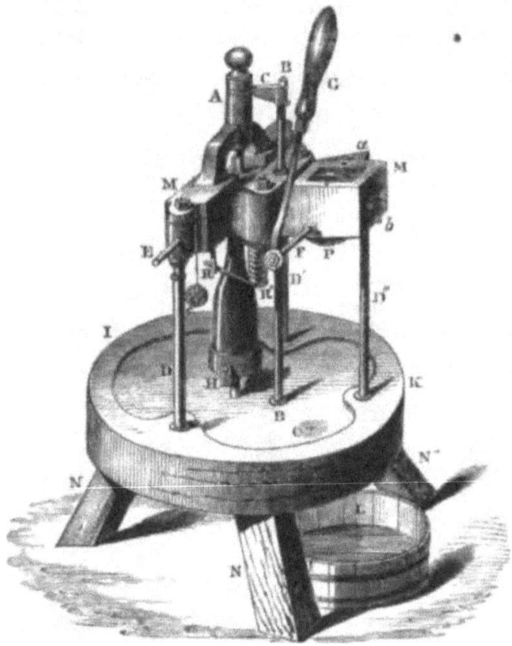

Champagnes formerly became often 'scuddy,' which means that they lost their limpidity and brilliancy; but this is now rarely the case. In consulting growers as to the cause of the change and improvement, I have heard it generally attributed to the previous ignorant habit of making their wine solely from one vineyard or plant, or locality; instead of observing the law so forcibly made known to us in the human species as well as in the animal and vegetable world, that all become feeble if continuously reared from the same stock. Probably it is also owing to this improved knowledge that *one*

disgorging is now generally found sufficient, while *three* were, at one time, not unusual.

The power, and the constant pressure of the gas against the cork, show how absolutely necessary it is to have the bottle always on its side; for then the cork is kept wet and swollen; but if the bottle remains on end it becomes dry, contracts, and the gas and the wine escape. If the wine is of good body and quality, although it will not sparkle as the others that are full, it will be found excellent, even if it has been half full for a month.

It is a mistake to suppose that champagne is spoiled if not drunk the day that it is opened. By corking it again, tying the cork firmly down, then turning the bottle mouth downwards, it will be found good for a long time. This is worth knowing; but those who value champagne according to the flight of the cork, will be disappointed if they expect this to be rapid, if the carbonic acid gas has been allowed to fly off.

I think champagne excels every white wine in delicious, high bouquet, and, when old, it surpasses them in taste; but it is rarely met with in possession of all these qualities.

In the first place, it must be of one of those vintages that seldom occur—there was not one fine year between 1846 and 1857; and, in the next place, it must be at least five years old, and it will improve for twice that period. I have never tasted champagne equal to one which the Mayor of Chalons lately gave me, made by himself, in 1834. Of course there was no report when the cork came out, and there was no 'froth,' but there was a beautiful creamy head, showing, by the way it spread and stood, the solidity of its foundation.

With drinkers in general it seems to matter very little what quality of champagne is placed on table, so long as it 'froths' well; but those who seek 'froth' should avoid age, for, the older it becomes, the more does it lose its effervescence. Unless it be of such a vintage as '34, '46, '57, '58, '61 or '62, it is best to drink it when two or three years old; but when it can be secured, truly, of such a year as any of these, several years' supply should be laid in, or kept abroad, and in five or six years it should be brought into use. I suspect that it will not be so much liked by many as if it had been half as old; but those who appreciate a true old, firm, creaming champagne, will value it.

In the old country residences there are large, cool cellars, where wine may be kept in the most perfect state, but in few modern or town houses are such to be found.

Champagne should be not only cool but cold, and, if it be not kept in a temperature sufficiently low, it must be iced. In a hot room, even in winter, the coolness is pleasant; but when the bottle is allowed to remain in the ice-pail until the wine becomes nearly as cold as the ice itself, it is wasting fine champagne to give it in that state, for flavour and taste become what wine-merchants call 'locked up.'

Ten minutes' iceing, or, as the French call it, *frappé*, does not deteriorate the wine; but even then it is not equal to that which is brought fresh out of a cold cellar, where it has lain long undisturbed. The practice of putting pieces of ice into the wine itself shows that a cool refreshing drink is wanted, but it is destructive to the quality.

The warmth of the hand on the bottle heats the wine, but this may be counteracted by a simple, neat instrument, shown in the accompanying drawing.

BOTTLE HOLDER.

The famous Sillery derives its celebrity from a village of that name at the foot of a range of hills, called the Montagne, a few miles from Reims. The vineyard, of about 100 acres, is hardly deserving of its reputation. This arose, in the first instance, from the splendid cellars built by the widow of a Marshal D'Estrées, at her Château-Sillery, and from the care she used in procuring the very finest grapes from the neighbouring vineyards, and devoting the utmost attention to making good wine.

The château and vineyards have been sold; and, although some excellent wine is still made by the larger proprietors, into whose possession they have fallen, many of the smaller ones have been very regardless of quality, hoping to sell their produce at high prices on the credit of a past renown.

There are, on the Montagne, the vineyards of Verzenay, Muilly, Bouzy, and several others, possessing all that could be desired in soil and exposure, with fine old vines, producing wine of great body, life, and bouquet.

To Sillery, the epithets *sec-non-mousseux* are usually attached; but, although such qualities as I have described are alone suited for yielding fine dry-still-sillery, it must not be supposed that other kinds, from Cramant, Pierry, &c., could not produce a similar kind, if similarly prepared. The usual way of preparing wine to become *Sillery-sec-non-mousseux* is, when there is a very fine vintage, to leave the desired number of casks in the coldest part of the cellar till the December or January after the succeeding vintage (about sixteen months), when they are bottled, and left in the cellar for eight or ten years. I have searched in many a cellar in Champagne for such sillery, and have occasionally found a little. When truly good, it is very fine, and those who have had it usually dislike all other; but I have seldom met with any who liked it at first. It is both troublesome and unsatisfactory to have to do with; for, after you have discovered a little forgotten bin, as still as sherry, the prize is sent off, probably in summer, and forthwith the heat and the shaking make it *mousseux*, and, whoever has ordered it, very angry. If it has actually got into 'mousse,' the remedy is to put it in a cold cellar, and, before drinking it, to place it for an hour in ice, leaving the cork out.

The price, of course, is very high. I am here attempting to describe true sillery; but there are many imitations, most of which are the result of mixtures of brandy, sherry, &c., to give body, and check effervescence.

Champagne, although made chiefly of black grapes, being entirely from the juice, is almost colourless, and consequently those kinds called amber, *rosé*, and pink, have been coloured.

For the first, a very slight quantity of a preparation called *fismes*, from the name of the place where it is made, is used. This is composed of the elderberry, boiled with cream of tartar, and filtered. To produce *rosé* or pink, more is required; but no one can carefully compare even the amber with that which is pure, without discovering a coarse, extraneous flavour; and in the deeper colours, this is still more perceptible. Sometimes any shade of colour is given by adding more or less must from red grapes, of which the husks have been pressed, and their colour allowed to mix with the juice; and this being put into the fermenting-tub, the whole is fermented together.

This has always appeared to me a better way of colouring than the other; for the *fismes* generally deposits a portion, injuring the limpidity of the wine; while the other, by the amalgamation by fermentation, and having nothing extraneous added, is both brighter and better.

Almost every house professes to have a secret and mystery in the preparation of its liqueur, but the process and details are well known. It is curious to see the different kinds preferred in different countries. The average degrees of liqueur in England are from 12 to 13; in France, 14 to 15; in Belgium, the same as France, but more brandy; in Germany, 16 to 18; in Russia, 20 to 22; in Sweden and Norway, 24 to 28, and even 30; in India, about 9.

Northern countries generally prefer a very young wine, because it has a strong *grapey* flavour, and makes the cork fly to the ceiling. I have heard it alleged of the Russians, perhaps by way of a joke, that they keep their windows open, when they have a party, in order that those in and out of the house may hear the reports of the champagne-bottles, and so become duly impressed by the style of the entertainment.

Immense fortunes have been made by a few of the noted Reims and Epernay merchants, who enjoyed a practical monopoly during many years, and consequently received enormous profits. But serious competition has arisen, and wine-merchants in this and other countries have learned that these firms, which were supposed to have some peculiar means of possessing the finest wine, have no advantage over the smaller ones than making purchases on a larger scale. In every trade and profession, men, when money and years have accumulated, are inclined to avail themselves of the reputation gained by former labours; and as there is seldom, in France, more than the usual family complement of a son and a daughter, there is not the same inducement to continue at hard work as in England, with six, nine, or even eighteen to provide for!

The natural consequence is, that partners cease to go about the country inspecting the vines, noticing how they are manured, &c., visiting the cellars of the numerous growers, and much else that they attended to, before money and age had made them fat and lazy; and therefore they devolve these necessary duties upon their *chef des caves* (head cellarman). He is not likely to do this so keenly as one whose profits are dependent upon the result of his purchases, and, as a matter of course, growers pay him to buy from them. I have been told of one *chef des caves* who, in this way, adds 400*l.* or 500*l.* a year to his other receipts.

This practice (bribery) has always prevailed to a great extent in the sale of wines, and particularly with champagne, and other French kinds. Probably there is not in the world a street of such palaces as the Rue de Commerce (usually known as La Folie), in Epernay. One was lately built which is stated to have cost 80,000*l.*; and the rivalry appears to be as to who will expend the greatest amount of champagne profits in building and carving. The cellar and business establishment are within the gates and walls that encircle the house, and the value underground in some of them is immense; and yet it was only in the year 1780, that when a merchant in Epernay made 6,000 bottles (500 dozens), he was considered a daring speculator.

A few miles on the Paris side of Epernay may be seen a château, above the doorway of which is carved 'Mater Filiæ,' the mater being a lady of world-wide fame, exceedingly rich, but still living in a small house in Reims, as she did many a year ago; and although above eighty years old, it is said there is not a cuvée made without her opinion, nor a transaction of importance, without consulting her.

Others may have, and have, quite as good wine as hers; for they have the same opportunities which she enjoys of buying grapes or wine from growers; while the preparation of her liqueur is no mystery, and the fermentation must everywhere go on in its natural course.

The desire of her house is, not to make its wine better one year than another, but to keep it as close as possible to its known standard peculiarity, year after year. If all seasons were alike, this would be comparatively easy, but some are so bad that not a single grape will be admitted into cellars of repute; and as two, three, and more such years often succeed each other, her and every other house are compelled to keep up stock in the best way they can. The only plan of accomplishing this is by searching throughout the district for the best wine that can be found in the cellars of growers or merchants, and preparing them for their brand. Large firms such as hers, and a few more, will make several cuvées of 50,000 and 100,000 dozens, after a good vintage. Shortly after that of 1861, I saw in her cellars casks that reminded me of the quays of the London Docks; and as these had to be prepared, with much liqueur, for the shipments to Russia, &c., and less for the portion for England, it may be imagined what a serious undertaking it is, and how much experience and discrimination are required, to amalgamate these various qualities into a homogeneous whole.

But it is just to add that, in stating that she has no monopoly of the best grapes, nor of the knowledge of fermenting or converting them into wine, hers is the only house where no other kind but the best procurable quality is kept; and therefore, anyone buying a bottle with her true brand on the cork, may feel confident that it is the finest she can offer. She presses her grapes less than other growers, disposing of the surplus; while most houses retain theirs for further pressure, and then sell according to the result; probably branding with their own known brand that which proves good, and with a 'fancy' brand that which is inferior.

The system of forging names and brands is not so frequent in France as in Germany, the punishment in the former country being very severe. It is, however, practised; and, a short time ago, the following paragraph appeared in *The Times*:—

Advices from Reims state that the Tribunal at that city has just pronounced judgement against two persons who had forged the mark of Cliquot Ponsardin on 300 cases of wine. They had been condemned to 18 months' imprisonment and a fine of £1,200, and to the publication of the sentence in the journals and the costs of its insertion. Their head cellarman also has been sentenced to four months' imprisonment. Some of these wines were seized in London; and it is to be hoped that, under the existing treaties for the protection of trade marks, our own Courts will in all similar instances act with equal vigour.

Having lately visited Avize, where this occurred, I was informed by a friend that he was surprised one morning, about four o'clock, to see seven gens-d'armes, with their carbines, marching past his house, and proceeding to that of a Monsieur Cazin, which, with his garden, they surrounded; but he had probably received intelligence of the proceedings in London by telegram, and had taken to flight some hours previously. This M. Cazin is said to have been worth about £20,000.

It is just to the people of the district, of all classes, to state that I heard only one expression of opinion about such fraudulent acts.

Although it extends my remarks on these transactions to a great length, yet, as it is a question of much importance, and the facts are undeniable, and show how purchasers of wine, with brands apparently genuine, are deceived, it is not necessary to offer much apology for inserting the following extract from a well-known circular of July 9, 1863:—

FABRICATED TRADE MARKS.

We have received copies of three bills in Chancery, filed by Messrs. Moët & Chandon, of Epernay, praying that the several defendants may be restrained, by order of the Court, 'from selling, or offering for sale, any wines in bottle, corked with corks having thereon a brand which is a copy or imitation of, or only colorably differing from, that of the plaintiffs;' and that 'the defendants may be decreed to deliver to the plaintiffs all corks in their power or possession so branded, and also all bottles corked with such corks.'

Further, 'that an account may be taken, under the order and direction of the Court, of all wine so branded, not produced by the plaintiffs, which has been sold by the defendants, and of all gains and profits made by the defendants on such sales; and that they may be decreed to pay to the plaintiffs the amount of such gains and profits, &c.'

The second bill, filed under date 19th ulto., is against Edward Gandell, Junr., who is described as 'a German yeast-merchant, having premises at No. 5, Paradise Street, Lambeth, and doing a considerable business in inferior wines and spirits,' and who is charged, in a similar manner to the former defendant, with having in his possession, and selling large quantities of spurious 'Moët's' champagne. The third bill was filed on the same day against Max Hirsch, a wine-merchant, of Canning Chambers, Liverpool, and Mayence-on-the-Rhine, and Jacob Birkett, commission agent, of No. 5, Eldon Chambers, South

John Street, Liverpool, who are charged with having 'for some time past, fraudulently, and with great profit to themselves, sold large quantities of wine, as and for the plaintiffs', but which were not produced by them. On the 23rd April last, Birkett addressed a letter to Messrs. John Dale & Co., of Lancaster, enclosing Hirsch's card, and offering 700 dozen of Moët & Chandon's wine, at 38*s.* per dozen, duty paid; to which those gentlemen replied on the 29th April—'We duly received yours of the 23rd inst. The price is less than we are paying Moët's agents, but we suppose it is genuine, &c.' In answer, Birkett wrote, on the 10th May—'I am not quite certain that it is genuine.'

Messrs. Dale & Co. thereupon communicated with Moët's London agents, who on the 18th May wrote to Birkett, 'We see, by a letter signed by you, that you are offering a large quantity of wine, which, although bearing Moët & Chandon's brand, is, as we are enabled to show, spurious, &c., &c.' To this, no answer was returned, and at the plaintiffs' request, Messrs. Dale & Co., on the 1st June, wrote to the defendant Hirsch—'Be good enough to forward us (as sample) one case, one dozen bottles of the Moët champagne which Mr. Birkett wrote us about a short time since.' However, Mr. Hirsch being by this time wide awake to the object for which the sample case was required, wrote—'In reply to your favour of yesterday, we beg to enclose price list. We are not aware that Mr. Birkett has offered you any Moët and Chandon, as we very seldom sell any, and, in fact, have none in stock now.' Notwithstanding this, the plaintiffs charge 'that he then had, and still has, a large quantity of spurious wine, professing to be "Moët's," and continues to offer it for sale as the genuine article,' &c.

In addition to the large quantities of spurious champagne referred to in these bills, we are informed that about 600 dozens were last week discovered and seized at Liverpool by Moët's agents.

By reference to the following statistical Table, the rapid extension of the trade in Champagne wine with foreign countries, since 1845, is shown. It is here seen, that while in that year it was only 4,380,214 bottles (365,017 dozen), it was last year 7,937,836 (661,486 dozen); in 1861 it rose to 732,352 dozen:—

Table of the Trade in the sparkling Wines of Champagne, from April 1, 1844, *to April* 1, 1863. (*From Returns of the Chamber of Commerce of Reims.*)

Years	Bottles existing in Stock of Wholesale Merchants	Bottles sent Abroad	Bottles delivered in France to Wine Merchants and Consumers	Total Sale in France and Abroad
1844–45	23,285,818	4,380,214	2,255,438	6,635,652
1845–46	22,847,971	4,505,308	2,510,605	7,015,913
1846–47	18,815,367	4,711,915	2,355,366	7,067,281
1847–48	23,122,994	4,859,625	2,092,571	6,952,196
1848–49	21,290,185	5,686,484	1,473,966	7,160,450
1849–50	20,499,192	5,001,044	1,705,735	6,706,779
1850–51	20,444,915	5,866,971	2,122,569	7,989,540
1851–52	21,905,479	5,957,552	2,162,880	8,120,432
1852–53	19,376,967	6,355,574	2,385,217	8,740,790
1853–54	17,757,769	7,878,320	2,528,719	10,407,039
1854–55	20,922,959	6,895,773	2,452,743	9,348,516
1855–56	15,957,141	7,137,001	2,562,039	9,699,040
1856–57	15,228,294	8,790,198	2,468,818	10,959,016
1857–58	21,628,778	7,368,310	2,421,454	9,789,764
1858–59	28,328,251	7,666,633	2,805,416	10,472,049
1859–60	35,648,124	8,265,395	3,039,621	11,305,016
1860–61	30,225,260	8,788,223	2,697,508	11,185,731
1861–62	30,254,291	6,904,915	2,592,875	9,497,790
1862–63	28,013,189	7,937,836	2,767,371	10,705,207

CHAPTER VIII.

BURGUNDY, CÔTE D'OR, BEAUJOLAIS, ETC.

Côte d'Or—Nuits—Vosne—English Travellers—Chambertin—Clos-Vougeôt—Cellars in Nuits—Memo. of Tasting—Pommard—Beaune—Meursault—Montrachet—Chablis—Mâcon—Beaujolais—Sparkling Burgundy—Lyons—Tain—Tournon—Hermitage—The Rhône—Memo. of Tasting.

IN writing the word Burgundy, the difficulty of the task I have undertaken comes vividly before me; for this district extends fifty miles in length, and forms the departments of Yonne, Côte d'Or, and Saône et Loire. At Joigny, about a hundred miles to the south-east of Paris, the department of Yonne begins. Farther southward Dijon is reached, and as the next stations are Vougeôt and Nuits, we find ourselves in the midst of the most celebrated vineyards; and continuing the same route we arrive at Beaune, and still farther on at Mâcon, the central dépôt for Mâcon and Beaujolais wines.

This is a most favoured vinous district, as from Joigny we come upon the spots noted for the full-bodied kinds of wine produced along the Saône and Rhône, including every variety of red and white. Here are Richebourg, Romanée-Conti, Montrachet, Meursault, the finest imaginable; then Volnay,

Pommard, Chablis, Pouilly, Tonnerre, which are excellent, and not nearly so costly as the former. Also Auxerre, Epineul, Maligny, Fontenay, for general use. But it would be tedious to enumerate the varieties, for every parish has its own. The peculiarities in the growth of each little vineyard are known in its locality, and the wine is valued according to the estimation in which it is held.

I visited the principal cellars, and have attempted to describe a few of the best known kinds. For above a week I lived within half an hour's walk of the most celebrated vineyards in Burgundy; and I cannot refrain from remarking that, however agreeable the house of an Englishman may be, there is in that of a French gentleman a freedom from ceremony, an ease, and a charm that are not easily forgotten. If English travellers could pass some of their time in the domestic circles of French families, they would form an impression very different from that produced by coming in contact solely with those whose politeness is mercenary. Several of the vineyards belong to the gentleman I was visiting, and from him I learned the most minute details connected with them; but it would be tiresome and uninteresting to give here more than a general outline of their capabilities.

At Nuits, fifteen miles south of Dijon, are large cellars of wine, in which may be found all the kinds of the district. Vosne is a village two miles from Nuits, and close to it are Romanée-Conti, Romanée,

La Tache, Grande Rue, Richebourg, and about a mile from those is Clos-Vougeôt, and a little farther off, nearer Dijon, is Chambertin. A goodly array of names! Except Clos-Vougeôt and Chambertin, not one of these yield on an average above 70 hogsheads, and Romanée-Conti seldom produces more than 12.

I could not remark any difference of flavour while eating the grapes, but I was assured that those accustomed to taste the wine, can immediately decide from which vineyard it has been made. The vines are old and of the best kinds: Romanée, Richebourg, La Tache, and Grande Rue (the latter across the road), appear to have all an equally favourable aspect; but with all these apparent resemblances, there may be a stratum of soil which causes the difference perceptible to experienced local tasters. The palate, like the eye, the ear, or touch, acquires by practice various degrees of sensitiveness that would be incredible, were it not a well-ascertained fact. For instance, those who devote attention to it, can tell whether a salmon is Irish or Scotch, and others can distinguish those taken from different rivers. Anyone who has eaten a grouse from the southern parts of Scotland, can perceive how different the taste and flavour are from one from the Highlands, fed entirely upon the heather-berry.

These vineyards possess to the fullest extent the characteristics of the highest class of red burgundy, which are a brilliant deep colour, delicious aroma, full rich body, great softness and delicacy.

The Clos-Vougeôt is a large vineyard surrounded by a wall, and is so celebrated, that when a French regiment marches past, it halts and presents arms. It is much overrated, for, although the upper part on the acclivity produces wine, such as none other surpasses, still the declivity is not at all equal to it; and the lowest part is no better than many other vineyards in the neighbourhood. Such well cared-for vineyards will produce the best wines, even in the most unfavourable seasons; but like Château Lafitte of 1858, worth 70*l.* or 80*l.*, and in 1860 only 5*l.* per hogshead, so Clos-Vougeôt may be worth 70*l.* or 80*l.* one year, and dear at 5*l.* in another season. The average produce of Clos-Vougeôt is about 500 hogsheads.

Another vineyard of justly high reputation is Chambertin, not far from Clos-Vougeôt; it yields generally about 150 hogsheads, which in a good year has a remarkably fine flavour. As those names are known throughout the world, it may well be imagined how rarely they can be obtained in a genuine state. But, besides these, there are many that should satisfy even very fastidious connoisseurs; and, for my own part, I think some of them more agreeable than the celebrated growths, such as the La Tache or Richebourg, which are really too 'grand,' and require many years' keeping in wood and in bottle before they are fit for use.

Anyone ought to be satisfied with good Pommard, Volnay, or Musigny, or with other kinds even inferior to them, but excellent in themselves, and having, like all wines from this district, a peculiarly high bouquet.

In the Yonne, the first-class qualities are, the Vin de Tonnerre, the Olivottes and others; and in the Saône-et-Loire, there are the capital Moulin-à-vent, the Torins, &c. and the white Pouilly, and Fuissé. I retain a very favourable impression of the Moulin-à-vent, from having found it several times very excellent at Véfour's, in Paris.

The gentleman with whom I was staying, in the most handsome and liberal way, afterwards introduced me to the principal wine-broker in Nuits, requesting him to accompany me to other cellars, to enable me to form a comparison of their qualities and prices.

I was not previously aware that *sugaring* was so very common, and that there was not the slightest desire to conceal it. I was assured that in Paris, and in the north generally, the addition of sugar was preferred, as it gives an appearance of richness. But as it is not the natural saccharine of the grape, it probably explains, in a great measure, why burgundies and the wines of this part of France so often 'go wrong.' My friend's cellars and business establishment in Nuits are very spacious, and hold a splendid stock of all the wines of this and the neighbouring districts.

It is almost a loss of time to go into a cellar without making memoranda of every cask and bottle tasted, and I therefore made a point of invariably doing this, to gain knowledge, and for future reference. The following (without the prices) is a literal extract from my Note-book :—

No. 1011. Beaune, 1858, very pleasant.
1012. Ditto, 1858, higher flavour, but hard.
1015. Ditto, 1858, 4*l.* dearer, not worth it.
895. Pommard, 1859, do not like.
1118. Volnay, 1858, excellent.
884. Pommard, 1858, very soft flavour, excellent.
868. Chambolle, 1859, truly fine high character.
699. Nuits, 1858, thin.
870. Ditto, 1859, don't like.
692. Vosne, 1858, full, fine, great bouquet.
929. Richebourg, 1858, grand.
665. Chambertin, 1858, exceedingly fine.
666. La Loche, 1858, ditto.
910. Romanée, 1858, perfect.
731. Clos-Vougeôt, 1858, very fine, but not equal to the Romanée.
8. Mâcon, 1858, nice light flavour.
7. Ditto, 40 *fr.* dearer, worth it.
5. Ditto, 44 *fr.* dearer, excellent.
(Mâcons and Beaujolais are so like that they are sold as one or the other.)
1. Moulin à Vent, 1858, capital, great flavour.
942. Beaune, 1858, first growth, high flavour, much body, fine.
931. Ditto, 1858, 6*l.* dearer, equal to a fine Burgundy.
693. Volnay, 1858, same price as 931, very soft, full flavour.
843. Vosne-Beaumont, 10*l.* dearer than the above, worth it.
716. La Tache, 1858, superb for flavour and quality.
715. Grande Rue, 1858, same price as La Tache, but still finer.

No. 717. Romanée-Conti, 1858, 14*l.* dearer than the above, finest wine ever I tasted.
660. Chambertin, 1858, very high peculiar flavour, but not very agreeable.
548. Richebourg, 1857, 6*l.* cheaper than the 1858, not so good.
545. La Tache, 1857; I prefer the 1858.
541. Chambertin, 1857, extraordinarily delicate, and fine flavour.

White kinds:—

No. 13. Mâcon, 1858, excellent at price.
12. Ditto, not dearer, more body.
9. Pouilly, 1858, 8*l.* dearer, fine, but too dry to please generally.
789. Chablis, 1858, 4*l.* dearer than the Pouilly, very dear for quality.
788. Meursault, 1858, 6*l.* dearer than 789, very excellent.
786. Chevalier-Montrachet, 1858, very fine, but too young.
787. Montrachet-Ainé, 1858, immense price, an amazing high powerful fine flavour, with great full richness. I am assured that when it has been four or five years in bottle, it will be wonderfully fine.

Volnay, Nuits, Vosne, vintage 1859, all excellent, with the Burgundy character, but each possessing a bouquet and taste peculiar to itself.

Richebourg, 1859, wonderful high grand flavour.

La Tache, 1859, splendid.

In Bottle—Volnay, 1854, too old.

Nuits, 1854, but better two years ago.

St. George-Nuits, 1854, very fine, great bouquet.

Romanée, 1854, exceedingly good.

Corton, 1857, capital.

In Bottle—Romanée, 1857, perfection.
Nuits, 1857, very excellent at the price.
White—Chevalier-Montrachet, 1849, fine and great flavour.
Montrachet-Ainé, 1857, great price and fine, but requires more keeping; 1858 will be much grander.

Leaving Nuits for Beaune by the road, we passed several well-known vineyards, among others Pommard; and here, as everywhere, I was struck with the fallacy of names, for anyone could perceive, by looking at the vineyards on the hill to the right, above the village, that the wine from them must be very different from the equally genuine Pommard grown on the plain extending to the road:—

Apertos colles amat Bacchus.

At Beaune, I went to the Hôtel du Chevreuil, which I can confidently recommend for its strong smells, and excellently-cooked frogs.

Having already tasted in Burgundy most of the red and white kinds of Beaune, I saw little here to call for remark; and shall only repeat that, although not to be compared to the first-class burgundies, the wines of this neighbourhood are generally moderate in price, and possess a most agreeable taste and bouquet.

Meursault is a little farther south; and close to it is the land of the splendid white wines, grown on the brow of the range of hills about two miles distant.

The most celebrated is the Montrachet-Ainé, after which comes the Montrachet-Bâtard, more usually called Montrachet-Chevalier.

Chablis is produced in the Yonne, farther north; and the best is very pleasant, and so likewise are the second-class growths, for almost all the white kinds about Chablis are good. Not a few names have a heavy burden to bear, and none more so than Chablis; for there is scarcely a French white wine that is not called and offered for sale under this name.

Mâcon is about thirty miles to the south of Meursault, producing wines with somewhat more body than the Beaune, but, on the whole, very similar; and the same may be said of the adjoining Beaujolais, which are sold indiscriminately as Mâcon or Beaujolais, and are very similar in flavour and taste. The latter being good, with a pretty name, has lately acquired a popularity that it would have been long in attaining, if, at the clubs and other places, a bottle of the homely Mâcon, instead of the elegant Beaujolais, had to be called for.

All common cheap French red wines seem now to have got the name of Beaujolais, as white have that of Chablis. In Nuits and other parts, a sparkling wine, called sparkling burgundy, is made, but I saw none equal to good champagne.

After leaving Mâcon, we left what may be called the burgundy class; but the similarity continues until Lyons is passed, when the difference becomes very perceptible; for, instead of the light, high-flavoured, agreeable burgundies, beaunes, mâcons, and beaujolais, we then find the Rhône growths, more solid, but with less bouquet; and (with numerous exceptions in certain favoured spots) this increases until we get among the heavy, coarse kinds on the Mediterranean.

About fifty miles to the south of Lyons is Tournon, and across the Rhône is Tain, the head-quarters of hermitage wine. The very high hill of Hermitage almost overhangs Tain, and the view from the old building at the top, which gives name to the wine, is very extensive and grand. Below is the rapid Rhône, running between rocks and precipices, several of which are surmounted by old castles; while mountains succeed mountains, as far as the eye can carry.

I have been several times at Tournon, but never before had so good an opportunity of tasting the wines of this district as while there during the last vintage.

No one who has been in the habit of tasting true fine clarets or burgundies will say the best hermitages equal them in bouquet or in delicacy of taste; but it is rarely that one sees a first-rate claret or burgundy. The hermitage possesses these advantages over both—it is very hardy, and both red and white will keep for almost any length of time. Besides, it is full, soft, firm, with a fine delicious flavour, and has a deep, beautiful colour. In thus describing it, I am of course alluding to some of the best; but even the common, cheap kinds have the same character, though in an inferior degree. Instead of giving an elaborate description of the various growths, I have copied from my memorandum-book my remarks upon those I tasted, excluding the quotations of price. They are but a small number of the kinds grown in the district, and along the banks of the river.

The Rhône so frequently overflows its banks, and floods the houses, that they have no underground cellars in Tain. Hermitage is still much used for giving colour and body to clarets, but not so much as formerly, for there is now a more correct appreciation of pure wine, of every kind. At first, such admixture creates a very favourable impression, as it gives fullness and softness to claret, which tastes very thin to our palates, accustomed to port and sherry; but I have invariably remarked, after such mixed wine has been three or four years in bottle, it becomes hard and flavourless.

I subjoin the following extract from my Notebook, with the remarks I made in one of the best stocks in Tain:—

TAIN: *Sept.* 22, 1862.

Jean Jullien Miseri, 1858, most excellent, full flavour.

Jourdan, 1858, a little bitter in taste, not equal to the former.

Deloche, 1858, grand.

Guerby, 1859, capital, deep fine colour, ready for bottling.

De la Blanche, 1859, splendid.

Machon, 1859, very fine, but requires longer in wood.
De Loche, 1859, perfect.
White—De Loche, 1859, excellent.
Château-Grillet, very excellent.
Croze, 1859, capital at the price.
Mercurol, very good, nice, cheap, nearly equal to chablis, fuller.
In Bottle—Red Croze, 1858, excellent.
Deloche, 1858, first rate.
White—Croze, 1858, very good at price, stout.
Hermitage, 1858, ditto.
Do. 1856, fine, but too clear.
Do. 1858, body, flavour, capital.
Deloche, 1858, delicious.
St. Peray, sparkling, clear, good.
Vin de Paille, 1849, very high price, but he has a little still higher, not worth the money.

CHAPTER IX.

SOUTH OF FRANCE.—MARSEILLES, ETC.

Marseilles — St. George — M. Gordon — Languedoc — Châteauneuf du Pape—Nismes—Banyuls—Letter from Montpellier, 1805—List of Prices — Gette — Undeserved bad Character — False Brands—Lunel and Frontignan — The Hérault — Beziers — Narbonne — Rivesaltes—Perpignan—Vintage—No Singing or Dancing—Port Vendres — Pyrenees — Magnificent Views — Elne Wine Shop — Collioure—A Bottle threescore Years old—Stone Rooms with 8,000 Gallons—Skins for Cattle—Origin of Masdeu—From Port Vendres to Bordeaux.

THE important town of Marseilles carries on a large trade in wine, being admirably situated for receiving into its cellars white and red, of every kind produced in this part of France.

To enumerate the various growths, and to describe the peculiarities of each, would fill a volume, which would prove to be an exceedingly useless and tiresome book. In reading or writing on this subject, it should never be forgotten, that statements correct to-day may be the reverse to-morrow, for it often happens that the circumstance of a vineyard having gained a high reputation is the very cause of its losing it. This arises from the temptation to increase the quantity by the use of manures and other means, which deteriorates the quality.

Every parish has its own distinctive name, and brokers are well aware that in each parish various qualities are grown, though all bear one general designation. I cannot better illustrate this than by reference to the parish of St. George, four or five miles from Montpellier, and which, among the numerous St. Georges throughout France, is the one understood by French wine-merchants as the *real* St. George. I know the parish well, as a fine hill in it belongs to M. Gordon, a very old friend.

In September I was there, and the care used in excluding bunches with rotten or green grapes, and in separating the stalks from the grapes, sufficiently explains why the result should be better than from the fields of the peasants and proprietors, who give little attention to these and other matters.

The difference in quality in the wine not even a week old was perceptible; and although that in the cellar of the possessor of a couple of hogsheads is as true St. George as that of M. Gordon, and a few others who are equally careful, still those who know the circumstances and treatment, or who taste the produce, will give three times as much for the one as for the other. Certainly no skill or attention could make that which I mention so good, were it not that M. Gordon's vineyard is upon a hill with a fine aspect, whence it enjoys a decided advantage over all others on the flat ground and on the plains; but unless there be also capital, skill, and patience, quantity may be got, but assuredly not quality.

The same reasoning applies to every vine-grower and vineyard in every place and country; but in some, and especially in the south of France, *quantity* is generally the object sought, provided it be such as will give body and colour to others.

I have tasted, however, some capital good-flavoured kinds, both red and white, in this quarter; and I may mention Tavel, Roquemaure, Lédénon, Saint Gilles (white), Laudun, and Cavisson, all from Languedoc; nor would I omit the Château-neuf-du-Pape, near Avignon, which, when genuine, of a good year, and old, is excellent.

The demand, for some years, for the wines of the south, from Nismes to the Banyuls, at the foot of the Eastern Pyrenees, has been so great, that prices have attained a height never before known, and there has been, in consequence, a great accession of wealth among all classes. Every nook and corner have been searched, and many who formerly used to take almost any price offered for their wines for *burning*, as it is called, that is, for distillation, are now aware that wine is valuable property. Such growers have, in consequence, been paying more attention to their vines; and in all quarters, from east to west, and north to south, new vineyards are seen; so that from these, and the greater care applied, we may expect, if favoured with a few abundant vintages, to see a great increase in the production of good wine.

As a proof of the rise in the price, owing to the oïdium, the following statements furnished by the

Chamber of Commerce of Montpellier, of the medium quality produced in the Hérault, is annexed; but it should be remembered these quotations are always for the wine itself, and in its new state, in the grower's cellar, exclusive of cask: —

In 1848,	7 francs per hectol. of 22 galls., which is	£0	12	0	per hhd.
In 1852,	9 „ „	0	15	0	„
In 1852,	15 „ „	1	5	0	„
In 1853,	30 „ „	2	10	0	„
In 1856,	40 „ „	3	7	0	„
In 1857,	28 „ „	2	7	0	„
In 1863,	15 common „ „	1	5	0	„
In 1863,	25 best „ „	2	0	0	„

The following letter, dated in 1805, with a Price Current of the same date, shows the prices of that period. How the expressions 'neutral on simulation' bring to our memory the days of convoys, privateering, forged papers, and Custom-house oaths!

MONTPELLIER: December 18, 1805.

PRICE CURRENT.

EXPORTS.

White Wines on board, commission excepted.

A Hogshead of 30 *velts.*

Rivesaltes Muscat wine, 1st quality, from 260 frs. to 250 frs., which is about £10 per hhd.

Frontignan Muscat wine, 1st quality, from 200 frs. to 210 frs., which is about £8 per hhd.

Lunel Muscat wine, 1st quality, from 200 frs. to 210 frs., which is about £8 per hhd.

Beziers Muscat wine, 1st quality, from 160 frs. to 180 frs., which is about £7 per hhd.

A Hogshead of 29 *velts.*

White Hermitage, 1st quality, from 380 frs. to 400 frs., which is about £16 per hhd.

White Hermitage, 2nd quality, from 310 frs. to 330 frs., which is about £13 per hhd.

Saint Peray, 1st quality, from 180 frs. to 200 frs., which is about £12 10*s.* per hhd.

Red Wines on board, commission excepted.

A Hogshead of 29 *velts.*

Red Hermitage, 1st quality, from 380 frs. to 400 frs., which is about £17 per hhd.

Red Hermitage, 2nd quality, from 310 frs. to 330 frs., which is about £13 per hhd.

Côte Rotie, 1st quality, from 260 frs. to 280 frs., which is about £11 per hhd.

Côte Rotie, 2nd quality, from 230 frs. to 240 frs., which is about £9 10*s.* per hhd.

Fine wine called Claret, 1st quality, from 100 frs., which is about £4 per hhd.

A Hogshead of 36 *velts.*

Red Tavel, 1st quality, 110 frs., which is about £4 per hhd.

Lirac, 1st quality, 105 frs., which is about £4 per hhd.

Saint Genies, 1st quality, 100 frs., which is about £4 per hhd.

Chusclan, 1st quality, 110 frs., which is about £4 5*s.* per hhd.

A Hogshead of 45 *velts.*

St. George's, 1st quality, 105 frs., which is about £3 10*s.* per hhd.

St. Drezery, 1st quality, 105 frs., which is about £3 10*s.* per hhd.

Roussillon strengthened alike Porto, 140 frs., which is about £4 15*s.* per hhd.

MONTPELLIER: December 18, 1805.

GENTLEMEN,—We confirm you our last respects of August 7th last, and beg your reference to the wishes we often expressed you, of being useful to your respectable house; and as we think it proper to acquaint you with the new prices of our articles, we take the liberty to hand you here annexed our price current, with the hope that the actual statement of the brandy and its good quality will induce you to favour us with your commands. Our punctuality and exertions will be such as will give you satisfaction, and insure us the continuance of your confidence.

You will find mentioned in the said price current the quotation of the colonial produces here; and should you determine to address us a *neutral on simulation*, loaded with such articles, you may rely upon our cares to sale them at your best advantage.—Waiting for your kind reply, we subscribe ourselves, very respectfully,

Gentlemen,

Your most humble, obedient Servants,

(Signed) B. Martin Lainé & Co.

Messrs. Yeats & Brown,
London.

It is the fashion to allude to Cette as a place where all sorts of adulterations are practised. Adulteration means the admixture of foreign matters with the juice of the grape. This is practised in Cette as well as in many other places, but probably comparatively little there; because there is such an ample choice of every description of grape-juice for honest blending, that some of the kinds are cheaper, and more suitable for the imitations desired than anything else. It is alleged, that if you tell a Cette merchant at 9 A.M. you wish to have 50 pipes of port, 50 butts of sherry, and 50 hogsheads of claret, he will promise to deliver them at 4 P.M. There is a good deal of (exaggerated) truth in this; but he can accomplish it, because he possesses an almost unlimited supply of a great variety of wines, with body and flavours which his experience has taught him how to use; so that, by certain combinations, he will produce a remarkably close resemblance to that of any other quality or country.

Walking along the quays, one is reminded of the London Docks, for there are rows of pipes, butts, hogsheads, quarters, and puncheons, made exactly like Portuguese, Spanish, and Madeira casks, and with very deceptive marks and brands, which are sent to all parts of the world, where they are not likely to be distinguished from the originals.

Marseilles and Cette are the great dépôts for the reception and exportation of the growths of several vinous departments; and in these towns enormous quantities are collected. The only way to procure a particular growth in its original state, is to go to the farmer who has it still in his cellar, and then you may generally trust in its purity; though not entirely, for some, when they have sold off their own stock, contrive, in the dark, to bring more into their stores and sell it as their own growth.

It does not follow that because a wine is only of one growth, and unmixed with any other, it is therefore better. On the contrary, it very frequently happens that it might be much improved by being mixed, not only with one, but with several others, so as to combine body and bouquet. No rules can be laid down for effecting this; but it should be remembered that what is desired by the seller, as much as by the buyer and consumer, is the quality that is most liked, and which will be most saleable and agreeable; for no business will continue to improve, if not founded on this basis. It must also be recollected, that although very excellent wine may often be found in a farmer's cellar, in general it is only that kind which he himself has grown and made; and should the various qualities of the district be wanted, they must be sought for throughout the department.

This is how the Paris and other wine-merchants of France, and often of Belgium, Germany, and Holland act, viz. *blending*, when they have got them in their own cellars, to suit their trade. So also must English merchants do, if they hope successfully to compete with others. But, although it is essentially necessary to be accompanied by a respectable broker of the locality, it is useless to attempt to purchase in this way, if one is ignorant of the language. It is surprising how few of the old English wine-merchants speak even French.

Should the operation here described be properly conducted, the same wine, which would be charged 100*l.* in a town merchant's cellar, might probably be bought from the grower for 80*l.*

Even in Frontignan and Lunel, so noted for their few casks of delicious sweet wine, much of the land is now used for the common dark quality. The best liqueur wines of that district are now from Marasson.

In the neighbourhood of Toulon, Avignon, Nismes, and wherever there are hills and loose calcareous or volcanic ground, there is sure to be good wine; but after leaving Montpellier, the country is nearly a plain as far as Perpignan in the Roussillon, and until it approaches the base of the Eastern Pyrenees.

From L'Hérault and Languedoc, through Beziers and Narbonne, the railway reaches as far as Perpignan, passing through Rivesaltes, celebrated for its delicious liqueur wine. Being there late in

September, it was wonderful to see vines, vines, vines, as far as the eye could reach; and strange to look upon the vineyards, with their green leaves and masses of black grapes, giving the whole a most peculiar appearance. Men, women, and children were busy cutting, gathering, loading, and conveying; and immense tubfulls of grapes were on little carts drawn by oxen, mules, or horses, or slung over the backs of the latter; but in vain one sought for dancing or singing, or the romance of the vineyard. All was very unpoetical hard work.

Except having a fortification, with a large garrison, and being an old, irregularly-built town, formerly belonging to the kings of Arragon, there is nothing much worth seeing in Perpignan; but I remarked that the farther south I went the less courteous and polite the people appeared to be, contrasting unfavourably with Northern France; and this drawback to the pleasure of travelling seemed to prevail still more on getting into Spain.

The next morning I hired a cabriolet, which took me in three or four hours to Port-Vendres. I wish I could describe in adequate language the journey. On leaving the town, there is a magnificent view of the range of the Pyrénées Orientales, which divide France from Spain, varying in height, shape, and colour with the shades and reflections produced by the almost tropical sun; and in the distance was the ever snow-capped Carrigou. Stopping at Elne, I went into a wine-shop, where I tried several kinds of the wine made in the neighbourhood, and found one bottle, which my host brought from some quiet

THE WINE-SHOP AT ELNE.

corner, covered with cob-webs, very good indeed. The country from Elne is one of hill and dale, with a loose argillaceous soil, and with such aspects that growths might be produced there that would vie with any in Médoc or Burgundy.

The driver informing me that he knew one of the principal growers in Collioure, I requested him to take me to his house, and, after winding through two or three narrow streets of that little place, we halted at his door, which was opened by a nice-looking old man, who invited me to enter. Nothing could exceed his or his wife's kindness, and from him I gained a great deal of information. He gave me some of the wine he drinks himself, which, like all other that I saw in this country, was common, and without fine flavour, but being almost invariably taken as a beverage, diluted with water, is as good as he and others care to have. After chatting and becoming good friends, he told me he would give me a bottle that had never left the bin it was put in at first, and that it was as old as myself. I thought this must be old wine indeed, for he might easily see I was past the three-score; but down he went, and soon returned with a venerable-looking, strange-shaped bottle, from which he drew the cork with great care, filled a glass for himself, his wife, and me. After hob-nobbing, I put it to my nose, looking very solemn and thoughtful; then, repeating the same ceremony, put it to my lips, and having moved it in my mouth long enough to appear a very critical judge, I pronounced the word *Doux* (sweet)! This was enough to set him agoing. He then told me that it was part of a cask of white sweet wine which his father had made, and that there were still half-a-dozen bottles remaining. It had never been equal to a good Rivesaltes, and I was again forcibly reminded of the proverb about the 'silk purse.'

During the whole ride, the Mediterranean was in full view close on the left, Collioure being washed by its waves; while on the right there is a succession of hills and vineyards; and in and around the village are trees covered with figs, oranges, olives, and also flowers of the most brilliant hues. Ascending a very steep hill, we soon arrived at Port Vendres; a very unpretending little place, but with a deep harbour, completely protected by hills and mountains from any gales that can blow. As the railway will soon be finished, it is probable that its proximity to Algiers will ere long make it a town of considerable importance. At present, it is known for a safe harbour, and as a great dépôt for the wines of the district. I went through the two largest establishments, and found both on a scale of such magnitude, that, although I have seen many in various countries, these altogether exceeded every other.

Here, for the first time, I saw wine-rooms formed entirely of masonry, each capable of containing about 8,000 gallons. They are called *cuves*, and are used to form cuvées of one quality from the growths of many vineyards, which have been put into this cuve to remain till the whole has become homogeneous. Ascending by a ladder to the top, I experienced a strange sensation, on looking, through an opening, into the lake of grape-juice contained in each of these vast chambers.

When the various kinds have lain long enough there to be sufficiently amalgamated, the clear wine is conveyed by tubes to the great store-casks, containing two or three thousand gallons each.

It is easy to imagine the mass of 'marc,' of stalks, and of skins which must be left in each 'room.' In parts where wine is not so plentiful, these are collected together, water is poured over them, and they are put into the press; and that which is pressed out is made into wine for the workmen. In other places it is converted into brandy, but here the residues are usually thrown into one or two chambers, to keep them fresh; when pieces are cut off as from a haystack, to feed the mules, pigs, and sheep during winter; and are found very strengthening and fattening. We must not go to that quarter to seek for fine qualities; still, it is from the South that France receives her great supplies, and from which the means are gained of rendering more palatable many kinds from the more northern provinces, which are usually too thin and poor without admixture; likewise those which, though excellent generally, require invigorating in bad years.

As a rule, in all wine countries, the actual farmers or growers of wine rarely keep it even for a year, selling it, if they can, to merchants, so as to have their casks ready for the next year's vintage; and, for some time past, there has been so great a run upon the South wines, that scarcely such a thing exists in the growers' sellers as even a '61. They are now all in the hands of merchants and speculators.

The first time I tasted the wine of this department was about forty years ago, when I was shown sample hogsheads sent over to try the London market; and the same have ever since been known as Masdeu. This name is given from a very extensive property a few miles from Perpignan, on the road to

Spain, belonging to a rich banker, who has bestowed upon it such care as is rarely known in France.

The first arrivals were not much liked, they had a mawkish, sweetish flavour and taste; but Ports were then dear, and, although it was generally thought the price fixed for the Masdeu was much too high, yet, being evidently a true wine, and suited for cheapening Ports, considerable quantities were sold.

Ports fell in price, and many were disappointed with their Masdeu, and its very name seemed to have vanished; but about ten years ago the same gentleman who had first introduced it, took it again in hand, and it is now sold to a large extent. He has been well supported by rich, intelligent men, who had always a just, well-grounded confidence in him, and acceded to almost any suggestion he offered. As an instance, I have been told, that when he informed them that the peculiar flavour and taste were attributed to the casks being of chestnut wood, they immediately put those aside and incurred a great expense in getting oak casks made.

Their wealth enabled them to act according to his wish to keep up a regular stock, as is done in Oporto and Xeres; so that those who give an order this year for the same class they had received one, two, or three years before, may get it, as nearly as nature will admit.

I am not aware of any other house in these great districts which holds stock in the same way. This gentleman has assuredly had such support and cooperation as seldom fall to the lot of anyone; but his friends have shown a shrewd appreciation of their own interest; for I have no hesitation in saying there is not one other man in the wine trade of London who could have accomplished what he has done by his straightforward indomitable energy, perseverance, and resolution.

The next day I returned to Perpignan, and thence to Toulouse, through vines on all sides; and thence to Bordeaux, passing the vineyards of Langon, Preignac, Barsac, and Graves, a few miles from Bordeaux.

It was easy to remark in all parts a decided improvement in the care of the vines during the last few years. Every weed extracted gives additional vigour to the plant and its produce.

The encouragement of high prices has induced many to root out their olive-trees, and to plant vineyards; which, with the greater care bestowed upon them, will lead to the production of increased quantities and superior quality.

CHAPTER X.

PARIS, BERCY.

Great Dépôt for Wines — Large Cellars at Bercy — Entrepôt des Vins—Octroi and Charges in Paris—Counting-houses at Bercy—Water— Restaurants—Consumption of Wine in Paris and in England—Extension of Octroi—'Liberté et Égalité'—The 'Marseillaise'—'Ordre Publique'—Wine Adulterations severely punished.

PARIS being a great dépôt for the wines from every part of France, not only for its own consumption, but as a general market, it ought not to be omitted in a treatise upon the wines of France. At Bercy, in the suburbs, there are very extensive cellars and warehouses for the storing of wines and spirits, which are justly considered one of the sights of Paris.

Each merchant rents a cellar, and has the entire control of all within it. Some are of immense size, full of liquids. The charge on a hogshead varies according to the rent of the cellar, but it is usually estimated at about 10*d.* per hogshead per annum, and the octroi and other town dues amount to about 10*d.* per gallon. Every holder of wine at Bercy has a counting-house attached; and here he may be found almost every afternoon, often accompanied by his wife or daughters, who occupy themselves in sewing; and a party of whist is often formed. The gentlemen may be seen smoking, but never drinking anything but coffee. A friend was so good as to accede to my request to be allowed to pass a few hours with him in his cellar, where he showed me his

BERCY.

various qualities, almost all of which were of a common kind—the usual character of the wines deposited in Bercy. Most of them were stout, deep-coloured, and young, and far from being agreeable. Upon my expressing this opinion, he said, laughingly, 'Wait a little, and I shall soon make you change your opinion.' I have often heard of the 'watering' of wines, but never saw it practised till he brought a little water, and, pouring some into a tumbler of new Narbonne, made a light

INTERIOR OF CELLAR AT BERCY.

pleasant wine. How long it would 'stand' I cannot say; but he informed me that about ten per cent. of water is generally added to such as I have described, and does not injure it. He further volunteered to state that these are the kinds supplied to restaurants; and that, if our countrymen and others desire to have the next bottle, *à la* Estèphe or

Larose, or any other *la*, instead of the St. Emilion, &c. which they disapprove of, the change of bin, effected by a good dash of water, will be found to possess the peculiar bouquet and body of their favourite vintage and growth!

My friend informed me that every cask in his cellar is fined and racked into fresh casks in March and September, and then filled to the bung; and that he generally does this four times a year to such as are quite new, in order to forward and *age* them. To attain this object, white wine is also very frequently added. Invariably, before racking into a fresh cask, he inserts a lighted sulphur-match to see if it burns bright; for, if it does not, he is sure it is not quite clean, and therefore has it thoroughly rinsed before trying it again. While I was with him, many customers, mostly restaurateurs, hotel-keepers, &c., called, each of them buying a few hogsheads; on each of which he told me he got a profit of 10, 20, or 30 francs.

According to the official statement, it appears that the consumption of all kinds of liquids in Paris, in 1861, was, with its population of 1,616,141, as follows:—

Wine	49,993,839	galls., which is	185	bottles per head.
Spirits and liqueurs.	2,278,408	,,	8	,,
Cyder	1,927,838	,,	7	,,
Beer	8,276,708	,,	31	,,
	62,476,793 gallons.			

There are no means of making the comparison with

London, but the total consumption of wine in the United Kingdom, in 1861, with 29,500,000 inhabitants, was 10,787,209 gallons, or two bottles per head.

Within these few years, the precincts of the city have been considerably extended, including many parts within the octroi, which formerly escaped this municipal tax. Such has been the case with an immense establishment where I remember getting a well-cooked substantial dinner (whether of horse or bullock I know not) for 4*d.*, and a bottle of wine for 3*d.* This was in 1848, when the expulsion of Louis Philippe was succeeded by the most enthusiastic rejoicings over the fact that, at length, had arrived for France, *Liberté et Égalité*—words which met one's ears and eyes at every corner.

The master of the place assured me that he sold yearly upwards of 500 hogsheads, about 132,000 bottles; which I can fully believe, because it was crammed full; and never did I see a more jovial set of people, resolved to express their happiness by song, and noise, and dancing. Entering into their feelings, and joining in the hope (futile it has proved) that they had at length gained the liberty they have so well deserved, I joined vociferously in the *Parisienne* and *Marseillaise*; touching glasses, and shaking hands with all around, and receiving embraces from a few who rejoiced to see a son of their old enemy—*la perfide Albion*—sympathising with them so heartily. Throughout the large room, mirth and songs resounded, and, above all, were heard the words associated with so many fearful scenes in the history of France:—

Allons, enfants de la Patrie,
Le jour de gloire est arrivé,
Contre nous de la tyrannie
L'étendard sanglant est élevé.
Aux armes, citoyens!
Formez vos bataillons;
Marchez! marchez! &c., &c.

Français! pour nous, ah! quel outrage,
Quels transports il doit exciter,
C'est nous qu'on ôse méditer
De rendre à l'antique esclavage.
Aux armes, citoyens! &c.

Quoi! des cohortes étrangères
Feraient la loi dans nos foyers!
Quoi! ces phalanges mercenaires
Terrasseraient nos fiers guerriers!
Aux armes, citoyens! &c.

Amour sacré de la patrie,
Conduis, soutiens nos bras vengeurs;
Liberté, Liberté chérie,
Que tes ennemis expirants
Voient ton triomphe, et notre gloire.
Aux armes, citoyens! &c.

It was a short time afterwards that I saw the blood of, perhaps, some of those same men, on the boulevards and other places; and some of the finest buildings nearly destroyed by round shot and musketry; with the flag of 'Liberté,' 'Egalité,' and 'Fraternité,' so conspicuous formerly, now converted into 'Ordre Publique.'

The punishment for adulterations is severe in France, as the following extract from a newspaper shows:—

Boille, 10 Rue Feutoier.—Falsification, eight days' imprisonment, 2*l*. fine.

Dauvois—Bercy.—For falsification, and for employing mixtures injurious to health, in the Entrepôt des Vins, at Bercy, one month's imprisonment, 2*l*. fine, seizure of the wine, public notification of the trial and sentence on the gates of the Entrepôt, and on the door of Dauvois' cellar.

Pasqualini, 136 Rue d'Allemagne.—Falsification of wine, one month's imprisonment, 2*l*. fine, ten advertisements.

CHAPTER XI.

RHINE AND MOSELLE.

Im Kühlen Keller — Rheingau Vineyards — The Press — White and Red Wines — Palatinate — Racking — Prices — Rüdesheim, Johannisberg, &c. — Schloss Johannisberg — Cabinet Wines — Steinberg — Rüdesheimer — Geisenheimer Rothenberg — Hochheimer — Assmannshausen — Rheinhessen — The Pfalz — Rhenish Bavaria — Bocksbeutel — Moselle — Trêves — The Saar — Sparkling Moselle — Preparation — Information as to Buying — Old Brown Hock — Gauges in Nassau, Hesse, Frankfort — Das Gläschen — Consumption, Quantity, and per-Centage, from 1831 to 1862.

IM KÜHLEN KELLER.

**Im kühlen Keller sitz' ich hier, auf einem Fass voll Reben,
Bin frohen Muth's, und lasse mir vom Allerbesten geben.
Der Küper zieht den Heber voll, gehorsam meinem Winke,
Reicht mir das Glas, ich halt's empor, und trinke, trinke, trinke.**

**Mich plagt ein Dämon, Durst genannt, doch um ihn zu verscheuchen,
Nehm' ich mein Deckelglas zur Hand, und lass' mir Rheinwein reichen.
Die ganze Welt erscheint mir nun in rosenrother Schminke;
Ich könnte Niemand Leides thun, ich trinke, trinke, trinke.**

**Allein mein Durst vermehrt sich nur bei jedem vollen Becher,
Dies ist die leidige Natur der echten Rheinweinzecher!
Doch tröst' ich mich, wenn ich zuletzt vom Fass zu Boden sinke,
Ich habe keine Pflicht verletzt, ich trinke, trinke, trinke.**

OF all wine-producing countries, no vineyards are cultivated with such care as those in the wine districts of Germany. There is a universal interest taken in the growth of the vines, and a universal pleasure in their progress. Even the poor man, ill paid for his hard labour, prefers employment in the vineyards, although obtaining considerably less wages, than by working in the mines of the neighbourhood. His daily pay is only 1*s.* 4*d.*; his toil begins in summer at five in the morning and finishes at seven in the evening, with only an hour-and-a-half's rest in the middle of the day.

The larger proprietors seldom engage their men by the day, but contract with some one to take charge of their vineyard for a stipulated sum, usually about 50*s.* per acre.

The vineyards are small, and in various localities. The ground is very unequal, and in a few minutes' walk many varieties of soils are found. The best is on the hills in the Rheingau, consisting of hard gravelly clay and stones; the latter, by retaining the heat of the sun, diffuse warmth to the neighbouring earth.

The worst soil is a soft, yellow clay, on which the wine is generally abundant; but, owing to its being wet and cold, of poor quality. On the left, or Hessian bank, the soil is sandy, and there the grapes ripen earlier than on the heavy soils opposite.

There is now a conviction that wine made from grapes perfectly ripe is much the best; indeed, is so very superior, that the vintage is often delayed to such a late period of the season as to incur the danger of injury from frost, and still more so from continued wet, which rots and withers the grapes. In the best vineyards it is usual to gather the fine ripe bunches first, from which is obtained what is called the 'auslese,' or 'first gathering.' Some owners of noted growths even pick out the faulty grapes from these fine bunches, in order to make the choicest wine possible. There is a very careful second gather-

BOY TREADING GRAPES.

ing; and the remainder is used to make the general and common kinds. The grapes are usually gathered by women and children, who carry them to the intersecting footpaths, where men are waiting to receive them, who immediately throw them from the baskets into a small perforated tub, in which a boy treads and crushes them so that all pass through the holes into the larger tub below.

Sometimes the grapes are put into a wooden vessel, in which they are broken by means of heavy pieces of wood; and at other times they are placed in a cask similar to a churn, which reduces them almost to a state of pulp. When a sufficient quantity is thus prepared, large tubs, formed to be strapped to the back, are filled and carried by men to a cart brought as near as possible, upon which is a large cask with a funnel, into which are poured juice, skins, and stalks, which are then conveyed to the press-house.

DISCHARGING THE TRODDEN GRAPES.

By means of a large opening at the end of the cask, the whole flows into tubs, which are carried to the press, where the operation of pressing is effected.

The accompanying sketches will render the description more intelligible.

The pressure at first must be gentle, to prevent the overflowing of the juice, but it is afterwards gradually increased. The pure juice, without admixture of either skins or stalks, then passes out through two holes which are in front of the wine-press, and runs into a small vat underneath, and is thence conveyed by pipes into casks in the cellar. The colour of the juice is yellow; it is thick, and its taste is pleasant and sweet. The casks into which it is passed must be well cleaned with hot water, and afterwards sulphured.

After the press has been screwed down for about three hours, little juice remains, and it is then loosened. The residue is now a hard mass, but the action of the presses not being so strong at the sides as in the centre, the edges are cut away all round, then broken up small, and replaced under the press. This wine has not nearly so much body as the other, and is seldom mixed with it, but kept apart, being of a very inferior quality.

It was formerly the custom of the larger proprietors to give their labourers a great entertainment at the close of the harvest. These festivities are becoming rarer every year, but instead, they receive a small present. It is often November before the vintage in the Rheingau begins, so that frost has frequently set in; the grapes become frozen, and the skins of a reddish-yellow colour. It is believed that this does not deteriorate the quality of the wine, and that the saccharine matter and the alcohol cannot be injured by the cold.

There is no doubt, however, that the quantity is

considerably diminished, and that the wine obtained from frozen grapes requires more time to become bright, and ripe for bottling.

The greater part are white, but a certain proportion of black are always to be found among them. Should the wine ferment before it is separated from the stalks, the colour in the black skins would be extracted, and, being mixed with the white juice, would give to the whole a pinkish colour, which is never liked in Rhine wine. Besides, the fermentation would draw out the bitter taste of the stalks and impregnate the wine with it. It is of the greatest importance for the grapes to be pressed as soon as possible; and on this account large proprietors employ three or four wine-presses at once.

With red wine the case is quite the reverse. The grapes must ferment with the stalks in vats for nearly eight days; so that the red colour may be extracted from the stalks and skins, as well as the bitter taste.

After the juice has been left quiet in the cask in the cellar for two or three days it begins to ferment, and continues working often for four weeks or more. Should the weather be so cold as to hinder the fermentation, the necessary warmth is supplied by means of a stove. It is important to notice whether the wine really ferments fully at harvest-time. If this is not so, it begins again in June, and therefore takes much longer to ripen.

A fermenting-machine instrument is placed upon

each cask, by means of which the carbonic acid gas is prevented from escaping into the cellar. Before this was invented, it was necessary to burn straw in order to expel the gas, or a windmill was put in motion to disperse it, and thus prevent the danger of suffocation.

In the Rheingau, as well as in the Palatinate of Hesse, the wine is generally put into stück or half stück casks; but in Rhenish Bavaria casks of from four to six stücks or more are used. During the time of fermentation, it is frequently roused by the application of a heavy iron chain, that the thicker portion may rise and all properly ferment together.

In spring it is, for the first time, drawn off from the lees. In a stück there are usually about 10 gallons of lees and *thick* wine. This has a clayey appearance, and yellow colour. It is put into sacks, and pressed in the wine-press; the wine which oozes out being used for filling up, after it has been made clear.

Six weeks after the first drawing off from the lees, the wine is racked off a second time. This is again done in the following autumn, when it is one year old. Afterwards it is racked every spring and autumn. Every four or five weeks the wine has to be filled up. When it is from two to three years old, it may be safely bottled.

There is, perhaps, a greater variety in Rhine wine than in any other, both as regards price and quality. For instance, in Rüdesheim, Geisenheim, or Johannisberg, wines are to be had from about 5*l.* up to 60*l.* per aum.

It is evident from this that the difference does not consist merely in the names of the several growths; since there are some of the finest and most inferior sorts produced in Rüdesheim and Johannisberg, as well as in most of the other districts in the Rheingau. It often happens that on the same hill two or three kinds are growing which differ widely from one another in quality; for example, the lower or north side of a hill produces a wine which is not half so valuable as on that which faces the south.

Besides this, the age, the treatment and manuring of the vineyard, all exercise an important influence on the quality. The difference of price in the Palatinate is not so great as in the Rheingau—arising from the fact that the country is much flatter, and the varieties of soil are not so numerous.

The growths of the Palatinate and of Rhenish Bavaria, &c. are generally sold at low prices compared with those of the Rheingau. The larger proprietors generally have their wine sold by auction, while the smaller ones dispose of theirs through brokers. The former realise by auction proportionately higher prices, as their wines are in great repute. These rich owners of large vineyards are certainly entitled to distinction for their fine wines, inasmuch as they possess the best vineyards, which are exceedingly expensive. The middle class of land-owners are seldom able to purchase vineyards of this description. The prices which are obtained for this first quality, are generally far beyond their value. Every wine-dealer is desirous of having in his cellar a little of these fine growths; and, as the quantity is small, they reach 'fancy prices.' But persons who do not absolutely require the very finest do best to make their purchases, by means of a broker, from one of the middling-class proprietors.

It is to be regretted that there are so few good vintages on the Rhine. Extraordinarily fine as its wine is in good years, it is proportionately bad in others; it is then unpleasant, and its consumption is almost confined to the country itself. A slight acidity is a natural characteristic; but, from the reports of medical men, it appears that this is by no means prejudicial to health.

A few proprietors are in the habit, in bad years, of mixing sugar with their wine, to make it more agreeable.

The following song in praise of Rhine wine is well known everywhere, and much sung by Germans:—

Rheinweinlied.

Bekränzt mit Laub den lieben, vollen Becher,
  Und trinkt ihn fröhlich leer!
In ganz Europia, ihr Herren Zecher,
  Ist solch ein Wein nicht mehr!

Er kommt nicht her aus Ungarn, noch aus Polen,
  Noch wo man franzmänn'sch spricht!
Da mag Sanct Veit, der Ritter, Wein sich holen,
  Wir holen ihn da nicht.

Wie wär' er sonst so edel, wäre stille
  Und doch voll Kraft und Muth!
Ihn bringt das Vaterland aus seiner Fülle
  Wie wär' er sonst so gut!

Er wächst nicht überall im deutschen Reiche,
Und viele Berge, hört,
Sind wie die weiland Kreter, faule Bäuche,
Und nicht der Stelle werth.

Thüringens Berge, zum Exempel, bringen
Gewächs, sieht aus wie Wein,
Ist's aber nicht; man kann dabei nicht singen,
Dabei nicht fröhlich sein.

Im Erzgebirge dürft ihr auch nicht suchen,
Wenn Wein ihr finden wollt.
Das bringt nur Silbererz und Kobaldkuchen
Und etwas Lausegold.

Der Blocksberg ist der lange Herr Philister,
Er macht nur Wind, wie der;
D'rum tanzen auch der Kuckuk und sein Küster
Auf ihm die Kreuz und Quer.

Am Rhein, am Rhein, da wachsen unsre Reben,
Gesegnet sei der Rhein!
Da wachsen sie am Ufer hin und geben
Uns diesen Labewein!

So trinkt, so trinkt, und lasst uns alle Wege
Uns freu'n und fröhlich sein!
Und wüssten wir wo Jemand traurig läge,
Wir gäben ihm den Wein.

THE RHEINGAU.

The wine district most favoured by nature is the Rheingau. It is situated on the right bank of the Rhine, extending about twenty-five miles, *i.e.* from Walluf to Lorch; and is about eight miles in width. The whole region is a chain of hills, which, extending along the river, produces the world-renowned Rhine wine. The steep hills are formed into terraces, one above the other, to prevent the soil giving way. On smaller hills this is not necessary. The greater part of the grapes grown here are Riesling; besides these, there are a large number of Oestreicher, Kleinberger and Kleb-Roth. Orleans grapes are more scarce; they are for the most part only on the Rüdesheim hill. The Riesling wine is, in good years, considerably better than Oestreicher, Kleinberger, or Kleb-Roth. It is distinguished by its flavour, aroma, and strength, and always improves by age.

In bad years, however, the Oestreicher, &c. are preferred, as they become ripe earlier than Riesling, and consequently yield in those years a more agreeable wine. The Orleans grapes cannot be cultivated in cold flat soils, as they require much warmth. They are generally planted on warm sunny hills, as for example on the Rüdesheim-Berg; and, even there, in cold wet years they do not thrive. In favourable seasons they yield a remarkably fine quality, distinguished by body and flavour.

In the centre of the Rheingau the castle of Johannisberg stands on the summit of the hill, surrounded by splendid vineyards, producing a wine that may be fearlessly compared with any in the world. The late Prince Metternich received this estate as a present from the Emperor of Austria.

The annual produce is from 320 to 400 aums, but the quantity which is sold by wine-merchants under its name is greatly more. The price of the genuine 'Schloss Johannisberg' is enormous. The charge for a bottle at the castle is about 20*s*. But the previous remark, that the quality of the wines produced on every hill varies considerably, is confirmed by the fact, that on the very hill of Johannisberg they have also wine which can be had at about 4*s*. per bottle!

Everyone may purchase the Johannisberg wine direct from the cellar, and there is no need to apply to an agent. Many German wine-merchants are agents for the sale, receiving a commission of 10 per cent. The Cabinet wines were formerly sold in bottle only, bearing the seal of the prince as a guarantee that they were genuine. Of late, however, a portion is sold in casks by auction.

An equally high reputation is enjoyed by the Steinberg, which is situated between Hattenheim and Erbach. This magnificent vineyard was formerly the property of the monastery of Eberbach; but its present proprietor is the Duke of Nassau, who does his utmost to uphold its character.

The Steinberg produces about twice as much as the Johannisberg, and is planted exclusively with Riesling grapes.

The most beautiful and most extensive of all the hills on the Rhine is the Rüdesheimer Berg. It is 400 acres in extent, and is covered almost to the summit with vineyards. As it is very precipitous, it is divided into a large number of terraces, supported by thick walls. Many of the grapes are Orleans, and the wine from this hill is in great repute.

The Rüdesheimer Hinterhaus is also much

esteemed; the grapes are chiefly Riesling, producing a very aromatic wine. The vineyards are divided among numerous proprietors, who can generally afford to keep them in good order.

About two miles farther up the Rhine is the Geisenheimer Rothenberg, but not nearly so extensive, producing a wine of similar quality to that grown on the Rüdesheimer Berg. The soil is quite red, and hence the hill derives its name.

The Marcobrunnen, in the upper Rheingau, is also a wine of first quality. Its principal proprietor is the Count of Schönborn.

Hochheimer is usually considered among the finest of the Rhenish wines; the Hochheimer Dom Dechaney is especially noted. The village does not lie on the Rhine, but on the Maine; notwithstanding, its produce is included among the Rhenish wines. It is supposed that the English name of 'Hock' is derived from Hochheim.

The principal wine districts in the Rheingau are Rüdesheim, Geisenheim, Winkel, Mittelheim, Oestrich, Hallgarten, Hattenheim, Erbach, Eltville, Assmannshausen, and Lorch.

These places produce in good years a great quantity, both at low and high prices. The wine produced is everywhere white, with the exception of Assmannshausen and Ingelheim. The latter place has a high reputation in Germany for its red wines. As the quantity is not very great, it sometimes realises exceedingly high prices.

RHEINHESSEN.

The wines of Rheinhessen, or the Palatinate, grow on the left bank of the Rhine. This district produces twice as much as the Rheingau, but, as regards quality, is not to be compared with it. Those of Hesse, which grow in Nierstein, Oppenheim, Bodenheim, Laubenheim, and on the Scharlachberg, near Bingen, are classed among the second quality of Rhenish wines. The rest are considered third quality; but are, nevertheless, very agreeable, though deficient in body.

RHENISH BAVARIA.

A large quantity of wine—good, but not first-class—is grown here. The Riesling and Traminer growths are very excellent. The inferior wines, on the other hand, have often an earthy taste. The principal wine districts are, Deidesheim, Dürkheim, Forst, Wachenheim, and Ungstein.

The Stein, or Leisten wines—the former generally kept in peculiar-shaped bottles, called 'Bocksbeutel'—are from the neighbourhood of Würzburg. They are well known for their body, strength, and sweetness, but possess little flavour.

MOSELLE DISTRICT.

The wine territories on the Moselle, properly speaking, extend only from Coblentz to Trêves; but it is customary also to include amongst them a few places which lie above Trêves, on the Saar, under the designation of the Saarwein land. The soil consists of small slate, which, with the vines, is not unfrequently swept away by heavy rains.

It is only in good years—that is to say, hot summers and warm autumns—that the quality is fine.

The grapes are Kleinberger, Rieslinge, and Klebroth. The Kleinberger are the most abundant throughout the whole district. In Zeltingen and Brauneberg, Rieslinge are principally grown. The Klebroth produces red wines at Kersten, and on the lower Moselle.

Moselle is known as the oldest German wine. It is quite bright, with a somewhat greenish-yellow colour, like the small young wines in Rhenish Hesse—never gold-coloured—with a certain amount of freshness; it possesses little fire, and is even cold and very dry. It has a light, agreeable flavour, and is well adapted for a cool refreshing summer drink. Its flavour is principally developed from grapes which have not been much exposed to the sun. It is the fault of the cultivators that it has such a green appearance; for the vines are trained too high, and sufficient care is not used in making the wine.

Moselle will not keep longer than from six to ten years, and this is also the case with the red. It is well known that it is very wholesome, and less heating than any other.

As the Palatinate wine can be had much cheaper than Moselle, it is frequently sold under the name of the latter.

On both sides, from Lorch to the Ahr, a great

number of pleasant wines grow, which are, nevertheless, little known in the trade. The Ahr may be called the lower boundary of the Rhine growths.

Baden, Wurtemberg, and Austria, produce a great quantity, scarcely known beyond their localities.

The following pretty lines describe the progress of wine, from the state of grape till it has gone into the bottle, has been drunk, and is at length exhaled in the fumes of poetry :—

Kreislauf des Wein's.

Aus der Traube in die Tonne,
Aus der Tonne in das Fass,
Aus dem Fasse dann, o' Wonne,
In die Flasche und in's Glas.

Aus dem Glase in die Kehle,
Aus der Kehle in den Schlund,
Und als Blut dann in die Seele,
Und als Wort dann in den Mund.

Aus dem Worte etwas später
Formt sich ein begeisternd Lied,
Das durch Wolken in den Aether
Mit dem Menschen Jubel zieht.

Und im nächsten Frühling wieder
Fallen diese Lieder fein,
Dann als Thau auf Reben nieder,—
Und sie werden wieder Wein!

SPARKLING RHINE AND MOSELLE WINES.

Although the making of these wines is still of recent date, it has already increased considerably, and is gaining more and more attention every day. The principal places for their manufacture are Hochheim, Mayence, Frankfort, and Coblentz.

Most of them are made from Palatinate wines, as these are particularly adapted for the purpose. The so-called 'Sparkling Moselle' is also generally made from the growths of the same district, and has a peculiar flavour, supposed to belong to the wines of the Moselle, but with which it has no similarity, being imparted by the following process. In a slight degree, it is not disagreeable, and is much liked by ladies; but it is frequently overdone to a nauseous extent:—

The small flowers of the elder-tree are carefully plucked from the stalks, and steeped in wine for some hours, after which they are passed through a very fine strainer, and added to the wine. This decoction improves much by age.

The process of making the wine sparkle, and all other preparations, are exactly the same as those in use with champagne.

Many German sparkling wines are fraudulently sold as champagne, under the assumed names of various well-known French firms; and for this object, the brands on the corks and cases, and the labels on the bottles, are imitated so exactly, that they cannot be distinguished.

A great drawback to the success of German wines in England may be traced to the high prices at which they are sold. The merchant on the Rhine usually charges 100 per cent., and even more, on the price of the grower, when for sale in England, Russia, &c.; and as, of course, the English merchant must charge his profit, it thus often happens that, before the wine reaches the consumer, it has risen enormously. The proper way is for the English wine-merchant to purchase direct from the grower, and thus to save the intermediate profit; but he must then buy not less than a stück, for growers have rarely even half stücks for sale.

He should find out who is the most trustworthy broker in the locality, get him to send samples, and, when he has decided upon what he wishes, should transmit the amount; for, as a rule, the farmers and proprietors are always paid as soon as the cask is placed on the buyer's cart.

Generally it may be arranged with the broker to have the stück racked into aums, if the extra expenses are paid. It is evident that it is scarcely possible to purchase in this way, unless there be a knowledge of the language. The broker's commission is usually 2 per cent. besides travelling expenses, &c. It is not advisable to buy very young wines, as these generally suffer from the voyage, and few in England know how to treat them. They should be at least two years old, and may then be kept in wood for a year longer, provided they be once, at least, drawn from the lees and kept filled up. The most advantageous time to purchase is after the vintage, for there are then many who, being in want of money, are anxious to sell. It cannot, of course, be taken as a uniform rule, that the wine is then cheapest, but it occurs, not unfrequently, that a vintage, considered fine at first, may not prove so in the end, and that prices will consequently fall.

Dealers usually keep wines in casks of a stück and half stück, rack them frequently off the lees, and fine them, so as to make them ready for sale as soon as possible. When a small cask has been filled from a larger, the one that the wine has been drawn from must be again filled up, as it is injurious to Rhenish wine to be left on ullage. If, from any cause, this cannot be avoided, a sulphur-match should be burned in the empty space, which will be a protection for two or three weeks. The empty casks ought to be well rinsed, placed in a fresh, airy store-room, often examined, and occasionally sulphured.

In bad seasons, the wines are often quite undrinkable, on account of their acid taste; and it is then usual, in order, in some degree, to counteract this, to put chalk into the cask, and, after it has lain for about a week, the wine is transferred to another cask. To impart a favourite amber colour, a little sugar is burned till it becomes brown, when a glass full is put into an aum, and the whole stirred about. Sometimes sherry, madeira, or teneriffe are employed to make what is called 'old brown hock,' formerly in great repute in this country, but now replaced by purer, young wines. On the Rhine itself quite new kinds are preferred, on account of the richer taste which these possess.

Merchants who have a foreign trade, generally add brandy in order to give more strength, but even the smallest quantity injures the delicate flavour of the growths of this district. Purchases by the merchants from the growers or farmers are always in stück (pieces), which are everywhere of the same gauge; but in Nassau and Hesse the stück fills only 7½ aums, while in Frankfort, where the aums are smaller, it fills 8 aums. It is not to be wondered at, according to the usages of trade, that the *sales* are according to the *Frankfort* aum.

Das Gläschen.

Ich nehm' mein Gläschen in die Hand,
  Vive la Compagnia!
Und fahr damit in's Unterland,
  Vive la Compagnia!
Vive la, vive la, vive la va,
Vive la, vive la hopsassa,
Vive la Compagnia!

Ich nehm' mein Gläschen wieder empor,
  Vive la Compagnia!
Und halt's an's recht und linke Ohr,
  Vive la Compagnia!
Vive la, vive la, vive la va,
Vive la, vive la hopsassa,
Vive la Compagnia!

Ich setz' mein Gläschen an den Mund,
  Vive la Compagnia!

Und trink' es aus bis auf den Grund,
Vive la Compagnia!
Vive la, vive la, vive la va,
Vive la, vive la hopsassa,
Vive la Compagnia!

Dem Gläschen ist sein Recht gescheh'n,
Vive la Compagnia!
Was unten ist, muss oben steh'n,
Vive la Compagnia!
Vive la, vive la, vive la va,
Vive la, vive la hopsassa,
Vive la Compagnia!

Das Gläschen muss nun wanderen,
Vive la Compagnia!
Von einem Freund zum anderen,
Vive la Compagnia!
Vive la, vive la, vive la va,
Vive la, vive la hopsassa,
Vive la Compagnia!

It is seen by the table of consumption, &c., that the consumption, and the per-centage which Rhenish bore to all other kinds, was:—

In 1831,	consumption	57,888	gallons and	0·93	per centage.
In 1841,	"	55,242	"	0·87	"
In 1851,	"	58,957	"	0·94	"
In 1859,	"	125,408	"	1·72	"
In 1860,	"	222,725	"	3·3	"
In 1861,	"	345,647	"	3·20	"
In 1862,	"	316,440	"	3·22	"

In reference to this statement, it is right to observe that it does not give a correct view of the actual increase in the consumption of Rhenish, for many other wines, shipped from Rotterdam, are included under the designation of rhenish; but, in reality, many of them are compounds, and mixtures, prepared in Holland, similar to the sherry from Hamburgh.

CHAPTER XII.

MARSALA.

Marsala—Soil similar to Xerez—Albariza—Barro—Argil—Excellent Red Wines—Mostly sent to America—Consumption fallen off—Sometimes called Bronti—Great care of the Vines—Strong Wine wanted—Unsaleable if imported Light—Remarks about Gauges—Wine production of Sicily—Shipments to Cette and Marseilles—Consumption and Percentages from 1831 to 1862.

THE town of Marsala, whence Marsala wine derives its name, is situated on the promontory of Lilybæum, at the west corner of Sicily; where Garibaldi landed on his memorable expedition in May, 1860. The vineyards extend along the coast, east and west, for about twenty-four miles, and about twelve miles inland.

The soil is very similar to that about Xerez, and the best wine here, as there, is grown on the albariza soil, or on a union of the albariza and barro soils, and on the barro alone. The albariza is of a yellow white colour, and chalky, consisting of carbonate of lime and argil, with oxide ot iron. This soil is very favourable for the vine in all countries, but especially under the hot climate of Sicily; for it is an absorbent, spongy substance, loose, always fresh and open, not caking. The albariza, with the barro, forms a sandy soil, mixed with a loamy, red earth and gravel, and, though not quite as valuable as the former, produces excellent wine.

The barro is sand mixed with a clayey earth and gravel, and yields a lighter quality than the others. The arena is sand on which the vine thrives well, and produces abundantly, but of a thin kind.

The bugeo is a blackish compound of clay, vegetable earth and gravel, and is usually found in the valleys and low grounds. The produce is also very abundant, but still, inferior to the arenas.

There are also red wines which are grown in the island, and are shipped largely to Italy and America, and occasionally to England. They are stout, with strong flavour, and might be of advantage in giving body and flavour to many wines that require it. It is difficult to explain how Marsala wine has made such slow progress in England; indeed, it has retrograded, which is doubtless owing to the effects of the vine disease upon the price.

An impression prevails that it is grown on a volcanic soil, and has a sulphureous flavour, but there is no sulphur within a hundred miles of the places where it is produced.

The late enormous rise in Marsala drove merchants to seek for a substitute; which was found in so-called Sherries, especially in Cape (South African), with the bounty which this enjoyed of paying only half duty. Another reason against its use, well known to every dealer, is, that when sold under its own name it is the most unprofitable of all wines. Sometimes it is called Bronte, from the name of an estate presented to Lord Nelson.

Not even in France is there more attention paid to the vines than in many of the vineyards in the district of Marsala, and other favourite parts inland, where shippers have stores.

While the sherry houses have been lately again raising their prices, and many at the same time deteriorating the quality, the Marsala houses, seeing the necessity of reducing their prices in order to recover their former position, have acted on this principle; and I am informed that, since they have done so, the sales have greatly increased. Looking to the geographical position of Sicily, its fine climate and its soil, almost exactly the same as that of Xerez, wine of as good quality might fairly be expected.

I think it might still be much improved by a change in the vines, to give finer flavour and vivacity, even if less strong; but, as I have often repeated, wine-shippers and wine-merchants seek to supply the kinds that are in general demand; and the demand is for a stout kind, well-brandied, in order to blend with other wines, or to sell it as sherry. Were a fine, delicate, slightly-brandied quality shipped, it would probably be objected to in England.

The duty on Marsala is about 68 per cent., and if, instead of 2*s.* 6*d.* per gallon, it were only 1*s.*, the per centage would still be about 25 per cent. on the cost. It is very likely that at least 20 per cent. of the

Sicilian wine entered as consumed or paid duty upon, has not passed through an English wine-merchant's hands, as many casks are shipped direct to private people. This arises from the number of military and naval men who have been stationed in the Mediterranean, or others who have travelled in Italy or Sicily, and become acquainted with this wine.

Importers are likely to make erroneous calculations of the cost of a pipe when comparing it with sherry; for the former contains only 93 gallons, while the latter is 108; so that if a pipe of Marsala costs 24*l.* the same quantity of sherry at the same price per butt would cost only 20*l.* 13*s.* The quantity of wine produced in Sicily is usually estimated at about 200,000 pipes; and of these about a fifth part is suited for exportation. I have it, however, from excellent experienced authority, that, if the demand arose, there would be little difficulty in making double the present quantity, for there are thousands of acres suited to the vine.

Vines are slow of growth, and old habits are difficult to be eradicated, as we well know by our own agricultural history.

Considerable shipments are made to Marseilles and Cette, where it is used for assisting in making up the 'London particular,' 'madeira,' and 'sherry,' which grow in such abundance in the cellars of those towns.

The accompanying sketch represents the stores of one of the principal houses at Marsala.

WINE ESTABLISHMENT AT MARSALA.

It is seen by the Table of consumption, &c., that the consumption and the per centage which Marsala bore to all other kinds was:—

In 1831	consumption	259,916	gallons,	and 4·18	per centage
In 1841	"	401,439	"	6·49	"
In 1851	"	394,225	"	6·28	"
In 1859	"	227,657	"	3·13	"
In 1860	"	209,154	"	2·84	"
In 1861	"	231,270	"	2·13	"
In 1862	"	214,125	"	2·18	"

CHAPTER XIII.

ITALY.

Its Wines disappointing—Climate and Soil offer high expectations—Vino d'Asti — Monte Pulciano — Extract from French Wine Journal—Progress in Wine-making.

VIEWING the geographical position of Italy, and knowing that it is mountainous and hilly from north to south, it is surprising it has never yet acquired the reputation of producing any good wine.

Not having been in that country, I cannot express myself with the same confidence as of others in which I have travelled; but, after having tasted the growths from various localities, I must say I have not seen one that is fine. The vino d'Asti is occasionally praised, but there is nothing in the least good in it.

The Lachryma Christi is coarse in taste and flavour. The Monte Pulciano is sweet, but not to be compared to a Frontignan, or Rivesaltes.

Throughout the whole country vines are grown, and wine made; and I do not believe that better qualities could be produced in any part of Europe; but it must never be forgotten that there is no plant which requires such incessant care as the vine, and no operation demanding more skill, experience, and patience than making wine. The exercise of patience requires the combination of capital, and capital seeks a compensating benefit.

In countries where wine is so abundant that all may drink it, little money value is attached to it, and it is consequently neglected; a remark which applies to every wine-land, where there is not an external demand.

In other countries and cities, natives and foreigners have established themselves, buying from the growers, laying in stocks to mature, to sell in the markets of the world; thus remunerating the proprietors and farmers for their labour, and encouraging production, rivalry, and improvement.

The only way, apparently, to account for this not having yet been done in Italy, is the disordered state of the country until a very late period. But even already, influential Italians are directing attention to this source of wealth, and I have no doubt that, in a few years, the trade in Italian wines will be important.

Few in England, even wine-merchants, have any idea of the anxious and constant care which wines need before they have been brought to the mature state in which they have hitherto been shipped to us; and, unless dealers acquire and practise that care, they must import at much higher prices than others who purchase new wine, and ripen it in their own cellars. It will give some idea of the correctness of this statement if I translate here the advice in a French wine journal, warning all of the danger of the peculiarly warm winter of 1862 :—

But it is the cellar which demands the most anxious and intelligent cares, and the operations usual in March must be employed in February. Thus, the racking and fining ought not to be delayed. Vaults and cellars should be thoroughly ventilated, and the atmosphere impregnated with sulphuric acid gas, either by burning matches or by dispersing the flour of sulphur, to destroy the fermentative principles in the air. In the present atmospheric circumstances, it will be unpardonable in proprietors or head cellarmen, to intrust to their men the examination of the casks, hoops, chimes, and especially the bungs.

If the bung frets, it shows working of the wine, and a hole must be immediately bored by its side to let the enemy escape. If a stave sweats, enlarge the hole, and stop it with a fosset. If the hoops show white spots, rub them off, and inspect them every day, for there may be danger of their giving way.

So much for the exterior: and now for the contents, which is certainly not less important and urgent. Instead of filling up the casks once a week, do so every three days. Examine the limpidity of the wine in different depths of the cask. Rack without delay, if the lowest is full of lees. Rack into well-sulphured casks, give a smart fining, even if it should impoverish the wine. A weak wine is preferable to one that is going wrong.

This, as well as much more which might be added, shows that the art of wine making is not so very easy as is generally supposed; and the Italians, who desire to gain a reputation, would do well to get some intelligent vine-growers and wine-makers, and cellarmen from France and Germany.

CHAPTER XIV.

GREECE.

Bacchus, the God of Wine—Pan—His Conquests by Wine—Homer's description of a celebrated Wine—Its Potency—Polyphemus—Ulysses—The Islands of the Archipelago—Cyprus—Commanderi—Malmsey—Santorin—Smyrna—Tenedos—Currants.

ABUNDANT evidence exists, both in sacred and profane writings, that vinous beverages were known to nations whose very existence has been lost in the lapse of time. It does not therefore surprise us that the Greeks should have placed Bacchus, the god of Wine, and of wine-drinkers, in the highest rank, making him the son of Jove himself, and his most especial care, after the death of Semele.

Although his birth-place is not stated, we learn that his youth was passed in the vine-covered islands of the Archipelago. They generally represented him as a handsome, effeminate young man, possessing eternal youth, thus denoting the pleasure and good effects to be derived from the moderate use of wine; but they also gave the reverse of this picture, by sometimes painting him as old and infirm, to warn his followers that inordinate indulgence will reduce us to weakness and decrepitude.

Accompanied by Pan, Silenus, fauns, and satyrs,

he extended his victories over the human race, making some of the greatest monarchs and philosophers his slaves. His crown was the vine, his thyrsus the wine-cup.

The greater part of Greece proper, the islands of the Grecian Archipelago, and Asiatic and European Turkey, are well adapted for the cultivation of the vine; and the Christian population bestows incessant care upon it. They have an ancient custom in many places of mixing rosin, chalk, and tar with their new wine, which makes it very unpalatable to those not used to it. In the Islands of Cyprus, the kind known as Commanderi (evidently derived from the time of the Crusades), is mixed with about one-third of tar, which is said to impart mellowness and softness, when kept for some years. It is a most luscious wine. Napoli de Malvasia, in Laconia, in the Peloponnesus, gives its name to the malmsey, once much used in England, and known to all as connected with the death of George Duke of Clarence.* The mode of preparing it has been lost there, but it is still made in the Island of Tinos.

The small Island of Santorin, being comparatively level, and of volcanic origin (as, indeed, are most of the islands), is almost covered by vineyards, and produces about one-tenth of the whole quantity made in Greece. In ancient times some of the most celebrated

* It is related that the Duke was such a connoisseur of his favourite wine, that when almost drowned he raised his head, and exclaimed, 'It is not fair: this is bad Malmsey!'

kinds came from the neighbourhood of Smyrna; and now much of that which is used in Constantinople is said to be grown in the Island of Tenedos and on the contiguous plains of Troy. That very strong wines were made in Greece and Thracian Ismarus, we know; for Homer, in the Ninth Book of the Odyssey, writes of Maron, the minister of Apollo:—

> He fetch'd me gifts of varied excellence;
> Seven talents of fine gold; a book all framed
> Of massy silver; but his gift most famed
> Was twelve great vessels, fill'd with such rich wine,
> As was incorruptible and divine.
> He kept it as his jewel, which none knew
> But he himself, his wife, and he that drew.
> It was so strong, that never any fill'd
> A cup, where that was but by drops instilled,
> And drunk it off, but 'twas before allay'd
> With twenty parts in water; yet so sway'd
> The spirit of that little, that the whole
> A sacred odour breath'd about the bowl;
> Had you the odour smelt, and scent it cast,
> It would have vexed you to forbear the taste.
> But then, the taste gain'd too, the spirit it brought
> To dare things high, set up on end my thought.
>
> *George Chapman's translation*, 1609.

We further learn that, through its potency, the Cyclop king, Polyphemus, not only lost his eye, but that Ulysses and his companions escaped from the doom prepared for them.

To have written thus of wine about 3,000 years ago, proves that the culture of the vine must have been well understood, even at that remote period.

At present, the Greeks find a ready market for their crude wines in Russia and in Turkey, but they are beginning to turn their attention to the establishment of a trade with England: They have made rapid strides in commercial enterprise, and Greek merchants are now to be found throughout the world. Not only individuals, but the Greek Government have been directing their attention to the improvement of their wines. Young Greeks have been sent to Burgundy, Champagne, &c. to be instructed in wine-making, and Frenchmen have been brought to Greece for the same purpose. Several wine companies have also been formed.

Is is a curious and interesting fact, that some of the finest grapes (the sultanas, for instance) are devoid of stones, which is accounted for by the great age of the vines. The fact is undeniable, but the explanation dubious; and, as such grapes do not appear to exist elsewhere, they are probably of some peculiar species.

Underground cellars are not known in Greece, which of course militates against the preservation of her wines.

I have not had much opportunity of tasting the different qualities, but enough to form a decided opinion that many possess body and flavour which only require time, capital, and skill to make them severe competitors with the growths of other countries.

There is also a very large trade in currants, which might be made to produce a tenfold quantity of wine, should it become more profitable to apply the currant grapes to that purpose.

CHAPTER XV.

HUNGARY.

Lines on the Vintage—Great Varieties—'Imperial' Tokay—Erroneous Ideas—Peculiar Properties—Natural Phosphor.

Dithyrambus in Vindemia Horna.

Gaudeamus igitur,
Hungari dum sumus!
Nam dant vinum copiosum
Jam in uvis gloriosum,
Almus sol et humus.

Cælitus vindemia
Tollit vinitores:
'Vinum vetus ebibemus;
Horno locum præparemus,'
Clamant potatores.

Semiusti clausimus
Spatium æstatis;
Sed autumnus restaurabit
Debiles, et Bacchus dabit
Novam vim prostratis.

Gaudeamus igitur,
Hungari dum sumus!
Vino patrio et more,
Jubilantes uno ore
Cætera sunt fumus.

FR. HUNAK, DR.

ALL accounts concur in describing Hungary as very fertile, with hills and mountains, on the slopes of which the vines attain the greatest perfection.

The estimated quantity is about 360,000,000 gallons, which, of course, rests on supposition; but, even were it correct, there is no doubt that the supply might soon be much increased, with improved quality. The delay and expense of bringing wines from Hungary are serious drawbacks, as may be seen by reference to the relative position of Pesth, &c. and the nearest shipping ports, Hamburg or Bremen. By Trieste the expense is less, but there is a very long sea voyage.

In some cellars there are said to be immense stocks of old wine remaining, because the demand from abroad is so small; but, although property is not subdivided as in France, this holding of stocks for years, with little or no demand, is not easily comprehended.

In other great wine-growing countries, the producers are generally anxious to get their casks empty for the new vintage, even the first year; and few have the capital, with the skill and patience essential for the preservation of natural wines.

It would be uninteresting to give the names of the places in which the various kinds are grown, but they are stated to be upwards of 600.

When Hungary is alluded to, 'imperial Tokay' is usually associated with it, and the idea prevails that this is a wine of transcendently high quality; but a little practical experience would disabuse those who have this impression. On the contrary, it is coarse, sweet, and disagreeable, yet possessing qualities which cause it to be sought for by certain classes.

The following description has been given to me by one well acquainted with the produce of Hungary:—

The district which produces this wine, and which takes its name from the principal town of Tokay, extends over an area of 24 English square miles. Prince Metternich never owned one foot of ground either in Tokay or anywhere in Hungary. According to the law of Hungary, in force up to 1848, no foreigner could hold land (and in that respect Austrians were considered aliens) unless by obtaining the *indigenat*, or naturalisation, by special act of parliament. Now, that great diplomatist never asked for this privilege, never was inscribed on the roll of the Hungarian nobility, and thus never had any property in Hungary. Neither has the Emperor of Austria any property in Tokay; though, as king of Hungary, of course, all the crown lands belong to the successor of St. Stephen, and thus he owns two vineyards in Tokay. But, as with all crown lands, these two vineyards are among the worst managed in that district, and the wine they produce is very indifferent. The boastful title 'Imperial' has misled people; that is all.

Although the law of entail (or, as our *corpus juris* calls it, *avicitas*) was the law of the land up to 1848, there is no land in Hungary more democratically parcelled out in small plots than the vine district of Tokay. Most magnates make it a point to acquire some property in Tokay, partly from a desire to have the (so-called) Imperial Tokay they want for their own use from their own vineyards, but especially to have a pretext for repairing thither with their families during the vintage—a season of festivities and general rejoicings. Many a noble proprietor spends on these balls, fêtes, &c. ten times the value of the whole produce of the vintage.

The average yearly produce of all kinds of Tokay wine (dry Tokay) is not less than 1,500,000 gallons in round numbers, and that of Imperial (sweet) Tokay not less than 50,000 gallons.

The scarcity of this last description, and the consequent high price, arise from the multiplicity of proprietors who are consumers of their own produce; so that little is left for the general purposes of commerce, and for that little there is, and always will be, a great demand for medical purposes; it being well known that the wines of Tokay, the dry as well as the sweet, hold a larger proportion of natural phosphor than any other wine prescribed as a restorative for debilitated persons. In this light must Tokay be viewed to be appreciated. As a *vin de luxe* it will never be popular in England.

But the grey-headed roués on the Continent will have it, and would swallow it were it as bitter as wormwood. This may account for the raptures of some poets about it, and may also explain its popularity at a certain period at Court here.

From another source I learn that—

Hungary is said to produce some of the most exquisite wines in Europe, but I must say that I never had the felicity to meet with them. Those which are found in ordinary use are detestable.

The vineyards of Hungary are chiefly in the hands of the peasants, who attend much more to the quantity than the quality of their produce: hence the wine commonly used in Hungary, generally a white wine faintly coloured from the mixture of grapes of every kind, is to a foreigner, and especially to an Englishman, who sets a value upon port, sherry, and madeira, altogether undrinkable. The country, however, round the town of Tokay is justly celebrated for its vintage. It extends over a space of about twenty English miles. The grapes are permitted to remain until they become sweet; they are then gathered carefully one by one, and collected in a cask, the bottom of which is pierced with holes, to let that portion of the juice escape which will run from them without any pressure, and which, under the name of Tokay Essence, is very highly prized. To the expressed liquor is added an equal quantity of other very fine wine; and the compound being allowed to stand for twenty-four hours, thoroughly to amalgamate, it is then strained. The juice thus obtained becomes the well-known wine of Tokay, which sells at Vienna at the rate of 12*l.* a dozen; and even at that price is difficult to be obtained.

The Meneses wine is by some judges said to be equal to Tokay. The secondary wines are Ædenburg, Rusth, St. Gyorgy, and Ofen.

CHAPTER XVI.

CRIMEA.

Prince Woronzow's Vineyards — Highly-cultivated Massandra — Aïdanil — Aloupka — Fine, pure Wines — Memorandum of Tasting.

ON the southern coast of the Crimea, there are three valuable properties belonging to Prince Woronzow. It is well known that his father, the late Prince, devoted much care and money in procuring the finest vines, and the most experienced cultivators and cellarmen, from France, Spain, and Germany. The wine produced on his estates of Massandra, Aïdanil and Aloupka, both red and white, is of very high quality and bouquet, but so delicate that it requires to be tasted in the open air in order to be fully appreciated.

I believe that no spirit is added to those Crimean wines; and that they are kept in the wood until quite mature.

The average annual produce is stated to be about 5,000 gallons of red, and the same of white. I cannot learn the estimate for other vineyards, nor have I tasted others that I could rely upon as being genuine.

The following is my memorandum of tasting:—

1st. Massandra, white, 1857; light, soft, fine, high flavour.

2nd. Aïdanil, white, 1857; fuller than the first; very fine wine, great flavour.

3rd. Massandra, white, 1856; exceedingly fine, high flavour.

4th. Aloupka, white, 1856; very perfect.

5th. Aïdanil, white, 1856; a little sweet, very fine, delicate, high flavour.

6th. Aloupka, red, 1858; great body in comparison with the white; fine flavour, as between Burgundy and Claret.

7th. Aloupka, red, 1856; full body, flavour, but taste and flavour as if a blend.

CHAPTER XVII.

MADEIRA.

Madeira Thirty Years ago—Now greatly Changed—Importation Trifling—Replaced by Sherry—Imitations from all Quarters—High Prices—Replanting necessary—Consumption and Percentage from 1831 to 1862.

THE following account of this island was furnished to me about thirty years ago by a friend who had long resided in it:—

Madeira, from its geographical situation (long. 16 W., lat. 32 N.), the genial heat of its climate, and the regularity of its seasons, is capable of producing not only all European, but mostly all tropical fruits and vegetables. Wine, however, being its staple article of production and exportation, of which it produces a great variety, of most delicious flavour and the finest qualities, deserves a more minute description.

When the Portuguese discovered Madeira they found it entirely covered with wood (madeira is the Portuguese word for wood). They selected a site on the south side of the island, at Funchal Bay, for the capital of the colony, than which a more delightful spot could not have been chosen; and having set fire to the woods (as the speediest mode of clearing the land), it is said they continued to burn for several years. This having, of course, denuded that side of the island of wood, they found, after planting the vines, there was no natural support for them, and they adopted the method of training them on a framework of canes, raised from 3 to 6 feet from the ground — a method which prevails at the present day. On the north side, on the contrary, the woods still remain, and the vines are trained on the trees, and form a delightful shade from the summer heats.

From the mountainous surface of the island, and the periodical rains that fall so abundantly, it will be readily understood that a vast quantity of the soil would be washed away, were precautions not taken to retain it. These consist principally in the erection of stone walls, built across the front of the mountains, above each other at convenient distances, which keep in the earth as it is washed down by the rains, or is tumbled down in masses, which always happens more or less during the wet season.

This earth is a composition of a soft rock (Pedra Molla), which never becomes a fine mould, but is generally in a crumbly state, like small coal. In this the vines are planted, and there they flourish best; as, from the loose nature of the earth, the moisture gets more readily at the roots, and the sun's rays dart with more immediate effect into it. The training, trimming, and pruning of the vines occupy the husbandman from the time they begin to expand their luxuriant foliage till the fermentation of the grape; they are then left to come to maturity, sooner or later, as the weather may be more or less favourable. Various are the appearances of the vineyard during the year; in the rainy season, being cleared of foliage, and the cane framework blanched by the rain, wind, and sun, the whole face of the mountains, occupied by vineyards, looks as if covered with a vast net. This is the appearance presented from the beginning of October to the middle of March, when the vines begin to bud, and in a few weeks put out the luxuriant foliage that makes these same bleak mountains exhibit, as far up as the vine will grow, a thick mass of that beautiful green which is so peculiar to the vine.

Next come the flowering months, May and June, when it is a treat to walk through the vineyards; the delightful scent of the flower, strongly resembling that of mignonette, as indeed it does also in appearance, makes you fancy yourself in a flower-garden. The great fear of injury to the vines is in June, when it sometimes happens that there is such a degree of cold—it is even called frost—during the nights of that month, as suffices to cause a complete blight; but this rarely happens. When it does not, the rapidity with which the grapes come to maturity is astonishing. Indeed, the progress of vegetation in this island is wonderful; a piece of land may be ploughed, sown with wheat, and reaped in three months.

The vintage commences in the south towards the

end of July, and from three to four weeks later in the north. Now, the presses and casks are put in a state of preparation—the latter ought to be well cleaned and seasoned. The mode of expressing the juice is just that mentioned in Scripture, 'treading the winepress.' Boys and girls (after the press has been filled with grapes) are put into it; then hands and feet go to work, to express as much juice as possible; after which a rude press finishes this stage of the process.

As the juice runs out it is received into casks, and, if left to the farmer to prepare for exportation, undergoes the process of fermentation on the spot where it is made. If not, it is sent from the vineyard to the merchant's stores in the state it issues from the press; only, in the latter case, it is received in small casks called barrils, or into goat-skins, and thus brought down from the hills—the barrils being slung across mules, the goat-skins laid on men's shoulders—to be deposited in the stores of the purchasers. This is called buying wine in 'mosto'—that is, immediately from the press; the other, made when the farmer has prepared the wine, is called buying in 'limpo,' or in a clear state.

After the new wine has been put into the casks in which it is intended to be treated, half a gallon of brandy is poured into each pipe, and it is allowed to remain quiet, with a few fig-leaves laid over the bung-hole, and the bung placed lightly over these. Then begins the fermentation; and, if all goes on well, the wine, after twelve or fourteen days, has become much clearer. If it remains so, after three or four days more, they prepare another set of pipes, well cleaned, put into each another half-gallon of brandy, and rack all the *clear* wine into fresh casks.

These are allowed to remain undisturbed for eight or ten days, by which time the wine will have become still clearer. Frequently one or more casks continue turbid, pouring out like a syrup, when it is called 'acra doce.' When such is the case, it is necessary to rack it into a clean pipe, making it pass from the cock to the bucket, through a whisk, so as to divide the particles thoroughly. The whole ought to be now sufficiently clear, and, after another fortnight or three weeks, ready for another racking —that is, provided fermentation has ceased.

The wine is then racked a second time, fined, and another gallon of brandy added to each. In ten days it ought to be bright, and fit to be put into the larger butts, where it remains to ripen, till sold, when it is drawn off into pipes, hogsheads, or quarters, and, with another gallon of brandy for each pipe, is ready for exportation.

The madeira in common use is made from both a white and black grape of a small size, generally mixed together, either at the time of pressing or treating; two or three rackings or finings being sufficient to take off all the dark colour.

The wines called Sercial, Boal, and Malmsey are delicious. The first two are very dry, the last is remarkably sweet; all three are made from a white grape, rather dear and scarce, very little being grown. The island is capable of growing 25,000 to 30,000 pipes annually, about 10,000 to 15,000 of which may be exported; the remainder being drunk or converted into brandy, very considerable quantities of which are now made on the island. By a law of the last Cortes, all foreign brandy was prohibited, and thus the growers were thrown upon the resources of the island.

The beneficial effects of this measure were twofold:—1st, they saved their specie which was paid for foreign brandy, and, what was much more important, all the low green acid grapes, in place of being mixed with Madeira wine, were made into brandy of very good quality. The wines exported for the last ten years are so superior to those of the previous twenty, that the improvement in quality can only be accounted for as the effect of this wise regulation.

The contract between landlord and tenant in this island is rather singular. The latter cultivates the ground, and is at all the expense of bringing the produce to maturity; the half of which he takes, and the landlord the other. Tenants are rarely put off the estates, if they can manage, with the assistance of their neighbours, which they generally do, to build a wall to keep in the soil. They cannot be turned off till the landlord has paid them for the wall the value put upon it by two sworn appraisers.

This, however, not one in fifty of the landlords is able to do, as they all live up to their incomes, and are generally in debt.

Almost all landed property is entailed, and is called 'morgado property;' it cannot be sold without the consent of all the heirs; even the guardians of infants who may possibly be heirs, however remote, must consent. This is productive of many lawsuits, which are multiplied by the fondness of the Portuguese for litigation; it is often a boast amongst them that they will leave their 'demandas' (lawsuits) as a bequest to their children. Three-fourths of their suits are carried to Lisbon by appeal, and for final decision.

Madeira is a gem in the Portuguese crown; and a sparkling and valuable jewel it is, not only for its beauty, but for its valuable produce and healthy climate. No one that has ever visited it can fail to be struck with the beauty of its scenery and the luxuriance of its produce; and were its revenues fairly collected and accounted for to the government, it would form a large item in the resources of Portugal. The seasons are remarkably regular, and it is never visited by those awful hurricanes so common and so destructive in tropical climates. Its healthiness is proved by the recovery of many who have resorted to it as a last resource in consumptions and similar complaints.

This account of Madeira and its wines was given to me, as I have already remarked, nearly thirty years ago, when the island was truly 'the gem of the ocean;' but 'tempora mutantur' may be now applied, for its wines are as of things gone by.

I think it was in Madeira, in 1851 or 1852, that the vine disease first showed itself, and there it has worked with the most destructive effect.

During the last four years the average yearly consumption has been 312 pipes, and its proportionate consumption to all kinds about 0·35 per cent.; whereas, from 1804 to 1828, there were annually about 3,500 pipes paid duty upon, and the percentage to the whole was about 5. It should, however, be added, that the use of Madeira had been diminishing for more than twenty years previous to the oïdium. The demand for some time had much exceeded its power of producing the fine quality, which is grown only in the south of the island, and the northern part was brought into requisition. Madeira wine thus fell in repute, and sherry usurped its place.

When madeira is originally fine, and kept till quite ripe, there is a soft fullness, with a delicious, pungent, delicate high flavour that surpasses every other kind, and compared to which even the best sherry is tasteless and flavourless.

The price is now, of course, very high, and it is difficult to meet with any very good.

In the northern and other parts of the island

many of the vines have been rooted out and replaced by the sugar-cane grain, &c., but they have been replanted in the south; so that, from the new and the old plants, a small supply may be looked for. Time, however, is demanded for the new plants, as the vine requires to be at least six years old before it yields good grapes for wine.

In the meantime, all sorts of compounds, under the name of Madeira, are shipped from the island; while Cette, Marseilles, &c., likewise furnish their quota, in handsome 'Madeira' casks.

It is seen by the Table of Consumption, &c., that the consumption and the percentage which Madeira bore to all other kinds was,

In 1831,	consumption	209,127	gallons and	3·56	percentage.
In 1841,	"	107,701	"	1·58	"
In 1851,	"	71,025	"	1·14	"
In 1859,	"	29,566	"	0·41	"
In 1860,	"	28,242	"	0·39	"
In 1861,	"	28,749	"	0·27	"
In 1862,	"	31,906	"	0·32	"

CHAPTER XVIII.

TENERIFFE, VIDONIA, CANARY, ETC.

Teneriffe, one of the five Canary Islands—Vidonia, from the Vidogne Grape—Teneriffe much used Forty Years ago—Canary Sack—Not denoting Dryness—Vine Disease.

THE Canaries consist of five islands opposite the coast of Africa, of which Teneriffe and Canary are the most important; and it is within the recollection of many that there was a large trade in Teneriffe, more usually called Vidonia, owing to the principal grape being the Vidogne.

There is no doubt that considerable quantities of these wines, under the name of Canary Sack, were brought to this country even three hundred years ago; and, as there is sometimes allusion to 'sack with sugar,' and even to 'sacke sweete,' and the same is applied to 'Malaga sack' and 'Sherris sack,' it is evident that the word 'sack' cannot be understood to have denoted sec (dry). Indeed, as far as I can make out, our forefathers, like the Greeks and Romans, seem to have had very coarse tastes, and could drink no wine without such admixtures as to make it a compound, and not a wine.

The very name of Teneriffe or Vidonia is now

almost forgotten, and instead of a yearly consumption of 150,000 gallons, not the tenth part is consumed. The oïdium attacked the Canary Islands' vines as severely as those of Madeira, and the sufferings have been consequently great in both places.

Like Madeira, which it resembles, though far from possessing its flavour or body, Teneriffe participated in the diminished demand when George IV. gave his royal preference to sherry. Both of these wines had been going out of fashion long before the vine disease came upon them, as if to obliterate them for ever.

It is supposed that these islands have suffered peculiarly, owing to the great age of the vines, which rendered them less able to withstand the disease.

CHAPTER XIX.

CAPE.—SOUTH AFRICAN.

Bounties on Cape—Complaints of Cape Merchants—Huskisson—Poulett Thomson—South African—Fatal Day for Cape—Unfair Competition—Constantia—Colonial Interests overpower the Government—Indulgence granted to Cape—Frauds with Drawback claimed—Consumption and Percentage from 1831 to 1862.

IN 1812, the rate of duty on Cape was 9/, the same as on port and sherry; on French wine, 13/6; on Rhenish, 11/3. In 1813, French was 19/8; others remaining the same, except Cape, which was reduced from 9/ to 3/.

After the battle of Waterloo, the restoration of our dear friends the Bourbons, and the expulsion for ever (!) from France of the family of Napoleon, we lowered the rate on French wine to 13/9.

In 1825, on the occasion of the reduction of French to 7/3, and all others to 4/10, the Cape merchants were exceedingly indignant that Cape was made 2/5 instead of 1/9, as they declared it ought to be, to stand in the same relative position as before; but fortunately our finance ministers were then Huskisson and Poulett Thomson, and *not* Nicholas Vansittart, Goulburn, Herries, and Courtnay, who, himself, likened his mind to a sheet of blank paper.

In 1831, when French wines were placed on an equality with others, at 5/6 per gallon, Cape was still favoured by being charged the half rate, 2/9; and again, in 1840, when 5 per cent. was added to all Customs' rates, others were 5/9, and Cape was 2/11.

I remember well, when I was a boy, hearing the words 'Cape wine' often mentioned, with much praise bestowed on Vansittart for his wisdom in supporting our own colony, and not giving away our money to foreigners; but although encouragement was offered to Germans from the Rhine, and to others, to settle there and enrich themselves by making Cape wine agreeable to British tastes, the attempt has proved unsuccessful. For my own part, I have never yet met with anyone courageous enough to place a bottle on his table.

Soon after the reduction in 1815, from 9/ to 3/, the annual consumption became about 440,000 gallons; in 1825, it was 670,639 gallons; in 1835, 522,941; in 1845, 357,953; in 1851, 234,672; in 1859, 785,926; and in 1862, 182,282 gallons. For some years previous to 1859, the word 'Cape' was discarded, and, being replaced by the euphonious 'South African,' the perseverance of some enterprising firms succeeded in making many believe in the discovery of a wine hitherto unknown.

The 29th of February, 1860, was a fatal day for

Cape, when the edict went forth that it was to pay the same rate as every other kind.

Two or three times I have tasted Constantia remarkably fine, but only a few pipes are produced. Occasionally there have been shipments of the general kind, both red and white, tolerably good; but the falling-off during the last two years proves that Capes were imported solely on account of the differential rate in their favour. This protection was not only unjust, but was contrary to the law, as I more than once stated, and (presumptuous as it may appear for me to say so) explained to Mr. Gladstone; for the circumstances had evidently been entirely forgotten.

When Mr. Robinson reduced the duties in 1825, he acceded to the entreaties of the Cape merchants to extend for still three years the protection which they had enjoyed since 1813; but when the time had expired, no alteration was made. The low rate on Cape continued till 1831, when French and others were to be equalised by diminishing the former by 1/9, and adding 8*d.* to the latter, making both 5/6. Cape was to have been included, but the colonial interests were then powerful, and actively cooperative, and the three or four Cape-wine firms in particular left no stone unturned; while no one troubled himself in the matter against their interest.

Many a discussion I listened to on this question in the House of Commons; for the West India, the East India, the timber, the corn-growing, and other trades, felt that, if protection was taken from Cape, it would probably soon be taken from them; and they consequently united in a strong phalanx to overwhelm Poulett Thomson. He then had really no assistance, for no one else had studied the question; but he made an admirable fight. Seeing him so greatly overmatched by numbers, without assistance, I took the liberty to write to him, giving him some practical information, and facts.

He expressed himself much obliged, and requested me to call, which I did; and I remember his remark when leaving his room,—'Well, I am glad you think I have fought them well; but you see it is useless, and we must give in.'

The Bill for equalisation passed, granting Cape the continuance of half duty for five years longer; but when this period had elapsed, all about the matter was forgotten, and, instead of five, it retained the privilege for thirty years.

While it paid only half duty there was no fairness of competition, because it was used solely to mix with other kinds, the mixture being sold as sherry, &c., which respectable houses would not do; indeed, many refused to allow a gallon of Cape to enter their cellars, lest it should be imagined that they had anything to do with it.

It was also mixed with sherry, &c., that was to be exported, and the duty of 5/9 per gallon claimed as drawback, and received; while probably 2/11 had been paid on two thirds of the quantity.

It is seen by the following statement that the consumption and the percentage which Cape bore to all other kinds was:—

In 1831,	consumption	539,584	gallons and	8·48	per centage.
In 1841,	„	441,238	„	7·10	„
In 1851,	„	234,672	„	3·74	„
In 1859,	„	785·926	„	10·84	„
In 1860,	„	427,698	„	5·81	„
In 1861,	„	340,082	„	3·16	„
In 1862,	„	182,282	„	1·86	

CHAPTER XX

AUSTRALIA.

Its Wine generally Bad—Vines sent to Adelaide—Better to apply her Capital and Labour to her natural Productions—Vineyards at Beechworth and Albury—Newspaper Extracts.

THE first Australian wine I ever tasted was shown to me by the late Mr. Porter, then Secretary of the Board of Trade, and it was very bad. Since that time I have tasted it frequently, but only once have I found it so good as to dispose one to take a second glass. With this single exception, it has been poor, flavourless, and thin. The exception was a six-dozen case of white and of red, sent as a present to a gentleman who has large property near Melbourne. Both of these were good, clean-flavoured qualities; but not better than may be easily procured in Germany and France.

So far as I can learn, Australia is not well adapted, either by soil or climate, for growing wine, and this opinion seems confirmed by the unsuccessful efforts of many years.

So long ago as 1835 I sent many hundreds of vines to Adelaide, by desire of a very intelligent wine merchant; but no good came of it. Even if soil and climate were favourable, the fact of its being a thinly peopled land must prevent the cultivation and making of fine qualities. It is almost literally true that the vine requires daily manual labour from the 1st of January to the 31st of December, and this can be done only in old countries, with a large population and low wages.

Australia must wait many years before she is in such a position; and she will, in the mean time, be more profitably employed in cultivating her great natural resources, and exchanging these for the wines of Europe. Being one of our colonies, her produce was charged the same as that of the Cape; but, even with such assistance, the importations of wine never rose above two or three hundred pipes a year.

Since writing the above, I find the following remarks by the correspondent of *The Times*, dated Melbourne, April 20, 1863. They confirm the opinion I have expressed as to the little progress in wine-making in Australia. The 1*l.* per gallon which Mr. Zimmermann gets at his vineyard is 2*l.* per dozen; and this appears to be without bottles, corks, &c.:—

'At Beechworth and in all the surrounding country extending to Albury, in New South Wales, the finest vineyards abound. By far the most successful wine-makers are Germans. A Mr. Zimmermann, at Beechworth, has a well-managed vineyard of an acre and a quarter in extent. Upon the proceeds of the sale of wine and fruit from this small bit of ground, he, his wife, and a very nearly grown-up son live comfortably. He gets 1*l.* a gallon on the spot for all the wine he can make, and for the table he obtained this year, from 200 three-year-old vines, the enormous quantity of 1,600lbs. of the finest grapes. But the vineyard is cultivated like a trim garden, and is so much his pet that he sleeps in it. Like his namesake of the Treatise, Mr. Zimmermann seems to have a taste for solitude, and he passes his nights (until his crop is in) concealed in a little tent, in the midst of his vines, with a gun by his side, and surrounded by a system of strings connected with bells, so that when larcenous Chinamen venture into his ground the bells ring, and the owner is aroused against his invaders. Mr. Zimmermann is merely one of many German cultivators in this part who are doing equally well. The statistical returns of the first quarter of this year for the Albury district (which, as well as Beechworth, is in the neighbourhood of the Murray River) give, besides wheat, hay, maize, barley, oats, potatoes, &c., 60,840lbs. of tobacco, and 40,360 gallons of wine.

I find in a Sydney newspaper the following very interesting and instructive information upon the production of wine in Australia. Notwithstanding the attempt to make it appear that the growth is increasing, and that wine-making may become a profitable investment, the facts do not appear to justify the hope :—

Australian Wine.—The production of wine now constitutes so important a branch of colonial industry, that the annual vintages are looked forward to with considerable interest. Every year shows a marked increase in the amount of capital invested, and in the number of people employed in the vineyards, although, owing to the precariousness of the crops, that increase is not necessarily attended with a corresponding increase in the quantity produced. The vintage of 1863 has been by no means a prosperous one. The actual quantity of wine produced is not perhaps much less than that of previous seasons, but it is considerably less as compared with the acreage of vines in bearing, many of the growers having, for some time past, been extending their operations. The accounts received, generally express disappointment at the results of the gathering. In the Hunter River district, where the greater portion of wines are produced, the continuance of dry weather during the early part of the summer was very propitious, and promise was given of an unusually abundant crop; but just before the ripening of the grapes heavy rains set in, accompanied with violent hail storms, causing great damage, and interrupting the gathering—the rains continuing during the vintage. In other districts the want of rain in the early part of the summer checked the growth of the vines. Altogether it would appear that fully a third of the crop has perished. It is estimated that in the Paterson district the produce has not exceeded two hundred gallons to the acre. Other circumstances besides the weather have operated to frustrate the expectations of plentiful crops, amongst these may be mentioned the depredations of flying foxes, parrots, and other birds.

At the Camden Park Vineyards, belonging to Sir W. and Mr. J. Macarthur, the dry weather favoured the growth and ripening of the grapes, but a considerable loss was sustained by the depredations of birds, and only between two and three thousand gallons of wine were made. Three years ago a succession of devastating floods swept over the Camden Park Vineyards, completely destroying the vines, and though they have been extensively replanted, they have not yet been restored to their condition prior to those disasters. Messrs. Wyndham, the largest growers in the colony, have made about 14,000 gallons from their vineyards at Dalwood, on the Hunter, which are above sixty acres in extent; of these about thirty-five are in bearing. They have also made nearly

5,000 gallons at Bukkulla, in the Gwydir district, after losing about a thousand gallons through the unseasonable rains. The yield at Cawarra Vineyards, on the Upper Paterson, belonging to Dr. Lindemann, has been about an average. The long-continued drought, which ruined other crops, was extremely favourable to the development of the vines, and the abundance and fine quality of the grapes augured a splendid vintage, it being expected that, from some parts of the vineyard, a thousand gallons would be obtained to the acre. Heavy rains set in, however, just before the grapes ripened, and a further loss was sustained by the depredations of parrots, who visited the vineyards in immense swarms, destroying a great quantity of fruit. Dr. Lindemann has made about 6,000 gallons, rather more than half of what he expected. His vineyards are about twenty acres in extent.

Messrs. A. and J. Park, of Lewinsbrook, on the Allyn, a branch of the Paterson, made about 4,000 gallons, but unfortunately a fire broke out soon after the vintage, and the whole was destroyed. At Orindinna, on the Paterson, Mr. Glennie made about 1,500 gallons from sixteen acres. Mr. A. Windeyer's vineyards, at Kinross, near Raymond Terrace, comprising about fifteen acres, yielded 3,000 gallons, considerable losses having been sustained by the rains and birds. At the Kaludah Vineyard, near Lochinvar, on the Hunter, the prospects in December were very good, but a hailstorm in the middle of that month did considerable damage, and although this vineyard did not suffer so much as others in the district, the loss from that and subsequent rains was at least 2,000 gallons. The produce is nearly 6,000 gallons, which is a little in excess of last year, and is considered a fair average as to quantity, but it is doubted whether the quality will be equal to that of last year's wines. Mr. Carmichael has made about 4,000 gallons of wine, from ten acres of vines at Porphyry, near Raymond Terrace. At Irrawang, Mr. C. Linz has made 950 gallons, from eight acres. At Mulgoa, near Penrith, Mr. Edward Cox has made about a thousand gallons from ten acres. This is only about half an average, the vines having suffered considerably for want of moisture during the early part of the summer, and the grapes being small, and not abundant. In the Albury district, the vines to some extent suffered from the rains, but the vintage is reported to be on the whole a successful one. It is satisfactory to notice the steady advance which our wines have made in public estimation, *and the extent to which they are displacing foreign importations.* The Australian wines are now supplied at all the hotels, clubs, and other places of resort, and also at public and private dinner tables. They have become generally popular sooner than might have been expected, considering the influence of custom *and deeply-rooted prejudices.* The demand is certainly increasing at a much faster rate than the production. This year's vintage will be far from supplying a twelvemonth's consumption; and it is not unlikely that its partial failure may, by making the article comparatively scarce, enhance its value.

Already the price of colonial wines is complained of as being too high, and as tending to check consumption amongst the classes by whom they ought especially to be drunk. It may seem surprising that the growers generally do not largely extend their operations, so as to be prepared to meet the increasing demand. The reason is probably the large, and for a long time unremunerative, outlay it would involve, as the vines do not yield till the third year after planting; besides which, experience proves the vine crop to be an extremely precarious one. It is one indication of the supply not keeping pace with the demand, that although wine does not attain maturity under three years, there is now none for sale older than 1861. Some wines find their way to the Sydney market under foreign titles, having undergone some 'improvement' for the purpose of assimilating their flavour to that of the wines they are intended to represent. It is quite possible that the wines of this colony may be made to resemble certain European vintages; but it does not follow that they should be the better appreciated, for having undergone that sophistication. The wide popularity of the Camden, Cawarra, and Dalwood wines proves the existence of a *relish for the pure juice of the grape*; and so highly are they esteemed, that with colonial wine-drinkers the names of those vineyards are a greater recommendation than the most pretentious French title. However well meant may be the intentions of those who endeavour to 'improve' our wines, there are significant indications that their services are not much appreciated.

On July 1, next, the Sale of Colonial Wines Encouragement Bill will come into operation, and any person will then be able to sell a single bottle *of colonial wine*—not, however, to be drunk on his premises; but it appears likely that the scarcity and consequent high prices will prevent that advantage being taken of the Act which its authors expected and promised for it.

The following extract from a South Australian paper gives a more flattering description of the production in that part of the great continent. It is, however, very evident that the person who has written it knows very little of the subject he is writing about, or of the capabilities of the wine countries of Europe:—

South Australian Wines.—It has been known for some time past that large quantities of the wines produced here were being shipped to Victoria, and were taking a high position in the Melbourne market; but, except to a few persons interested in the trade, it was not known that the business had assumed such large dimensions. It had been supposed by many that our produce hitherto has not been much greater than was necessary for our own consumption; and yet it appears from an article in the *Argus* that by far the largest portion of Australian wines imported by our neighbours comes from this colony. The taste for these wines is growing, and there can be but little doubt that for some time to come there will be a market in Melbourne for as much as we can send them. The writer says: — ' In New South Wales they produce so little, or else are so fond of what they have got, that but little finds its way into this market. Not so with South Australia, whose wines come here in large quantities, and are in deserved high favour. Messrs. Ritchie and Farrington, who perhaps stand at the head of the colonial wine trade in Victoria, give an estimate of the relative demand for colonial wines, taking the lowest as 1, as follows:— 'South Australian. *White*: Erlana, 4; Verdeilho, 5; Pedro Ximenes, 1; Malvasia, 2; Muscatella, 3; Hock, 1; Riesling, 3. *Red*: Hermitage, 6; Richebourg, 3; Constantia, 2.' Our best wines are placed much higher by these experienced merchants, and are in larger demand than those of either New South Wales or Victoria, and we hope our wine-growers will do their best to maintain the good character which they have already obtained. So high is the value of colonial wines in Victoria, that unscrupulous persons are actually buying up low-priced and inferior German wines, and, by a kind of doctoring which they know how to perform, are working them up into a semblance of Australian wine. This is a fact much to be regretted, because the character of our pure and nutritious wines will in all probability suffer if inferior stuff, charged with drugs and fortified with strong spirit, is put into the market and sold as colonial wine.

According to the *Argus*, South Australian wines realise in Melbourne from 20*s.* to 25*s.* a dozen, in addition to the duty of 3*s.* a gallon which they must pay. This is a fair price, and one which ought to be highly remunerative to the producer. Of course it is the better class of wines which obtain this price. Others, we are told, are often invoiced in the wood at 2*s.* 6*d.* a gallon without the duty. We question this latter statement. A very small portion, we should think, at this price ever leaves the colony of

South Australia. It must be wine which, from its inferior quality, is utterly unsalable here, and which the people in this land would hardly accept as a gift. The humblest harvest wines would bring a better price than this. There can be no doubt that much wretched stuff has been made in South Australia. In the case of many persons the manufacture has been tentative and experimental, and much good fruit has been converted into bad wine; this is the price which has been paid in acquiring the art of winemaking. It is possible that the results of some of these experiments may have found their way to Melbourne at 2*s.* 6*d.* a gallon; but we think we may very confidently assert that no samples which would be drunk here would be exported at such a price.

The most mischievous restriction to the sale of South Australian wine in the Melbourne market is that which arises from the Customs' duty of 3*s.* a gallon. We hope the Conference may have agreed upon some scheme which will admit colonial productions to all the colonies free of duty. From the high character which our wines have taken, and which, from the enlarged experience of our vignerons, we have no doubt they will be able to maintain, there is no reason why we should not command the Melbourne market for many years to come.

We have been assured on good authority that certain qualities of South Australian wines would, if supplied regularly and in sufficient quantities, very fairly compete with those of European production. It is something, in drinking wine, to know that it is what it professes to be —the pure juice of the grape; and we believe that, with respect to the great bulk of the wine produced in this colony, this confidence is warranted. It would be a great pity if, for the sake of assimilating them either in strength or taste to the wines of Europe, our wine-makers were to resort to fortifying or doctoring their productions. They have a character of their own by which their value will be tested and determined. It would be as absurd for the manufacturers of French claret by a kind of doctoring to work that delicious wine into a bad imitation of old Port, as for our vignerons to destroy the distinctive character of South Australian wines, to adapt them to the taste of those who have been accustomed to the heavy-bodied productions of Spain and Portugal. That the lighter wines will commend themselves to the taste of the great majority of Englishmen we have but little doubt. Indeed, the heavy brandied wines of the south-west of Europe have become popular in England only in late years. Every person acquainted with the social life and habits of the wine-drinking people of Great Britain, before the commencement of the present century, must know that the wines of France were chiefly used. When Mr. Gladstone introduced his Budget to the English House of Commons—the chief point in which was the reduction of the duties on French wines—he gave several interesting and conclusive illustrations of this fact; and he maintained that the taste for full-bodied wines was a modern and an acquired taste. And the success which has attended the introduction of French wines to the English market proves that the sagacious Chancellor was right.

Now we have every reason to believe that in South Australia we can produce wines in all respects equal, and in some respects superior, to those of France. Let our first-class vignerons have faith in the wines they make pure and simple, and carefully eschew all tampering with them, and doctoring them, and let them sell them at as moderate a price as they can afford until the taste for them be firmly established, when they will become a necessity, and then we have no doubt they will be able to command highly remunerative prices. It is as certain as anything can be that the manufacture of wine will become one of the chief articles of South Australian produce. Taking the colony throughout, there is no description of grapes which cannot be grown, and with all the advantages we possess we cannot fail to become a large wine-producing colony.

CHAPTER XXI.

AMERICA—CALIFORNIA.

Longfellow's Song in praise of Catawba—Different Opinion—Hotel Charges before the time of Greenbacks—Cock-tail—Brandy Smash—Carolina—Scuppernong—California—Good Wines—Angelico—Aliso—Large Production—German Vine-Growers.

THE following beautiful lines by Longfellow, in praise of Catawba, make me somewhat timid in expressing opinions so very different from his; nor would I have ventured to do so on my own limited knowledge, had they not been confirmed by others. The greatest respect, however, is due to such a man and writer, even on the subject of wine; and I, therefore, call attention to the poet's remark about that which is 'shipped o'er the reeling Atlantic.'

Catawba Wine.

This song of wine
Is a song of the vine,
To be sung by the glowing embers
Of wayside inns,
When the rain begins
To darken the drear Novembers.

It is not a song
Of the Scuppernong
From warm Carolinian valleys,

Nor the Isabel
And the Muscadel
That bask in our garden alleys:

Nor the red Mustang,
Whose clusters hang
O'er the waves of the Colorado,
And the fiery flood
Of whose purple blood
Has a dash of Spanish bravado.

For the richest and best
Is the wine of the West,
That grows by the Beautiful River;
Whose sweet perfume
Fills all the room
With a benison on the giver.

And as hollow trees
Are the haunts of bees
For ever going and coming,
So this crystal hive
Is all alive
With a swarming and buzzing and humming.

Very good in its way
Is the Verzenay,
Or the Sillery soft and creamy;
But Catawba wine
Has a taste more divine,
More dulcet, delicious, and dreamy.

There grows no vine
By the haunted Rhine,
By Danube or Guadalquivir,
Nor an island or cape,
That bears such a grape
As grows by the Beautiful River.

Drugged is their juice
For foreign use,
When shipped o'er the reeling Atlantic,

To rack our brains
With the fever pains
That have driven the Old World frantic.

To the sewers and sinks
With all such drinks,
And after them tumble the mixer;
For a poison malign
Is such Borgia wine,
Or at best but a Devil's Elixir.

While pure as a spring
Is the wine I sing,
And to praise it, one needs but name it;
For Catawba wine
Has need of no sign,
No tavern bush to proclaim it.

And this song of the vine,
This greeting of mine,
The winds and the birds shall deliver
To the Queen of the West,
In her garlands dressed,
On the banks of the Beautiful River.

It is with much diffidence that I write upon the wines of the United States, for I am conscious of my ignorance about them. The American wine best known by name in this country is the Catawba (Longworth's) just mentioned, which reminds me of the sparkling Vouvraye made near Tours, but is not so good. I have heard it compared to champagne, but the comparison ought to be made with a very coarse, common kind of champagne.

Almost every important wine merchant has (or had) an agent in the (United) States, which was an excellent market. Even before the introduction of green-back currency, and the increased tariff, the prices charged at hotels were very high. By reference to the bill of fare of Astor House, New York, in 1836, I see that no sherry was less than 8/, and some 12/ a bottle. But madeira seems to have been the favourite, for it begins at 8/, and ascends to 12/, 16/, 20/, 24/, 28/, 40/. The 24/ per bottle is called 'Smith & Huggins' (Dyker's white top), bottled 1800, in St. Eustatia.' The 40/ is 'Gov. Kirby's original bottles, 00.'

The most important vineyards are those of Ohio, Missouri, and Indiana. Wine is also made in Western Virginia, the State of New York, Pensylvania, and Maryland. But the most celebrated is in Cincinnati, where there are large vineyards, especially those belonging to Messrs. Longworth and Zimmermann, who have gained a high reputation for their sparkling Catawba, about which I have expressed my own opinion. In the Northern and North Western States, wines of all kinds, generally in imitation of favourite European, are made; but all have a peculiar—what we should call an *American*—flavour and taste; and the Americans themselves appear to prefer those which are imported.

A *drink* in great demand consists of Isabella and sweet Catawba, mixed with sugar and spirits and poured upon pounded ice, and sold at the 'bars' of hotels and taverns. These are somewhat aristocratic luxuries; but there are numerous others, usually sucked through a straw, bearing the elegant names of 'cock-tail,' 'brandy-smash,' 'mint-julep,' 'cobbler,' &c.

There is a wine grown in the Carolinas, called 'Scuppernong,' resembling Rhenish, but with a sweetish flavour. It is too light to be sent to a distance.

California seems better adapted for producing good wine. Its growths are best known as Angelico, Aliso, Porto, Champagne. One firm—Sausserain & Co.—is stated to have produced, in 1858, 9,400 gallons white, and 4,000 gallons red Aliso; 9,000 gallons Angelico, and 1,000 gallons brandy; in all, 23,000 gallons. It is stated that in the district of Angelos there were produced, in that same year, about 200,000 gallons of wine of various qualities.

Since that time a wealthy German company have established themselves about twenty miles from Angelos, and, in one year, had planted half a million of vines. Indeed, large districts are yearly planted.

The wines of California can offer a fair comparison with those of Europe; and the Germans have already shipped them to their countrymen in Bremen and Hamburg. Aliso has a good body, and somewhat resembles Barsac. A San Francisco house has an agent in Paris for its sale.

CHAPTER XXII.

PERU.

Letter from a Traveller in Peru—Peruvian Sherry—Doubtful if made in Peru.

> 'In the summer it is intensely hot during the day, with clouds of saline dust and sand, and there is no shade to protect from the ever-scorching sun. This very arid district is a portion of a great desert which, with little intermission, extends 1,500 geographical miles, from Coquimbo in Chili to Paytu in Peru. About south-east are the rather large towns of Pica and Matilla, where the vineyards are nourished by waters of irrigation.'
>
> Bollaert's *Antiquities of South America.*

SOME wines, closely resembling sherry, said to be from Peru, having been brought to England, a friend, well acquainted with that country, has given me the following information:—

As early as 1825 I have known and drunk the wines of Peru, and the peculiar but very nice brandy of Pisco, often called Pisco de Italia. These wines and brandies are produced in about lat. 14° S., in deep valleys, which are irrigated by water produced by the melting of snow on the sides of the Cordilleras. Peru itself is a 'rainless' land. In the interior of the province of Tarapaca, between 20° and 30° S., and about 70° W., at more than 4,300 feet above the sea, but at the foot of the Cordilleras, some good red and white wine was produced at Pica, by irrigation, but in very small quantities. For many years great attention has been paid in Peru to agriculture, and particularly to the cultivation of sugar and of the vine; and Señor Elias now produces yearly from his estate at Hojos, near Pisco, about 100,000 gallons of the wine said to be similar to madeira. Señor Urrutea's vineyard, in the same district, yields about 200,000 gallons. Connoisseurs would probably not much like this Peruvian madeira, but it is pretty good, and is drunk in the country, and even on board the steamers plying along the coasts. Aguardiente (brandy) is mostly made at Teâ, near Pisco; it is a sweet brandy, made from the muscatel grape.

Another similar quality is grown and made in the province of Mocqueber. In 1860, there were produced in the valley of the Teâ, upon 116 estates (independent of the Indian farms), from 70,000 to 80,000 botijas (earthen jars) of brandy of eighteen degrees; and 10,000 barrels of wine, to imitate sherry, madeira, and malaga; 8,000 cwt. of cotton, and 30,000 to 40,000 lbs. of cochineal.

I have several times carefully tasted this (so-called) wine of Peru, but have each time become more strongly convinced that the proportion of Peruvian, if any, in the casks is very small, and that it is composed of a common clean-flavoured white wine from Spain, prepared, and reshipped to England. Several circumstances strengthen this opinion.

Anyone acquainted with wine countries will doubt whether such as is imported as Peruvian can have been made in that country of scattered population; most of the labourers Indians, with a soil dependent for moisture entirely on dew and irrigation from mountains, and with miserable roads. The shape and make of the casks still further increase this supposition.

CHAPTER XXIII.

CELLARS—DECANTING—FININGS—BOTTLES—BOTTLING.

Bad Cellars in modern Houses—Iron and movable Bins—Architects ignorant about Cellars—Mr. Farrow's decanting Machines—All Wines should be decanted—Articles required in the Cellar—How to carry a Bottle—Fining—Corks—Bottling—Best to employ a Wine-cooper—Bottles—Uniform Size impracticable.

ALLUSION has already been made to the confined, ill-placed, and ill-arranged cellars in most modern houses—a great contrast to those in old buildings. This drawback may be partly owing to the small stocks gentlemen have been in the habit of keeping for some years past, and also because wine has generally ceased to be a subject of conversation and of rivalry as formerly.

This, however, hardly accounts satisfactorily for the inconsistency of houses having magnificent rooms, large kitchens, &c., but only a little poking wine-cellar, into which it is often difficult to get even a hogshead.

Frequently the space under a staircase is thought good enough for the purpose, but even this is better than being next the kitchen fire or laundry flues.

Others, again, are in some back or front area, enjoying a temperature of zero in winter, and 60° or 70° in summer.

When the so-called cellar is 'fitted up,' it is found to be provided with two or three brick partitions. and stone slabs, forming half a dozen bins, not suited, either in width, depth, or height, for any conceivable arrangement of bottles. If six or eight kinds only are to be kept, these bins might hold them conveniently; but in most cellars there are a few dozen of different kinds of port, sherry, claret, and probably a little champagne, and other descriptions, with a few bottles of spirits. Those who have had experience of the usual London cellars can describe the annoyance and the confusion which are caused by those ill-adapted places. If three dozen are put in one of the bins, it may be said to be rendered useless for anything else, for breakage and mixing of the bottles are sure to arise from placing even another three dozen on the top of the first.

There should be a separate and distinct place for even six bottles of any one quality or kind, and this is practicable only by having many subdivisions. In a large cellar this can be done, though not easily, with the old-fashioned thick brick bins. Iron bins, such as are represented in No. 1, have been in use among wine merchants for many years; and many private gentlemen have had them put up, according to the size of their cellars. As they are clean, take up very little space, and are fitted so as to receive shelves when wanted, and to be made of sizes to hold large or small quantities, there cannot be a doubt of their superiority.

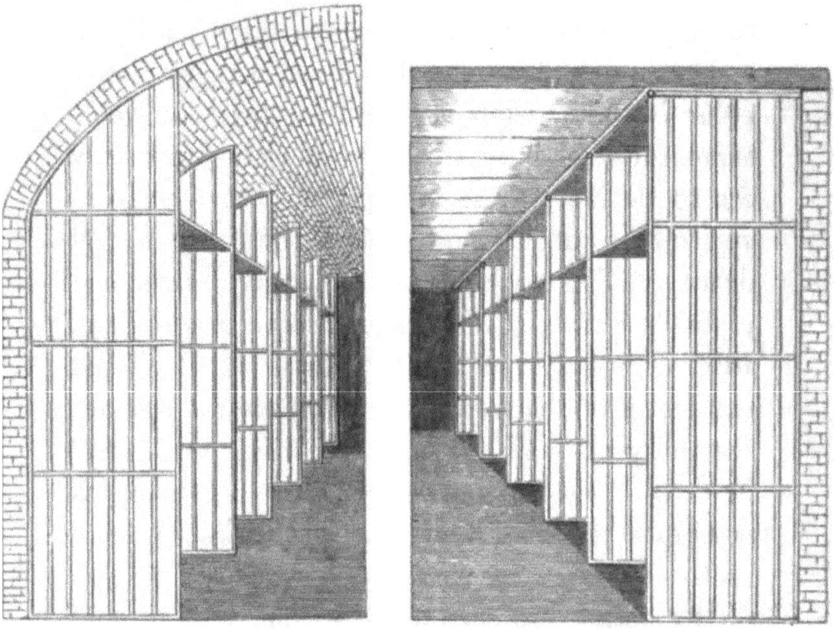

For Arched Vaults For Flat Ceilings.

WROUGHT-IRON WINE BIN. No. 1.

A few years ago I was greatly pleased with a light movable iron bin which I saw in Paris. It is now well known here, and is much improved by a slight projection, which prevents the bottle from falling out, or being stolen; and, as a lock and key or padlock may be attached, the bin may be safely placed anywhere. It is made of what is called hoop-iron, which is very light, and allows it to be easily moved to any suitable situation.

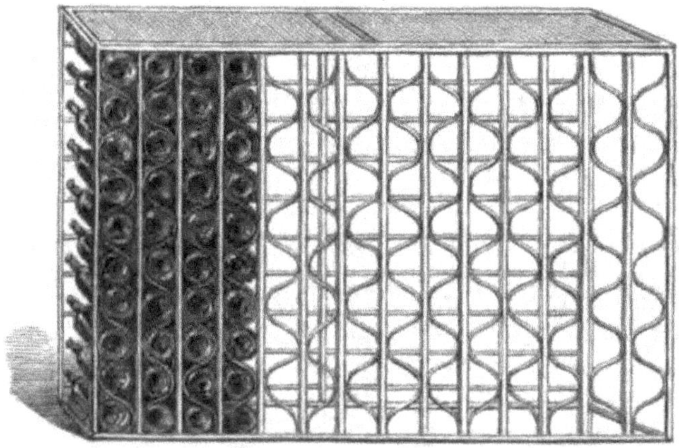

REGISTERED CELLULAR WINE BINS; REST FOR EACH BOTTLE. No. 2.

No. 2 shows one of these movable bins partly filled; and No. 3 shows another, with a guard and

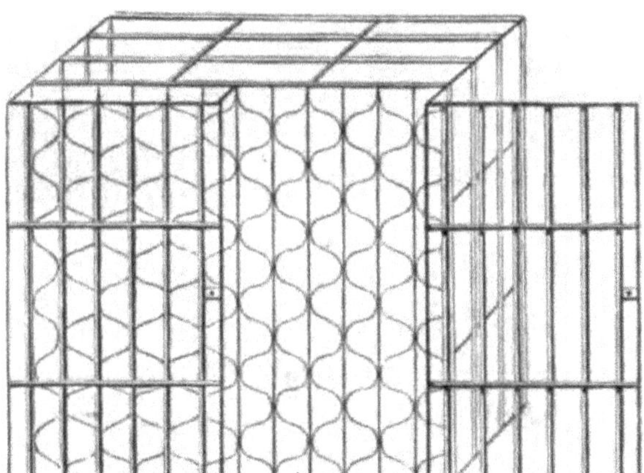

MOVABLE IRON BIN, WITH LOCK. No. 3.

padlock, so that it may be safely put in any open place. They may be had of any size, from Farrow

and Jackson, of Tower Street, the manufacturers of all kinds of things for wine merchants.

The one without the guard costs about 6/, and the other about 8/ per dozen.

The following sketch represents cases and bins combined, now much used instead of the common cases; for they possess the great advantage of being made to hold the bottles securely, without the annoyance of straw and the mess it causes

WOODEN PACKING-CASES, SUITED ALSO FOR BINS.

in unpacking. But their peculiar advantage consists in being convertible into bins, by being merely stood up. It will be easily understood what a convenience this often is—especially when in lodgings. It is seen that they may be fitted with a lock and key. The cost is not greatly more than for the usual cases. As wood decays soon in damp, unventilated places, these wooden bins should not be left long in damp cellars. They are made by many, but Spencer and Co., of Billiter Street, are probably the largest makers. Although every kind may be kept safely and separately by those iron and wooden bins, it would be no great trouble to label each bottle before being put in, so that it may be at once seen what it is. This should be done, in large letters or figures, on a piece of paper about an inch square, gummed into the punt, or hollow part of the bottom of the bottle, which is the most visible when in the bin.

Architects have yet to study that part of their profession connected with cellars. As a general rule, they ought to be in the part of the house least likely to be affected by changes in the atmosphere or temperature; for all important changes in the latter are injurious, especially to every kind of unbrandied wine. It ought not to exceed 54° of Fahrenheit, nor to fall below 48°; but, even so great a variation should, if possible, be avoided.

The cellars in the Marne are about 40°, and I recommend everyone, who has a place of that temperature in his house, to put his champagne and sparkling Rhenish there.

I have already alluded to the practice of icing wines, which may be said to be destructive to every kind except champagne and other sparkling kinds; but even champagne, after it has been so long in ice as to become very cold, is not to be compared to the same wine when brought out of a cold cellar.

The flavour gets *locked up*, and it is difficult, when in that chilled state, to distinguish the finest from a common quality.

Few houses have cold cellars, and, as it is bad when warm, ice becomes necessary; but ten minutes or a quarter of an hour is usually long enough to make it what the French call *frappé*.

Grievous as it is to see fine wine half frozen, this is nothing in comparison with the barbarous act of putting lumps of ice into it. It would be well if those who do such a thing would remember, besides the spoiling of the wine, the 'bloody flux' which it caused Lord Dorchester.

We learn this from Dean Swift's journal of his visit to London in 1710, and from him we also know that London had such summers at that period as we have just experienced in 1863, and that the bad practice of putting ice into wine is of very old date.

The Dean writes:—

> I take Patrick with me to hold my night-gown, shirt, and slippers, and borrow a napkin of my landlady for a cap. I have been swimming in the river this half hour and more, and when I was coming out, dived, to make my head and all through wet, like a cold bath; but as I dived, the napkin fell off, and is lost, and I have that to pay for. It is pure warm; I never felt so hot a day since I was born. I lie with nothing but the sheet over me, and my feet quite bare. Nothing makes me so peevish as hot weather. Mr. Bertie would not let me put ice in my wine, saying, 'It was the worst thing in the world, and gave my Lord Dorchester the bloody flux.'

It is convenient to have a small cellar attached to

the larger, with shelves and a few small bins, or, rather, with one of the movable iron kind, in which a few bottles of different kinds may be kept. A strong deal table is also useful for decanting; but to this important and last stage of manipulation of the wine, for which so much time, labour, and money have been bestowed, I must devote a few special observations.

DECANTING.

All know the difficulty of attempting to decant wine of any kind, old in bottle; and very few possess the requisite steadiness of hand, with the eye ready to stop as soon as the sediment begins to move. The difficulty can be obviated only by mechanical means.

One plan has lately been invented by Mr. Ellis, of the 'Star and Garter,' Richmond, which I have heard much praised, but it appears to me heavy and complicated.

I would rather avoid the mention of my own contrivance for this object, but I have not yet seen anything so good and simple as that which I designed some years ago; but in which I have now no interest whatever, nor do I even know whether, or where, it can be procured.

Nos. 1 and 2 give an idea of that machine, and it is easy to describe it. The bottle is laid upon the frame, and tightly screwed in at the neck, so that, with Lund's or any other good screw, the cork can be drawn with ease, and without shaking the bottle. This being done, the frame may be raised by the tip of the finger, and, on withdrawing this, the same position is retained till it is again raised or depressed.

MACHINE FOR DECANTING. No. 1.

The explanation is simple. The engraving shows that the head part of the frame is between two pieces of iron; and the whole mystery of the beautiful smooth movement is, that it is so formed that, as the frame is moved up or down, there is a pressure against both sides, and the elasticity contained in iron causes resistance sufficient to hold the weight of the bottle in whatever position it has been placed or left. The operation may be performed as quickly as by hand, and far better.

I would recommend that one of these, or a better one, if it can be found, should be placed, not only in all wine merchants', but in every gentleman's cellar; for, if he is in the habit of drinking wine, he will save a glass out of every bottle, and will not have the rest displeasing to the eye and the palate, as is so frequently the case. It ought to be firmly fixed in a table in the outer or inner cellar, on a strong pillar, as in No. 2, high enough for any decanter; and

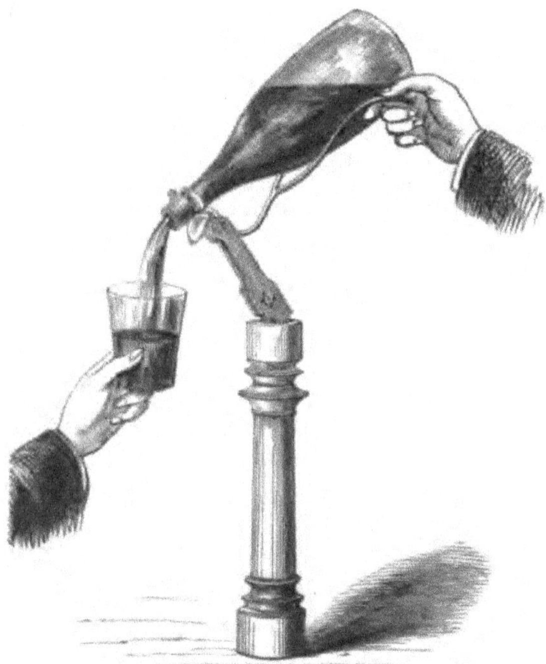

MACHINE FOR DECANTING. No. 2.

it is an improvement to have a candle attached to the frame on the opposite side, so fixed that, in moving the frame, the bottle is seen through, and the state of its contents observed from the beginning to the end.

Since the days of old port, the criticisms upon it, and the rule that the gentleman alone could and should decant his wine, little attention, comparatively, is paid to this subject; but there is no wine whatever, white or red, that is not greatly deteriorated in value by being drunk without being decanted. All wines form a deposit, and (excepting sparkling) the only others I would name as not injured in taste and appearance are, port that has been many years in bottle, and is bright and full of bees-wing, and very old white kinds, whose particles have become crystallized by age.

Many a bottle of claret or other French wine, which would be much liked had it time for repose, and had been then carefully drawn from its lees, is condemned, solely because it has been 'badly treated.' I may mention here, that not only ought all wines to be decanted, but this ought to be done two or three hours before they are to be used, because they require time for the flavour to be evolved and developed. This is still more necessary when the bottles come out of a cold cellar, for cold has what wine merchants call the effect of 'locking up the flavour.'

Along with the decanting machine, it would save much trouble if all the requisite tools were hung up beside it, so as to be ready for use. These are, a glass funnel, which ought to be curved, so that the wine may pour down the side, and not splash into the middle of the decanter; a champagne opener, for removing the wire; a corkscrew; a brush, for brushing off the dust, &c., which collects about the top of the cork; a strong knife, for cutting corks, string, &c.

There is also an article which is seldom seen, though it should be in general use, as it is scarcely possible to decant well without it; for it is inevitable that when a bottle containing liquid is turned down, the air will force itself in, and thus cause a gurgling and disturbance of the flow, until sufficient liquid has passed out to let it enter without difficulty. This instrument is what I call an Air-conductor, in the form of a bent hollow tube.

AIR-CONDUCTOR FOR DECANTING.

By placing the tip of the finger very tightly upon one orifice, and inserting the other end in the bottle till it reaches the small vacuum in the upper shoulder when a little slanted, and *then* removing the finger, the air rushes into the vacuum, exerting a pressure on the liquid which causes it to flow in a steady continuous stream. The accompanying sketch shows what it is like.

One observes even the most experienced men, in carrying bottles, hold them horizontally; and baskets are made for laying them in this position, when they

METAL BOTTLE-CARRIER.

are to be moved. Owing to the empty space thus left in the upper shoulder, it follows that when the bottle is moved the liquid also moves with it, from one end to the other. It seems much better, therefore, on taking the bottle from the bin, to change it very gradually and gently to the perpendicular; since it is almost impossible there can be any motion when it is thus steadily held.

There has been lately introduced from Paris, a very compact little metal bottle-carrier, having the advantage over the usual kinds, that it is smaller, does not collect sawdust, &c., and is not injured by being left in a damp cellar. The drawing on the preceding page is a sketch of it.

FINING, CORKS, ETC.

Fining is very simple; and I believe there is nothing better than the whites of fresh-laid eggs and real *sturgeon*-isinglass; but I have abandoned my intention of describing the operation, as it would require entering into many details. Whites of eggs are generally used for red, and isinglass for white wines; but the rules laid down in books as to a certain number or weight are, necessarily, often wrong; since it is evident that one pipe of port, &c., or butt of sherry, young, stout, and strong, may require twelve eggs, or one ounce of isinglass, while for others, old and mature, half these quantities may be sufficient.

The best way is to request the merchant from whom the wine is bought to put in the finings before sending it off; and, if it is for bottling, I would recommend the purchaser to procure from him also the proper quantity of the very finest corks.

Many a cask is spoiled, owing to bad corks and dirty bottles; and it is money well bestowed to employ a person who understands these matters, and will act fairly. If a wine cooper in London is wanted, I believe Mr. Rolfe of Great St. Helens may be relied upon in every respect.

It is greatly to be desired that there were one legal measure for bottles, but this seems impracticable; and the only way to escape being deceived is to act as is done in the other transactions of life—by dealing only with those who are considered respectable, or else to purchase in cask and bottle at home.

Among respectable wine merchants the recognised fair bottle is six to the gallon; but many others use a much smaller size; and consequently, when they sell at the same nominal price, receive a greater profit. While millions of old bottles exist, there seems no way of compelling the use of any certain size.

When gentlemen purchase in cask, there is no use in their incurring the expense of buying new bottles if they have old ones already; for, of whatever shape or size they be, they are of *glass*; and port, sherry, claret, &c., will keep as well in one shape as in another, provided both be perfectly clean. With wine merchants whose object in bottling is to sell, it is different, for they must use regular shapes.

CHAPTER XXIV.

GOUT.

No personal Experience—Letter from a Physician—Average annual Consumption in Mayence—Gout almost unknown there—Produced by too much Azote—Bi-carbonate of Potash—Letter from Bordeaux—Letters from a Gentleman in London, and from a Country Gentleman.

HAVING, happily, no personal experience of gout, I cannot say much about it, but I have sought for information; and I copy letters from Mayence, on the Rhine, from Bordeaux, and from two English gentlemen who are sufferers from its attacks. Whatever may be the cause, I do not presume to guess; there is, however, no doubt that it is infinitely more common among ourselves than anywhere abroad.

MAYENCE: January, 1863.

If we wish to arrive at a correct knowledge whether the use of Rhenish wines tends to produce Gout, we must, in the first place, acquaint ourselves with certain facts as existing in those towns, which form the centre of the country which produces them.

1st. In what number do cases of real gout occur, distinct from rheumatism, with which it is frequently confounded?

2nd. What is, approximately, the quantity of Rhenish wines consumed in those towns?

Within my own positive knowledge, I can, with reference to the above points, only speak of Mayence and Bingen, the towns in which Rhenish wines are consumed in the greatest proportion.

The yearly consumption of Rhenish wines in Mayence, amounts to 15,000 aums, or 500,000 English gallons, with a population of 40,000 souls; the adult man, therefore (women and children are of course left out of consideration), drinks on an average 60 gallons yearly, or 360 bottles.

The fact, however, that some individuals drink no wine, and that the proportion consumed by others is very unequal, serves to show that many of the wine-consuming population must indulge in a very large quantity indeed.

Yet the cases of Gout are so scarce, that during the last twenty years, only four cases came under my observation; and those cases were persons who led a sedentary life, and were addicted to the pleasures of the table, confining themselves by no means to the use of Rhenish wines. In Bingen, the consumption of Rhenish wine, in proportion to the number of inhabitants, is even larger than that of Mayence, yet Gout is there almost unknown; and equally rare in both these towns are those affections so intimately connected with Gout; as diseases of the bladder and kidneys.

In Frankfort, the consumption of Rhenish wines is considerably less. With a population of 70,000 souls, only 120,000 gallons are consumed.

As to the number of cases of Gout occurring there, I am less minutely informed, but it is certain that they do not occur in a much larger proportion. Eighty years ago the condition of the people in the Rhine country was different from what it is at present.

At that time there was among the population a greater difference in the relations of life, a more marked separation of classes, a greater number of 'fruges consumere nati,' who, in easy circumstances, indulged in idleness and excess, thereby generating a predisposition to Gout. Since then, however, a decided change has taken place, and Gout has all but disappeared from our part of the country; while the production and consumption of Rhine wine has become greater and more general.

From these facts we may conclude that those Rhine wines contain no properties productive of Gout. This can also be proved theoretically, so far as the present state of knowledge admits. Gout is produced by admitting into the system an immoderate quantity of azotic nourishment, by an insufficient secretion of human matter, and insufficient bodily exercise and respiration. As wine does not contain any azotic parts whatever, its alcoholic properties can only indirectly conduce to the production of Gout. But the Rhenish contains less alcohol than any of the southern wines; less than those of Portugal, Spain, Sicily, Cyprus, and Madeira; and is distinguished by its acid properties, which form Kali-bicarbonicum (Bi-carbonate of potash), a remedy for Gout. These remarks apply equally to still and to sparkling kinds.

DR. GOERIS.

From Bordeaux, a friend writes:—

It is a mistake to suppose that the wines of Bordeaux are a cause of Gout. Our medical men prescribe them for those whose blood is poor, and who require strengthening. Certainly, if *too much* is taken, it will do harm, as too much food will: but it is otherwise considered beneficial for the health of everyone, to drink true Bordeaux wine.

The following letters are from gentlemen in London, and in the country:—

LONDON: January 6, 1863.

In reply to your enquiry as to which wine I find it prudent to avoid, as most likely to bring on Gout,

I must first tell you that my Gout is hereditary; that my father and two of my brothers have died from it, and that I myself have what physicians describe by the term 'Gouty diathesis.' In other words, I am susceptible, and compelled to watch against any of those causes likely to develope the latent tendency. Under other circumstances my own experience has led me to the conclusion that Gout is never (in my own case at least) developed except during indigestion. I do not mean that indigestion always produces Gout in me, but this I know, I never had an attack except after this had set in. Hence, my system of self-treatment is to anticipate indigestion rather than to cure it. I do my utmost to forestall it, and prevent a recurrence.

I find its occurrence depends on a multitude of circumstances very different from the taking of wine; but I also find that certain wines are much more likely to produce it than others; and these, therefore, I avoid. The two which I am obliged to be most cautious about are Port and Burgundy. All others I take freely, without any reason to believe them at all injurious. Even Burgundy and Port I can take in moderation, with perfect impunity.

Ten or fifteen years ago, before I understood how to manage myself so well as I have since learned by experience to do, I used to have Gout three or four times every year. I then adopted my present precautionary system, including great moderation in Port, and taking principally white wines, and I found immediate benefit. For the last ten years my principal wine daily is fine Madeira, and frequently Champagne; and my attacks have been reduced from three in twelve months to four in twelve years!

You will observe that I condemn no wine in moderation, as in itself a provocation; but those I find least likely to cause indigestion, and consequently the best to avoid Gout, are Champagne and Madeira; that is, assuming them both to be fine wine, pure, and of the best quality; but the grand prophylactic is, not merely to keep down indigestion, but to forestall and prevent its approach.

WARWICK: January 13, 1863.

I have more fear from the liver than from indigestion. I never know, beforehand, when the Gout is coming, but I could bring it on at any time by eating and drinking sweets and acids.

LISTS OF ALL KNOWN WINES.

I. WINES OF FRANCE.

II. WINES NOT FRENCH.

LISTS OF WINES.

THE following alphabetical lists of every kind of wine known throughout the world will be useful for reference. The departments in which those of France are produced, and their general quality and colour, are here seen.

Others are not so minutely described, but to each is attached the country of its growth, and to many, their usual reputation, and colour (red or white); but, as both colours are found in almost all wine districts, this last column is not of much use.

In the compilation of these lists I have derived much assistance from the last edition of Jullien's valuable work, *Topographie de tous les Vignobles connus.*

I. WINES OF FRANCE.

Wine	Department	Quality	Colour
Achain	Meurthe	Common	Red
Agde	Herault	do.	do.
Aginois	Guienne	fine and ordinary	red and white
Agnac	Aveyron	ordinary	red
Aiglepierre	Jura	do.	do.
Aignes Vives	Gard	common	do.
Ain	Indre	ordinary and common	red and white
Airvault	Deux-Sevres	ordinary	red
Aisne	Indre	ordinary and common	red and white
Aix, Ile d'	CharenteInférieure	common	do.
Aix	Savoie	ordinary	do.
Aixe	Haute-Vienne	common	do.
Ajaccio	Corsica	ordinary	do.
Alais	Gard	common	red
Alan	Drôme	ordinary	do.
Albi	Tarn	common	do.
Aleth	Aude	ordinary	do.
Algajola	Corsica	do.	white and red
Allassac	Corrèze	do.	do.
Allauch	Bouches-du-Rhône	do.	do.
Allier	Indre	ordinary and common	do.
Allonnes	Maine-et-Loire	ordinary	do.
Allouveaux	Meuse	do.	do.
Aloxe	Côte-d'Or	fine	red
Alpes	Basses-Alpes	ordinary and common	white and red
Alpes	Hautes-Alpes	do.	do.
Alpes	Alpes-Maritimes	ordinary	red
Alsace	Alsace	dry, sweet, fine, and ordinary	white and red
Ambarés	Gironde	common	red
Amberieux	Ain	ordinary	do.
Ambés	Gironde	do.	do.
Amboise	Indre-et-Loire	common	white and red
Ammerschwihr	Haut-Rhin	dry, sweet, fine	white
Ampuis	Rhône	fine	red
Ancenis	Loire-Inférieure	ordinary	white
Ancirville	Marne	common	do.
Andresy	Seine-et-Oise	ordinary	red
Angé	Loire-et-Cher	do.	do.
Angers	Maine-et-Loire	do.	do.

Wine	Department	Quality	Colour
Anglefort	Ain	Ordinary	Red
Anglet	Basses-Pyrénées	liqueur	white
Angoulême	Charente	ordinary	white and red
Angoumois	Do.	ordinary and common	do.
Anjou	Maine-et-Loire	do.	do.
Annecy	Savoie	ordinary	do.
Antoigné	Maine-et-Loire	common	white
Apremont	Meuse	ordinary	red
Arancy	Aisne	do.	do.
Arbanats	Gironde	fine	white
Arbois	Jura	ordinary and fine	red and white
Arcet	Landes	ordinary	white
Arcins	Gironde	fine	red
Arcy-sur-Cure	Yonne	ordinary	do.
Ardèche	Ardèche	fine and ordinary	do.
Ardennes	Ardennes	common	do.
Argelès	Hautes-Pyrénées	do.	do.
Argelliers	Aude	ordinary	do.
Argence	Calvados	common	red and white
Argentat	Carrèze	do.	do.
Argenteuil	Seine-et-Oise	do.	do.
Argentière	Ardèche	ordinary	do.
Arles	Bouches-du-Rhône	do.	do.
Armagnac	Gers	do.	do.
Arnaville	Meurthe	do.	red
Ariége	Ariége	common	do.
Ars	Moselle	ordinary	do.
Arsac	Gironde	do.	do.
Arsures	Jura	do.	do.
Arthezé	Sarthe	do.	red and white
Artuis	Loire-et-Cher	common	white
Arveyres	Gironde	do.	red
Asnières	Charente	ordinary	do.
Asgues	Gironde	do.	do.
Athée	Indre-et-Loire	do.	do.
Athis	Seine-et-Oise	do.	do.
Aubagne	Bouches-du-Rhône	do.	do.
Aube	Aube	fine, ordinary, common	do.
Aubenas	Ardèche	ordinary	do.
Aubertin	Basses-Pyrénées	do.	do.
Aubigny	Haute-Marne	do.	do.
Aubons	Basses-Pyrénées	do.	white and red
Aude	Aude	ordinary, common	
Audignon	Landes	ordinary	white
Aules	Do.	do.	white and red
Aunis	Vendée	ordinary and common	do.
Aussac	Tarn-et-Garonne	do.	do.
Auvergne	Puy-de-Dôme	fine, ordinary & common	do.
Auxerre	Yonne	fine and ordinary	red
Avallon	Do.	ordinary	do.
Avenay	Marne	do.	do.
Avensan	Gironde	fine	do.
Aveyron	Aveyron	ordinary and common	do.

Wine	Department	Quality	Colour
Avignon	Vaucluse	Fine	Red
Avirey	Aube	do.	do.
Avize	Marne	do.	white
Ay	Do.	do.	do.
Aydie	Basses-Pyrénées	ordinary	white and red
Ayrans	Gironde	do.	white
Azay	Aisne	common	do.
Azay	Indre-et-Loire	ordinary	red
Babelheim	Haut-Rhin	dry and fine	do.
Bacalan	Gironde	ordinary	do.
Bagneux	Aube	fine	do.
Bagnères	Hautes-Pyrénées	common	do.
Bagnols	Gard	fine	do.
Bahus	Landes	ordinary	do.
Baixas	Pyrénées-Oriental.	do.	do.
Ballan	Indre-et-Loire	do.	do.
Balnot	Aube	fine	do.
Bandols	Var	ordinary	do.
Banos	Landes	do.	white
Banyuls-s.-Mer	Pyrenées-Oriental.	fine, sweet	red
Bar-le-Duc	Meuse	ordinary	do.
Bar-sur-Aube	Aube	do.	do.
Bar-sur-Seine	Do.	do.	do.
Barbantanne	Bouches-du-Rhône	sweet	do.
Barbezieux	Charente	ordinary	white and red
Barolles	Rhône	do.	red
Barsac	Gironde	fine	white
Bassan	Hérault	sweet	do.
Bassanèse	Corsica	ordinary	white and red
Bassens	Gironde	do.	red
Bastennes	Landes	do.	white and red
Bastia	Corsica	do.	do.
Bats	Landes	do.	white
Baule	Loiret	do.	red
Baulette	Do.	do.	do.
Baurech	Gironde	do.	do.
Bayon	Do.	do.	do.
Bayonville	Meurthe	do.	do.
Bazas	Gironde	common	do.
Bazouges	Sarthe	ordinary	white
Béarn	Basses-Pyrenees	fine, ordinary, common	white and red
Beaucaire	Gard	fine	red
Beauce	Loiret	common	do.
Beaugency	Do.	ordinary	do.
Beaujolais	Rhône	fine, ordinary, common	do.
Beaumarche's	Gers	ordinary	do.
Beaumes	Vaucluse	sweet	white and red
Beaumont	Dordogne	ordinary	do.
Beaumont	Marne	do.	white
Beaune	Côte-d'Or	fine	red
Beausset	Var	ordinary	do.
Beautiran	Gironde	do.	white and red
Beauvais	Charente-Inférieure	do.	do.

Wine	Department	Quality	Colour
Behonne	Meuse	Ordinary	Red
Bellac	Haute-Vienne	common	do.
Belleville	Rhône	ordinary	do.
Belleville	Meuse	do.	red and white
Bellevue	Aisne	do.	red
Bennes	Yonne	do.	white
Begerac	Dordogne	fine	red and white
Bergholtzell	Haut-Rhin	dry, fine	white
Bernouil	Yonne	ordinary	do.
Berry	Indre	ordinary and common	red and white
Béru	Yonne	ordinary	white
Besançon	Doubs	do.	red
Besse	Var	common	do.
Bessins	Isère	ordinary	do.
Beurre	Doubs	do.	do.
Béziers	Hérault	sweet, ordinary	do.
Bièvre	Aisne	ordinary	do.
Bigorre	Pyrénées	ordinary and common	do.
Blacé	Rhône	ordinary	do.
Blagny	Côte-d'Or	fine	do.
Blaisois	Loire-et-Cher	ordinary and common	do
Blandans	Jura	ordinary	do.
Blanquefort	Gironde	fine	do.
Blanquette	Aude	ordinary	white
Blanzac	Charente	do.	red
Blaye	Gironde	common	do.
Bléré	Indre-et-Loire	ordinary	do.
Blois	Loire-et-Cher	do.	do.
Boissy	Seine-et-Oise	do.	do.
Boen	Loire	do.	do.
Boesse	Loiret	do.	do.
Bommes	Gironde	fine	white
Boncourt	Meuse	ordinary	do.
Bonifacio	Corsica	do.	do.
Bonnaville	Savoie	do.	do.
Bordelais	Gironde	fine, ordinary, common	do.
Bouches-du-Rhône	Bouches-du-Rhône	sweet, ordinary, and common	white and red
Boudonville	Meurthe	common	red
Bouilh	Hautes-Pyrénées	ordinary	white
Bouillé	Deux-Sèvres	do.	white and red
Bouilly	Aube	do.	red
Boulennes	Landes	do.	
Bouliac	Gironde	do.	do.
Boulin	Landes	ordinary, common	
Bourbonnais	Indre	ordinary	
Bourdeilles	Dordogne	do.	
Bourg	Gironde	do.	
Bourges	Cher	common	white
Bourgneuf	Saône et Loire	ordinary	do.
Bourgogne (Burgundy)	Côte-d'Or	fine, ordinary, common	
Bourré	Loire-et-Cher	ordinary	do.

Wine	Department	Quality	Colour
Bouzeron	Saône-et-Loire	Ordinary	white
Bouzigues	Hérault	do.	red
Bouzy	Marne	fine	do.
Brantôme	Dordogne	ordinary	do.
Brassac	Do.	do.	do.
Brassempouy	Landes	do.	
Bresse	Ain	common	
Bretagne	Loire-Inférieure	ordinary, common	
Brezé	Maine-et-Loire	ordinary	
Brie	Oise	common	
Brion	Maine-et-Loire	do.	white
Brionde	Haute-Loire	do.	red
Brives	Corrèze	ordinary	do.
Brochon	Côte-d'Or	do.	do.
Brouassin	Sarthe	do.	
Brouilly	Saône-et-Loire	do.	do.
Bruley	Meurthe	do.	
Buanes	Landes	do.	white
Budos	Gironde	fine	do.
Bugey	Ain	ordinary	
Burosse	Basses-Pyrénées	do.	
Bussac	Charente-Inférieure	do.	
Bussy-la-Côte	Meuse	do.	red
Buxerulles	Do.	do.	do.
Buxières	Do.	do.	do.
Buxy	Saône-et-Loire	do.	
Buzet	Lot-et-Garonne	fine	white
Buzet	Haute-Garonne	ordinary	
Byans	Doubs	do.	red
Cadillac	Gironde	fine	white
Cadillon	Basses-Pyrénées	ordinary	
Cagnes	Var	fine	red
Cagny	Somme		
Cahors	Lot	ordinary	
Caissaguet	Tarn	do.	do.
Calenzana	Corsica	do.	
Calvados	Calvados		
Calvi	Corsica	do.	
Calville	Puy-de-Dôme	do.	
Calvisson	Gard	do.	
Cambes	Gironde	do.	white
Camblanes	Do.	do.	do.
Camiac	Gironde	do.	red
Campagne	Ariége	common	do.
Campsas	Tarn-et-Garonne	ordinary	do.
Camy	Lot	do.	
Canon	Côte-de-Gironde	fine	do.
Cantal	Cantal	common	
Cantefort	Savoie	ordinary	
Cantenac	Gironde	fine	do.
Capbreton	Landes	do.	
Cap-Corse	Corsica	ordinary, sweet	
Capens	Haute-Garonne	ordinary	red

Wine	Department	Quality	Colour
Carnoules	Var	Common	Red
Cassis	Bouches-du-Rhône	sweet	
Castelvieilh	Hautes-Pyrénées	ordinary	white
Castellet	Var	do.	red
Castelnau	Hautes-Pyrénées	do.	do.
Castelnau	Landes	do.	
Castres	Gironde	do.	white
Castries	Hérault	do.	red
Caupenne	Landes	do.	white
Cazalis	Do.	do.	
Cazouls	Hérault	sweet	do.
Celles	Dordogne	ordinary, common	
Cercié	Rhône	ordinary	red
Cerons	Gironde	fine	white
Certaux	Saône-et-Loire	ordinary	do.
Cerveyrieux	Ain	do.	red
Cette	Hérault		
Cévennes	Lozère		
Chablis	Yonne	fine and ordinary	white
Chabris	Indre	ordinary	do.
Chaînette	près Yonne	fine	red
Chamtrè	Maine-et-Loire	ordinary	
Chaise	Allier	common	white
Châlons	Maine	do.	
Châlons	Saône-et-Loire		
Chalosse	Landes		
Chambertin	Côte-d'Or	fine	red
Chambéry	Savoie	fine, ordinary	
Chambolle	Do.	do.	do.
Chambon	Loire-et-Cher	ordinary	
Chamery	Marne	do.	do.
Champagne	Ain	do.	do.
Champagne	Sarthe	do.	white
Champagne	Marne	fine, ordinary	
Champagne	Charente	ordinary	
Champagney	Haute-Saône		
Champigny	Vienne	do.	red
Champigny	Maine-et-Loire	do.	do.
Champillon	Marne	do.	do.
Champlitte-le-Château	Haute-Saône	do.	do.
Champougny	Meuse	do.	do.
Champs	Yonne	do.	white
Chancelade	Dordogne	do.	
Chanes	Saône-et-Loire	do.	red
Chantagne	Savoie	do.	
Chanturgue	Puy-de-Dôme	fine	do.
Chapelle	Loire	ordinary	white
Chapelle	Loire-Inférieure	do.	do.
Chapelle	Loiret	do.	red
Chapelle	Sarthe	do.	
Chapelle-de-Guinchay	Saône-et-Loire	do.	do.

Wine	Department	Quality	Colour
Chapniers	Charente-Inférieure	Ordinary	Red
Chardogne	Meuse	do.	do.
Charentay	Rhône	do.	do.
Charente	Charente	ordinary, common	
Charente-Inférieure	Charente-Inférieure	do.	
Charey	Meurthe	ordinary	do.
Chargé	Indre-et-Loire	common	
Chariez	Haute-Saône	ordinary	do.
Charlieu	Loire	common	do.
Charly	Rhône	ordinary	do.
Charmes	Vosges	do.	do.
Charnay	Saône-et-Loire	do.	
Chartres	Eure-et-Loir	fine	
Chassagne	Côte-d'Or	do.	do.
Chassagne	Rhône	ordinary	do.
Chassé	Maine-et-Loire	do.	
Chassors	Charente	do.	do.
Château-Châlons	Jura	fine	white
Château-du-Loir	Sarthe	ordinary	do.
Château-Gombert	Bouches-du-Rhône	do.	red
Château-Grillet	Loire	fine	
Château-Haut-Brion	Gironde	do.	do.
„ Lafitte	do.	do.	do.
„ Latour,	do.	do.	do.
„ Margaux	do.	do.	do.
Châteauneuf-de-Chabre	Hautes-Alpes	ordinary	do.
Châteauneuf-de-Gadogne	Vaucluse	do.	do.
Châteauneuf-du-Pape	Vaucluse	fine	do.
Châteauneuf-du-Rhône	Drôme	ordinary	do.
Château-Renard	Bouches-du-Rhône	do.	do.
Chateauroux	Indre	do.	
Château-Thierry	Aisne	common	red and white
Château-Vilain	Haute-Marne	ordinary	red
Châteldon	Puy-du-Dôme	do.	do.
Châtillon-le-Duc	Drôme	do.	do.
Châtre	Sarthe	do.	white
Chaumont	Loir-et-Cher	do.	
Chauriat	Puy-de-Dôme	do.	
Chauvigny	Vienne	do.	red
Chaux	Puy-de-Dôme	do.	
Chavau	Marne	do.	do.
Chavenay	Loire	do.	do.

Wine	Department	Quality	Colour
Chavignol	Cher	Ordinary	
Chemilly	Yonne	do.	
Chénas	Rhône	fine	red
Chenay	Mârne	ordinary	do.
Cheney	Yonne	do.	do.
Chenonceaux	Indre-et-Loire	do.	do.
Chenove	Saône-et-Loire	do.	
Chenove	Côte-d'Or	fine, ordinary	
Cher	Cher	ordinary, common	
Chérac	Charente-Inférieure	ordinary	
Chereubles	Rhône	do.	do.
Chevagny	Saône-et-Loire	do.	do.
Chichée	Yonne	do.	white
Chigny	Marne	fine	red
Chinon	Indre-et-Loire	ordinary	
Chissay	Loire-et-Cher	do.	red
Chisseaux	Indre-et-Loire	do.	do.
Chouilly	Marne	do.	white
Chouzelot	Doubs	do.	red
Chusclan	Gard	fine	do.
Chuynes	Loire	ordinary	do.
Ciotat	Bouches du-Rhône	ordinary, com., sweet	do.
Cissac	Gironde	fine	do.
Civrac	Do.	ordinary	do.
Civray	Indre-et-Loire	do.	
Clairac	Lot-et-Garonne	fine	
Clairegoutte	Haute-Saône		
Clarette	Drôme	ordinary	
Classun	Landes	do.	do.
Claveau	Marne	do.	do.
Clessé	Saône-et-Loire	do.	
Cognac	Charente		
Collioure	Pyrénées Orientales	fine, sweet	
Colmar	Haut-Rhin	do.	white
Colombier	Dordogne	do.	
Commensac	Gironde	fine	red
Commissey	Yonne	ordinary	do.
Compiègne	Oise	common	do.
Comps	Gironde	ordinary	do.
Comté de Foix	Aude	common	
Conchez	Basses-Pyrénées	ordinary	
Concremurs	Indre	do.	do.
Condrieu	Rhône	fine	white
Confolens	Charente	ordinary	
Conserans	Hérault	common	
Corent	Puy-de-Dôme	ordinary	white
Cornas	Ardèche	fine, ordinary	red
Corneilla-de-la-Rivière	Pyrénées Orientales	ordinary	do.
Corrèze	Corrèze	ordinary, common	
Corse	Corsica	ordinary	
Corte	Do.	do.	
Corton	Côte-d'Or	fine	

Wine	Department	Quality	Colour
Cosperon	Pyrénées Orientales	Fine, sweet	Red, white
Coteau-Brûlé	Vaucluse	fine	red
Côte-d'Or	Côte-d'Or	fine, ordinary	
Côte-Rôtie	Meurthe	fine	do.
Côte Saint André	Isère	ordinary	white
Côtes	Gironde	do.	
Côtes-du-Nord	Côte-du-Nord	do.	
Coudes	Puy-de-Dôme	do.	red
Coulange-la-Vineuse	Yonne	do.	do.
Courchamps	Maine-et-Loire	do.	white
Courchverny	Loir-et-Cher	do.	do.
Courgy	Yonne	do.	do.
Cournon	Puy-de-Dôme	do.	red
Couronne-la-Palud	Charente	do.	do.
Coutras	Gironde	do.	do.
Couture	Vienne	do.	do.
Couzon	Rhône	do.	do.
Cramant	Marne	fine	white
Craonelle	Aisne	ordinary	red
Craonne	Do.	do.	do.
Cravant	Yonne	do.	do.
Créancey	Haute-Marne	do.	do.
Crépy	Aisne	do.	do.
Crèpy	Savoie	do.	
Creuë	Meuse	do.	
Creuse	Creuse		
Creuziers	Allier	common	
Creysse	Dordogne	fine	do.
Croix-de-Bléré	Indre-et-Loire	ordinary	do.
Crolle	Isère	do.	
Cromières	Sarthe	do.	
Croze	Drôme	fine	do.
Cruon	Aveyron	ordinary	do.
Cubzac	Gironde	do.	
Cuers	Var	ordinary, common	do.
Cugnaux	Haute-Garonne	ordinary	
Culoz	Ain	do.	do.
Cumières	Marne	fine	do.
Cumèges	Dordogne	ordinary	do.
Cunac	Tarn	do.	do.
Cuqueron	Basses-Pyrénées	do.	do.
Cuques	Bouches-du-Rhône	do.	
Curis	Rhône	do.	
Cussac	Gironde	do.	do.
Cussy	Aisne	do.	
Dâle	Moselle	do.	do.
Dallet	Puy-de-Dôme	do.	
Damery	Marne	do.	do.
Dampierre	Maine-et-Loire	do.	
Damoulens	Landes	do.	white
Dannemoine	Yonne	fine, ordinary	

Wine	Department	Quality	Colour
Dauphiné	Drôme	Fine, ordinary	
Davayé	Saône-et-Loire	ordinary	
Denicé	Rhône	do.	red
Designy	Savoie	do.	do.
Deuil	Seine-et-Oise	common	do.
Deux-Sèvres	Deux-Sèvres	ordinary	
Die	Drôme	do.	
Dié	Yonne	do.	white
Dierre	Indre-et-Loire	do.	
Dijon	Côte-d'Or	do.	red
Dissay	Vienne	do.	do.
Distré	Maine-et-Loire	do.	
Disy	Marne	fine	
Diusse	Basses-Pyrénées	ordinary	
Dôle	Jura	common	white
Domgermain	Meurthe	ordinary	
Domme	Dordogne	do.	red
Dompcevrin	Meuse	do.	do.
Donzacq	Landes	do.	
Donzenac	Corrèze	do.	
Donzère	Drôme	do.	do.
Dordogne	Dordogne	fine, ordinary	
Dornot	Moselle	ordinary	white
Doubs	Doubs	do.	
Douillon	Marne	do.	red
Drôme	Drôme	fine, ordinary	
Durette	Rhône	ordinary	do.
Echaillon	Savoie	common	do.
Ecrouves	Meurthe	ordinary	do.
Ecueil	Marne	do.	do.
Egry	Loiret	common	do.
Eguilles	Bouches-du-Rhône	ordinary	
Emeringes	Rhône	do.	do.
Enguisheim	Haut-Rhin	do.	white
Engraviés	Ariège	common	red
Entre deux Mers	Gironde	ordinary	
Epeigné	Indre-et-Loire	do.	
Epernay	Marne	fine	
Epinal	Vosges	common	
Epineuil	Yonne	fine	
Ernolsheim	Bas-Rhin	ordinary	white
Esparron	Pyrénées Orientales	do.	red
Espira de l'Agly	Do.	do.	do.
Essey	Meurthe	do.	do.
Essey-les-Ponts	Haute-Marne	do.	do.
Estroy	Saône-et-Loire	do.	do.
Etoile	Jura	do.	white
Etoux	Rhône	do.	red
Eure	Eure	ordinary, common	
Euvezin	Meurthe	ordinary	do.
Eyres	Landes	do.	white
Farques	Gironde	fine	do.
Fau	Tarn-et-Garonne	ordinary	

Wine	Department	Quality	Colour
Faverolles	Loire-et-Cher	Ordinary	
Finistère	Finistère		
Fiton	Aude	do.	red
Fixey	Côte-d'Or	do.	do.
Fixin	Do.	fine, ordinary	
Flavigny	Do.	ordinary	do.
Fleury	Loiret	common	do.
Fleury	Rhône	fine	do.
Fleury la Rivière	Marne	ordinary	do.
Fley	Yonne	do.	white
Florac	Lozère	common	
Florentin	Tarn	ordinary	red
Flotte	Sarthe	do.	white
Foix	Comté-de-Foix	ordinary, common	
Fondettes	Indre-et-Loire	ordinary	
Fontenay	Yonne	do.	white
Force	Dordogne	fine	red
Fores	Cantal	sweet, ordinary	
Fougerolles	Haute-Saône		
Fouquebrune	Charente	ordinary	
Fourneaux	Loiret	do.	do.
Foy	Maine-et-Loire	do.	white
Foy-Monjault	Deux-Sèvres	do.	red
Franche-Comté	Doubs, Jura	fine, ordinary	
Francillon	Loir-et-Cher		black
Francueil	Indre-et-Loire	ordinary	
Fronsac	Gironde	do.	
Frontignan	Hérault	sweet	
Fronton	Haute-Garonne	ordinary	
Fuissé	Saône-et-Loire	fine	white
Fussy	Cher	ordinary	red
Gabarnac	Gironde	do.	white
Gaillac	Tarn	do.	
Gan	Basses-Pyrénées	fine	
Gard	Gard	fine, ordinary, common	
Gardanne	Bouches-du-Rhône	ordinary	
Garde-Adhémar	Drôme	do.	red
Gardes	Charente	do.	do.
Garenne-du-Sel	Allier	do.	do.
Garonne	Haute-Garonne	ordinary, common	
Garrigues	Hérault	ordinary	do.
Gascogne	Gers, Landes	fine, ordinary	
Gatinais	Indre	ordinary, common	do.
Gaude	Var	fine	do.
Gaujacq	Landes	ordinary	
Gazonfière	Sarthe	do.	
Gelos	Basses-Pyrénées	fine	white
Gemenos	Bouches-du-Rhône	ordinary	
Génissac	Gironde	do.	red
Geraise	Jura	do.	do.
Gers	Gers	ordinary, common	
Gervant	Drôme	fine	do.
Gévaudan	Lozère		

Wine	Department	Quality	Colour
Gevrey	Côte-d'Or	Fine	
Gex	Ain	common	
Ginestas	Aude	ordinary	red
Ginestet	Dordogne	fine	do.
Gircourt	Vosges	ordinary	
Gironde	Gironde	fine, ordinary	
Givry	Saône-et-Loire	ordinary	
Givry	Yonne	do.	do.
Goûts	Gers	do.	do.
Goûts	Dordogne	do.	do.
Gradels	Aveyron	do.	do.
Grande Côte	Yonne	fine	do.
Grasse	Aude	ordinary	do.
Grattay	Saône-et-Loire	do.	do.
Grauve	Marne	do.	white
Grave	Gironde	common	red
Grave	Tarn	ordinary	do.
Grave	Gironde	fine	
Grenier	Savoie	ordinary	
Gresivaudon	Isère	do.	
Grignon	Do.	do.	
Groslée	Ain	do.	do.
Guebviller	Haut-Rhin	dry, fine	
Guienne	Gironde	fine, ordinary	
Guignes	Loiret	ordinary	do.
Guilherand	Ardèche	do.	
Gy	Haute-Saône	do.	do.
Gyé	Aube	common	do.
Habsheim	Haut-Rhin	dry	white
Hattonchâtel	Meuse	ordinary	red
Haut-Brion	Gironde	fine	do.
Haute-Saône	Haute-Saône	ordinary	
Hautvillers	Marne	fine	
Haux	Gironde	ordinary	white
Haye	Loire-Inférieure	do.	do.
Heiligenstein	Bas-Rhin	sweet	
Hérault	Hérault	do., ordinary	
Hermitage	Drôme	fine	
Hernouville	Marne	ordinary	red
Homme	Sarthe	do.	
Hourcade	Basses-Pyrénées	do.	do.
Huis	Ain	do.	do.
Hunneveyr	Haut-Rhin	dry, fine	
Hurigny	Saône-et-Loire	ordinary	
Hyères	Var	do.	do.
Igé	Saône-et-Loire	do.	do.
Ile-de-France	Seine, Oise	common	
Illats	Gironde	fine	white
Ille-et-Vilaine	Ille-et-Vilaine	common	
Imbsheim	Bas-Rhin	ordinary	do.
Indre	Indre	ordinary, common	
Indre-et-Loire	Indre-et-Loire	do.	
Ingersheim	Haut-Rhin	dry, fine	do.

Wine	Department	Quality	Colour
Irancy	Yonne	Fine, ordinary	Red
Irigny	Marne	ordinary	do.
Irigny	Rhône	do.	
Isère	Isére	fine, ordinary	
Issoudun	Indre	ordinary	
Izon	Gironde	do.	do.
Jadousse	Basses-Pyrénées	do.	
Jailleu	Isère	do.	do.
Jallerange	Doubs	ordinary, common	
Jambles	Saône-et-Loire	common	
Jarday	Loir-et-Cher	ordinary	
Jargeau	Loiret	do.	do.
Jarnac	Charente	do.	
Jarrie-Haute	Isère	do.	do.
Jasseron	Rhône	do.	do.
Jasnières	Sarthe	do.	
Jaulnay	Vienne	do.	do.
Jaulnay	Meurthe	do.	do.
Javernant	Aube	do.	do.
Joigny	Yonne	do.	
Joinville	Haute-Marne	do.	do.
Jonquières	Gard	do.	do.
Joué	Indre-et-Loire	do.	do.
Julienne	Charente	do.	do.
Jullié	Rhône	do.	do.
Julliénas	Do.	do.	do.
Jumigny	Aisne	do.	do.
Junay	Yonne	fine, ordinary	
Jura	Jura	do.	
Jurançon	Basses-Pyrénées	do.	
Jussy	Moselle	ordinary	do.
Jussy	Yonne	do.	do.
Kaysersberg	Haut-Rhin	do.	
Katzenthal	Do.	fine	white
Kientzheim	Bas-Rhin	dry, fine	
Kientzheim	Haut-Rhin	fine, sweet	
Labarde	Gironde	ordinary	red
Labrède	Do.	do.	white
Lacadière	Var	do.	red
Lacénas	Rhône	do.	do.
Lachau	Puy-de-Dôme	do.	do.
Lacostière	Gard	do.	do.
Lagnieux	Ain	do.	do.
Lagos	Basses-Pyrénées	do.	do.
Laines-aux-Bois	Aube	do.	do.
Laisnes	Saône-et-Loire	do.	do.
Laizé	Do.	do.	
Lamarque	Gironde	fine	do.
Lambin	Isère	common	
Lancedat	Aveyron	ordinary	do.
Lancié	Rhône	do.	do.
Landes	Landes	fine, ordinary	
Landes	Puy-de-Dôme	do.	do.

Wine	Department	Quality	Colour
Landiras	Gironde	Fine	White
Landreville	Aube	common	red
Langeais	Indre-et-Loire	ordinary	
Langlade	Garde	do.	do.
Langoiran	Gironde	fine, ordinary	
Langon	Do.	fine	white
Languedoc	Gard, Garonne	fine, ordinary, common	
Lantigné	Rhône	ordinary	
Laon	Aisne	do.	red
Larronin	Basses-Pyrénées	fine	white
Larroque	Gironde	ordinary	do.
Larroque	Tarn	do.	do.
Lascazères	Hautes-Pyrénées	do.	do.
Lasseras	Savoie	do.	white
Lasseube	Basses-Pyrénées	do.	red
Latour	Gironde	fine	do.
Latour du Breuil	Indre	ordinary	
Latresne	Gironde	do.	do.
Laudun	Gard	do.	
Lavans	Doubs	do.	do.
Lebas	Lot	do.	
Lédenon	Gard	do.	do.
Lembras	Dordogne	fine	
Lénye	Côte-de-Landes	ordinary	
Léognan	Gironde	fine	
Lestiac	Do.	ordinary	white
Letret	Hautes-Alpes	do.	red
Leucate	Aude	do.	do.
Lezandre	Puy-de-Dôme	do.	do.
Libarde	Gironde	do.	do.
Libourne	Do.	do.	
Liesle	Doubs	do.	do.
Ligny	Meuse	do.	do.
Ligny le-Châtel	Yonne	do.	
Limerai	Indre-et-Loire	do.	
Limony	Ardèche	do.	do.
Limosin	Haute Vienne	ordinary and common	
Limoux	Aude	ordinary	white
Linars	Charente	do.	red
Linde	Dordogne	do.	do.
Lionville	Meuse	do.	do.
Lirac	Gard	fine	do.
Listrac	Gironde	do.	do.
Livron	Drôme	ordinary	
Loché	Saône-et-Loire	do.	
Loir-et-Cher	Loir-et-Cher	ordinary, common	
Loire	Loire	sweet, ordinary	
Loire	Haute-Loire	common	
Loire-Inférieure	Loire-Inférieure	ordinary, common	white
Loiret	Loiret	do.	
Loisey	Meuse	ordinary	
Lombard	Doubs	do.	red
Longeville	Meuse	do.	do.

Wine	Department	Quality	Colour
Lons-le-Saulnier	Jura	Ordinary	
Lormont	Gironde	do.	red
Loroux	Loire-Inférieure	do.	white
Lorraine	Meurthe, Meuse	ordinary, common	
Lot	Lot	do.	
Lot-et-Garonne	Lot-et-Garonne	fine, ordinary	
Laudun	Vienne	ordinary	do.
Loupiac	Gironde	fine, ordinary	
Loupian	Hérault	ordinary	red
Loupmont	Meuse	do.	do.
Loury	Loiret	common	white
Lozère	Lozère	do.	
Luc	Basses-Pyrénées	ordinary	red
Lucey	Meurthe	do.	do.
Ludes	Marne	fine	do.
Ludon	Gironde	do.	do.
Lunel	Hérault	sweet	
Lupé	Loire	ordinary	do.
Lure	Haute-Saône	common	
Lusillé	Loir-et-Cher	ordinary	do.
Lussac	Gironde	do.	
Lussan	Gers	do.	do.
Luynes	Indre-et-Loire	do.	do.
Luzech	Lot	do.	
Lyonnais	Rhône	sweet, fine, ordinary	
Macau	Gironde	ordinary	do.
Maccaticcia	Corsica	do.	
Machurat	Ain	do.	do.
Mâcon	Saône-et-Loire	fine	
Madiran	Hautes-Pyrénées	do.	do.
Magrie	Aude	do.	white
Mailly	Marne	fine	red
Maine	Sarthe	ordinary, common	
Maine-et-Loire	Maine-et-Loire	ordinary	
Maisdon	Loire-Inférieure	do.	white
Malgue	Var	fine	red
Maligny	Yonne	ordinary	white
Manche	Manche		
Mancy	Marne	do.	do.
Mantes sur Seine	Seine-et-Oise	ordinary, common	red
Maraussan	Hérault	sweet	
Marchand	Rhône	ordinary	do.
Mauzé	Charente	ordinary, common	
Marcillac	Aveyron	ordinary	do.
Marçon	Sarthe	do.	white
Mardeuil	Marne	do.	red
Mareil	Sarthe	do.	white
Marennes	Charente Inférieure	do.	
Maretel	Savoie	sweet	do.
Mareuil	Dordogne	ordinary	red
Mareuil	Loir-et-Cher	do.	do.
Mareuil	Marne	fine	
Margaux	Gironde	do.	do.

Wine	Department	Quality	Colour
Marignane	Bouches-du-Rhône	Ordinary	
Mariol	Puy-de-Dôme	do.	
Marmande	Loire-et-Garonne	do.	white
Marne	Marne	fine, ordinary	
Marne	Haute-Marne	ordinary, common	
Marnoz	Jura	ordinary	red
Marseillan	Hérault	sweet	white
Marseille	Bouches-du-Rhône	ordinary	
Marthon	Charente	do.	red
Martigné-Briante	Maine-et-Loire	do.	white
Martignac	Gironde	fine, ordinary	do.
Martres	Puy-de-Dôme	ordinary	red
Marvejols	Lozère	common	
Mauves	Ardèche	ordinary	do.
Mauzé	Deux-Sèvres		
Mayenne	Mayenne	common	
Mazan	Vaucluse	sweet	
Mazères	Basses-Pyrénées	fine	white
Mazères	Gers	ordinary	red
Médoc	Gironde	fine, ordinary	
Mées	Basses-Alpes	ordinary	do.
Mel-la-Garde	Lot	do.	
Melun	Seine-et-Marne	do.	
Menetree	Jura	do.	do.
Menil	Marne	fine	
Mer-la-Ville	Loir-et-Cher	ordinary, common	
Mercurey	Saône-et-Loire	ordinary	do.
Mercurol	Drôme	fine	
Merignac	Gironde	do.	do.
Messanges	Landes	do.	
Meung	Loiret	ordinary	do.
Meursault	Côte-d'Or	fine, ordinary	
Meurthe	Meurthe	ordinary, common	
Meuse	Meuse	do.	do.
Meusnes	Loir-et-Cher	ordinary	
Méze	Hérault	do.	
Mézel	Puy-de-Dôme	do.	
Miélan	Gers	do.	do.
Mignaux	Seine-et-Oise	do.	
Mihervé	Maine-et-Loire	do.	white
Milery	Doubs	do.	do.
Milhars	Tarn	do.	red
Millery	Rhône	do.	do.
Milly	Yonne	do.	white
Miradoux	Gers	do.	red
Mirebeau	Vienne	common	do.
Mirepeisset	Aude	ordinary	do.
Mitteleveyer	Haut-Rhin	dry, fine	
Molesme	Yonne	ordinary	do.
Molins	Marne	do.	white
Molsheim	Bas-Rhin	dry, fine	do.
Momuy	Landes	ordinary	

Wine	Department	Quality	Colour
Monbazillac	Dordogne	Sweet	
Monbogre	Saône-et-Loire	ordinary	
Monein	Basses-Pyrénées	do.	
Monistrol	Haute-Loire	do.	
Monmarvès	Dordogne	fine	red
Monprinblanc	Gironde	do.	white
Mons	Seine-et-Oise	ordinary	
Monsec	Meuse	do.	red
Montagne	Gironde	do.	do.
Montagny	Saône-et-Loire	do.	
Montargis	Loiret	common	do.
Montbartier	Tarn-et-Garonne	ordinary	do.
Montbazin	Hérault	sweet	white
Montchâlons	Aisne	ordinary	red
Montélimar	Drôme	do.	do.
Montelivaut	Loir-et-Cher	do.	white
Montemaggiore	Corsica		
Mont-en-Saint Martin-de-Sanzay	Deux Sèvres	do.	red
Montesquieu-Volvestre	Haute-Garonne	do.	
Montferrand	Gironde	do.	
Montflanquin	Lot-et-Garonne	do.	do.
Montford	Landes	do.	do.
Montgrimault	Marne	do.	white
Monthelie	Côte-d'Or	do.	red
Monthelon	Marne	do.	
Monthou	Loir-et-Cher	do.	
Montignac	Charente	do.	
Montigny	Jura	do.	white
Montluçon	Allier	common	red
Montmelas-St. Sorlin	Rhône	ordinary	do.
Montmelian	Savoie	fine	do.
Monton	Puy-de-Dôme		
Montpellier	Hérault	ordinary	do.
Montpeyroux	Puy-de-Dôme	do.	do.
Mont-Rachet	Côte-d'Or	fine	white
Montrelais	Loire-Inférieure	ordinary	do.
Montrichard	Loir-et-Cher	do.	
Montsaugeon	Haute-Marne	do.	red
Montségur	Drôme	do.	do.
Morancin	Landes	fine	do.
Morbihan	Morbihan	common	
Morey	Côte-d'Or	fine	
Morgon	Rhône	ordinary	do.
Morières	Vaucluse	do.	do.
Mornac	Charente	do.	do.
Moselle	Moselle	ordinary, common	
Moulidars	Charente	ordinary	do.
Moulin-à-Vent	Saône-et-Loire	fine	do.
Moulix	Gironde	do.	do.

Wine	Department	Quality	Colour
Moussy	Marne	Ordinary	Red
Mouthier	Doubs	do.	do.
Muides	Loir-et-Cher	do.	white
Murinais	Isère	do.	red
Mutzig	Bas-Rhin	do.	white
Naives	Meuse	do.	red
Nantes	Loire-Inférieure	do.	white
Narbonne	Aude	do.	red
Navarre	Basses-Pyrénées	common	
Navarrenx	Do.	ordinary	
Navenne	Haut-Saône	do.	do.
Néac	Gironde	do.	do.
Neffles	Hautes-Alpes	do.	
Nersac	Charente	do.	do.
Nerthe	Vaucluse	fine	
Neufchâteau	Vosges	ordinary	do.
Neuillé	Maine-et-Loir	do.	
Neuville	Aube	do.	do.
Neuvy-Sautour	Yonne	do.	
Neuviller	Bas-Rhin	do.	white
Nevers	Nièvre	do.	red
Nevian	Aude	do.	do.
Nice	Alpes Maritimes	do.	do.
Nièvre	Nièvre	ordinary, common	
Niort	Deux-Sèvres		
Nivernais	Indre	do.	
Nord	Nord		
Normandie	Manche, &c.	common	
Noulliers	Charente Inférieure	ordinary	
Nouilly	Moselle	do.	do.
Nuits	Côte-d'Or	fine	do.
Ordenas	Rhône	ordinary	do.
Oger	Marne	fine	white
Oise	Oise	common	red
Oléron, Ile d'	Charente Inférieure	do.	
Ollioules	Var	ordinary, common	
Oleviller	Haut-Rhin	dry, ordinary, sweet	white
Omet	Gironde	ordinary	do.
Onzain	Loir-et-Cher	do.	red
Orange	Vaucluse	sweet	
Orgeval	Aisne	ordinary	do.
Orgon	Bouches-du-Rhône	do.	do.
Orléanais	Loiret	ordinary, common	
Orléans	Loiret	do.	
Orne	Orne		
Pagny	Meurthe	ordinary	do.
Paillet	Gironde	do.	white
Palet	Loire-Inférieure	do.	do.
Palus	Girondes		
Pannes	Meurthe	do.	red
Pargnan	Aisne	do.	do.
Pargny	Marne	do.	do.
Parnac	Lot	do.	

Wine	Department	Quality	Colour
Parmay	Maine-et-Loir	Ordinary	
Paroisse, la-grande	Seine-et-Marne	ordinary, common	red
Paron	Yonne	ordinary	do.
Parsac	Gironde	do.	do.
Pas-de-Calais	Pas-de-Calais		
Pauilhac	Gironde	fine	do.
Perche	Eure-et-Loire	common	
Pereuilh	Hautes-Pyrénées	ordinary	
Peri	Corsica	do.	
Péricard	Lot-et-Garonne	do.	do.
Périgord	Dordogne	fine, ordinary	
Pérols	Hérault	ordinary	do.
Peronne	Saône-et-Loire	do.	do.
Pessac	Gironde	fine	do.
Peyricguère	Hautes-Pyrénées	ordinary	
Pezilla	Pyrénées Orientales	do.	do.
Pian	Gironde	do.	do.
Pfaffenheim	Haut-Rhin	fine	
Picardie	Somme	common	do.
Pierreclos	Seine-et-Loire	ordinary	
Pierrefeu	Var	do.	do.
Pierry	Marne	fine	
Pignans	Var	ordinary	do.
Pistoule	Lot	do.	
Pizay	Rhône	do.	do.
Plaisance	Gers	do.	do.
Plant de Cugnes	Bouches-du-Rhône	do.	
Ployard	Aisne	do.	do.
Poce	Indre-et-Loire	do.	do.
Podensac	Gironde	fine	white
Poilly	Yonne	ordinary	do.
Poinchy	Do.	do.	do.
Poinvillers	Doubs	do.	red
Poitou	Vendée, Vienne	ordinary, common	
Poleymieux	Rhône	ordinary	
Poligny	Jura	do.	do.
Pomerol	Gironde	do.	do.
Pomerols	Hérault	sweet	white
Pommard	Côte-d'Or	fine	red
Pomport	Dordogne	do.	white
Pont du Château	Puy-de-Dôme	ordinary	red
Pont-en-Royans	Isère	do.	do.
Pontigny	Yonne	do.	do.
Ponts	Basses-Pyrénées	do.	
Portel	Aude	do.	do.
Portet	Basses-Pyrénées	do.	do.
Portets	Gironde	do.	white
Portieux	Vosges	do.	
Porto-Vecchio	Corsica	do.	
Port-Vendre	Pyrénées Orientales	fine	red
Pouillé	Loire-et-Cher	ordinary	do.
Pouilley	Doubs	do.	do.

Wine	Department	Quality	Colour
Pouilly	Saône-et-Loire	Fine	
Pouilly	Niévre	ordinary	
Poujeaux	Gironde	fine	red
Pourly	Yonne	ordinary	do.
Poussan	Hérault	do.	do.
Praissac	Lot	do.	
Prauthoy	Haute-Marne	do.	red
Preignac	Gironde	fine	white
Prémeaux	Côte-d'Or	do.	
Prémiac	Lot	ordinary	
Prépouille-de-Salses	Pyrénées Orientales	do.	white
Prigonrieux	Dordogne	fine	red
Princens	Savoie	ordinary	do.
Prissé	Saône-et-Loire	do.	do.
Provence	Var, Basses Alpes	fine, ordinary, sweet	
Pujaut	Gard	ordinary	red
Pujols	Gironde	fine, ordinary	
Puligny	Côte-d'Or	fine	white
Pupillin	Jura	do.	do.
Puisseguin	Gironde	ordinary	red
Puy-de-Dôme	Puy-de-Dôme	fine, ordinary	
Puynormomo	Gironde	ordinary	red
Pyrénées	Basses-Pyrénées	fine, ordinary	
Pyrénées	Hautes-Pyrénées	ordinary	
Pyrénées-Orientales	Pyrénées Orientales	fine, ordinary, sweet	
Quercy	Lot-et-Garonne	ordinary, common	red
Queyries	Gironde	ordinary	do.
Quincey	Haute-Saône	do.	
Quincié	Rhône	ordinary, common	red
Quinsac	Gironde	ordinary	
Quintigny	Jura	fine	white
Rabastens	Tarn	ordinary	red
Rablay	Maine-et-Loire	do.	
Rambucourt	Meuse	do.	red
Ray	Haute-Saône	do.	do.
Rebréchien	Loiret	do.	white
Regnié	Rhône	do.	red
Rembercourt	Meurthe	do.	do.
Renaison	Loire	ordinary, common	do.
Reuil	Marne	ordinary	do.
Reuilly	Indre	do.	white
Reventin	Isère	fine	red
Rhin	Bas-Rhin	dry, fine	
Rhin	Haut-Rhin	do.	
Rhône	Rhône	fine, ordinary	
Riaillé	Loire-Inférieure	ordinary	white
Ribeauvillé	Haut-Rhin	dry, fine	
Ribérac	Dordogne	common	red
Riceys	Aube	fine	do.
Richebourg	Côte-d'Or	do.	do.
Rilly	Marne	do.	do.

Wine	Department	Quality	Colour
Rioms	Gironde	Ordinary	
Riqueivihr	Haut-Rhin	dry, fine	
Ris	Puy-de-Dôme	ordinary	red
Rivesaltes	Pyrénées Orientales	sweet, fine, ordinary	
Rivières-les-Fosses	Haut-Marne	ordinary	red
Rixheim	Haut-Rhin	dry, ordinary	white
Roche	Hautes-Alpes	ordinary	red
Rochecorbon	Indre-et-Loire	do.	white
Rochefort	Maine-et-Loire	do.	
Rochelles	Meuse	do.	red
Rochenard	Deux-Sèvres	do.	do.
Roches	Isère	do.	do.
Rochette	Savoie		
Rodès	Pyrénées Orientales	sweet	
Roffey	Yonne	ordinary	white
Roiffé	Vienne	do.	do.
Romanèche	Saône-et-Loire	fine	red
Romanée-Conti	Côte-d'Or	do.	do.
Romanée-de Saint-Vivant	Do.	do.	do.
Romont	Marne	do.	white
Roquemaure	Gard	ordinary	red
Roquevaire	Bouches-du-Rhône	ordinary, sweet	do.
Roucy	Aisne	ordinary	do.
Rouergue	Aveyron	ordinary, common	
Rouillac	Charente		
Roulet	Do.	ordinary	red
Roussas	Drôme	do.	do.
Roussillon	Pyrénées Orientales	fine, ordinary, sweet	
Roustignon	Basses-Pyrénées	fine	white
Rouzieres	Meuse	ordinary	red
Rufach	Haut-Rhin	dry, fine	white
Rully	Saône-et-Loire	ordinary	
Rumilly	Savoie	do.	
Ruy	Isère	do.	red
Saillac	Corrèze	do.	
Saillans	Drôme	do.	red
Saint-Aignan	Loir-et-Cher	do.	
" Amand	Cher	ordinary, common	
" Amarens	Tarn	ordinary	red
" Amour	Saône-et-Loire	do.	do.
" André	Isère	do.	do.
" André	Loire	do.	do.
" André	Pyrénées Orientales	do.	white
" Aubin-de-Luigné	Sarthe	do.	do.
" Avertin	Indre-et-Loire	do.	
" Ay	Loiret	do.	red
" Basle	Marne	fine	do.
" Benoît	Ain	ordinary	do.
" Benoist	Sarthe	do.	white
" Bris	Yonne	do.	

Wine	Department	Quality	Colour
Saint-Chef	Isère	Ordinary	Red
,, Christol	Hérault	do.	do.
,, Christoly	Gironde	do.	do.
,, Christophe	Do.	do.	do.
,, Cyprien	Dordogne	do.	do.
,, Cyr	Maine-et-Loire	do.	
,, Cyr	Var	do.	do.
,, Cyr	Indre-et-Loire	do.	do.
,, Denis-de-Jargeau	Loiret	do.	do.
,, Denis-en-Val	Do.	do.	do.
,, Dié	Loir-et-Cher	do.	white
,, Drézéry	Hérault	do.	
,, Emilion	Gironde	do.	red
,, Estèphe	Do.	fine	
,, Étienne-la-Varenne	Rhône	ordinary	red
,, Faust	Basses-Pyrénées	fine	white
,, Fiacre	Loire-Inférieure	ordinary	do.
,, Gengoux-le Royal	Seine-et-Loire	dry, sweet, ordinary	red
,, Geniés	Gard	fine	do.
,, Geniez	Hérault	ordinary	do.
,, Genis	Charente	do.	do.
,, Georges, le clos	Côte-d'Or	fine	do.
,, Georges	Gironde	ordinary	do.
,, Georges	Indre-et-Loire	do.	white
,, Georges	Loir-et-Cher	do.	red
,, Georges	Sarthe	do.	white
,, Georges-d'Orques	Hérault	do.	red
,, Georges-les-Baillargeaux	Vienne	do.	do.
,, Gereon	Loire-Inférieure	do.	white
,, Germain	Gironde	do.	red
,, Gervais	Do.	do.	do.
,, Gilles-les-Boucher	Gard	do.	do.
,, Gy	Loiret	do.	do.
,, Henry	Lot	do.	
,, Herblon	Loire-Inférieure	do.	white
,, Hilaire	Indre	ordinary	red
,, Innocent	Savoie	sweet	white
,, Jean	Ardèche	ordinary	do.
,, Jean	Savoie	do.	red
,, Jean-d'Angély	Charente Inférieure	do.	
,, Jean-d'Ardière	Rhône	do.	white
,, Jean-de-Bray	Loiret	do.	red

Wine	Department	Quality	Colour
Saint-Jean-de-la-Porte	Savoie	Fine	Red
" Jean-le-Priche	Saône-et-Loire	ordinary	do.
" Jean-le-Blanc	Loiret	do.	do.
" Jean-Poudge	Basses-Pyrénées	do.	
" Jérôme	Bouches-du-Rhône	do.	red
" Joseph	Ardèche	fine, do.	do.
" Juéry	Tarn	ordinary	do.
" Julien	Bouches-du-Rhône	do.	white
" Julien	Meuse	do.	red
" Julien	Rhône	do.	do.
" Julien	Gironde	fine	white
" Julien	Savoie	ordinary	red
" Lager	Rhône	do.	do.
" Lambert	Gironde	fine	do.
" Laune	Hautes-Pyrénées	ordinary	
" Laurent	Bouches-du-Rhône	sweet	
" Laurent	Dordogne	do.	
" Laurent	Gironde	fine	red
" Laurent	Do.	ordinary	do.
" Laurent	Jura	do.	do.
" Laurent	Var	fine	do.
" Laurent	Gard	do.	
" Léger	Viénne	ordinary	white
" Leon	Dordogne	do.	red
" Lothain	Jura	do.	do.
" Loubès	Gironde	do.	do.
" Loubouer	Landes	do.	
" Louis	Bouches-du-Rhône	do.	
" Loup	Tarn-et-Garonne	do.	red
" Luygne	Maine-et-Loire	do.	white
" Marc	Indre-et-Loire	ordinary, common	
" Marcel	Bouches-du-Rhône	ordinary	white
" Martin	Gironde	do.	red
" Martin	Marne	fine, ordinary	white
" Martin	Saône-et-Loire	ordinary	
" Martin	Yonne	ordinary, common	red
" Martin-de-la-Porte	Savoie	ordinary	do.
" Martin-la-Rivière	Vienne	do.	do.
" Maximin	Isère	do.	
" Médard	Gironde	do.	white
" Michel	Meuse	do.	red
" Michel-sous-Condrieu	Loire	sweet	white
" Mihiel	Meuse	ordinary	red
" Naixant	Dordogne	sweet	
" Nazaire	Var	ordinary	red
" Nazaire	Aude	do.	do.

Wine	Department	Quality	Colour
Saint-Nicolas de	Indre-et-Loire	Ordinary	Red
,, Bourgueil	Do.	do.	do.
,, Orse	Dordogne	do.	do.
,, Pantaly	Do.	do.	do.
,, Paul	Var	fine	do.
,, Peray	Ardèche	do.	white
,, Pey-Langon	Gironde	do.	do.
,, Pierre-de-Bœuf	Loire	ordinary	red
,, Rambert	Ain	do.	do.
,, Romain	Vienne	do.	do.
,, Satur	Cher	do.	white
,, Saturnin	Charente	do.	red
,, Sauveur	Vaucluse	fine	do.
,, Sauveur	Gironde	do.	do.
,, Savin	Isère	ordinary	do.
,, Selve	Gironde	do.	white
,, Sernin	Charente	do.	red
,, Seurin	Gironde	do.	do.
,, Seurin-de-Cadourne	Do.	fine	do.
,, Sever	Landes	ordinary	white
,, Sorlin	Ain	do.	red
,, Salpice-d'Izon	Gironde	do.	white
,, Thierry	Marne	fine, do.	red
,, Tropez	Var	ordinary	do.
,, Urbain	Haute-Marne	do.	do.
,, Vallerin	Saône-et-Loire	do.	
,, Vérand	Do.	do.	
,, Vérand	Sarthe	do.	red
,, Victor	Dordogne	do.	do.
,, Vincent	Lot	do.	
Sainte-Cécile	Sarthe	do.	
,, Croix	Gironde	do.	red
,, Eulalie	Do.	do.	do.
,, Foi	Do.	do., common	
,, Foy	Rhône	ordinary	red
,, Foy	Dordogne	fine	do.
,, Gemme	Gironde	do.	do.
,, Luce	Do.	common	do.
,, Marthe	Bouches-du-Rhône	ordinary	
,, Raffine	Moselle	do.	red
Saintes-Maries	Bouches-du-Rhône	do.	do.
Saintes	Charente Inférieure	ordinary, common	do.
Saintonge	Do.	common	
Saix	Vienne	ordinary	white
Sâle	Rhône	do.	red
Salins	Jura	do.	do.
Salival	Meurthe	do.	
Salses	Pyrénées Orientales	do., sweet	
Samonac	Gironde	ordinary	do.
Sampigny	Meuse	do.	do.

Wine	Department	Quality	Colour
Sancé	Saône-et-Loire	Ordinary	Red
Sancerre	Cher	do.	do.
Sandillon	Loiret	do.	red
Santenay	Côte-d'Or	fine	white
Saône	Haute-Saône	ordinary	
Saône-et-Loire	Saône-et-Loire	fine, ordinary	
Sara	Ardèche	ordinary	red
Sargoin	Savoie	do.	
Sari	Corsica	do.	
Sarlat	Dordogne	common	red
Sarraziet	Landes	ordinary	
Sarthe	Sarthe	do., common	
Saujon	Charente-Inférieure	do.	red
Saulce	Hautes-Alpes	ordinary	white
Saules	Saône-et-Loire	do.	
Sault-de-Navailles	Basses-Pyrénées	do.	red
Saumousset	Maine-et-Loire	do.	white
Saumur	Do.	do.	do.
Sauternes	Gironde	fine	do.
Sauvian	Hérault	fine, sweet	red, white
Savagnac	Lot	ordinary	
Savenay	Loire-Inférieure	do.	
Savennières	Maine-et-Loire	do.	white
Saverne	Bas-Rhin	do.	
Savigny	Côte-d'Or	fine	red
Savoie	Savoie	sweet, fine, ordinary	
Savennières	Meuse	ordinary	do.
Schelestadt	Bas-Rhin	do.	
Scy	Moselle	do.	red
Seine	Seine	common	
Seine-et-Marne	Seine-et-Marne	ordinary	
Seine-et-Oise	Seine-et-Oise	do.	
Seine-Inférieure	Seine-Inférieure		
Selles	Loir-et-Cher	common	red
Selve	Gironde	ordinary	white
Semécourt	Moselle	do.	red
Semur	Côte-d'Or	do., common	
Sennecé	Saône-et-Loire	do.	
Senouche	Charente-Inférieure		
Séon-St-André	Bouches-du-Rhône	ordinary	red
Séon-St-Henri	Do.	do.	do.
Septeuil	Seine-et-Oise	do.	
Serigny	Yonne	do.	white
Sèvres	Deux-Sèvres	do.	
Seyssel	Ain	do.	
Seyssuel	Isère	fine	red
Sigolsheim	Haut-Rhin	dry, fine	
Sijean	Aude	ordinary	red
Sillery	Marne	fine	
Solliés-Farlede	Var	ordinary	red
Sologne	Loir-et-Cher	do.	
Solomé	Vienne	do.	white

Wine	Department	Quality	Colour
Solutré	Saône-et-Loire	Ordinary	
Somme	Somme	do.	
Sommensac	Lot-et-Garonne	do.	
Sorgues	Vaucluse	fine	red
Soublecauze	Hautes-Pyrénées	ordinary	
Souligny	Aube	do.	
Soupir	Aisne	ordinary, common	
Soussans	Gironde	fine	red
Soustons	Landes	do.	
Souzay	Maine-et-Loire	ordinary	white
Strasbourg	Bas-Rhin	common	do.
Surgères	Charente-Inférieure	ordinary	
Synex	Corrèze	do.	
Tâche	Côte-d'Or	fine	red
Tain	Drôme	do.	do.
Taissy	Marne	do.	do.
Talence	Gironde	do.	do.
Tallissieux	Ain	ordinary	do.
Tallano	Corsica	do.	
Talmont	Vendée	do.	
Tanlay	Yonne	do.	white
Tarantoise	Savoie	ordinary, common	
Tarascon	Bouches-du-Rhône	ordinary	red
Tarbes	Hautes-Pyrénées	do.	
Tarn	Tarn	ordinary, common	
Tarn-et-Garonne	Tarn-et-Garonne	do.	red
Tauriac	Gironde	ordinary	do.
Tavel	Gard	fine	do.
Tecou	Tarn	ordinary	do.
Terrasse	Isère	do.	
Terres-fortes	Gironde	do., common	
Thann	Haut-Rhin	dry, fine	white
Théssée	Loir-et-Cher	ordinary	red
Thézac	Lot-et-Garonne	do.	
Thiaucourt	Meurthe	do.	red
Thieffenthal	Bas-Rhin	do.	
Thoissey	Ain	do.	red
Thonac	Dordogne	do.	do.
Thonon	Savoie	do.	
Thouarcé	Maine-et-Loire	do.	white
Thouars	Deux-Sèvres	do.	
Tinery	Meurthe	do.	
Tissery	Yonne	do.	white
Tonnerre	Do.	fine	
Torcieux	Ain	ordinary	red
Torins	Saône-et-Loire	fine	do.
Torremila	Pyrénées Orientales	ordinary	do.
Touches	Saône-et-Loire	do.	
Toul	Meurthe	do.	
Toulene	Gironde	fine	white
Touraine	Indre-et-Loire	fine, ordinary, common	
Tourne	Gironde	ordinary	

Wine	Department	Quality	Colour
Tournus	Saône-et-Loire	Common	Red
Touvière	Savoie	ordinary	
Treffort	Ain	do.	do.
Treille	Bouches-du-Rhône	do.	
Treilles	Aude	do.	red
Trois-Moutiers	Vienne	do.	white
Tronchoy	Yonne	do.	red
Turckheim	Haut-Rhin	dry, fine	white
Turquant	Maine-et-Loire	ordinary	
Tursan	Landes	do.	
Ubexy	Vosges	ordinary	red
Urgons	Landes	do.	white
Usseau	Basses-Pyrénées	do.	
Uzès	Gard	fine	red
Vadans	Jura	ordinary	do.
Vadoux	Rhône	do.	do.
Vailly	Aisne	common	do.
Valançay	Indre	ordinary	do.
Valence	Gers	do.	
Valentine	Bouches-du-Rhône	do.	
Valentons	Gironde	do.	red
Valet	Loire-Inférieure	do.	white
Valeyrac	Gironde	do.	red
Vandelainville	Meurthe	do.	do.
Vanteuil	Marne	do.	do.
Var	Var	fine, ordinary, sweet	
Varades	Loire-Inférieure	ordinary	
Varets	Corrèze	do.	
Varneville	Meuse	do.	red
Varney	Do.	do.	do.
Varrains	Maine-et-Loire	do.	
Varreins	Dordogne	do.	do.
Vars	Charente	do.	do.
Vasselay	Cher	do.	do.
Vassogne	Aisne	do.	do.
Vassy	Haute-Marne	do.	do.
Vaucluse	Vaucluse	fine, ordinary, sweet	
Vaucouleurs	Meuse	ordinary	red
Vaulichères	Yonne	do.	
Vaux	Ain	do.	red
Vaux	Haute-Marne	do.	do.
Vaux	Vienne	do.	do.
Vauxrenard	Rhône	do.	do.
Velay	Puy-de-Dôme	do., common	
Vendée	Vendée	common	
Véragues	Hérault	ordinary	red
Vercheny	Drôme	do.	
Véretz	Indre-et-Loire	do.	do.
Vergisson	Saône-et-Loire	do.	white
Verinay	Rhône	fine	red
Verlus	Gers	ordinary	do.
Vermanton	Yonne	do.	do.
Vernet	Pyrénées-Orientales	do.	do.

Wine	Department	Quality	Colour
Vernon	Indre-et-Loire	Ordinary	White
Verteillac	Dordogne	do.	red
Verteuil	Gironde	fine	do.
Vertus	Marne	fine, ordinary	do.
Verzé	Saône-et-Loire	do.	do.
Verzenay	Marne	fine	do.
Verzy	Do.	do.	do.
Veuil	Indre	ordinary	do.
Vezannes	Yonne	do.	white
Vézelay	Do.	do.	red
Vezinnes	Do.	do., common	do.
Vic	Meurthe	do., "	do.
Vic-Fezensac	Gers	do., "	do.
Vic la Moustière	Indre	do., "	
Vic-le-comte	Puy-de-Dôme	do., "	do.
Vico	Corsica	do., "	
Viella	Gers	do., "	do.
Vielle	Landes	do., "	white
Vienne	Vienne	do., "	
Vienne	Haute-Vienne	common	
Vienne	Isère	ordinary	
Vieux-Boucau	Landes	fine	
Vigneulles	Meuse	ordinary	red
Vignot	Do.	do.	do.
Villaudric	Haute-Garonne	do.	
Ville-aux-Clercs	Loir-et-Cher	do.	do.
Villebarou	Do.	do.	
Villebois	Ain	do.	do.
Ville-Comtal	Gers	do.	do.
Villedaigne	Aude	do.	do.
Villedieu	Tarn-et-Garonne	do.	do.
VilleDommange	Marne	do.	
Villefranqueux	Do.	do.	do.
Villemort	Vienne	do.	do.
Villenave-d'Ornon	Gironde	fine	white
Villeneuve	Var	do.	red
Villeneuve-de-la-Rivière	Pyrénées Orientales	ordinary	do.
Villeneuve-le-Roi	Yonne	ordinary, common	do.
Villenoxe	Aube	common	do.
Villers-Allerand	Marne	fine	do.
Villers-aux-Noeuds	Do.	ordinary	white
Villers-sous-Preny	Meurthe	do.	red
Villesecron	Loir-et-Cher	do.	
Villetoureix	Dordogne	do.	red
Villeveyrac	Hérault	do.	do.
Villié	Rhône	do.	do.
Villy	Yonne	do.	white
Vinay	Marne	do.	red

Wine	Department	Quality	Colour
Vincelottes	Yonne	Ordinary	Red
Vincey	Vosges	do.	
Vinzelles	Saône-et-Loire	do.	
Vion	Ardèche	do.	do.
Virelade	Gironde	fine	white
Virieux	Ain	ordinary	red
Vivarais	Do.	ordinary, common	
Viviers	Yonne	ordinary	white
Voiteur	Jura	do.	red
Volnay	Côte-d'Or	fine	do.
Vosges	Vosges	ordinary, common	
Vosnes	Côte-d'Or	fine	do.
Vougeot	Do.	do.	do.
Vourcienne	Aisne	ordinary	do.
Vouthon	Charente	do.	
Vouvray	Indre-et-Loire	fine, do.	white
Vouziers	Ardennes	common	
Walbach	Haut-Rhin	ordinary	
Wissembourg	Bas-Rhin	do.	
Woinville	Meuse	do.	
Wolxheim	Bas-Rhin	dry, fine	
Xaronval	Vosges	ordinary	red
Yonne	Yonne	fine, ordinary	

II. WINES NOT FRENCH.

Wine	Country	Quality	Colour
Abymes-de-Myans	Savoy	Common	
Abyssinia	Africa		
Acqui	Italy	ordinary	
Acre	Syria		
Aderbijan	Persia		
Affiney	Russia	do.	
Affghanistan	Asia	sweet, fine	
Africa		fine, ordinary	
Africa, South		sweet, fine	
Agosta	Sicily	ordinary	
Agosta	Italy		
Agria	Hungary	do.	red
Ahsberg		dry, ordinary	white
Akerman	Russia	do.	
Albania	Turkey	do.	
Albano	Italy	sweet, fine	
Alcala-la-Real	Spain	ordinary	
Alcamo	Sicily	do.	red
Alemtejo	Portugal	do.	
Algarves	Do.	do.	
Alghieri	Italy	sweet, ordinary	
Alicante	Spain	sweet	
Altenahr	Lower Rhine	ordinary	
Amelia	Italy	do.	
America		sweet, ordinary,	
Amorgo	Greek	ordinary	
Amphiloquie	Turkey	do.	
Ana	Arabia		
Anatolia	Turkey	sweet, fine, ordinary	
Andalusia	Spain	do.	
Andrianople	Turkey	ordinary	
Andros	Greece		
Anduxar	Spain	do.	
Annemasse	Switzerland	do.	
Antella	Italy	sweet, ordinary	
Antignana	Istria	ordinary	
Appenzel	Switzerland	ordinary, common	
Aragon	Spain	sweet, ordinary	

Wine	Country	Quality	Colour
Arbourg	Switzerland	Ordinary	White
Arcadia	Greece	fine	
Ardola	Italy	ordinary	
Argolide	Greece	fine	
Argovia	Switzerland	ordinary	
Arica	Peru	ordinary	
Arinse	Isle of Scio	fine	
Armenia	Persia	fine, ordinary	
Arnfels	Styria	ordinary	
Artiminio	Italy	sweet, ordinary	
Arva	Hungary	ordinary	
Aschaffenburg	Bavaria	sweet	
Asia		sweet, ordinary	
Asia, Little	Turkey	sweet, fine	
Assmannshausen	Nassau	fine	red
Astia	Italy	ordinary	
Astracan	Russia	do.	
Asturias	Spain	do.	
Athamanie	Turkey	do.	
Aussig	Bohemia	fine	red
Austria	Austria	sweet, fine, ordinary	
Averne	Italy	fine	white
Avola	Do.	ordinary	
Azano	Do.	do.	
Azores Islands	Portugal	do.	
Bacharach	Nassau	dry, fine	white
Baden	Switzerland	ordinary	
Baden	Grand Duchy	dry, fine, ordinary	
Badenweiler	Baden	dry, fine	white
Bagaria	Sicily	ordinary	red
Bagdad	Turkey	do.	
Bakou	Russia	do.	
Basel (Bâle)	Switzerland	do.	do.
Banalbusa	Majorca	do.	
Banat	Hungary	do.	
Barbacena	Greek	fine, ordinary	
Barbary	Africa		
Bardolino	Venice	ordinary	
Bari	Italy	sweet	
Barko	Hungary	do., fine	
Barra-a-Barra	Portugal	fine, ordinary	
Basilicata	Naples	sweet	
Bavaria	Bavaria	do.	
Becherbach	Lower Rhine	dry, fine	white
Beira	Portugal	fine, ordinary	
Belgium	Belgium	ordinary	
Belgrade	Turkey	ordinary	
Bellaggio	Italy	do.	
Bellinzona	Switzerland	do.	
Bellet	Nice	do.	red
Bender	Russia	do.	
Bonesalem	Majorca	do.	
Benicarlo	Spain	do.	do.

Wine	Country	Quality	Colour
Berchtolsdorf	Austria	Ordinary	
Berfschetz	Istria	sweet	
Berg-Fabern	Bavaria	dry, ordinary	
Bergame	Italy	ordinary	
Berghausen	Baden	dry, fine, ordinary	
Beringfeld	Bavaria	ordinary	
Bernang	Switzerland	do.	
Berncastel	Lower Rhine	dry, ordinary	
Berne	Switzerland	ordinary	red
Bessigheim	Würtemberg	dry, fine	do.
Bettola	Italy	ordinary	
Biella	Italy	do.	
Bingen	Hesse-Darm-stadt	dry, fine	
Birthalmen	Transylvania	sweet, ordinary	
Biscay	Spain	common	
Bischofsheim	Hesse	ordinary	white
Blegno	Switzerland	do.	
Bobbio	Italy	common	
Bodendorf	Lower Rhine	dry, ordinary	white
Bodenheim	Hesse-Darm-stadt	do.	
Bodwar	Würtemberg	dry, fine	
Bohemia	Bohemia	fine, ordinary	
Bolivia	S. America	ordinary	
Bolzano	Tyrol	do.	
Borja	Spain	sweet	white
Bormio	Italy	ordinary	
Bosa	Sardinia	sweet, ordinary	
Bosnia	Turkey	ordinary	
Bossey	Switzerland	do.	
Bossi	Hungary	fine	
Bouchberg	Switzerland	ordinary	
Boudistan	China		
Boudry	Switzerland	ordinary, common	white
Bouillon	Belgium	fine	
Bourg	Lower Rhine	dry	
Boutchica	Greece	ordinary	
Brannenberg	Lower Rhine	dry, fine	white
Breitensee	Austria	ordinary	
Brescian	Venice	sweet, do.	
Brazils	S. America	common	
Brunn	Austria	ordinary	
Brunn	Moravia	do.	
Bucellas	Portugal	fine	white
Bude	Hungary	fine, do.	
Buenos-Ayres	S. America	common	
Bukowetz	Croatia	ordinary	
Bulgaria	Turkey	common	
Bungert	Lower Rhine	dry, ordinary	white
Bunslau	Bohemia	ordinary	
Buti	Italy	do.	
Cabezon	Spain	common	

Wine	Country	Quality	Colour
Cabuli	Asia	Ordinary	
Cadafaes	Portugal	do.	
Cadiz	Spain		
Calabria	Italy	sweet	
Calamota	Ragusan	do., ordinary	
Calatrava	Spain	ordinary	
Calcavellos	Do.		
Calenberg	Austria	fine	
California	U. States	do.	
Cambodja	Asia		
Campania	Italy	ordinary	
Canada	N. America		
Canary	Canary Isles	sweet, fine, ordinary	
Candahar	Affghanistan		
Candia	Turkey	fine, ordinary	
Canelli	Italy	sweet	
Canstadt	Wurtemberg	fine	
Cape of Good Hope	S. Africa	sweet, fine	
Capo-d'Istria	Austria	sweet	
Caprés	Italy	fine, ordinary	
Capris-Trano	California	do.	
Carcavellos	Portugal	sweet	
Cardona	Spain	fine, ordinary	
Carigliano	Italy	sweet	
Carinena	Spain	do.	
Carinthie	Austria	common	
Carmignano	Italy	sweet, ordinary	
Carniola	Austria	fine, do.	
Carthagena	Spain	sweet, do.	
Casal	Italy	do. do.	
Cashmere	Asia	sweet, fine	
Castalen	Switzerland	ordinary	
Castellamare	Sicily	do.	red
Castelleno	Genoa	do.	
Castellina	Italy	do.	
Castel-Vetrano	Sicily	dry, fine	
Castiglione	Italy	sweet, ordinary	
Castile	Spain	fine, do.	
Catalonia	Do.	sweet, fine, do.	
Catania	Sicily	ordinary	red
Catzenellinbogen	Nassau	dry, do.	
Caucasus	Russia	common	
Cauzem	Lower Rhine	dry, ordinary	white
Cephalonia	Greece	sweet	
Cerigo	Ionian Islands	fine, ordinary	red
Cezena	Italy	ordinary	
Chamakhi	Russia	fine	
Chambave	Italy	sweet	
Champs-Elysées	Naples	ordinary	
Chamusca	Portugal	do.	
Chan-si	China		
Chan-tong	Do.		

Wine	Country	Quality	Colour
Charcas	Peru	Ordinary	
Chatista	Turkey	sweet, fine, ordinary	
Chaumont	Italy	ordinary	
Cheronea	Greece	sweet, do.	
Cherso	Austria	ordinary	
Chiavenne	Italy	sweet, do.	
Chianti	Do.	do. do.	
Chili	S. America	ordinary	
Chinchon	Spain		
Circassia	Russia	ordinary	
Citta-Nova	Austria	sweet	
Ciudad-Real	Spain	ordinary	
Clavezana	Genoa	do.	
Cobern	Lower Rhine	dry, common	white
Coblentz	Do.	do., ordinary	do.
Collares	Portugal	ordinary	red
Cologne	Lower Rhine	dry, common	white
Coligny	Switzerland	ordinary	
Colombia	S. America		
Commanderie	Cyprus	sweet, fine	red
Como	Italy	ordinary	
Conegliano	Do.	do.	
Constantia	Cape of Good Hope	sweet, fine	
Cordova	Spain	sweet, ordinary	
China	China		
Corfu	Ionian Islands	do.	
Corinth	Greece	ordinary	
Cornios			
Cortaillot	Switzerland	fine	red
Coskina	Greece	sweet, ordinary	
Cotbus	Prussia	common	
Côte	Switzerland	ordinary	
Cotnar	Moldavia	sweet, fine	
Contourachi	Turkey	ordinary	
Cracow	Poland		
Craef	Lower Rhine	do.	white
Crépy	Savoy	do.	
Creta	Italy	do.	
Cretzingen	Baden	dry, fine, ordinary	
Creutzberg	Lower Rhine	ordinary	red
Creutznach	Do.	dry, do.	white
Crimea	Russia	ordinary	
Croatia	Austria	fine, do.	
Crossen	Prussia	common	
Crotova	Turkey	ordinary	
Cschepreg	Hungary	do.	
Cuba	America		
Cully	Switzerland	do.	red
Cusel	Lower Rhine	dry, ordinary	white
Cuyo	Chili	fine, do.	
Cuzco	Peru	ordinary	
Cyprus	Turkey	sweet, ordinary	

Wine	Country	Quality	Colour
Daghestan	Russia	Ordinary	
Dalmatia	Austria	fine, do.	
Dalmatia	Turkey	ordinary	
Damas	Syria	do.	
Dante	Teneriffe	sweet, fine	
Deidesheim	Bavaria	dry, fine	white
Denderah	Egypt		
Derbent	Russia		
Dernau	Lower Rhine	ordinary	red
Devescher	Hungary	fine, do.	
Didymia	Italy	sweet, ordinary	
Diebach	Lower Rhine	dry, do.	white
Dimi	Russia	ordinary	
Doebling	Austria	do.	
Dolce-Aqua	Italy	do.	
Domech	Switzerland	do.	red
Don	Russia	fine, do.	
Dormbach	Austria		
Douchet	Russia	ordinary	
Doudels-Kirchen	Hungary	fine	
Douro	Portugal	do.	
Durkheim	Bavaria	dry, fine	white
Dussemond	Lower Rhine	do.	
Eberbach	Baden	ordinary	
Eglisau	Switzerland	do.	red
Egypt	Africa	do.	
Elba	Italy	sweet, ordinary	
Elide	Greece	fine, do.	
Elvas	Portugal	do.	
Ekaterinoslav	Russia	common	
Engehelle	Lower Rhine	dry, ordinary	
Entre-Douro-e-Minho	Portugal	fine, ordinary	red-white
Enzersdorf	Austria	ordinary	
Epire	Turkey	do.	
Erdo-Benye	Hungary	sweet, fine	
Erivan	Persia	fine, ordinary	
Erlac	Switzerland	sweet, do.	red
Erlau	Hungary	ordinary	
Escherndorf	Bavaria	do.	white
Eslingen	Wurtemberg	dry, fine	
Estramadura	Spain	ordinary	
Do.	Portugal	sweet, fine, ordinary	
Etna	Sicily	do.	
Etsey	Hungary	fine, ordinary	
Farnese	Italy	sweet	
Faro	Sicily	ordinary	
Faro	Portugal	do.	
Farsistan	Persia	sweet, fine	
Faverge	Switzerland	fine	red
Fayal	Azores Islands	ordinary	
Fayoum	Egypt	do.	
Felicuda	Italy	do.	

Wine	Country	Quality	Colour
Fenerbach	Baden	Dry, fine	White
Ferro	Canary Islands	ordinary	
Ferrara	Italy	do.	
Flaach	Switzerland	do.	
Florentin	Italy	sweet, fine	
Flores	Azores Islands	common	
Forst	Bavaria	dry, ordinary	white
Forli	Italy	ordinary	
Fortaventura	Canary Islands	common	
Francavilla	Italy	sweet	
Frankfort on Maine	Germany		
Franconia	Bavaria	fine, sweet	
Frangy	Switzerland	ordinary	red
French-Grant	America	common	
Freyenthurn	Austria	fine, ordinary	
Fribourg	Switzerland	common	
Friul	Austria	ordinary	
Fuencaral	Spain	sweet	
Fundi	Italy	ordinary	
Gal-Szech	Hungary	sweet, fine	
Galicia	Austria	common	
Galicia	Spain	ordinary	
Galka	Russia	do.	
Garda	Italy	do.	
Garnaccia	Sardinia	sweet	
Gatinara	Italy	ordinary	
Geisenheim	Nassau	dry, fine	white
Genoa	Italy	sweet, ordinary, com	
Geneva	Switzerland	ordinary	red
Genzano	Italy	do.	
Georgia-	Russia	do.	
Gharthis-Kari	Do.	do.	
Ghend'je	Do.	do.	
Ghilan	Persia	common	
Gierace	Italy	sweet	
Giogoli	Do.	sweet, ordinary	
Ginpana	Austria	do.	
Glan	Lower Rhine	common	
Glaris	Switzerland	do.	
Glodova	Hungary	sweet	
Goesgen	Switzerland	ordinary	do.
Gomera	Canary Islands	ordinary, common	
Gonowitz	Styria	ordinary	
Graach	Lower Rhine	dry, fine	white
Gracieuse	Azores	common	
Grafenberg	Nassau	dry, fine	
Gratz	Austria	fine	
Gravosa	Do.	ordinary	
Grinzig	Do.	do.	
Grisons	Switzerland	sweet, ordinary	
Grunau	Hungary	fine, ordinary	
Grunstadt	Bavaria	dry, ordinary	do.
Grusinie	Russia	ordinary	

Wine	Country	Quality	Colour
Guamanga	Peru		
Guatemala	Cent. America		
Guimar	Canary Islands	fine	
Guiana	S. America		
Guinea	Africa	do.	
Gumpoltskirchen	Austria	ordinary	
Gundermansdorf	Do.		
Gyoengyoesch	Hungary	fine	
Gyorok	Do.	sweet	
Haïti	W. Indies		
Hamptberg	Nassau	fine	white
Harxheim	Bavaria	dry, fine	do.
Heidelberg	Baden	do.	
Heilbronn	Würtemberg	do.	
Heiligenstadt	Austria	ordinary	
Herzegovina	Turkey	do.	
Hesse-Cassel	Hesse-Cassel	dry, fine	
Hesse-Darmstadt	HesseDarmstadt	dry, fine, ordinary	
Hidgschig	Hungary	fine	
Hindustan	Asia	fine, ordinary	
Hochheim	Nassau	dry, fine	
Hoeflein	Austria		
Holland, New	Asia		
Hungary	Austria	sweet, fine, ordinary	
Ica	America	ordinary	
Illyria	Austria	fine	
Immiretia	Russia	ordinary	
Imola	Italy	do.	do.
Ingelheim	HesseDarmstadt	fine	
Irak-Adgeny	Persia	sweet	
Ischia	Italy	sweet, ordinary	
Ispahan	Persia	fine	do.
Istria	Austria	ordinary	
Italy	Italy	fine, ordinary, common	
Ithaca	Ionian Islands	fine	red
Iviza	Spain	ordinary	
Jannina	Turkey	do.	
Japan	Asia		
Java	Do.		
Jerusalem	Syria	ordinary	white
Jobbagy	Hungary	fine, ordinary	
Johanisberg	Nassau	dry, fine	
Kaisersthul	Switzerland	ordinary	
Kahlenberg	Austria	do.	
Kaketie	Russia	do.	
Karlowitz	Austria	fine	
Kartalinie	Russia	ordinary	
Katschdorf	Hungary	fine, ordinary	
Kawkaskoi-Uswat	Russia	ordinary, common	
Keroan	Syria	sweet	
Kesseling	Lower Rhine	ordinary	red, white
Kherson	Russia	do.	
Kiedrich	Nassau	dry, fine	white

Wine	Country	Quality	Colour
Kiew	Russia	Common	
Kirchenberg	Austria	ordinary	
Kissamos	Candia	sweet, ordinary	
Klingenberg	Baden	dry, fine	
Kloster Neuberg	Austria	ordinary	
Koenigsbach	Bavaria	do.	
Koos	Russia	do.	
Kos-Rad	Hungary	fine, ordinary	
Kostheim	Nassau	dry, fine	white
Kreutz	Hungary	fine	
Kryvostyan	Do.	sweet, fine	
Lac	America	fine	
Lacryma Christi	Italy	sweet	
Laconia	Greece	sweet, fine	
Ladikieh	Austria	do.	
Laguna	Canary Islands	dry, sweet	
Lahor	Hindustan	fine, ordinary	
Lamporechio	Italy	sweet, ordinary	
Laos	Asia		
Larnica	Cyprus	sweet, fine	
Laubenheim	Hesse-Darmstadt	fine	
Laufen	Baden	dry, fine	do
Laybach	Austria	ordinary	
Lebrixa	Spain	do.	
Leinenborn	Lower Rhine	do.	
Lentzburg	Switzerland	do.	
Lepsguigne	Russia	sweet	
Leon	Spain	ordinary	
Lepanto	Greece	sweet, ordinary	
Lesina	Dalmatia	ordinary	
Leutmeritz	Bohemia	do.	
Lichtenstein	Austria	do.	
Lieser	Lower Rhine	dry, ordinary	
Liesing	Austria	ordinary	
Lima	Peru	do.	
Lintz	Lower Rhine	dry, fine	red
Lipari	Italy	sweet, ordinary	
Liptau	Hungary	ordinary	
Lisbon	Portugal	sweet, fine	
Lissa	Ragusa	sweet	
Litzerhecken	Lower Rhine	dry, fine	
Livadia	Greece	sweet, ordinary	
Locarno	Switzerland	ordinary	
Lodi	Italy	do.	
Logrono	Spain	do.	
Lombardy	Italy	sweet, fine, ordinary	
Lonato	Do.	sweet, ordinary	
Lopud	Ragusa	do.	
Louisburg	Bavaria	sweet	
Louisane	N. America	ordinary	
Lucena	Spain	do.	
Lucerne	Switzerland	common	

Wine	Country	Quality	Colour
Lucomba	America	Fine	
Lucea	Italy	ordinary	
Lugano	Do.	do.	
Lusace	Lower Rhine	dry, ordinary	white
Lutternberg	Styria	fine	
Luxemburg	Netherlands	ordinary	
Maas	Lower Rhine	dry, ordinary	
Macchia	Sicily	ordinary	
Maedoine	Turkey	do.	
Mada	Hungary	sweet, fine	
Madagascar	Africa		
Madeira	Portugal	sweet, dry, fine, ordinary	
Majorca	Spain	sweet, ordinary	
Malaga	Do.	do.	
Malvasia	Greece	sweet, fine	
Mancha	Spain	fine, ordinary	red
Manerba	Italy	ordinary	
Mantua	Do.	do.	
Manzanares	Spain	do.	
Marach	Egypt	do.	
Maraschino	Dalmatia	sweet	
Marcobrunnen	Nassau	dry, fine	white
Marocco	Africa		
Marsala	Sicily	ordinary, fine	
Martigny	Switzerland	sweet, ordinary	
Marzamin	Italy	fine, ordinary	
Mascoli	Sicily	sweet, fine	red
Massa	Italy	ordinary	
Masserano	Do.	do.	
Matanza	Canary Islands	dry, fine	
Mataro	Spain	ordinary	
Mauerkalksburg	Austria	do.	
Mayence	Hesse-Darmstadt	fine, dry, ordinary	
Mayschof	Lower Rhine	ordinary	do.
Medina-del-Campo	Spain	do.	do.
Medwisch	Transylvania	sweet, ordinary	
Mega-Spileon	Greece	fine	
Megara	Do.	ordinary	
Meilen	Switzerland	do.	
Melazzo	Sicily	fine	
Meleda	Turkey	ordinary	
Melnick	Bohemia	do.	do.
Mendrisio	Switzerland	do.	
Menes	Hungary	sweet, fine	
Merseburg	Baden	ordinary	
Mesopotamia	Turkish Asia		
Messina	Sicily	fine	
Mesta	Isle of Scio	do.	
Meyenfeld	Switzerland	ordinary	
Mezes-Male	Hungary	sweet, fine	

Wine	Country	Quality	Colour
Miconi	Greece	Ordinary	
Milan	Italy	do.	
Mindanao	Philippine Is.	do.	
Mingrelia	Russia	do.	
Minorca	Spain	ordinary, common	
Miranda-de-Ebro	Do.	fine, ordinary	
Misitra	Greece	sweet, fine	
Modena	Italy	ordinary	
Modern	Hungary	fine, ordinary	
Moedling	Austria	do.	
Moettling	Styria	do.	
Moguer	Spain	fine	
Mokozange	Russia	do.	
Moldavia	Turkey	sweet, fine, ordinary	
Molita	Russia	ordinary	
Moluccas	Asia		
Monacan	Virginia	do.	
Mongatchaour	Russia	do.	
Monnetier	Switzerland	do.	red
Montagne-Verte	Moselle	dry, ordinary	
Montalcino	Italy	sweet	
Montale	Do.	sweet, ordinary	
Monte-Catini	Do	sweet	
Monte-Fiascone	Do.	do.	
Monte-Pulcino	Do.	do.	
Monte-Serrato	Do.	ordinary	
Monte-Spertoli	Do.	sweet, ordinary	
Monterey	California	fine, ordinary	
Montferrat	Italy	ordinary	
Montilla	Spain	dry	
Mont-Termino	Savoy	fine	do.
Montzingen	Lower Rhine	dry, fine	white
Moravia	Austria	ordinary	
Mosyvina	Do.	do.	
Motril	Spain	do.	
Moukhran	Russia	do.	
Murcia	Spain	sweet, ordinary	
Nackenheim	Hesse	dry, fine	do.
Naples	Italy	fine, ordinary, sweet	
Narni	Do.	ordinary	
Nassau	Nassau	dry, fine	
Navarre	Spain	fine, ordinary	red
Neuchâtel	Switzerland	do.	
Neudorf	Austria	ordinary	
Neumagen	Lower Rhine	do.	
Neustadt	Bavaria	dry, fine	white
Neustift	Austria	ordinary	
Neustoed	Hungary	fine, ordinary	
Neu-Wied	Lower Rhine	fine	red
Neytra	Hungary	ordinary	
Nicosia	Sicily	dry	
Nieder-Breizig	Lower Rhine	dry, ordinary	white

Wine	Country	Quality	Colour
Nierstien	Hesse-Darm-stadt	Fine	White
Novi	Italy	sweet, ordinary	
Nubia	Africa		
Nussdorf	Austria	ordinary	
Oasis	Africa	do.	
Ober-Sifring	Austria	do.	
Ober-Stein	Lower Rhine	dry, ordinary	
Oberflach	Switzerland	ordinary	do.
Ober-Nusdorf	Hungary	fine, ordinary	
Oedenburg	Do.	fine	
Oeiras	Portugal	sweet	
Ogliastra	Italy	sweet, ordinary	
Ohio	America	ordinary, common	
Olisberg	Lower Rhine	dry, fine	do.
Olivença	Spain	fine	red
Oppenheim	Hesse-Darm-stadt	dry, fine	white
Orenburg	Russia	common	
Orotava	Teneriffe	dry, fine	do.
Orvieto	Italy	ordinary, sweet	
Otchacov	Russia	common	
Ottacring	Austria	ordinary	
Ouadnoum	Africa		
Padenghe		do.	
Palermo	Sicily		
Palestina	Syria	do.	do.
Palma	Majorca	do.	do.
Palme	Canary Islands	sweet, fine	
Panaria	Italy	sweet, ordinary	
Pantellaria	Do.	ordinary	
Paraguay	S. America	do.	
Parma	Italy	sweet, ordinary	
Parras	Mexico	sweet, fine	
Partiminio	Sicily	ordinary	red
Passo-del-Norte	Mexico	sweet	
Patisbanskaja	Russia	ordinary	
Patras	Greece	do.	
Paulis	Hungary	sweet	
Pavia	Italy	ordinary	
Paxarete	Spain	sweet, dry, fine	white
Paxos	Greece	ordinary	
Paz	Peru	do.	
Pennsylvania	N. America	do.	
Peralta	Spain	sweet, ordinary	
Perle	Cape of Good Hope	sweet, fine, ordinary	
Persia	Asia	do.	
Peru	S. America	fine, ordinary	
Peterwardein	Austria	ordinary	
Pezaro	Italy	sweet, ordinary	
Pezo-da-Regoa	Portugal	fine	red
Pickerne	Austria	ordinary	

Wine	Country	Quality	Colour
Philippine	Philippine Is.		
Philippseck	Hesse-Darmstadt	dry, ordinary	white
Piacenza	Italy	ordinary, sweet	
Piatra	Wallachia	sweet, fine	
Pico	Azores Islands	ordinary	
Piemont	Italy	sweet, ordinary	
Pirano	Austria	sweet	
Pisa	Italy	common	
Pisco	S. America	fine	
Pisport	Lower Rhine	dry, fine	do.
Plata	S. America	ordinary, common	
Poetzleindorf	Austria	ordinary	
Pokoinoi	Russia	ordinary, common	
Pola	Austria	fine	do.
Poleschowitz	Moravia	ordinary	
Pollenzia	Spain	sweet	do.
Pomerania	Prussia	ordinary	red
Poncino	Italy	sweet, ordinary	
Pont-Ercole	Do.	sweet	
Ponte-a-Mariano	Do.	do.	
Ponte-d'Allolio	Do.	ordinary	
Port-Sainte-Marie	Spain	dry	white
Porto	Portugal	fine	red
Porto-Longone	Italy	ordinary	
Porto-Santo	Madeira	dry, ordinary	
Portugal		sweet, fine, ordinary, and common	
Posega	Austria	ordinary	
Prawardie	Bulgaria	do.	
Presburg	Hungary	fine, ordinary	
Pressinge	Switzerland	ordinary	
Procida	Italy	sweet, ordinary	
Prosecco	Austria	ordinary	
Prussia		ordinary, common	
Psaffstaeten	Austria	ordinary	
Pulsgau	Do.	do.	
Pyrgos	Greece	fine, ordinary	
Quarta	Spain	ordinary	do.
Quigliano	Italy	do.	
Quillota	Chili	do.	
Radkersburg	Styria	do.	
Raen	Do.	do.	
Raffa	Italy	do.	
Ragusa	Austria	do.	
Rasdorof	Russia	fine	white
Ratchdorf	Hungary	sweet	
Rast	Austria	ordinary	
Rauenthal	Nassau	dry, ordinary	do.
Ravensburg	Würtemberg	do.	do.
Rech	Lower Rhine	ordinary	red
Redoute-Kale	Russia		
Reggio	Italy	sweet, ordinary	

Wine	Country	Quality	Colour
Reichenau	Baden	Ordinary	
Rems	Würtemberg	dry, fine	
Rensberg	Lower Rhine	dry	white
Retimo	Candia	sweet	
Rhinegau	Nassau	dry, fine	
Rhintal	Switzerland	ordinary	
Rhodes	Turkey	fine	
Ribadavia	Spain	ordinary	
Ribiera	Italy	do.	
Riccia	Do.	do.	
Riminese	Do.	sweet	
Rimini	Do.	ordinary	
Rio	Do.	sweet	
Riol	Lower Rhine	dry, ordinary	do.
Rioxa	Spain	fine, ordinary	
Riviera	Switzerland	ordinary	
Riviera	Italy	sweet, ordinary	
Riviere	Venice	do.	
Roaschio	Italy	ordinary	
Roben	Cape of Good Hope		
Rolle	Switzerland	do.	
Roman	Do.	do.	do.
Romania	Turkey	do.	
Ronagremalda	Italy	do.	
Rosenheck	Lower Rhine	dry	
Rota	Egypt	sweet, fine	red
Roth	Bavaria	dry, fine	white
Rothenberg	Hesse	dry	do.
Rüdesheim	Nassau	dry, fine	do.
Rugario	Italy	ordinary	
Russia Minor	Russia	do.	
Russia, South	Do.	ordinary, fine	
Rust	Hungary	fine	
Rutz	Lower Rhine	dry, fine	do.
Ryeck	Hungary	fine	
Sabayes	Spain	sweet, fine	
Saint Aubin	Switzerland	ordinary	red
„ Gall	Do.	do.	
„ George	Hungary	sweet, fine, ordinary	
„ George	Austria	ordinary	
„ George	Greece	fine	
„ Luis-de-la Paz	Mexico	sweet, fine	
„ Serf	Istria		
Sala-del-Cristo	Italy	ordinary	
Salatica	Do.	do.	
Salmersdorf	Austria	do.	
Salo	Italy	do.	
Saltzburg	Austria	ordinary, common	
Samos	Greece	sweet, fine, ordinary	
San-Buonaventura	California	fine, ordinary	
„ Diego	Do.	fine	

Wine	Country	Quality	Colour
San-Felice		Ordinary	
„ Gabriel	California	fine	
„ Giovanni	Sicily	ordinary	
„ Lucar	Spain	sweet	
„ Marino	Italy	ordinary	
„ Remo	Do	do.	
„ Vigilio	Do.	sweet, ordinary	
Sansal	Austria	ordinary	
Santa Barba	California	fine	
„ Cruz	Canary Islands		
„ Maria	Italy	sweet, fine	
„ Maura	Ionian Islands	sweet, ordinary	
Santarem	Portugal	ordinary	red
Santiago	Chili	do.	
Santo-Pretaso	Italy	do.	
Santo-Stefano	Do.	sweet	
Santorin	Greece	sweet, ordinary	
Saratof	Russia	ordinary	
Sardinia	Italy	sweet, fine, ordinary	
Sardinia	Island	common	
Sarepta	Russia	ordinary	
Sargans	Switzerland	do.	
Sassari	Italy	sweet, ordinary	
Sauritsch	Styria	ordinary	
Saxony	Germany	ordinary, common	
Schaffhausen	Switzerland	ordinary	
Schalksberg	Bavaria	do.	white
Schartsberg	Lower Rhine	dry, fine	do.
Schinanach	Switzerland	ordinary	do.
Schirvan	Russia	do.	
Schorapoma	Do.	do.	
Schweinfurt	Bavaria	do.	
Schwitz	Switzerland		
Sciarra	Sicily	fine	red
Scio	Turkey	sweet, fine	
Scoglitti	Sicily	ordinary	
Scopelo	Greece	fine, ordinary	
Sebenico	Dalmatia	sweet	
Segorde	Spain	ordinary	do.
Sellingen	Baden	fine, ordinary	
Seltz	Nassau		
Semlim	Austria	ordinary	
Senegal	Africa		
Sennori	Sardinia		
Serkar	Asia	do.	
Servia	Turkey	do.	
Setuval	Portugal	sweet	white
Seville	Spain	do.	
Sicily	Italy	sweet, fine	
Sienna	Do.	ordinary	
Sierre	Switzerland	sweet, ordinary	
Silesia	Austria		
Silesia	Prussia	common	

Wine	Country	Quality	Colour
Siloe	Canary Islands		
Simonetti	Russia	ordinary	
Sinac	Do.	do.	
Sines	Portugal	do.	
Sion	Switzerland	do.	
Sirmien	Hungary	sweet	red
Sitges	Spain	do.	
Slavonia	Austria	sweet, fine, ordinary	
Smyrna	Turkey	sweet, fine	
Sogd	Tartary	ordinary	
Soleure	Switzerland	do.	
Sommerach	Bavaria	do.	
Sorso	Italy	sweet	white
Spitz	Austria	ordinary	
Spoleto	Italy	do.	
Ssoetoesch	Hungary	fine, ordinary	
Stadtberg	Austria	ordinary	
Steeg	Lower Rhine	dry, ordinary	do.
Steegerberg	Do.	ordinary	
Steinberg	Nassau	dry, fine	do.
Steinfeld	Austria	ordinary	
Stellenbosch	Cape of Good Hope		
Stephansberg	Lower Rhine	do.	
Stettin	Prussia		
Stromboli	Italy	sweet, ordinary	
Stuttgard	Würtemberg		
Styria	Austria	dry, ordinary	
Sudagh	Russia	sweet, ordinary	
Sulm	Würtemberg	dry, fine	
Sumketie	Russia	common	
Switzerland		sweet, fine, ordinary	
Syracuse	Sicily	sweet, fine	
Syria	Turkey	sweet, fine, ordinary	
Syrmia	Austria	fine	
Szadany	Hungary	sweet, fine	
Sceghy	Do.	do.	
Tacaronte	Canary Islands	dry	do.
Tagamana	Do.	do.	do.
Taief	Arabia		
Tai-yuen	China		
Tallya	Hungary	sweet, fine	
Tangarog	Russia	ordinary	
Tangier	Morocco		
Taormina	Sicily	do.	red
Tarare	Italy	do.	
Tarczal	Hungary	sweet, fine	
Tarento	Italy	sweet	
Taroumoff	Russia	ordinary	
Tarrodant	Africa		
Taurida	Russia	do.	
Tauris	Persia	do.	
Tavira	Portugal	do.	white

Wine	Country	Quality	Colour
Tcheniedaly	Russia	Fine	
Tcherkask	Do.	ordinary	
Temeswar	Hungary	do.	
Tenedos	Turkey	sweet	
Teneriffe	Canary Islands	sweet, fine, ordinary	
Terceira	Azores Islands	ordinary	
Termini	Sicily	sweet, ordinary	
Terni	Italy	sweet	
Thayengen	Switzerland	ordinary	
Tarchof	Turkey	do.	
Theodosia	Russia	do.	
Thermina	Greece	sweet, ordinary	
Thessaly	Turkey	ordinary	
Thessaly	Greece	do.	
Thibet	Asia		
Thurgovil	Switzerland	do.	
Tidono	Italy	do.	
Tierra-del-Campo	Spain	fine, ordinary	
Tiflis	Russia	ordinary	
Tine	Greece	sweet, fine	
Tintilla	Spain	sweet	red
Tinto	Do.	do.	do.
Tizzanna	Italy	sweet, ordinary	
Toeplitz	Austria	ordinary	
Tokay	Hungary	sweet, fine	
Tokluk-Syrt	Russia	ordinary	
Toledo	Spain	ordinary, common	
Tolesva	Hungary	sweet, fine	
Tonquin	Asia		
Torre	Spain	ordinary	do.
Torres	Do.	do.	
Torres-Vedras	Portugal	do.	do.
Tortosa	Spain	sweet, ordinary	
Toscolano	Italy	ordinary	
Traben	Lower Rhine	dry, ordinary	white
Tranmontano	Chili	ordinary	
Transylvania	Austria	sweet, ordinary	
Trarbach	Lower Rhine	dry, ordinary	
Traz-os-Montes	Portugal	fine	
Treves	Lower Rhine	dry, fine	do.
Trieffenstein	Bavaria		
Trieste	Austria	ordinary	
Tripolitza	Greece	do.	
Troy	Turkey		
Truxillo	Peru	do.	
Tschernemble	Istria	fine	
Tucuman	S. America		
Tudela	Spain	ordinary	red
Turkey	Asiatic	sweet, fine, ordinary	
Turkey	European	do.	
Tuscany	Italy	sweet, ordinary	
Tuy	Spain	ordinary	

Wine	Country	Quality	Colour
Tyrol	Austria	Fine, ordinary	
Uberlingen	Baden	ordinary	
Udine	Austria	do.	
Ukraine	Russia	common	
Ungerberg	Lower Rhine	dry, ordinary	white
Ungstein	Bavaria	do.	do.
Unter-Kutzendorf	Austria	ordinary	
Unter-Sifring	Do.	do.	
Unterwald	Switzerland		
Uri	Do.	common	
Urzig	Lower Rhine	dry, ordinary	do.
Ustica	Italy	ordinary	
Vachery	Russia	do.	
Val-Maggia	Switzerland	do.	
Valais	Do.	sweet, ordinary	
Valdepenas	Spain	fine, ordinary	
Valdrach	Lower Rhine	dry, ordinary	do.
Valencia	Spain	sweet, fine, ordinary	
Valparaiso	Chili	ordinary	
Valpulezella	Venice	do.	
Valtelina	Switzerland	do.	
Vartsike	Russia	do.	
Vaud	Switzerland	do.	
Vaux	Do.	do.	red
Veglia	Dalmatia	do.	
Velez-Malaga	Spain	sweet, ordinary	
Venice	Austria	do.	
Verdetto	Plaisance	ordinary	
Veroetz	Slavonia	do.	
Verona	Italy		
Vesuvius	Naples	sweet, fine, ordinary	
Vevey	America	ordinary	
Vincenza	Italy	do.	
Vidiguiera	Portugal	do.	
Vinaroz	Spain	fine, do.	do.
Vinitza	Croatia	ordinary	
Virginia	America	common	
Viterbo	Italy	ordinary	
Vittoria	Spain	fine	white
Vittoria	Sicily	ordinary	
Voghera	Italy	sweet, ordinary	
Volkach	Bavaria	ordinary	do.
Waehring	Austria	do.	
Wallachia	Wallachia	sweet, fine, ordinary	
Walporzheim	Lower Rhine	dry, ordinary	do.
Warasdin	Austria		
Wehlen	Lower Rhine	dry, fine	do.
Weinberg	Würtemberg	do.	
Weinfelden	Switzerland	ordinary	
Weinhaus	Austria	do.	
Weinitz	Do.	fine, do.	
Weisskirchen	Do.	ordinary	
Wenzenheim	Lower Rhine	dry, ordinary	do.

Wine	Country	Quality	Colour
Wersitz	Hungary	Fine, ordinary	
Wertheim	Bavaria	dry, ordinary	white
Wiezlar	Prussia	do. do.	do.
Wiesel	Austria	ordinary	
Wikert	Hesse-Darmstadt	dry, fine	do.
Wildenstein	Do.	dry, ordinary	do.
Windisch Feistritz	Styria	ordinary	
Winningen	Lower Rhine	common	do.
Wintherthur	Switzerland	ordinary	
Wipach	Carniola	fine, ordinary	
Wisbaden	Hesse-Darmstadt	dry, fine	do.
Witteboom	Cape of Good Hope	sweet, fine	
Wittingen	Luxemburg	ordinary	do.
Wolfhalden	Switzerland	do.	
Worms	Hesse-Darmstadt	dry, fine	do.
Würtemberg	Würtemberg	do.	do.
Wurtzburg	Franconia	fine, sweet	
Wurtzgarten	Lower Rhine	dry, ordinary	do.
Xeres-de-la-Frontera	Spain	sweet, dry, fine	do.
Yverdun	Switzerland	ordinary	
Yvorne	Do.	do.	
Zabert	Würtemberg	dry, fine	
Zadany	Hungary	sweet, fine	
Zana	Peru	ordinary	
Zante	Ionian Islands	do.	
Zara	Austria		
Zeil	Bavaria	do.	
Zelaya	Mexico	sweet, fine	
Zeltingen	Lower Rhine	dry, fine	do.
Zemplin	Hungary	sweet, fine	do.
Zips	Do.	ordinary	
Zollicon	Switzerland	do.	
Zombor	Hungary	sweet, fine	
Zschelhoe	Do.	fine, ordinary	
Zug	Switzerland	common	
Zullichau	Prussia	do.	
Zurich	Switzerland	ordinary	
Zymslansk	Russia	fine	red

APPENDIX.

I.

Letter of Mr. Ballantyne.

THE following letter is extracted from 'The Times,' of December 24, 1807. It is evidently written by a person of much experience in the wine trade, and contains some very curious and interesting information:—

TO THE WINE DRINKERS OF BRITAIN.

DEAR SIRS,—There are many of you enjoying the happiness of living in this convivial island, who absolutely have, on an average of the last six years, drank of Portugal wine alone 38,973 pipes per annum, for which duty has been paid; and 11,000 butts of sherry and upwards per annum, for the last two years; and I suppose, in this year, you have kept up to the same quantity, exclusive of madeira, teneriffe, claret, hock, rhenish, mountain, &c.

Knowing, from long experience, that many of you enjoy it not so much as you ought, by the long and ill-founded prejudice against the wine-merchants, and in hopes of lessening that prejudice, and giving you a better relish for it, I make the following declaration, which, if deficient in point of elegance, shall not be so in point of fact.

On my return from Jamaica, 1767, with some judgment in making sugar and distilling rum, but much more of naval affairs (having been clerk of His Majesty's naval stores), I engaged as clerk with Mr. Robert Halcrow, of Mark Lane, who, previous to his death, gave me a share of one branch of his business. He was a general merchant, and a great importer of wine, and had one ship in the Oporto, and another in the Lisbon trade. I became very anxious to discriminate between the different qualities in all sorts of wines, and was assisted by an excellent cellar-man, whose father was the wine cooper to all the merchants of York. I made acquaintance with Mr. Tailleur, a very old wine-merchant, and a sensible and scientific man, who informed me of all the methods of managing wines for fifty years preceding that time; and also with Mr. Christopher Smith, a very old wine-merchant, who told me, when he had come to a state of manhood, and to drinking wine at taverns, it was eight-pence per quart, served up in a curious pewter measure, which turned round upon a little swivel with a spout, and if ten were in company one glass served them all.

The taverns were then like what paltry ale-houses are now, having old wainscot tables, covered with coarse blue-and-white cotton stuff; and the call was only for red or white, but frequently the red was called claret, and the white, sherry. Sherry was then generally, like other white wines, kept in a state of fermentation by sweet malaga, meade, cyder, or honey; pale wine was but just coming home on the lees, with which was mixed Spanish or small French wine; and a similar mixture was made of the various sorts of white wines. The dexterity of the wine-cooper then, was making the most palatable at the lowest prices. But much as both these gentlemen could give of the knowledge of wine, I got more from lectures on the art and mysteries of vintners delivered in Gresham College, by one of the professors, long before their time. Now, all wine comes in so clean and so perfect a state, that the wine-cooper's skill of former days is not required.

I believe it was not before the year 1750 that the first growth claret, properly prepared and of proper age, came to England from Boulogne, to Mr. Stewart of York Buildings, and Mr. Allen of Mark Lane. It was managed at Boulogne by the house, of which my relations, John and James Ballantyne, had the chief charge for more than fifty years. But of late years, the Forsters, the Johnstons, and two or more houses at Bordeaux, can ship it in the same excellent condition as formerly from Boulogne. As late as 1770, when I was at York, Newcastle and Durham, in the east, and Manchester in the west, I found all the five northern counties supplied from Edinburgh and Leith.

From 1767 to 1774 no pale wine was bottled but for immediate use; only draft wine was used in the principal taverns, with most of which I was acquainted, and many inns in the vicinity; and it was often very bad, not from the tricks generally of the vintners, but their bad management. When a good pipe in draught was grown flat, a hogshead was filled, and, in time, put in draught; and lastly, reduced to a half hogshead; and those casks were seldom clean. Now, I do affirm, that during these seven years we made no mixture of any kind; but if Lisbon was too thin, and not rich enough, we applied a portion of Calcavello-Lisbon, at a much superior price; and with white port (being subject to ferment in summer and grow foul in winter) we mixed a little fine teneriffe, which improved its flavour and prevented any further fermentation.

When a pipe of port became too old for our customers, we enriched it to their taste with newer wine; for at that time superannuated port was not esteemed. I think three years of the above had passed before I had seen a butt of sherry, but when I did, I recommended it in preference to white port. A man of quality recommended to me Mr. Duff, our late consul at Cadiz, to whom I sent orders from several friends, and white port soon became despised; although it had been in such esteem, that, even as late as 1782, I got orders in one week for shipping 80 pipes. Now it is forgotten; sherry has prevailed: but I beg— as many of you as have given up your affection for your palates, to gratify your eyes with what is extremely pale— that when you discover a hot, pungent, bitter taste, such as no grapes could ever give, you will not impute it to the wine-merchant, many of whom with reluctance import it, only to gratify your perverted tastes.

As a tribute to the memory of my friend Mr. Robert

Halcrow, I cannot refrain from telling you that he had been a seaman on board the Admiral Sir John Norris's ship. He was a Shetland man, of amazing strength; was a mate in the Portugal trade, then master, and afterwards owner of two ships, as before stated. He was also an elder brother of the Trinity House, and a governor of the Merchant Seamen's Hospital; he made three of his nephews masters of ships; and was so esteemed by the Portuguese that he became one of the greatest shippers of goods, both to Oporto and Lisbon. Like a seaman he would swear a little, but he was extremely generous and devout; he discoursed with me till the hour of his death, expressed no repentance for adulterating wine in his confessions, but desired me to write his epitaph without fulsome praise; which is in Stepney churchyard.

In 1775, I engaged with Mr. Paul Amsinck, a man of the highest pride in having good wine; he would as readily have committed robbery as have adulterated wine, and I think I know a hundred in London of the same disposition, and about as many in the outports, cities, and great towns. If you ask me, are there no wine-merchants who sell bad wine? I reply, that in places where there are three or four wine-merchants, there is one generally underselling the rest; and many of that sort are here. They do it not so much by the mixture of sloe, cyder, &c., as the vulgar error leads you to believe (especially in the last twenty-one years, since the exciseman comes in upon them unawares), as by purchasing inferior wine rejected by the wine-merchants, and sent on adventure or barter.

For instance, when I was buying some of Lynch's particular madeira on the quay at 65*l.*, which now would sell for 115*l.*, a madeira merchant offered me thirty pipes at 55*l.*, which, a year afterwards, I could have bought for 45*l.* I have seen wine shipped by shopkeepers of Oporto, that no wine-merchant of repute could have suffered to come into his vaults; so it is absurd to believe that all bad wine is made so here. These inferior wines are purchased by those who never presume to supply the tables of gentlemen or respectable men of business; and I am sorry the poorer sort, when they can regale themselves with a bottle, get any such in the houses whereon you see 'Wine neat as imported.'

In 1778, after my return from Oporto, where I had been on important business, and commenced agent for the (then) John Perry, in the quality of whose wines ten years' experience had given me confidence, I was kindly received by many of the most considerable importers, but particularly Mr. Allnutt, who was in the highest estimation, not only for the great extent of his business, but for his honourable spirit and generosity to all with whom he had any concern. I then set off to Bristol, and through Gloucester to Liverpool and Glasgow, making, as a seaman would say, a traverse course; and from thence to Edinburgh, returning by Newcastle, Durham, York, and Hull, and afterwards to Lynn and Norwich.

A man in my character, agent to a house of Oporto, and lately come from thence, with ten years' experience here, they had not before seen. I was most kindly received, and, except by one of the undersellers of Liverpool, I cannot recollect one who was not anxious to show me all his wine, and take my opinion. There seemed to be no fear of my discovering any that had been adulterated. The only fault I found, and which I corrected, was their having generally ordered their houses at Oporto to ship the very oldest wine, not regarding the price. Wines long kept at Oporto grow tawny in colour and vapid, and get what we call the country taste; but those who took my advice and ordered two-year-old wine, obtained more praise from their customers than they ever got before.

If you wish to have excellent port, and wait till it be of age at home, buy young wine here, not what has been in a fever four years at Oporto. It was true what my old friend Admiral Vandeput often said: 'He is a fool who thinks he gets better wine by importing than buying of the merchants here. I have been in all the ports in Europe, Madeira, Teneriffe, but even if our friend Mr. Duff would ship me a butt of sherry, it might not please my palate; and I know the foreign houses lay on more than the profit the wine-merchant would charge me here, if I buy on the quays, and pay ready money, which I must do if I import; and if I do not like the wine, I cannot send it back. If at unlimited prices you get orders to ship for such houses as Carbonell's, Paxton's, Allnutt's, and other houses here, for forty or fifty pipes, from Gourillet of Winchester, the Grangers at Exeter, or my old friend Major Balfour of Leith, and such houses, am I to expect my pipe better than theirs? No, no; I know the contrary.' He was the best judge of any gentleman I knew.

I have been in as much good company probably as any to whom I now address myself, here as well as in almost any considerable city and town in England, Scotland, and Ireland, and have found in most companies some troublesome pretender to a judgment in wine, thinking it a gentlemanlike accomplishment, but who generally tries to wake up your prejudice against the wine, till by the strength of imagination you fancy it sour; yet, if he has previously heard that his own esteemed wine-merchant has provided the wine, then it is indisputably the best in the world!

I beg, my good friends, that, to check these things, you would give your palates practice, and be not prejudiced in favour of Mr. Anybody's wine or Nobody's, nor in white wine by its colour. About the year 1790 and 1791 I had above 170 wine-merchants chiefly taking their port wine of me, among all of whom there were not ten who sought cheap wine; and these mostly great importers, who sold to publicans and the lesser dealers, making no pretensions to supply gentlemen's tables.

Your obedient Servant,

WM. BALLANTYNE.

II.

Letter from a London Hospital Surgeon, Sept. 1852.

A connection, for above a quarter of a century, with one of the metropolitan hospitals, has given me ample opportunities of observing the habits and constitutions of the labouring classes. Although the vice of habitual intemperance is one for which nothing in the spirit of apology will be received with favour, yet it behoves the charitable person to reflect on the peculiar temptations to exceed in the use of stimulating drinks to which the hard-worked artisan, close pent in populous towns, is exposed.

Everything in his mode of life tends to produce exhaustion of the physical powers. I will allude only to two of these. First, his lodging. Owing to straitened means, he must dwell (wherever his work may be) in a densely-crowded, cheap district; and there the atmosphere is noxious and oppressive. As regards public health, it is now a well-established point, that the assembling together of numerous human beings in a small space has of itself, independently of other circumstances, a wonderfully depressing influence on the system of those who live within the circle; so that, when disease breaks out in the locality, all its different forms, colds, fevers, &c., are characterised by being of a rapidly debilitating nature, calling for the administration of remedies which will most effectually sustain the powers of life, and counteract that weakening poison, as it may be called, of the surrounding atmosphere.

I may add, in regard to this subject, that for many years back a great change has taken place in the general treatment of the inmates of London hospitals, and with the most marked advantage. The system of giving lowering medicines, although required at the first onset of the majority of diseases, is pursued much more cautiously than heretofore, and continued for a shorter period, and the quantity of wine, porter, and ale administered has been increased to a most remarkable degree; so that, for the support of the charities, the wine-merchant's bill forms one of the most heavy and formidable items in the annual amount of expenditure. These facts, I think, prove that, for preserving the health of the labouring members of the community, a full and generous mode of living, *embracing the proper use of stimulants of a wholesome kind*, is necessary; and that, however praiseworthy it may be for those residing in comfortable houses to preach against intemperance, a total abstinence from such refreshing, invigorating, and restoring drink as sound, full-bodied wine, is contrary to the promptings of natural instinct and the observations of scientific men.

Next, as to the food of the poor. Necessity obliges the labouring man to purchase the cheapest articles left on the stall of the butcher after being rejected by the caterers for the rich; to him falls the choice of the tough, tendinous, skinny parts. If he takes a fancy for fish, it is coarse, soft, and slimy; even his wheaten bread is doughy, pasty, and sour; in short, his diet consists of articles the hardest of digestion that a human stomach can encounter. Moreover, it is wretchedly cooked, and commonly eaten at irregular periods, with little or no interruption of his hard labour.

Is it to be wondered at that the poor fellow should have a parched tongue and dried throat, and that he should experience a gnawing at his stomach, that makes a craving for some hot stimulant irresistible? Now, the liquors to which he has recourse are the very ones to make things worse. The spiced gin and the drugged beer satisfy the wants of his internal sense for a time, but they soon create a heat and parched sensation within him, that enforce a repetition of the indulgence; at length, stupefaction from the intoxicating effects of the liquor subdues his consciousness and sense of shame, and he recks not how he goes on adding glass to glass.

But mark what is the early consequence of this unhappy course of proceeding. The man's digestive powers fail. The bad food, I will not deny, has a great share in inducing weakness of stomach. But appeal to all the medical men of London, especially to those who have had experience, as hospital or dispensing doctors, in the treatment of the poor, and they will unanimously declare, that for producing indigestion and its manifold concomitant sufferings, nothing that enters the stomach is so fertile as the use of strong alcoholic drinks, or large potations of beer. And, in confirmation of this statement, I would point to the difference in the prevailing disorders of the poor in this country, as compared with the same class in wine-growing countries, where the poor drink wine with their meals, and are sparing in the use of spirits and beer.

I have credible authority for affirming that dyspeptic complaints (indigestion) are, in the latter, less frequently met with, and that in a very marked degree, than in Great Britain. And, in making this observation, I confine myself to the evil effects of what may be considered a moderate abuse of spirits and beer. I exclude that fearful malady—*delirium tremens*—the result of excessive addiction; and which, I believe, is rarely met with in the wine districts of the Continent.

Those poor patients in London who daily crowd the waiting-rooms of the hospitals and dispensaries, seeking out-door succour, are, in a very large proportion, sufferers from disordered stomachs and livers—diseases brought on principally by the pernicious qualities of the liquors they are forced to drink. My strong conviction is, that should the time arrive when wine will be accessible to the labouring classes of this nation as it is to those in neighbouring countries, it will in itself be a more wholesome beverage than that which they now indulge in; that its more general adoption will lead to improvement in the sanitary quality of the beer that will continue to be drunk; that it will probably drive out spirits from extensive consumption; and that, independently of a diminution of drunkenness, it will greatly ameliorate the general health of the working classes. A LONDON HOSPITAL SURGEON.

III.

On the Use of Wine among the Lower Orders in Scotland in the Seventeenth Century. By Joseph Robertson, Esq., F.S.A. Scot.

The discussion on Mr. Gladstone's Budget and the Commercial Treaty with France has raised this purely historical question—How far at any time has wine been in general use among the common people of this country?

I cannot pretend for myself to have had any doubt upon the point. Everything which I have observed has gone to satisfy me that, at least in Scotland, wine was one of the staple drinks of our forefathers, until they became politically and commercially estranged from France at the Revolution in 1688. This I firmly believe; and I venture to think that I could give reasons for my belief which should satisfy everyone possessed of patience enough to follow me through the multitude of necessary details and computations. The Society need not be alarmed. I am not about to put their forbearance to the proof of a long paper of statistics. I have no thought of asking their attention to more than one small fragment of the large mass of evidence; and I hope that I shall be able to say what I have to say in a very few words, and without any arithmetic.

If I were to ask you to name any one province of Scotland, or of Britain, of which it could be affirmed that its inhabitants must, from all their circumstances, have had both less will and less power than their neighbours to indulge in the use of wine, I think I may say that you would at once name the Western Isles. The people were poor even beyond the measure of Scottish poverty; their climate is proverbially raw and damp; and in the whisky of divers kinds which they made at home—their *usquebaugh*, their *trestarig*, and their *usquebaugh-baul*—they had a drink which might have been supposed to be the most congenial of all drinks, at once to their poverty, their climate, and to their taste. If I can show, therefore, that wine was in general use among the common people in the Western Islands, I think you will agree with me in holding that it would be superfluous to adduce evidence of its general use among the wealthier common people of the more favoured mainland of Scotland.

Now, in the official registers of the time preserved among our national records, we have proof that the passion for wine among the Islesmen, in the beginning of the seventeenth century, was so strong that the Government of the day found themselves unable to control or restrain it, except by means which went far beyond what I believe to be the provisions of the so-called Maine Law of our own time. The following ordinance was passed by the Privy Council in the year 1616:—

Act aganis the Drinking of Wynes in the Yllis.

Apud Edinburgh xxvj of Julij 1616.

Forsamekle as the grite and extraordinar excesse in drinking of wyne commonlie vsit amangis the commonis and tennentis of the Yllis is not onlie ane occasioun of the beastlie and barbarous cruelteis and inhumaniteis that fallis oute amangis thame to the offens and displesour of God and contempt of law and justice bot with that it drawis nvmberis of thame to miserable necessitie and powertie sua that thay ar constraynit quhen thay want of thair awne to tak from thair nichtbouris For remeid quhairof the Lordis of Secrete Counsell statutis and ordanis that nane of the tennentis and commonis of the Yllis sall at ony tyme heirefter buy or drink ony wynes in the Ylles or continent nixt adiacent vnder the pane of tuenty pundis to be incurrit be euery contravenare *toties quoties* The ane half of the said pane to the Kingis Maiestie and the vther half to thair maisteris and landislordis and chif-tanes Commanding heirby the maisteris landislordis and chiftanes to the saidis tennentis and commonis euery ane of thame within thair awine boundis to sie thir present act preceislie and inviolablie keept and the contravenaris to be accordinglie pvnist and to vplift the panes of the contravenaris and to mak reckning and payment of the ane halff of the said panes in [his] Maiesteis excheckar yeirlie and to apply the vther halff of the saidis panes to thair awne vse.

There is here, you will observe, a prohibition under high penalties, not only of the sale, but of the use of wine in the Isles. To make the prohibition more effective, it was not only provided that one half of the penalty should go to the landlord or chief, but these landlords and chiefs were further taken bound individually, by formal bonds fenced by good sureties and enormous forfeitures, to use only a certain limited quantity of wine themselves, and to take strict order that none of their tenants and country people should buy or drink any wine whatever.

The ordinance of 1616 which I have read was not the first piece of legislation on the subject. Seven years before, the Privy Council had prohibited the importation of wine and spirits from the mainland, without however prohibiting the use of either, and with a special declaration that the prohibition should be 'without prejudice always to any person within the Isles to brew aquavitæ and other drink to serve their own houses, and to the special barons and substantious gentlemen to send to the Lowlands, and there to buy wine and aquavitæ to serve their own houses.'

The Act of 1616, then, was not the first of its kind. I need scarcely add that it was not the last; for it would seem to be the fate of all such attempts to prevent mankind from gratifying the reasonable appetites of their nature; that as one law fails in its object, another and another, each more oppressive than its predecessor, is placed upon the statute-book, until at last either the accumulated mass proves more than human patience can bear, or the Legislature, gathering wisdom from experience, tacitly abandons an enterprise which it sees to be beyond its strength. In 1609, the Scottish Privy Council forbade the introduction of wine into the Isles from the mainland. In 1616, they forbade its use. And now in 1622, confessing the failure of their former attempts, they of new prohibit its importation from any quarter whatever, and its sale by any person whatever. The following ordinance was passed in July 1622:—

Act that Nane send Wynis to the Ilis.

Apud Edinburgh 23 Julij 1622.

Forsamekle as it is vnderstand to the Lordis of Secreit Counsell that one of the cheiff caussis whilk procuris the continewance of the inhabitantis of the Ilis in their barbarous and inciuile forme of leving is the grite quantitie of wynes yeirlie caryed to the Ilis with the vnsatiable desire quhairof the saidis inhabitantis are so far possest that quhen their arryvis ony ship or other veshell thair with wynes thay spend bothe dayis and nightis in thair excesse of drinking and seldome do thay leave thair drinking so lang as thair is ony of the wyne restand sua that being ouercome with drink thair fallis oute mony inconvenientis amangis thame to the brek of his Maiesteis peace And quhairas the chiftanes and principallis of the clannis in the Yllis ar actit to tak suche ordour with thair tennentis as nane of thame be sufferit to drink wynes yitt so lang as thair is ony wynes caryed to the Ilis thay will hardlie be withdrawne frome thair evill custome of drinking bot will follow the same and continew thairin whensoeuir thay may find the occasioun For remeid quhairof in tyme comeing The Lordis of Secreit Counsell ordanis lettres to be direct to command charge and inhibite all and sindrie marcheantis skipparis and awnaris of shippis and veshellis be oppin proclamatioun at all placeis neidfull that nane of thame presoume nor take vpoun hand to carye and transporte ony wynes to the Ilis nor to sell the same to the inhabitantis of the Ilis except so mekle as is alloued to the principall chiftanes and gentlemen of the Ilis vnder the pane of confiscatioun of the whole wynes so to be caryed and sauld in the Ilis aganis the tenour of this proclamatioun or els of the availl and pryceis of the same to his Maiesties vse.

Here, unfortunately, the register from which this information is derived fails us. Nor have I observed elsewhere any further information about the use of wine in the West Isles during the seventeenth century. We may safely presume, however, that there, as in other parts of Scotland, it gradually fell into disuse among the mass of the people, as war and a false commercial policy destroyed our trade with France, as excessive import duties raised the price above the reach of all but the more opulent classes, and as our improved Customs' police and a better tone of public feeling put an end to the smuggling by which these import duties were evaded. Wine has long ceased to be used among the common people of the Hebrides. Its place has been supplied by whisky; and of the extent to which that is consumed, Sir John M'Neill has given startling information in the Report on the West Highlands and Islands which he made to the Home Secretary in 1851.

We have seen that while wine was utterly prohibited to the common people, their chiefs were allowed to use it in certain limited quantities. The Society may perhaps wish to know what in those days was considered a reduced allowance of claret for a Highland gentleman. The smaller chiefs, then, such as Mackinnon of Skye, Maclean of Coll, and Maclean of Lochbuy, were restricted to one tun, or four hogsheads, each, in the twelvemonth. Chiefs of a higher rank, such as the Captain of Clanranald, had three tuns, or twelve hogsheads, a year. Potentates of still greater mark—Maclean of Duart, Macleod of Dunvegan, and Donald Gorme of Sleat—were permitted to have, each of them, four tuns, or sixteen hogsheads, yearly. Four

Scottish tuns, I should explain, contain rather more than 876 imperial gallons. In other words, there were, in 1616, at least three houses in the West Isles where the consumption of wine, under the jealous regimen of the Privy Council, amounted to 438 dozen every year. May I ask if there be *one* house now in all the Hebrides which uses so much?

IV.

Letter of the Author to 'The Times,' Oct. 19, 1860.

Subjoined is a letter from Mr. Shaw, the early and well-known advocate of a reduction of the wine duties to 1*s.* per gallon, and whose exertions on the question were made at an epoch when there was a surplus revenue to favour the experiment, when the produce, unaffected by the vine disease, was good and ample to meet any sudden increase of demand, and when our Continental relations were such that there was time to trust to the effects of a continuous increase of trade through several years to prevent the growth of a military feeling and the preparation of enormous armaments against this country.

It remained for others to neglect or oppose his arguments at the date when they were put forth, and then to take 1860 as the period for adopting them, and to claim, amid the usual flourishes about 'international progress,' the 'consummation of free trade,' &c., all the popularity and advantages of the measure, political and otherwise. In his present communication, the object of Mr. Shaw is to modify the bearing of certain statements recently put forth as to the disastrous character of the French vintage this season, and also regarding the probability of wine becoming a general article of consumption. In the latter respect his views continue sanguine, but he points out a serious drawback to their realisation. The public are almost universally under an impression that at the reduction of duties to their lowest point on January 1, next, all wines of the lighter class will come in at a duty of only 1*s.* per gallon. On the contrary, Mr. Gladstone and his advisers have arranged that 'the very weakest *vin ordinaire*, as well as the cheapest and dearest champagne and burgundy, and every wine imported *in bottle*,' must pay 2*s.* 5*d.* per gallon, or nearly the same rate as that at present chargeable. This is a result of the sliding scale imposed with regard to alcoholic strength. It being impossible to test that strength in the instance of wine in bottle, the high rate is therefore imposed indiscriminately.

This clumsy contrivance would be vexatious even if it were necessary, but it will appear especially disagreeable if Mr. Shaw's statement is accurate, that the alcoholic test is altogether a needless device of official obstructives—ever ready to apprehend that all the commercial world live only for the purpose of defrauding or outwitting them:—

'Nuits, Côte d'Or, France, Oct. 12, 1860.

'SIR,—In your paper of the 5th inst. there is a letter from Mr. Standen containing remarks upon the vintage of the present year in this country, and his opinion on the results to be expected from the late and prospective reduction of the duty on wine. Although apparently unaware that the vintage in the great southern districts has proved both excellent and abundant, it is unfortunately true that it is bad in all other quarters, and that prices have risen, and would have risen still more, were it not for the general depression of trade and the considerable stocks of former years still existing. It should be remembered that a rise of even 25 per cent. on the usual good descriptions is seldom more than 3*l.* to 4*l.* per hhd., or from 3*s.* to 4*s.* per dozen.

'Mr. Standen mentions that the present price of a choice bottle of claret at the Hôtel du Louvre is 20*s.*, and that little, if any, more would be charged in England. The experiment might be tried at Mivart's or the Clarendon, as a criterion of the prices of wine in each country, by asking for a bottle of 1820 port; the price of it in England would probably be found to be 40*s.*

'But I could take him to numerous restaurants in Paris where for 3*s.* or 4*s.* he would get an excellent dinner, in a room fit for a prince, and with his dinner a bottle of wine which satisfies French ladies and gentlemen who have been accustomed to wine from their infancy. Mr. Standen's assertion, that Englishmen are more choice in their selection than other nations, is open to much doubt. That they pay very high prices is unquestionable; but there is no country in Europe where such ignorance of pure, natural wines exists, though in a less degree than formerly. Not long ago the favourite clarets drunk in England were half hermitage, and champagnes were nearly the colour and strength of brown sherries; and ever since the Methuen Treaty, in 1703, they have been driven to the use of such kinds as have made them generally unable to appreciate any others in their natural state. Wine-merchants talk of their "experience" to prove that English people will never drink the wines of France; but it must be replied that there has been no "experience" to justify any such assertion, because, during the fifteen years from 1688 to 1703, the duty on the wines of France was raised 360 per cent., while those of Portugal, until 1831, were admitted at a duty of one-third less. This, with the permanent rate against the former, and the lowest duty on French from 1811 to 1820 being 13*s.* 9*d.*, and as high as 19*s.* 8*d.* per gallon, necessarily drove it almost entirely out of use; so that the consumption fell at one period to about 120,000 gallons for the whole United Kingdom, the percentage to the total quantity being less than 2 per cent. In 1859 it was 9·58 per cent. It is now much larger.

'Although still little known, there are probably as good light wines in other countries as in France, but, with the enormous duty which has so long prevailed, it has suited neither seller nor buyer to import them. It is a gross misapplication of the word to call this "experience" of the taste of the British nation. It is necessary to go a long way back; but the Battle of Waterloo is not more a historical fact than that almost the only wine drunk in England until the Revolution of 1688 was from France; while the duty was raised during a century from that period, from 4*d.* to 9*s.* 5*d.* per gallon. We learn that before the immense increase of duty, not less than 200 vessels loaded wines in Bordeaux for England in one year. Scotland cannot be said to be a very warm country for "light French wines," yet so general was its use there that when several vessels arrived in Leith about the same time, casks were carried in Edinburgh and other towns on carts, and sold to those who came with jugs, &c., as is now the case with milk.

'These are incontrovertible facts, and it is well known that, notwithstanding the endeavours of Governments to stop it, a great deal of French wine was smuggled both into Scotland and Ireland, long after it had been almost excluded from England. It seems almost impossible to convince English people that as strong, powerful wines are grown in France as in Portugal or elsewhere; but if the excellent Masdeu and other growths in the south had the same amount of spirit added as ports get, they would be quite as strong and as intoxicating, and such would also be the case with many of the excellent wines of the Herault, &c.

'It is not necessary, however, to refer to olden times to prove that it is not only in hot countries that the wines of France will be liked, for we may instance Norway, Sweden, Hamburg, &c., where they are preferred to the strong kinds; and surely we may thence infer by analogy that such will be the case with us.

'Even already since the late reduction from 5*s.* 9*d.* to 3*s.* per gallon the increase has been considerable, although, by deferring the further reduction till January, most of those who would have purchased are delaying to do so.

'One of the most important political, commercial, and financial measures ever carried has been that of reducing the duty of wine; but, although the proposal to make it 1*s.* per gallon on every description, which emanated from myself, and has been urged and advocated against the opposition of every wine-merchant, is at length admitted to be the best, and it might therefore be thought that I ought to be satisfied, I am grieved to feel compelled to add that I never saw a fine thing more thoroughly spoiled.

'I cannot believe that a man of Mr. Gladstone's knowledge and ability can have yielded to the representations of the officials of the Customs and Excise without great regret; but I have no hesitation in repeating what I expressed and endeavoured to prove while the question was under discussion, that he has acted on advice given in ignorance, which must inevitably prove very injurious to the success of the measure; and I have not heard any wine-merchant, whether opposed to or in favour of a reduction, express another opinion than that the differential rates are unnecessary for the protection of the revenue, that they will be a source of continual disputes and confusion, and will greatly interfere with the trade and consumption.

'During my stay in the wine districts of France I have met with many of the principal wine-growers and merchants, who all express the deepest sorrow at this regulation.

'The professed object has been to prevent loss to the revenue by the introduction of strongly alcoholised wine, not from the fear of illicit distillation (for of this they say they have no fear), but from its conversion into compounds which, as they allege, will be drunk instead of spirits, so that the revenue will thereby suffer.

'Others, as well as myself, have done all in our power to get the revenue officers to show a specimen of this fearful compound, but they evidently cannot; and thus, from a phantom held up before the Chancellor of the Exchequer, there is to be a duty on wine of 1*s.* per gallon up to 18 per cent. of proof spirit; above 18 to 26, 1*s.* 9*d.*; above

26 to 40, 2*s.* 5*d.*; above 40 to 45, 2*s.* 11*d.*; above 45, the spirit duty; and, owing to the same cause, the very weakest *vin ordinaire*, as well as the cheapest and dearest champagne and burgundy, and every wine imported in bottle, must all pay the high rate of 2*s.* 5*d.* per gallon, or 4*s.* 10*d.* per dozen, while no drawback is to be allowed on exportation.

'Independently of other objections, these enactments seem to have been made almost for the purpose of diminishing the success of the measure; because the very kind of wines which are both cheap and stout—and which therefore at the outset will be generally preferred in England for family consumption—are subjected to a rate of nearly 150 per cent. more than the light kinds; while a uniform rate of 1*s.* would have been simple, and have enabled all to drink on equal terms whatever they prefer.

'As to the taste which has arisen for pale ale, it is an excellent thing; but so is wine; though, unfortunately, almost all have been debarred from the use of the latter, the consumption not having been above one bottle and a half for each person per annum, though the total quantity and the revenue (with more than double the population, and probably fifty-fold the wealth) are almost the same as they were at the beginning of the century. Last year there was an apparent increase in quantity, but this arose from the use of wretched Cape, under the name of South African; which, moreover, as well as the substitution of British brandy for Cognac, proves that Englishmen, although willing to pay high prices for good, are also ready to drink what is bad, if procurable at a low price.

'You have already inserted so many letters from me on this subject during the last ten years, that I feel almost ashamed to be again obtruding myself; but when statements such as are contained in the letter referred to are published to the world, and allowed to remain uncontradicted, it is naturally inferred that they are incontrovertible.

'Your obedient servant,

'T. G. SHAW.'

To the Editor of the 'Daily News.'

'London, May 17, 1861.

'SIR,—Although the discussions during the last few years have tended to dispel much of the ignorance which prevailed about wine, there are still comparatively few who have a just idea of its abundance throughout a great portion of Europe; or who can believe that, instead of continuing to be regarded as a luxury attainable only by a few, it may become a general beverage, promoting temperance and health, and, at the same time, one of our great sources of trade and revenue.

'To Mr. Gladstone is due the honour of having accomplished this great measure, fraught with national benefits of the utmost importance; but it is deeply to be regretted that he allowed others to deter him from gaining the rapid development which the immediate reduction to a uniform rate of 1*s.* per gallon would have ensured.

'Having laboured during more than twenty years to prove that even 1*s.* per gallon was a high percentage on most kinds of wine, it is gratifying to find it realised, though grievously disappointing to see it accompanied by the new and unexpected system of alcoholic tests; while, on the other hand, there is the comfort of knowing that this is so universally disliked, that it must inevitably be soon abolished. Not even the revenue officers attempt to defend it as a protection to the revenue, and few will now venture to urge the application of fiscal means for weaning the taste of the nation from the strong kinds which a long period of enormous duties has rendered habitual, and which it will require time to alter, or modify.

'The following statement shows the operation of the test,

and it may be added, that if the strength on the quantity is even one-tenth above 18, the additional duty will be 75*l.*; above 26, it will be 66*l.*; above 40, it will be 50*l.*

Per centage of proof-spirit	Duty per gallon	Amount of duty on 2,000 galls.
18	1*s.* 0*d.*	£100
Above 18, up to 26	1*s.* 9*d.*	175
Above 26, up to 40	2*s.* 5*d.*	241
Above 40, up to 45	2*s.* 11*d.*	291

All in bottles 2*s.* 5*d.* per gallon, or 4*s.* 10*d.* per dozen.

'By this process the most delicate and costly growths may probably be charged 1*s.* per gallon, or 3 or 4 per cent. on their price, while other strong useful kinds may pay 2*s.* 5*d.*, or 70 to 80 per cent. No fermented juice of the grape yields above, and very few so much as, 28 per cent. of proof spirit, whether from Portugal, Spain, France, or anywhere else; and all above this strength have been made so by additional spirit.

'The alcoholic strength of wines is estimated in France according to Gay-Lussac, and in England according to the hydrometer of Sykes. They are as follows:—

18 of Sykes	equal to	10 of	Gay-Lussac.
26	"	15	"
40	"	22	"
45	"	25	"

'The grapes of southern countries contain more saccharine than the northern, but none are richer in this important principle than those grown in the great districts of France bordering on the Mediterranean; and the wines produced there differ from those of other parts of France, as they do from the innumerable growths of Spain and Portugal. Everyone travelling in wine countries must have observed a similarity in all natural, pure wine, fully fermented, while varying according to soil, exposure, &c.

'Almost every French red wine is here called claret, a name unknown anywhere but in England, and probably derived from Clairac, in Gascony, from whence large supplies were formerly imported, while the Médoc, which alone produces what is now considered true claret, was a barren waste.

'Remembering the few millions of inhabitants, the quantity of wine brought from various countries in olden times is astonishing, but numerous facts prove it. Even so early as the reign of Edward VI., in 1546, we see by records just published by Mr. Froude—"And for wines we have continually from France and Spain, as also out of Almaine and out of Candia, great quantity of the best that grow in these parts. The Flemings do buy much of our beer, because it is better than theirs, and pay almost as much for it as we do to the Frenchmen for our wine."

'Documents prove that it was often so abundant in Scotland, that when ships from Bordeaux or Rochelle arrived in Leith, casks were placed on wheelbarrows, and the "claret" sold off in the streets, in stoups; and long after French wines had been almost driven out of England, the wild shores of Scotland and Ireland enabled the smuggler to bring them in; which accounts for the fact, perceptible even now, and much more so some years ago, that claret remained on Scotch and Irish tables long after port had usurped its place in the south.

'Dr. Somerville, in his Memoirs descriptive of the manners of the Scotch about a hundred years ago, says:—"In families of my own rank the beverage offered to ordinary visitors consisted of home-brewed ale and a glass of brandy; or, when there was greater ceremony, claret, and brandy punch." Proofs are innumerable that people in England, Scotland, and Ireland drank little else than the red and white wines of France for several centuries; but although some are now beginning to waver, it seems almost an impossibility to induce most Englishmen, and especially wine-merchants, to believe that anything but port ever was or ever will be drunk by John Bull. I have been informed by an eye witness that, about the year 1770, large bodies of armed men were organised in

Galloway, the scene of Dirk Hatteraick's exploits, within a short distance of that famous smuggling dépôt, the Isle of Man, and, assembling to receive the cargoes from thence, traversed the district on horseback with their pack-horses laden with tea, brandy, wine, &c.; and, in order to conciliate the resident magistrates and ladies and gentlemen, used to leave in their stables, or other understood places, a piece of silk, some tea, or a cask of brandy or wine. Occasionally there were deadly conflicts between them and the dragoons assisting the customs officers.

'Railways are opening up districts hitherto inaccessible, and those who have not studied the subject, can have a very slight idea of the quantities of wine produced. Besides many other striking proofs, they will find that in many parts of Spain, wine is more abundant than water, and has been used for dissolving the lime required for building! If this is doubted, let the consular reports to our Government be referred to. During the last few years vine proprietors have generally been very prosperous, and have got prices that have induced them to devote greatly more care to their vines and the making of wine; and at this moment, in France, thousands of acres, hitherto appropriated to olives, &c., are being cleared of these, and planted with vines.

'It is a very simple matter to trace the cause of the decrease in the use of French wines. When the war with France, in 1688, broke out, the duty, which had formerly been 8*d.* per gallon, was raised to 4*s.* 10*d.* within fifteen years; and in 1703 we bound ourselves to admit Portugal wines at one-third less than those of France.

'For eighty-five years the difference against France was 120 per cent., and until 1831 was never less than 50; and I may add that, in 1813, the duty was 19*s.* 8*d.* per gallon, or 39*s.* 4*d.* per dozen; while port, sherry, &c. were 9*s.* 1*d.* per gallon, or 18*s.* 2*d.* per dozen. It was only in 1831 that the duties were equalised.

'At the end of the last century the wines of Portugal

constituted about 75 per cent. of the whole, but some of this was white port, and a large part Lisbon, which was then a favourite wine, though now almost forgotten. Last year, port was 25 per cent., during many years French was about 3, continuing till very lately about 7; but in 1860 it was 15, and by the returns of the first quarter of this year it is shown to have been nearly 20 per cent., while port was 26, and sherry 39. The comparative proportions of the different strengths on which duty was paid are, at 1*s.*, 10·72 per cent.; at 1*s.* 9*d.*, 3·20 per cent.; at 2*s.* 5*d.*, 76·30 per cent.; at 2*s.* 11*d.*, 2·23 per cent.; in bottle, 7·54 per cent.

'As it offers an interesting view of the change which has already occurred in the taste and the habits of the country, I give the relative quantities of red and white wines now drunk, by which it is seen how greatly white wines preponderate over red.

'The total duty paid in 1860 was on 7,358,192 galls.; whereof red was 3,001,413 galls., or 40·79 per cent., and white 4,356,779 galls., or 59·21 per cent.

'Even notwithstanding the intolerable alcoholic test, there is no doubt, and indeed it is seen already, that wines, good enough for general family use, will be now introduced for sale at prices greatly lower than have been known during a long period; while there will be also the fine rare qualities for those who are willing to pay the prices which such will always fetch. Spain and Portugal during many years have had practically the monopoly of the supply of this country, and it has been abused, like every other monopoly.

'Nowhere can finer wine be grown, or at less cost, than in these countries; but the system which has been generated in Oporto and Xerez will require to be adapted to the competition which will now be brought against them. It is an undeniable fact—and there are still alive those who remember when the usual price of fine old port was a guinea per dozen, and the dozen was thirteen bottles. The duty was then 3*s.* 1*d.*, but the price of the wine itself was scarcely a third of what it is now, and much less than it was even before the appearance of the oïdium.

'For many years the annual consumption for each person in the kingdom has been a bottle and a third, and the revenue about 1,900,000*l.*

'In Paris, where the consumption is estimated at 216 bottles, the duty is about 10*d.* per gallon.

'If, instead of 216 bottles, our consumption were only 12 bottles per head, this would give about 60,000,000 of gallons, which, at 1*s.* per gallon, would produce 3,000,000*l.* of revenue.

'I know I am alone in this opinion, which is considered very utopian; but I believe that if it were not for the alcoholic test it would be realised within two years.

'Although champagne is usually considered here one of the important wines of France, it is very little drunk there, being considered a *vin de luxe.* The district has been long celebrated, but it seems doubtful whether its wines were made "sparkling" till not many years ago.

'Even in Russia, to which immense quantities are now shipped, it was not known till 1815, when a Russian general, quartered in the house of Veuve Clicquot, in Rheims, was so much delighted with it, that he advised her to send some to St. Petersburg, and hence the origin of its great use in that country, and of her celebrity.

'The ancients do not seem to have drunk spirits, nor can we trace their use in Europe till about the beginning of the last century, when it was brandy from distilled wine. It is generally supposed that whisky has always been the drink of Scotchmen, but it can be shown that whisky was scarcely known in Scotland a hundred years ago, having been forced into use when it became difficult to smuggle Brandy and Hollands.

'The average consumption of spirits since 1846 has been as follows:—The revenue derived last year (1862) was 11,849,154*l.*; a fearful sum to be paid in duty alone for the great evil and curse of this country.

Average of 5 years.	1846 to 1850	1851 to 1856	1856 to 1860	1861	1862
	gallons	gallons	gallons	gallons	gallons
Rum . . .	2,288,306	3,092,547	3,510,174	3,452,576	2,820,181
Brandy . . .	1,741,775	1,808,156	1,339,705	1,600,304	1,700,183
Hollands . .	20,515	26,292	73,779	101,017	say 100,000
British spirits .	22,782,223	24,611,846	23,741,226	20,045,159	19,790,250
	27,541,819	29,538,841	28,664,884	25,199,056	24,820,614

'During the year ending March 31, 1860, the quantity of British spirits was 24,985,192 gallons; and to the same date in 1861, 20,147,824; showing a diminution of 4,837,368 gallons; and, as duty has been paid during the first three months of this year only on 4,670,797 gallons, if the same ratio continues for nine months, the total quantity will be 18,683,188 gallons during 1861.

'THOMAS GEORGE SHAW.'

V.

Operation of the Differential Rates in India.

It is satisfactory to see, by the following correspondence, that the trouble arising from the differential rates and strengths extends even to our Eastern possessions. The dictatorial, self-satisfied tone of the Collector of Customs in Calcutta, in expressing himself so decidedly about what he evidently does not understand, is amusing.

The authority he refers to here is not such as will carry much influence among those who have studied the question; neither will that of his analytical chemist in Calcutta. If he wishes for valuable information, he should apply to Mr. Johnston, the head of the gaugers in the London Custom House, who understands the whole subject thoroughly.

Although I have already given the result of the official

testing of the wines of Bordeaux, I copy it here in order to show still more strikingly the fallacy of the principle in operation in India, of rating the duty upon wine according to its being 'light' or 'strong,' estimating the value by this criterion. It is seen that the Château Lafitte of 1858, for which 80*l.* and 90*l.* per hogshead was paid, is the lightest of all in alcohol in that year—actually two per cent. weaker than a common vin de Blaye, worth 4*l.* or 5*l.*

Again, some of the cheapest wines, in reference to quality, are produced in the south of France, and some of these show as much as twenty-seven per cent. of proof spirit, by Sykes's hydrometer, which is as much as ports, sherries, or marsala yield in their natural state.

Strengths tested of Samples selected in Bordeaux, as being free from any addition of Spirit, by Officers sent by Government to the Wine Countries.

Description of Wine	1858 Per cent. of proof-spirit	1859 Per cent. of proof-spirit	1860 Per cent. of proof-spirit
Château Lafitte	16·5	17·7	14·8
St. Estéphe—supérieur . .	17·7	18·3	13·7
Médoc—paysan	17·7	18·3	14·8
St. Emilion—supérieur . .	18·9	18·9	16·0
St. Emilion—Bourgeois . .	16·6	15·4	16·0
Blaye—Bourgeois (very cheap, comn.)	18·3	17·1	14·8
Blaye—paysan " "	17·1	17·1	14·8
Latour Blanche (very fine Sauterne)	23·9	26·5	20·8

'*Bombay Chamber of Commerce.*

'CUSTOMS DUTY UPON LIGHT WINES.

'No. 409 of 1863.

'FROM GEORGE INVERARITY, ESQ., COMMISSIONER OF CUSTOMS, TO H. BROOKE, ESQ., SECRETARY, CHAMBER OF COMMERCE.

'February 28, 1863.

'SIR,—In continuation of Mr. Secretary Robertson's letter to your address, No. 3964, of October 31 last, and with reference to your communication, No. 137, of November following, I do myself the honour to transmit, for the information of the Chamber of Commerce, copies of the correspondence containing the decision of the Government of India on the subject of the duty to be levied upon light wines generally.—I have, &c.

'GEORGE INVERARITY,
'Commissioner of Customs.'

'No. 1697 of 1862.—REVENUE DEPARTMENT.

'FROM GEORGE INVERARITY, ESQ., COMMISSIONER OF CUSTOMS, TO THE HONOURABLE A. D. ROBERTSON, ESQ., ACTING CHIEF SECRETARY TO GOVERNMENT.

'Bombay Custom House, November 11, 1862.

'SIR,—With reference to the second para. of your letter to the Secretary to the Chamber of Commerce, No. 3964, of the 31st ultimo, copy of which was received with your endorsement, No. 3965, of the same date, I have the honour to bring to the notice of His Excellency in Council, that practically very great difficulty is experienced in giving satisfaction to the mercantile community generally in carrying out the provisions as to light wines contained in Schedule A of Act XI. of 1862.

'2. Two communications have been received from the Customs Department at Calcutta on the same subject—one a telegram, dated May 21 last, stating, as a general rule, that only the wines of France and Germany imported into this country are light wines; and the second, also a telegram, dated June 10 following, stating the Calcutta office considered all kinds of champagne and hock to be light wines; but that it admitted at the lower duty only wine which did not exceed twelve rupees per dozen in value.

'3. It appears doubtful, therefore, whether the Customs Departments at Calcutta do not admit at the lower rate of duty all wines of rupees twelve per dozen in value and under.

'4. Very great difficulty must always be experienced in strictly defining the term "light wine." And the merchants themselves, as I learn from a communication from the Secretary to the Chamber of Commerce to my address, are in doubt where to draw the limit at which a wine ceased to be a light wine. If the term is confined to the wines of France and Germany alone, as implied by your letter, No. 3964, above quoted, then injustice will be done to the producers of the light wines of Spain, Portugal, and the Cape, as well as of some Mediterranean ports, who would be placed at a great disadvantage in respect to the producers of France and Germany, Tinto, Bucellas, Lisbon, red Spanish wines, but of low value on account of their poorness of flavour and deficiency of strength. Tinto and Lisbon, especially, can be imported into Bombay for considerably less than twelve rupees a dozen; and yet, because they may be considered as inferior kinds of port and sherry, and scarcely capable, therefore, of being classed with the light wines of France and Germany, they must, under the existing interpretation of the law, be charged with the higher duty of nearly four rupees per dozen, a rate which must eventually act as entirely prohibitory. I beg further to add that none of these wines are "adulterations" (*vide* para. 2 of your letter above quoted); they are all pure wines, and in considerable demand amongst the middle classes of Portuguese and others.

'5. It appears, therefore, that the public have strong grounds for complaint against existing arrangements. Enquiry has satisfied me that all discontent would be removed by admitting at the lower duty, by one rupee the imperial gallon, all wines indiscriminately which did not exceed Rs. 12 per dozen in value, without attempting to lay down minute distinctions between "light wines" and others, such as even those practically acquainted with the trade find it impossible to draw; and I would respectfully solicit the early sanction of His Excellency in Council to this arrangement being adopted. It might result in a small sacrifice of revenue; but that would be of inferior importance to the removal of what is at present very generally considered an unfair and unnecessary restriction on the importation of certain classes of wines.—I have, &c.,

'GEORGE INVERARITY,
'Commissioner of Customs.'

No. 301.

'FROM A. M. MONTEATH, ESQ., UNDER-SECRETARY TO THE GOVERNMENT OF INDIA, TO H. L. ANDERSON, ESQ., CHIEF SECRETARY TO THE GOVERNMENT OF BOMBAY.

'Fort William, January 12, 1863.

'SIR,—I am directed to acknowledge the receipt of Mr. A. D. Robertson's letter, No. 4303, dated November 26, submitting for the decision of this Government a question as to the proper application of the term "light wines," contained in Schedule A of Act XI. of 1862, with reference to the discriminating duties on wines at Bombay levied under that Act.

'2. In reply, I am directed to forward, for the information of the Government of Bombay, the accompanying copy of a memorandum from the Collector of Customs, at Calcutta. The Governor-General in Council considers that the Calcutta practice as therein exhibited is correct, and that no sufficient reason for altering it has been shown.—I have, &c.,

'A. M. MONTEATH,
'Under-Secretary to the Government of India.

'Memorandum by the Collector of Customs in reply to the three following questions:—

1. What is the practice of the Calcutta Custom House?
2. Is any inconvenience experienced in carrying out that practice?
3. What do you think of Mr. Inverarity's suggestions?

'1. The practice of the Calcutta Custom House is to admit at the one rupee duty only the wines of France and Germany, and then solely when of less value than twelve rupees a dozen.

'Ginger wine has been admitted at one rupee when the value was below twelve rupees, and the analysis showed the absence of almost any spirit.

'An attempt was made by a Calcutta firm to get port wine admitted at one rupee duty. This I opposed; and the Board upheld my views. The wine had been valued at fourteen shillings a dozen. I was so satisfied that port could not be considered a light wine, that I wrote to my own wine-merchants, Messrs. Maxwell & Keys, of James Street, Haymarket, as to what was considered "light wine." Messrs. Maxwell & Keys were exporters of wines to India when only three firms in all were engaged in the trade. Their answer to my query is as follows: —

'"In answer to your enquiry respecting the term 'light wines,' we give that definition only to the French and German wines, and any there may be of that kind when the spirit is about twenty per cent. and under. Neither port nor sherry, nor even wines coming from Spain or Portugal, as far as we have seen (and they are shipping the ordinary country wines, we have heard), are in our opinion entitled to be called 'light wines.' With respect to the cost, possibly they may be costing as little as you quote (that is fourteen shillings a dozen above referred to); but it is very likely to be a blended wine from our docks. It has been usual to require a certificate of cost where duty is payable according to value."

'In fixing the spirit at twenty per cent. and under, Messrs. Maxwell & Keys have, I think, fixed it favourably for the trade. Sixteen per cent. of spirit and under is generally the line of distinction between light wines and other descriptions.

'2. I am not aware of any inconvenience attending the practice of the Custom House here. The wine is approved by sample; and if a French or German wine, and valued by the appraiser at twelve rupees and under, it is passed at the one rupee duty. If not, and it should exceed twelve rupees, the higher duty is taken.

'3. I have no objection to a uniform rate of one rupee duty on all wines of less value than twelve rupees a dozen, with the exception of sherry, port, madeira and marsala. These are not light wines, and cannot be called such in any sense of the word. Burgundy and some clarets are not light wines; but when of the quality to exclude them from the class of light wines, they cannot be imported at twelve rupees the dozen. An analytical chemist in this town, when I spoke to him as to whether port at fourteen shillings the dozen could be a light wine, replied, "Port, sherry, and madeira are not light wines, even at a cost of one rupee the dozen." Marsala I have known myself to give twenty-six per cent. of spirit.

'I imagine a good deal of the confusion at Bombay arises from parties who have not been brought up to the wine trade, and acting as agents for shippers from England, and proceeding on their own ideas as to what ought to be the rule, instead of, or what is the recognised practice of, the trade. 'J. A. CRAWFORD.'

June 5, 1863.—By the receipt of Sir Charles Trevelyan's Budget, we learn that all differential rates on wine are abolished in India, and that there is now a uniform tax of (one rupee) 2*s*. per gallon, instead of 2*s*. on what were considered light kinds, and 4*s*. on all others. This is a great improvement, but it is a very different amount of tax from about 13 per cent., *ad valorem*, as the correspondent of 'The Times' estimates it, and as that journal, in a leading article, states the duty now to be—viz. 13 per cent. on the value. Two shillings per gallon on a hogshead of French wine of forty-six gallons, is 4*l*. 12*s*, which is more than 100 per cent. on the cost of many common growths.

The percentage will, of course, diminish, according to the price of the wine, and 13 per cent. is on the estimated value of 37*l*. for a hogshead, which is a high estimate. It is 92*l*. 10*s*. for a pipe of port.

VI.

Letter in the 'Moniteur Vinicole.'

The following letter, which lately appeared in the 'Moniteur Vinicole,' gives a correct view of the discontent existing in the wine districts of France, owing to the slight increase of demand from this country. The writer's statement, that wines here are generally valued according to their body and strength, regardless of delicacy or bouquet, is not far from the truth; and his advice to his fellow-dealers to assimilate their wines to those of port and sherry, if they desire to extend their trade with England, is probably sound.

The relative proportions of alcoholic strength of wine, calculated according to the English standard of Sykes's hydrometer, and the French of Gay-Lussac, are as above given.(page 454). In the translation, I state the strengths by Sykes:—

'England, Belgium, Holland, Northern Germany, Denmark, Sweden, Russia, are not wine producers, but use considerable quantities. Their palates, however, are generally spoiled by drinking spirits and strong beer. Consequently they find our wines, the chief merit of which consists in the fineness and delicacy of the bouquet, too light. What they want is something that is rough, strong, and that catches the throat. Talk not to them of flavour, of softness—these terms are, to them, incomprehensible: for them, the stronger the better.

'All the world knows that our fine Bordeaux wines intended for the English market are strongly fortified by hermitage, and other stout growths; and yet our insular neighbours call these mixtures claret. London claret often contains 26° of proof spirit, but sherry and port have often as much as 40° to 45°, and sometimes even more!

'Is it then that the natural produce of Spain and Portugal contains a greater quantity of alcohol than that of some parts of our country? Not at all. They have not more spirit than some of the growths of the Roussillon, and other districts in the south, which are, without any addition, 26° and 28°. When shipped to Britain, they are made much stronger, in order to please the taste of the wine-drinkers there.

'Well, what must our wine-merchants do, if they hope to compete successfully with their rivals of the Peninsula? They must assuredly make our wines as strong. The intelligent merchant studies and follows the taste of his customer, however strange and bad it may be.'

VII.

Extract from Cunningham's 'History of Britain.'

The following extract, from the Translation of 'Cunningham's Latin History of Britain, from the Revolution to the Hanover Succession,' gives a very curious and interesting picture of the state of society at that period, and shows the feeling and excitement caused by the introduction of port, and the prohibition of French wines:—

'And now I shall take this opportunity to speak of the French wine-drinkers as truly and briefly as I can. On the first breaking out of the confederate war, the merchants in England were prohibited from all commerce with France, and a heavy duty was laid upon French wine. This caused a grievous complaint among the topers (who have great interest in Parliament), as if they had been poisoned by port wines. Mr. Portman Seymour, who was a jovial companion, and indulged his appetites, but otherwise a good man; General Churchill, the Duke of Marlborough's brother, a man of courage, but a lover of wine; Mr. Pereira, a Jew and smellfeast, and other hard drinkers, declared that the want of French wine was not to be endured, and that they could hardly bear up under so great a calamity. These were joined by Dean Aldrich, who, though nicknamed the priest of Bacchus, was otherwise an excellent man, and adorned with all kinds of learning. Dr. Radcliffe, a physician of great reputation, who ascribed the cause of all diseases to the want of French wines, though he was very rich, and much addicted to wine, yet, being extremely covetous, bought the cheaper wines; but, at the same time, he imputed the badness of his wine to the war, and the difficulty of getting better. Therefore the Duke of Beaufort and the Earl of Scarsdale, two young noblemen of great interest among their acquaintance, who had it in their power to live at their ease, in magnificence or luxury, merrily attributed all the doctor's complaints to his avarice.

'All those were also for peace rather than war; and all the bottle companions, many physicians, and great numbers of the lawyers and inferior clergy, and, in fine, the loose women too, were united together in the faction against the Duke of Marlborough.'

VIII.

Frozen Wine.

Were the statements contained in many books (and often repeated, on their authority, as undeniable facts) to be believed, it would not be doubted that it was a common custom in Burgundy for wine-growers and merchants to convert a portion of their wine into ice, in order to enhance the value of the remainder.

Notwithstanding these assertions, the fact seemed to me so questionable, that I would not have entered upon the subject had it not been lately brought forward in a report to our Government, by one of the gentlemen deputed to gain information as to the strengths of the wines of various countries.

In my visits to Burgundy, the freezing of their wine

was never even alluded to by those who were giving me information; and, if it had been mentioned as a *usual practice*, I certainly would have expressed some astonishment as to the annual supply of ice and snow in that quarter; for I know, by experiments, that wine, unless very weak, requires intense cold to freeze even the surface; and it seemed strange that one should never have heard of the operation except in this district. Below is an extract from the report of the Government Commissioner, Mr. Ogilvy, and, following this, is a letter from a friend in Burgundy, who is one of the very highest authorities in that country:—

Extract from the Report of Mr. Ogilvy, Inspector-General of Customs.

'In Burgundy, the strength is also artificially increased, after the wine is made, by the process called "congélation," or freezing. Formerly, this operation was effected in the winter, during the frosty weather, by rolling the cask into the open air, opening the bungs, and covering the cask up with snow and ice; but this method, though cheap as regards the means of operating, often proved dear in the end, as the weather was uncertain, and, if too cold, the wine froze too rapidly; and if the frost, as was frequently the case, suddenly broke up before the completion of the operation, the wine was spoilt. It has been found better, therefore, to freeze the wine by artificial means, by putting it in large tin vessels, which are immersed in a mixture of pounded ice and salt, and the operation is carefully watched, to prevent it being carried too far.

'The principle on which this process is based is, that water freezes more readily than spirit or wine. The water naturally contained in wine is in part frozen, and thereby separated, when it is taken out and thrown away; by which the bulk of the wine is decreased, and all its properties are condensed, and made more perceptible; but, as the bad qualities are condensed as well as the good, this operation is only useful in very fine and faultless wines.'

Extract from a Letter of a Grower, dated Vosne, in the Côte d'Or, June 21, 1863.

'The freezing of wine in the Burgundy district is of *rare occurrence*; and the few who have tried it express strong doubts as to its being beneficial.

'The professed object is to increase the strength by diminishing the watery part, which alone freezes, and it is naturally inferred that the portion unfrozen, and reduced in bulk, must contain a greater proportionate amount of alcohol.

'It is alleged that the process rids the wine of the mucilage which is held in suspension, and thus protects it against fermentation, which might cause decomposition.

'It is also stated that it renders it more full-bodied and strong; but experience has proved that this is invariably effected at the expense of delicacy and of bouquet, which are essentially important elements in fine wines.

'The only hope of a good result is by operating on high qualities during the winter after the vintage. Supposing there has been a good supply of ice and snow, a certain quantity of sea-salt is mixed with these, and after having placed about twenty gallons of wine in a tin vessel, well closed, this is covered over with the mixture, and in eight or ten hours the temperature of zero to 5° above zero, of Fahrenheit, is reached. Ice is formed in the interior of the vessel in greater or smaller quantities, according to the temperature; and, when it is considered that it has been continued long enough, the liquid wine is drawn off.

'The ice which remains is of no value, for, when melted, it is colourless and tasteless. The wine is allowed to remain in cask till March or April, when it is fined, and treated like the rest in the cellar.

'As in this process there is necessarily a great loss of quantity, perhaps even a fourth part, it would require such an improvement in the quality as to compensate the proprietor, by an increase of price, for the loss caused by the freezing; but any improvement is very questionable.

'It is a mistake to believe that the practice is general, for it is almost entirely limited to a few who wish to make the experiment from curiosity as to the result.'

Although not having much reference to frozen wine for a commercial object, yet, as it is an interesting fact, I may mention that I have been informed, by one of the most distinguished Arctic navigators, that the degree of cold experienced by him on some occasions was more than 100° below freezing point, and that his wine became a mass of ice, which, when melted, was found to have lost almost all the taste of wine.

IX.

Strengths of the Wines at the International Exhibition, and comparative Table of the English and French Degrees of Alcohol.

A very interesting and valuable report has been lately published on the authority of the Commissioners of H.M. Customs, showing 'the results obtained in testing samples of the various wines exhibited at the International Exhibition.' It is full of curious information, ably arranged by Mr. Keene.

I have desired to avoid encumbering this book by figures and statistics, more than seemed useful for elucidating opinions, and I therefore extract from Mr. Keene's report only the following: —

1. *Average Strength of the weakest Wines of each Country according to Sykes's Hydrometer.*

In Italy the average lowest strength is	19·5°
In the Zollverein	19·7°
In the Austrian Empire	18·4°
In France	19·0°
In Australia	21·3°

2. *Table showing the relative English and French Degrees of Alcoholic Strength, obtained by an experimental Comparison of the Hydrometers of Gay-Lussac and Sykes.*

English		French	English		French	English		French	English		French
Over Proof	Proof Spirit per Cent.		Over Proof	Proof Spirit per Cent.		Under Proof	Proof Spirit per Cent.		Under Proof	Proof Spirit per Cent.	
74·0	174·0	100	28·8	128·8	74	13·0	87·0	50	56·5	43·5	25
72·3	172·3	99	27·0	127·0	73	14·7	85·3	49	58·2	41·8	24
70·5	170·5	98	25·3	125·3	72	16·5	83·5	48	60·0	40·0	23
68·8	168·8	97	23·5	123·5	71	18·2	81·8	47	61·7	38·3	22
67·0	167·0	96	21·8	121·8	70	20·0	80·0	46	63·5	36·5	21
65·3	165·3	95	20·1	120·1	69	21·7	78·3	45	65·2	34·8	20
63·6	163·6	94	18·3	118·3	68	23·4	76·6	44	66·9	33·1	19
61·8	161·8	93	16·6	116·6	67	25·2	74·8	43	68·7	31·3	18
60·1	160·1	92	14·8	114·8	66	26·9	73·1	42	70·4	29·6	17
58·3	158·3	91	13·1	113·1	65	28·7	71·3	41	72·2	27·8	16
56·6	156·6	90	11·4	111·4	64	30·4	69·6	40	73·9	26·1	15
54·9	154·9	89	9·6	109·6	63	32·1	67·9	39	75·6	24·4	14
53·1	153·1	88	7·9	107·9	62	33·9	66·1	38	77·4	22·6	13
51·4	151·4	87	6·1	106·1	61	35·6	64·4	37	79·1	20·9	12
49·6	149·6	86	4·4	104·4	60	37·4	62·6	36	80·9	19·1	11
47·9	147·9	85	2·7	102·7	59	39·1	60·9	35	82·6	17·4	10
46·2	146·2	84	0 9	100·9	58	40·8	59·2	34	84·3	15·7	9
44·4	144·4	83	Under			42·6	57·4	33	86·1	13·9	8
42·7	142·7	82	proof			44·3	55·7	32	87·8	12·2	7
40·9	140·9	81	0·8	99·2	57	46·1	53·9	31	89·6	10·4	6
39·2	139·2	80	2·6	97·4	56	47·8	52·2	30	91·3	8·7	5
37·5	137·5	79	4·3	95·7	55	49·5	50·5	29	93·0	7·0	4
35·7	135·7	78	6·0	94·0	54	51·3	48·7	28	94·8	5·2	3
34·0	134·0	77	7·8	92·2	53	53·0	47·0	27	96·5	3·5	2
32·2	132·2	76	9·5	90·5	52	54·8	45·2	26	98·3	1·7	1
30·5	130·5	75	11·3	88·7	51						

X.

Wine Duties in 1806 and 1863, with the Standard Gauges of the Casks of each kind of Wine.

	1806 Old Gallons Gauge	1806 Rate of Duty per old Gallon	1806 Total Duty per Cask	1863 Imperial Gallons Gauge	1863 Total Duty per Cask, at the rate of 2*s.* 6*d.*	1863 Total Duty per Cask, at the rate of 1*s.*	Usual Run in Bottles about
		s. d.	£ *s. d.*		£ *s. d.*	£ *s. d.*	doz.
Lisbon . pipe	140	7 7	53 1 8	117	14 13 3	5 17 0	55
Port . pipe	138	7 7	52 6 6	115	14 8 3	5 15 0	54
Sherry . butt	130	7 7	49 5 10	108	13 10 8	5 8 0	52
Teneriffe . pipe	120	7 7	45 10 0	100	12 10 8	5 0 0	48
Sicilian . pipe	112	7 7	42 9 4	93	11 13 1	4 13 0	44
Cape and Madeira, pipe	110	7 8	42 3 6	92	11 10 7	4 12 0	43
Tent . hhd.	63	7 7	23 17 9	52	6 10 0	2 12 0	29
French . hhd.	56	11 5	31 19 5	46	5 15 0	2 6 0	22
Rhenish . aum	36	9 5	16 19 0	30	3 15 0	1 10 0	14

XI.

Mr. Croft's Pamphlet.

The following extracts are from a pamphlet published in 1788, and lately found on a book-stall in Edinburgh. Its title is, 'A Treatise on the Wines of Portugal since the Establishment of the English Factory at Oporto, anno 1727. By John Croft, S.A.S., Member of the Factory at Oporto, and Wine Merchant, York.'

I am informed that this John Croft is the original Mr. Croft, of the still-existing and much-respected house of Thompson & Croft, of Oporto.

What he means by his allusion to 'the decadence and falling off of the Florence vintages,' I cannot comprehend:—

'It was about a hundred years ago that the Portugal wines were at the first imported into England, and chiefly or principally about the reign of Queen Anne, on the decadence or falling off of the Florence vintages, that the wines from Oporto came into any sort of draught or use; for, before the introduction of the Ports, there were also imported the Ribadavia wines from Galicia, a province in Spain, though of this sort there only used to come about two or three thousand pipes yearly. They were a thin sort of wine; the red not unlike what is called or termed in Portugal "Palhete," or Methuen wine, from one Mr. Paul Methuen, who was the first that mixed the red and white grapes together; and you may suppose a liquor nearly the same as red and white port being mixed. When the demand for this sort of wine became greater than its produce, especially in a scanty vintage, it put some English supercargoes, who resided there and at Viana, near Oporto, at that time, on teaching the Portuguese to cultivate the vineyards on the heights or mountains bordering on the river Douro, from whence the district takes the name of Sima de Douro: it is about forty or fifty miles distant from the city of Oporto, where the harbour is, and where it runs into the sea. It is vulgarly called by the English factory residing there *the wine country*, and from thence it is that the wines are transported and conveyed down to the city of Oporto in proper vessels, being a sort of lighters or keels.

'At the first cultivation of the vineyards, owing to more care and labour being employed, and the summer seasons in Portugal being intensely and excessively hotter than of later years, the wines were then undoubtedly found richer, and of superior strength and mellowness to those produced at present, at least by the account of them from the old people in that country. It is chiefly owing to the delicacy and tenuity of the soil, and its being at a proper distance from the sea, that the situation is certainly the best suited or most favourable of any in Europe for the growth of red wines of a superior mellowness or body, which, owing to the system of modern luxury, is so much familiarised to us by custom in England, and so much adapted to the taste and constitution of the Northern climates as to become a staple commodity; and an Englishman of any decent condition or circumstances cannot dispense with it after his good dinner, in the same manner as he uses a piece of Cheshire cheese for pretended digestion-sake.

'As vineyards are a long time before they can possibly come to maturity, or arrive at any degree of perfection, even with the greatest pains and cares in the cultivating them, it may not be improper to enlarge a little upon this matter, it being a great argument against the late projected scheme for planting and growing of vines in America, as well as the inconstancy of that climate.

'Such was the case with those of Sima de Douro; though the wines so immediately came into a repute in England, owing to many circumstances, but first and chiefly to the bad produce of the wines of other countries, their falling off and scanty vintages, as said before; and, secondly, to the advantage arising from the establishing a factory or body of merchants at Oporto, so far considered as beneficial in taking off the woollen manufactures of England, under the sanction of those most valuable privileges ceded by John IV., King of Portugal, in the year 1654, to Oliver Cromwell and the Government of England; from which time—for before that they went only as supercargoes, and returned again to England—we may date the first settlement of the English in Portugal; so that it does not appear that port wines have been at all known in the northern countries of Europe above seventy or eighty years at the farthest; and even so late as Queen Anne's time the importation was very small, for it is related traditionally that it was then customary in London, upon a meeting of two friends, to invite one the other to the tavern to drink, or, in vulgar phrase, to crack a bottle of claret dashed with port: this only to intimate the extreme scarcity of the latter and the plenty of the former.

'In the infancy of the trade, the first cost of a pipe of red port in Sima de Douro was about 16*l.* or 17*l.*, and the duty in England very inconsiderable to what it is at present, or has been of later years; all which served, as well as the high demand they had, to encourage the Portuguese to attend to their vineyards, and neglect their corn-lands; for at that time of day the province of Sima was chiefly corn-land, and, from the richness of the soil and the fruitfulness of the country, afforded as fine a produce as any in Europe, and so great a plenty as it was never known that the province of Entre Minho e Douro, or Oporto, wanted grain of any sort; nor was it ever known, at that time, that any corn was imported or wanted from abroad, there being a regular and sufficient supply from that rich and plentiful province.

'But by the settling of the Factory of Oporto, the mutual intercourse of the trade, and the encouraging demand from England for the wines, with the close attention of the natives to the growing and cultivating of the vines, it was soon seen, by degrees, that their corn-lands were changed into vineyards; and as the demand in England for the wines was still increasing, and even much greater quantities were called for there than what could be expected from the natural produce, the English factors and wine-coopers were induced to try the expedient of adulterating, and teaching the Portuguese to sophisticate them, and, according to the proverb, "What the lion's skin would not do, to eke it out with the fox's tail;" and this they effected principally with the juice of the elder-berry, inasmuch as a great many elder-trees were planted, and soon seen to flourish in the vineyards, the chief use of which was, not so much to increase the quantity as to give the wine a colour.

'The institution of the Portuguese Wine Company struck effectually at the root of the English privileges in Portugal.

'The Portuguese set about establishing this Company in the year 1756, when England was engaged in war with France and Spain, and they availed themselves of this critical conjuncture. Notwithstanding the repeated remonstrances made by the representatives of the English Factory, and the Portugal merchants in London, to the Minister, the grievances still lay unattended to, as Mr. Pitt, then Secretary of State, was employed, and entirely immersed, in schemes and plans of war. This belligerent Minister did not favour the commercial interest so much as he might have done, as fearful, at the same time, of giving umbrage to the Court of Portugal, whose friendship we were then soliciting; because a rumour was spread about of their coming into the family compact with France and Spain, which gave the Portuguese an opportunity of treating the English merchants with great insolence and contempt. Nay, they even went so far as to threaten imprisonment, upon a very slight pretence, to the English Consul at Oporto, and nothing was more common than their talking of expelling the English from their country.

'This conduct was considered so notorious, that it is handed down to us in history. Not to digress further on this subject, I shall only add, that they used to say, that as the privileges were granted to Cromwell, who was an usurper, they were not obligated to observe them. Afterwards, in the year 1762, when we saved Portugal from the Spanish yoke, their ratifying the treaty to the full extent should then most properly have been insisted on, as it was a fair and good opportunity for our Government to have determined on the Company's being abolished at that time.

'Davenant, inspector-general of the imports and exports, in his report to the commissioners for stating the public accounts in the year 1669, says that no Portugal wines were entered in the Custom-house books at that time. It was only at the epoch of the Restoration that the use of wines became at all common in England, at which juncture they were chiefly imported from France and Germany. In King William's time some wines were sent to England, but in no great quantity. In the year 1702 the war broke out with France and Spain, and the Portuguese, joining the Allies, the next year a new treaty, commonly called the Methuen Treaty, was concluded upon that occasion by Queen Anne, by which Portugal wines were to pay one-third less duty than French wines. From this time we may date the general use of port wines in Great Britain.

'At first, the export was about 5,000 pipes, and in the year 1780 it was found to be from 20 to 30,000 pipes a year. The wines about Viana, near Oporto, were at first in great repute. The wines of Sima de Douro came in demand afterwards.

'In the year 1701 the Douro wines were sold in the wine country at 10 millreas, about 2*l.* 15*s.* per pipe; in the year 1731 at 48 millreas, about 13*l.* per pipe; in the year 1755 at 12 millreas, about 3*l.* per pipe; in the year 1779 at 30 millreas, about 8*l.* per pipe. This is only mentioned in reference to what goes before, with respect to the demand of the wines for England, or the small quantity in point of vintage.

'The English supercargoes first established themselves under the sanction of the privileges granted by the Court of Portugal and authority of England, in the year 1656, when Cromwell gave the patent of consul-general to one Thomas Maynard, with a patent of vice-consul to his brother, Walter Maynard, of the vice-consulship at Oporto, in the year 1659. It was only in the year 1727 that the British merchants or factors at Oporto in a manner incorporated themselves, and made certain rules for their proceedings, which have been observed with very little alteration ever since.'

XII.

Board of Trade Returns, 1863.

The Board of Trade Returns for the first six months of this year (1863) being now published, I subjoin an estimate for the twelve months, calculating the latter six months on the ratio of the first. The progress of the trade in wine, since the reduction of duty, is seen to be very unsatisfactory; but I would refer to the arguments in the body of the work, and to copies of letters published while the subject was under discussion, to prove that the differential rates rendered such a result inevitable.

It would, however, be unfair to omit reference to another very important cause. I allude to the enormous rise in the shipping prices of port and sherry, which still constitute nearly 70 per cent. of the whole consumption.

The reduction from the former rate of 5*s*. 9*d*. per gallon to 2*s*. 6*d*. is 19*l*. on a pipe of port, and 18*l*. on a butt of sherry; but the increased cost of the former during the last ten years may be called from 20*l*. to 30*l*. per pipe, and of the latter from 25*l*. to 40*l*. per butt. Formerly, the use of sherry was almost exclusively among ourselves, but it is now a favourite wine throughout the world, and the demand exceeds the present power of supply.

In a circular of one of the principal shippers, dated June 15, 1863, it is stated, 'It is nine years since there has been an average vintage. Scarcely any wine was produced in 1855 or 1856, and the six following years did not give three vintages. The present year promises an abundant one; but this cannot influence prices for years to come. The demand for old sherry, existing now in very small quantities, is enormous; hence, our quotations are likely to be supported and increased.'

Perhaps a few houses do keep up quality in relation to prices; but I am not singular in thinking that it is now difficult to meet with sherry which there is any pleasure in drinking.

I refrain from again entering on the question of the unfortunate mistake of the differential rates; but I must repeat, that it is almost ridiculous to hear the duty spoken of as a reduction to a low rate. By reference to the following tables of calculations, we see that, of the whole consumption in the years 1861 and 1862, only 15 per cent. was of the 1*s.* rate, and, in the present year, it is only 12 per cent.! Of the total number of gallons, viz.: 10,787,171 in 1861, and 9,803,146 in 1862, the quantities which paid the duty of 1*s.* were, respectively, 1,495,666 and 1,287,511 gallons; and, by the estimate for this year, the total number of gallons will be 10,250,662, of which there will be only 1,259,376 gallons rated at THE SHILLING.

TABLE I.

Showing the total Quantities, Duty paid, in the Years 1859, 1860, 1861, 1862, *and* 1863, *specifying the Increase or Decrease of Gallons, and of Revenue in each. The Year* 1863 *is estimated for Twelve Months, calculated from the first Six Months.*

Year	Total Quantity, Gallons	Total Increase, Gallons	Total Decrease, Gallons	Revenue	Increase of Revenue	Decrease of Revenue	Rates of Duty per Gallon
				£	£	£	
1859	7,263,046	..	..	1,982,327	..	..	2/11 and 5/9
1860	7,358,192	95,146	..	1,444,790	..	537,537	3/
1861	10,787,171	3,428,979	..	1,223,240	..	221,550	1/, 1/9, 2/5 and 2/11
1862	9,803,046	..	984,125	1,123,605	..	99,635	1/ and 2/6 and above 42°, say 3/
estimate 1863	10,250,662	447,616	..	1,187,494	63,893	..	ditto

TABLE II.

Showing the Consumption (the quantity on which Duty was paid) in the Year before the Reduction (1859), *and in the subsequent Years till the end of* 1863 ; *the last Six Months of that Year being estimated on the ratio of the first Six Months.*

	Year	Consumption (Duty paid)—Gallons	Per Centage of Total	Increase in Quantity—Gallons	Decrease in Quantity—Gallons	Increase, per Cent.	Decrease, per Cent.
From Portugal . . .	1859	2,020,561	27·82				
	1860	1,776,138	24·14	..	244,443	..	3·68
	1861	2,702,649	25·06	926,511	..	0·92	
	1862	2,349,954	23·97	..	352,695	..	1·09
Estimated . . .	1863	2,464,020	24·05	114,066	..	0·08	
From Spain . . .	1859	2,876,554	39·60				
	1860	2,975,769	40·44	99,215	..	0·84	
	1861	4,032,274	37·38	1,056,505	..	..	3·06
	1862	3,956,213	40·35	..	76,061	2·97	
Estimated . . .	1863	4,339,518	42·33	383,305	..	1·98	
From France . . .	1859	695,913	9·60				
	1860	1,125,599	15·30	429,686	..	5·70	
	1861	2,227,662	20·65	1,102,063	..	5·35	
	1862	1,900,344	19·38	..	327,318	..	1·27
Estimated . . .	1863	1,937,336	18·89	36,992	..	..	0·49
From the Cape & Australia	1859	785,926	10·82				
	1860	427,698	5·81	..	358,228	..	5·01
	1861	340,082	3·16	..	97,616	..	2·65
	1862	182.282	1·86	..	157,800	..	1·30
Estimated . . .	1863	115,682	1·13	..	182,282	..	0·73
From all other countries, and mixed in bond, and compounds from abroad.	1859	501,465	6·90				
	1860	592,167	8·50	90,702	..	1·60	
	1861	878,838	8·15	286,671	..	..	0·35
	1862	851,782	8·68	..	27,056	0·53	
Estimated . . .	1863	1,394,106	13·60	542,324	..	4·92	

TABLE III.

Showing the Number of Gallons of each Class, on which Duty was paid in the first Six Months of the Years 1861, 1862, *and* 1863, *and the Percentage (proportion) which each Class bore to the Whole.*

Degree of Strength	Rate of Duty per Gallon	Year 1861, Gallons	Year 1861, perCent.	Year 1862, Gallons	Year 1862, perCent.	Year 1863, Gallons	Year 1863, perCent.
Under 26° .	1/	920,951	15·08	752,487	15·01	629,688	12·29
Under 42° .	2/6	4,619,753	75·67	3,792,732	75·63	3,980,839	77·64
Under 45° .	say 3/	..	..	..	..	12,439	0·24
In bottle .	2/6	564,874	9·25	469,423	9·36	502,365	9·83
		6,105,578	100	5,014,642	100	5,125,331	100

INDEX.

CPSIA information can be obtained
at www.ICGtesting.com
Printed in the USA
LVHW040357110522
718423LV00001B/160

9 783375 003548